FATE BORN

SECRETS OF SRATTA

SECRETS OF SRATTA

THE FATE BORN TETRALOGY
BOOK 1

MICHELLE L. ROBISON

OUTERLIMITS
PRESS

ISBN: 979-8-9891771-1-0 (Paperback)

ISBN: 979-8-9891771-2-7 (Hardcover)

Library of Congress Control Number: 2024901376

Any references to historical events, real people, or real places are used fictitiously. Names, characters, and places are products of the author's imagination.

Front cover image by Michelle L. Robison

Stock photos from DALL-E Image Generator

Printed by Outerlimits Press, in the United States of America.

First printing, 2024.

Outerlimits Press LLC

28515 N. North Valley Pkwy

Phoenix, AZ, 85085

www.michellelrobisonbooks.com

❀ Created with Vellum

DIESTRA

ANELLI

SRATTA

DRAMMAT

KARTZEL

PEDIAN

VITA DANTIS
SOLAR SYSTEM

To my husband

You are my greatest supporter and biggest fan. This book truly would not exist without you. Thank you for going along with me on this crazy ride.

ONE

"ARIA?" Her mom's voice rang in her ears like a distant echo. "Honestly, at this point, I can't tell if it's another episode or if she's purposely ignoring us."

"Lori, please," her dad's deep, soothing voice cut in. "Aria, can you hear us?"

Aria's erratic heartbeat quickened as the scene in her mind replaced the view of her parents' worried faces. A frustrated cry caught in her throat, but she restrained it as always.

This couldn't be happening. Not again. Not now.

She clamped her eyelids shut and bowed her head, focusing on her mantras. He wasn't real. None of this was real. The monochromatic room that filled her mind's eye was as depressing as ever, but the teenage boy in the small bed was peaceful in his sleep. It was the only state Aria knew of that made him look so young.

Her parents' voices floated around her, but none of their words reached her ears—not that she needed to hear them to guess what they were saying. "Is it Luca again?" and "Maybe we should wait a year," would certainly have been involved.

Aria's eyes roved beneath her eyelids, a pang of longing cutting through the fear as they rested on Luca's face. There was a time when her visions gave her comfort. That time ended years ago. Now all Luca brought her was a crippling fear surrounding everything she would lose if anyone found out—anyone other than her therapists and psychiatrists, anyway.

She had to snap out of it. He wasn't real.

Aria forced her eyelids open and locked her blue-green irises with her dad's deep brown ones. She clenched her fists under the table, fingernails digging into her palms.

"I'm fine." Aria's voice didn't even tremble. Lying was pretty much her default mode at this point. "I haven't had an episode in years. Why would they start up again now? I think I'm just a little nervous about tomorrow, but who wouldn't be?"

She unclenched her fists to take her dad's large hands in hers, and shifted her gaze to her mom, who was standing at the head of the table.

"You told me you puked the night before your orientation," Aria said. "I'm nowhere near that point." She turned to her dad and plastered on a small smile. "I probably just need to get some rest."

"Of course," he said. "You'll do great. The Academy was the best experience of both your mom's and my life, and if anyone can make an even bigger impact there, it's our girl."

He gave her a warm, proud smile, and a pang of guilt shot through her at the deception. The hulking man stood first, pulling Aria's much smaller frame up with him. He crushed her in a bear hug and gave her one last smile. When her mom's slender arms came around her, they were stiff. Aria extricated herself and bolted up the stairs and into her bedroom.

Finally, alone in her room, she allowed the shaking to set into her bones as she paced the floor. What was going on? This was the fifth time in as many weeks. How long had it been since her last true episode? Five, six years? She had beat this thing fair and square! All but for the dreams, at least, but everyone had strange dreams. Dreaming didn't make her crazy. Seeing visions in the middle of her daily life, on the other hand, might do it.

Aria bolted to her vanity and gave the silent command for the drawer to open. She searched haphazardly in the deep drawer until her fingers caught hold of a small, cold cylinder. Relief poured over her. She still had a few doses left. She hadn't needed her meds in so long. How would she get more without alerting her parents, or worse, the Academy?

She fell into bed, lifted her shirt, and placed the end of the cylinder to her stomach. The sting of metal pricked the soft flesh as she pressed down on the injector. Immediately, the drugs began to take effect. Her anxiety lessened and her eyes drooped, but her thoughts unfortunately didn't quiet. The pull of temptation intensified as her senses dulled, and she fell into unconsciousness with a smile.

Aria's eyes fluttered open to a familiar profile silhouetted by a dim, yellow light. A forbidden smile tugged at the corner of her lips as a ripple of tiny butterflies filled her stomach. A distant part of her remembered to feel ashamed for indulging in the warmth of Luca's presence, but the guilt was too slippery to hold. For every second she studied the curves of his face, her feeble resolve wavered. Why should she feel ashamed? She couldn't stop the dreams. She had tried ten years to do that, and here she was. Besides, who wouldn't be utterly smitten by this boy? He was the kind of handsome that no one could be unaware of, yet somehow she never saw him act arrogantly. If anything, the tall, muscular boy with dark chestnut skin and tight ebony curls seemed genuinely lonely. Because he was essentially her imaginary friend, perfection would make sense, but he wasn't perfect. Sometimes he got angry and lashed out, just like anyone else. Maybe that was why he seemed so undeniably real.

Aria would have given anything to be able to reach out to him, but that thinking was pointless. As real as he felt, she could never seem to make him see her, not even after sixteen years of trying. So, she contented herself with being a ghost in his bleak world.

Luca stirred and swung his bare feet to the cold, metal floor, rubbing the sleep from his eyes. He stood from his tiny bed and stretched, hands grazing the low ceiling as he yawned. He pulled the same gray T-shirt he always wore over his head and exited his tiny room. He stretched more freely in the spacious hall as he strode toward the dark porthole at the end of the passage.

Aria followed, a silent observer. It always struck her as odd that he looked nearly the same every night, and not only because of his drab clothing choices. For as long as Aria could remember, Luca had been more or less the same age, probably only a year or two older than she was now. A pang of sorrow shot through her as she watched him reach the porthole. The day would soon come when she would pass him by. How would it feel when she was an old lady ravaged by time, and he was still as young and handsome as ever?

A subtle feeling began to seep into Aria's mind from somewhere foreign, a familiar mix of grief and guilt. This was a ritual of Luca's: walk to the porthole, stare into space, and beat himself up over some past sin or loss. Most nights, the abyss he stared into was nearly black, with only distant stars streaking by. On rare occasions, the ship passed closer to planets and celestial bodies, providing a more spectacular but equally blurry landscape.

But tonight's view was not a star-streaked void nor even a bold, beautiful flash of color. Tonight, the ship was barely moving, and a vast ocean of space spread out in front of Luca as the ship slowly turned for the first time in Aria's memory. A blue, green, and white orb appeared, and Aria's heart stuttered.

"Drammat?" she whispered, unheard as always.

The brilliance of Aria's home planet gleamed in Luca's intense brown eyes as moisture gathered there. For the first time in a very long time, a new feeling flowed from him and filled Aria. As both terror and hope surged in his chest, the golden flecks in his eyes burned.

"So, *you're* Drammat," he muttered. "Let's see if you're all you're cracked up to be."

Aria's eyes snapped open to the sound of her alarm, and she lurched upright, nearly tumbling out of bed. The time and weather danced in bold symbols in the center of her vision and the scent of wild oranges invigorated her sleepy brain. She clumsily swiped at the bold lettering, and the intangible screen retracted, ending the assault on her senses. The complete memory of her dream overcame her, and overpowering guilt descended.

"What is wrong with me?" she moaned, swiping at the cold sweat beading her forehead and soaking the hem of her T-shirt. She dropped her head into her trembling hands and attempted to slow her breathing.

"He's not real," she whispered through trembling lips. "Focus on what's real."

After a few deep breaths, Aria threw her covers to the side, staggered out of bed, and stretched her arms above her head. She stumbled to her full-length mirror, trimmed with the medals and ribbons from her proudest accomplishments, and inspected her ragged image. Why did Luca always seem so alive? Her time with him felt more real than her actual life sometimes. A sudden burst of rage smashed through her defenses, and she slammed a fist down on the vanity before her.

"Pull it together," she hissed at the wreck in the mirror.

A pair of tears slipped down her cheeks and she wiped them away. She didn't have time to fall apart today. The waking visions must have been induced by the stress of starting at the Academy. Her mom and dad wouldn't let her start school a year early if she couldn't get her anxiety in check, so naturally, her treacherous brain was trying to ruin everything. But her brain wouldn't win this time. What her parents didn't know wouldn't kill them, and nothing would stop her from taking her rightful place.

At sixteen, Aria was the youngest student to ever be accepted to the Grand Drammatan Academy. Everyone of any significance went to the Academy, including her parents. The few lucky enough to work their way into the elite group of scientists, soldiers, engineers, politicians, lawyers, and medical experts who graduated from the Academy would shape the future of humankind. Aria had worked her entire life for this opportunity, and a little anxiety wasn't about to mess it all up. However, full-blown insanity might do the trick. She just needed to get through the day, and everything would be fine.

Aria jumped as her alarm went off a second time. Being

late probably wasn't the best way to commence her epic plans. She swiped up in front of her face, minimizing the intangible screen to its base embedded in the brain tissue above her right ear and connecting directly to her nervous system.

She darted frantically across her bedroom floor and into the bathroom, stripping off her shorts and T-shirt mid-run. As the shower's warm water rolled down her back and soothed her trembling body, her mind finally began to catch up with her. She rushed through her new morning routine, frantically dressing in the uniform she would wear for the next four years.

She examined the black leather pants and fitted forest-green T-shirt with her last name embroidered over the heart. She hated how the clothes hung on her, emphasizing her history-making young age, but pride overshadowed her self-consciousness. She laced up the black boots and slipped her arms into the sleeves of the light jacket a few shades darker than her shirt. After rushing through her mother-approved makeup routine and running her fingers through her damp hair, she frowned at herself in the mirror. Her mom would disapprove of her being so careless with such an essential first impression, but she had wasted precious minutes in a silly panic, so wet hair would have to do. She grabbed the pack of equipment for her classes and slung it over her shoulder, pausing in the doorway. She smiled back at her childhood bedroom, sixteen years of memories bringing moisture to her eyes.

"Aria," her mom shouted up the stairs. "You're going to be late. Get down here!"

"I'm ready!" she yelled, turning to bound down the stairs.

"Let's go! I don't see *you* waiting in the pod."

"Don't speak to your mother that way," her dad said.

Aria walked through the door to the garage, and her

parents rushed in behind her. Her dad lugged her suitcase and backpack from the house to the pod and lowered himself into the pilot's seat. As Aria and her mom slid in, restraints slinked across their bodies and locked into place. The pod registered Aria's dad's bio-signature as he sat, and it lifted off the ground. As the garage door opened and they sped off toward the rest of Aria's life, she couldn't help taking one final look back at her childhood home.

"Would you like a breakfast bar?" her mom asked, holding one out for her.

Aria took it. "Thanks, but I don't know how much I can eat. I'm still a little nervous."

"Well, at least you won't need to worry about bloating on the most important day of your life," she said with a tight smile.

Aria rolled her eyes as she picked at the bar. Unable to stomach much, she gazed over the coastline and let the minutes pass. She was lucky; living within an hour of the Academy, she might be the closest student to home. The terrain gradually changed from rocky seashore and sprawling fields to sandy beaches and tropical groves reaching up the side of a small mountain range.

Eventually, a large, metal gate obstructed her vision of the sparkling ocean, and all her hard-earned poise vanished. As the pod stopped behind a long line of arriving students, her stomach threatened to return the few bites of food she managed to get down. Clutching her new bag, she slid open the sleek, silver door and stepped onto the shimmering gray curb as her dad retrieved her luggage and set it beside her.

"It's really something, isn't it?" he asked, smiling at the imposing building. "I remember my first day like it was yester-day. You're going to love it here, kiddo."

"I know," Aria said. Her smile nearly broke as her eyes tracked along the ancient building. "Just don't expect me to be super popular, earn the top place in my discipline all four years, and find the time to fall in love like you did."

A booming laugh escaped him and he pulled Aria in with one strong arm. "Oh, honey, you're going to have an even greater time than we did."

Aria's mom arrived at her other side, slipped her arm around her waist, and guided her family through the crowd.

"You'll do great, darling," she whispered. "You were born for this."

"Thanks." Aria hesitated as a question waited temptingly on her tongue. "Why did they make this building look like something from ancient Earth?"

Her mom's head snapped to stare at her daughter. "Aria," she hissed. "Really?"

"Sorry," she whispered. "I just don't understand why one of our most important buildings is modeled after a lesser society. Why would our forefathers model their architecture after Earth's old buildings?"

Aria's mom narrowed her eyes at her, but her father laid a calming hand on his wife's shoulder and she visibly relaxed. Aria took in the vast quakestone building with enormous pillars holding up the slightly vaulted roof. It must have been a herculean undertaking to mine so much quakestone on Sratta and transport it through space to build not only this enormous structure but all of Drammat's first essential buildings. Of course, they still relied on quakestone in modern building projects, but now they had the process down to a science.

"This was one of the first buildings they erected when the Great Explorer arrived on Drammat," Aria's dad said. "I assume they chose a style of architecture representing the pursuit of knowledge on Earth. Or maybe they chose the most structurally sound design in their antiquated building style. Whatever the reason, the crew of the Great Explorer always made the best decision they could with the information they had. That's all we need to know."

"Sorry I asked," Aria muttered.

"It's good to ask questions, kiddo," he said. "Just don't dig too far into taboo subjects. For most kids your age, a simple question wouldn't be so bad. With your history, it's best not to make any extra waves."

Aria nodded and the trio sped up the stairs between two massive pillars as they entered the crush of people. Aria reflexively clenched her fists and held her breath as they passed through the oversized front door. A security screen skimmed over their bodies as they crossed the threshold, probing for weapons and other contraband. Dozens of new students and their parents piled through the doors around them. Aria forced a smile, straining to look like the rest of the ecstatic new students.

As they walked toward the elevators, her vision blurred and faded to black. She slowed, blinking repeatedly. Her sight returned as suddenly as it had disappeared, but something was off. Another vision? It couldn't be. She was still at the Academy, still walking through a crowd of people in the Grand Hall, but her vantage point was new. Amid the crush of students and parents, a single person came into focus. His back was turned to her, but his dark curls and strong, tall frame were unmistakable. Inextinguishable excitement with a familiar undertone of guilt flared inside her chest, and an involuntary gasp escaped her throat. The distinct urge to reach the top of the building struck her. The vision vanished, and the storm of emotions calmed as she forced them to retreat into herself. She blinked, and her vision returned her to reality, a startling picture of her mother peering at her with wide eyes and worry lines creasing her forehead.

"Is it Luca?" she whispered.

"Mom!" she hissed. "We agreed not to talk about this here."

"Tell me, Aria. Exposing your illness would cost you much more than simply waiting to start with the other kids your age."

"It's not him," she snapped, straining to keep her voice down. "I'm just nervous, okay? Let's go, please!"

Her mother's eyes narrowed, but she followed silently as Aria pushed past her. They walked another fifty paces to the elevators, stepped onto the first available platform, and waited for the thin disk to lift them through the air to the top floor. They coasted to a smooth stop as it reached the ballroom. Today, just like one late summer day when her parents were young, and just like every orientation day for centuries, the ballroom would host five hundred new Academy students as they said goodbye to their parents and began a new life. The trio walked into the large room, squeezing through the growing crowd. Aria's dad dropped her bags off in the Colonization pile at the back wall to be delivered to her room during the meeting.

"Noah Blake?" a gray-haired man asked, slapping Aria's dad on the back. "Good to see you! You still have to meet my wife, Maren." The man whisked Aria's parents away, leaving her alone, surveying the space awkwardly.

The massive ballroom was filled with five long tables covered from end to end with an incredible feast, though no one was seated yet. Each table was decorated in the color of one of the five disciplines: red for Medical, purple for Diplomacy, black for Engineering, blue for Defense, and green for Colonization. Even with the tables and the hundreds of young adults and their parents mingling, the ballroom was nowhere near capacity.

"Hey! Colonization green," a friendly voice said behind her. Aria turned to see a tall girl with long red hair, striking green eyes, and a thick spray of freckles holding a hand out to her. "I'm Dima. Looks like we'll be in the same cohort!"

Aria took Dima's outstretched hand with a smile. "I'm Aria."

"Aria," she said, drawing out the word as if testing the taste of it on her tongue. "I like that. So, are you a legacy or a first gen?"

"Legacy. Mom was in the Diplomacy program, and Dad was in the Defense program. They were kind of the 'it' couple when they were here, so no pressure, right? What about yours?"

"Mine came here too, but I doubt they ran in the same social circles. My parents are huge dorks, for lack of a better term. I love them, but they don't really get me."

"Trust me; I feel that," Aria said. "Sometimes, I swear I must be adopted."

"I dunno." Dima winked. "Looks like you could be a Diplomacy student to me."

A flush crept up Aria's neck. "Yeah, thank my mom for that. She has this thing about appearances. I'm looking forward to wearing a semi-normal amount of makeup for the next four years."

"To new beginnings," Dima said, turning up one corner of her mouth. "Hey, did you hear about our end-of-the-year field trip to Sratta?"

"Sure," Aria said. "I have some cousins who just graduated a few years ago from the Defense program, and they never shut up about the field trips."

"I can't wait to see what our mission will be!" Dima said. "I can hardly believe first-years go to such a dangerous planet! If the cold doesn't get us, the diseases might! There's a reason nobody visits our icy little neighbor"

A booming voice reverberated through the ballroom, and

although Dima's mouth continued moving for a moment, Aria couldn't hear anything over the powerful female voice.

"Attention, students and parents: please take your seats."

A strong hand soon clasped Aria's shoulder and led her quickly away from Dima. Her parents flanked her as they shepherded her to the far-left table where other Colonization students were already taking their seats.

Anxious and excited faces filled the long table, each surrounded by proud, older faces. Aria watched as Dima and her parents walked around the table to their seats. Aria stifled a laugh as she suddenly understood precisely what Dima had meant. She looked entirely out of place next to the two gangly, middle-aged redheads wearing clothing from at least a decade past. Yet, she couldn't help but notice how they seemed to dote on Dima as if she were all they had ever hoped for in a daughter. Despite a confusing pang of jealousy, Aria smiled for her new friend. Was it a little desperate for her to call Dima a friend already? Unless she could claim Luca from her subconscious as a friend, she had never really had one.

A tingle raced up Aria's spine as the sensation of being watched rippled across her skin. She scanned the room with narrowed eyes. Several students were gawking at her. Even some of the parents watched her. Was there something on her face? She opened the camera app through her neurolink and squinted at her image. She smiled, but she didn't have anything in her teeth.

An older woman stood from her place at the faculty table and walked gracefully to the podium. Aria fumbled to close her screen as the woman's identity crashed over her. President Emily Ann Gray was a legend. Every little girl on Drammat dreamed of being just like her. Most of the galaxy's important innovations in the last half-century could be attributed to her, either personally or through her students. Tears sprang to

Aria's eyes. President Gray's work had inspired Aria's interest in Colonization as a child.

"Welcome students and parents of the Grand Drammatan Academy class of thirty-one twenty-five," President Gray said. "Thank you, parents, for being here and supporting your students in this important next step on the road to excellence. I see many alumni among us, including some of our brightest stars. Would our alumni please stand and join me in reciting the mission statement of the Academy?"

Chairs glided out as Aria's parents, along with the rest of the hundreds of alumni in the ballroom, stood at attention. The voices of hundreds mingled as one as they chanted.

Forward and Upward.
As children of Drammat and followers of knowledge,
We strive to build up the human family.
We use our knowledge to expand the galaxy,
And ensure our eternal progress.
We place the good of humanity above our own,
Valuing bravery, loyalty, and the greater good.
Always remembering the Great Explorer which bore our forefathers
to paradise,
Never neglecting Drammat as our ancestors did the wasteland of
Earth.

The alumni sat in unison as they finished. President Gray scanned the faces in the ballroom as she spoke in a commanding tone.

"Our mission is simple: expand and improve the human family. Our methods, however, are complex and ever-changing. Over the next four years, our mission statement will become as much a part of you as the heart beating inside your chest. Only half of you will make it to graduation. Those who do not will enter a new, inferior career path, while those who do will stand here at the end of the fourth year, knowing they have what it takes to shape the future for all humankind. Now, enjoy brunch and celebrate the genesis of a new life."

Applause erupted from the hall as new students and parents stood, creating a wave across the room. A thrill shot through Aria's veins, and, for the first time in months, excitement overshadowed her fears. For a precious moment, the pressure melted away, and her own dreams and ambitions—not her parents' expectations—filled her mind's eye.

As the applause died, everyone sat and dug into the lavish meal. While Drammat had made food scarcity a thing of the past, the kitchens of the Academy were galaxy-renowned. Aria's mom closed her eyes with pleasure as she spooned fresh fruit salad into her mouth, some of the fruits grown on foreign planets. The sweet, tropical scent filled Aria's lungs, and she reached for a spoonful. She alternated bites of fruit with a decadent, flaky pastry that melted in her mouth, while her dad crammed a bacon-wrapped breakfast sandwich in his mouth and washed it down with an exotic red juice.

A tall, muscular boy with jet-black hair and almond-shaped eyes sitting across from her nodded with a sly smile. "Hey," he said. "What's your name?"

Aria finished chewing her pastry and swallowed, holding a hand over her mouth. "I'm Aria. You?"

The boy coughed violently. "Aria?" he wheezed as he wiped up the water he had just sprayed. "You wouldn't happen to be Aria Blake, would you?"

"Yeah," she said, drawing out the word. "Have we met?"

"No way," he said. "I would remember if we had. You're supposed to be some kind of kid genius. I bet almost everyone here has heard of you. You better expect to be a little famous when you're the youngest kid to *ever* attend the Academy."

"Oh, no." Aria blushed. "I'm really not a genius. I mean, not any more of a genius than everyone else here."

How could she possibly explain that her record-breaking age was nothing more than the result of exceptionally strict parents and a total lack of a social life? More importantly, how could she explain without spilling her parents' reason for keeping her locked away?

"So you're a humble genius?" he asked, popping a grape in his mouth. "My name's Nick. Nice to meet you. People are gonna look at you like you're a circus freak at first, but it'll die down. You'll make friends—starting with me, if you want."

Aria flashed a crooked smile. "You seem to have a lot of insight into life at the Academy. What, are you repeating your first year? I didn't think that's how this worked."

"Sorry, am I mansplaining? Honestly, I was just trying to get on your good side so you'd do all my homework." He smiled roguishly and winked.

Despite herself, Aria couldn't repress a snort of laughter as she rolled her eyes. "Something tells me you don't need a geek for hire," she said. "I bet—"

Aria's words broke off abruptly as a wave of anxiety enveloped her and her vision blurred again. An image of Luca's face forced itself into her mind. He sat at a table much like hers, but the green shirts and jackets were replaced by black ones. The urge to run, to find something, nearly propelled her to her feet. Was she so anxious that her subconscious was convinced the only solution was to run away? She pinched her eyes shut and sucked in a deep breath as she mentally shoved Luca into the furthest recess of her mind. Finally, her sight blurred back to reality, Nick's worried face staring back at her.

"Aria," he whispered. "Are you okay? Can you hear me?"

"Umm yeah," she muttered. "Sorry. I got, uh, distracted." She met Nick's eyes and flashed her best false smile.

"Students!" A new voice boomed through the speakers. "It's time to say farewell to your parents and follow your cohort leaders to the Boarding Halls. You have two hours to settle in, after which you will return here to the ballroom. You are dismissed."

Aria closed her eyes and let out a deep breath. As much as she loved her parents and would miss them, the last thing she needed now was their constant scrutiny.

"Well, I guess this is it," she said, turning to her mother.

"Come here, darling," her mom said, pulling Aria in for a hug. Her dad encircled them both in his powerful arms.

"We love you, Ari-bug," he said. "And we know you're going to do great things here. Work hard and have fun, but not too much fun!"

"I love you guys, too," she said, voice cracking. "Thank you for helping me get here."

"Goodbye, sweetheart," her mom said. "We'll see you for Colonization Day."

Aria's parents waved and turned to walk back to the elevators with the mass of exiting parents. She wiped a stray tear from her cheek and straightened; this was what she wanted.

Aria scanned the large room for her cohort leader. A young woman, just a few years older than her, wore the same green shirt and jacket, though hers had a unique silver emblem on the front. She directed students with large gestures toward the exit, where Nick and Dima stood talking.

"Hey, guys!" she said with a smile as she jogged up to them. "Do you know each other?"

"Not really," Dima said. "We met yesterday in the tech supply store. I guess we're both procrastinators."

"Only way to be." Nick winked. "Hey, I'll catch you guys later. Looks like I'm getting left behind." He pointed over the girls' heads at the swarm of young men in green jackets exiting the building.

"Sounds good," Dima said. "I'm sure we'll have tons of classes together."

"Hey," he shouted as he backpedaled toward the group. "Don't get into too much trouble without me!"

Dima elbowed Aria as Nick sprinted away. "Please," she whispered, grinning. "We're gonna get into plenty of trouble."

TWO

ARIA AND DIMA jogged to catch up with the other girls in green, filing out of the ballroom into a wide hallway and down an ancient, grand staircase. Scattered gasps floated from the front of the line as the group spilled out into the sunlight. As Aria crossed the threshold, her jaw dropped.

The Academy sat on the north side of the Camut Peninsula, a mere two-hundred and fifty kilometers from Kan City, the capital city of the Allied Nations. Aria had always been proud to grow up near Kan City. The tiny town of Miller Bay was considered a coastal gem, but the scene before Aria made her beautiful hometown's beaches pale by comparison. The sun sparkled off the turquoise water and the white sand beach. All kinds of trees and bushes grew to the beach's edge, heavy with colorful flowers and fruit. Beyond the gorgeous, warm water of the Gulf of Camut, tropical birds floated over the rolling Western Mountains. Tears welled up in Aria's eyes for the umpteenth time that morning.

Without warning, an image of Luca walking along the water's edge danced across her vision. The sensation of pure wonder doubled her already overwhelming emotion. Aria shook herself. Her vision finally returned as the cohort leader took her place at the front of the group. Aria shook her head, tempted to slap herself but careful not to follow the impulse.

"My name's Rhen," the older girl said. "Your other cohort leader is Jake. He's showing the guys to the Men's Boarding Hall. We're both happy to help with anything you need. I'm sure you're all nervous, but work hard, and you'll be fine. Let's get to the fun part!"

Rhen led the group to a fork in the path and veered toward the end of the peninsula.

"The Women's Boarding Hall is just a short walk down the beach," she said. "The men's hall is attached to ours by the common room where we can hang out with the guys. There's plenty of fun to be had on campus and in town. Just remember that your studies should always come first."

"Buzzkill," Dima whispered.

Aria grinned but didn't respond. She was busy reveling in the ocean breeze as she closed her eyes, tilted her head back, and filled her lungs with the sea air. This time of year was normally hot and humid, but today, the weather couldn't have been more perfect.

"Isn't this great?" Dima asked. "Aren't you from around here? I guess it must not be too special for you."

Aria cracked one eye open to look at the redhead. Dima's smile was infectious, and before Aria knew it, she was smiling back at her. "Yeah, pretty close. I'm from Kan City—well, Miller Bay. It's just outside the city, right on the beach."

"You're joking!" Dima said. "I would love to live in the capital! I'm from a tiny town in the north called Kreet. I wouldn't expect you to know it."

"I didn't spend much time in the city. I was only allowed to leave my house alone for school, sports, and school-sanctioned functions."

"Really?" Dima's breezy smile faltered. "That's kind of

messed up."

Aria winced. This was why she avoided this topic. Dima was so open that it was hard not to confide in her. Aria's mind grasped at any possible topic change.

"Wait," she said, turning to her new friend. "Why don't you have a northern accent?"

Dima's eyes lit up and all was forgotten. "You have no idea how glad I am that you asked!" she squealed. "I worked on my southern accent all summer. My country drawl might be cute to some people, but I didn't think it would do me any favors professionally. You might catch me with it now and then, but I'm getting pretty good."

"That doesn't seem right. Why would you have to change the way you talk?"

"It's just the way of things." Dima shrugged. "Most upper-class Northerners try to ditch the accent in professional settings."

The girls fell silent and pensive as they turned a corner and passed through a grove of palm trees, revealing the massive boarding hall. An artificial waterfall flowed over the surface of the west wall, overlooking the sea. The grounds outside were well-maintained and complete with fountains, fruit trees, and lush grass. The group walked up the stone path and through the hulking doorway, entering an expansive sitting room. They passed various entertainment and study rooms on their way to the elevators, where groups of giggling girls stepped onto the rising metal disks until all had made it to the next floor.

"The entire second floor is for first-year students," Rhen called loudly enough for everyone to hear. "The building is a pentagon, and each wall belongs to a different program. You'll be rooming with four other girls from the Colonization cohort. You and your roommates will be together a lot, so you might as well try to be friends. I'll call names to assign your room and your roommates."

Rhen had only called one other group when Aria heard her name. "Aria Blake, Dima Fitzgerald, Allison Hibbet, Gemma Osmund, and Jeslyn Ruiz, you'll be sharing room number 202, the second door on the right."

Dima's eyes widened and she threw her arms around Aria.

"No way!" she squealed. "Now that's what I call fate."

She wiggled her eyebrows at Aria, linked their arms together, and tugged her away. They had only skipped down the hall a few paces when they found the door numbered 202. Dima released Aria's arm and ran to the door, which slid open as it recognized her bio-signature. All five girls tumbled into the entryway only to pause with dropped jaws. The first-year dorms were supposedly the least comfortable, but Aria couldn't imagine how a college dorm room could get any more luxurious. Every surface glimmered with a clean, modern finish. The sitting room and kitchen areas were plenty big for the five of them, with room left over for a guest or two for every roommate. Everything was exquisitely decorated, and a transparent back wall with water running over its surface gave the room an extra air of opulence.

Aria whistled. "Great Explorer."

"You can say that again," said a short, pretty girl with deep caramel skin and thick black hair.

"This is amazing!" Dima screeched. "I can't believe we all get to live here! I mean, a waterfall! Are you kidding me?"

She took off down the hallway, setting off a stampede behind her. The girls followed through an arched doorway and into an elegant powder room. A circular plush bench sat in the center of the room, with five vanities spread out at even intervals around the room. Each girl would have a sink, mirror, and shelves to herself. Dima and Aria stepped through a second doorway into the bathroom, and the other three girls crowded in behind them. A massive jet tub sat opposite the luxurious shower.

"I think I'm gonna cry," Dima said with a huge smile. Her eyes widened, and she turned to the other girls. "I call the best bunk!" She squeezed between the two girls in the doorway and darted to the other side of the hall.

Aria's eyes bulged further as she followed Dima into the bedroom. Like the one in the living room, the far wall was transparent, and water poured over it. There were three sets of bunk beds along the left-side wall, although one of the bottom bunks was replaced by a couch. Each set of beds had a closet and desk on either side. The opposite wall was left blank, presumably for when the girls wanted to connect neurolink feeds and watch something together. Decorative pillows and artwork matched the rug in the middle of the floor.

"Oh yeah," Dima said, falling onto the bottom bunk against the water wall. "This one's mine."

"I get the top bunk!" Aria said. "As long as the window tints at night. I don't want random strangers watching me sleep."

"They aren't random strangers," Dima said. "They're future friends!"

Aria rolled her eyes but plopped down next to her new friend. The other three girls were claiming bunks of their own. Aria pretended not to notice the way they stared at her.

"Where are you three from?" Dima asked the others.

"I'm from the Central Region," the short, pretty girl said as she threw herself on the bottom bunk next to Dima's. "I grew up in a city called Vineyard."

"No way," Dima said. "You're Jeslyn, right? My family and I vacationed in Vineyard a couple of times. Isn't it one of the oldest cities on Drammat?"

"You can call me Jess if you want. But yeah, Vineyard was almost the capital city of the Allied Nations. I don't know why it ended up being Kan City instead."

"And you guys?" Dima asked the other two.

"I'm Allison," said the girl with deep brown skin, hip-length braids, and big brown eyes. Her accent was smooth, thick, and so recognizable that her following words were hardly necessary. "I'm from Brecken. It's the largest city in the Snotch Isles."

"I've always wanted to visit," Dima said. "Isn't it always freezing there?"

"Pretty much. This tropical weather is the opposite of what I'm used to."

"You know," Dima said, "it gets just as cold where I'm from in Kreet. It just doesn't stay that cold for very long."

"It gets pretty cold in Wenjin, where I'm from," said the girl with pale skin, silky black hair, and dark, almond-shaped eyes. "Wenjin is probably similar to Kreet."

"Well, aren't we just a world committee?" Dima said. "How cool is this? What else could have brought us together from all corners of Drammat but the Academy? Look out, world."

Dima jumped up from her bed and dug into the pile of suitcases on the floor. "We only have an hour until we have to meet back in the ballroom. We'd better unpack!"

Aria blinked as Dima began unpacking with all the energy of a toddler on a caffeine high. It might take her a few years to get used to a Dima-paced lifestyle. Aria lugged her bags out of the heap and opened them, emptying her belongings onto her new desk. When she finished putting the most essential items in their places, she stepped back and smiled at her work. She glanced at the ever-present timestamp overlaying the top left corner of her vision.

"Great Explorer!" Aria yelled. "We're gonna be late!"

All four of her roommates dropped what they were doing and bolted to their feet. Aria slung her jacket over her shoulder and sprinted out of the apartment, her roommates following behind. Ten minutes later, five sweaty girls burst through the Great Hall's back door and breathlessly sprinted up the wide staircase, arriving barely a minute late. They stopped to catch their breath for a few precious seconds before creeping into the ballroom.

As they snuck through the door, Luca's face flashed in Aria's mind, worry lines creasing his brow. Again, she felt the need to run—not away from the ballroom, but further into it. At least that was an impulse she could work with.

She closed her eyes for a moment and clenched her fists as she fought for control. A familiar fear tugged at her heart. Maybe she wasn't cut out for this life. Or maybe early enrollment *had* been a bad idea. There had to be a reason no one had ever done it, right?

"You good?" Dima's whisper penetrated the panic and Aria's eyes popped open.

"Sorry, yeah. I'm good."

Dima linked her long arm with Aria's and the pair trailed behind their roommates into the back row of the Colonization seating, the only seats remaining in the entire ballroom. Aria pasted a smile onto her face as she stared past the backs of hundreds of students' heads into the face of the woman who could take away her entire future if Aria gave her a reason.

"Welcome back, students," President Gray said from the podium. Silence fell over the crowd of young adults. Aria's hand went involuntarily to her chest as her heartbeat raced. It was so loud she was sure Dima could hear it. "Now that it's just us and you're all more settled, let's talk about why you're here. The Academy is the oldest and proudest school on Drammat. You are each joining the ranks of men and women who have helped advance humankind for centuries. While there are many valuable and necessary vocations that one might choose in life, five sectors are essential for progress.

These include Engineering, Medicine, Diplomacy, Defense, and Colonization."

Dima nudged Aria and smiled. She should be squealing with joy, but instead, her insides twisted and lurched. She smiled anyway.

"We dedicate our lives to the study and execution of these pursuits," Gray continued. "Engineering students, your calling is to build better tools for every aspect of human life. Medical students are called to enhance and lengthen human life. Diplomacy students, you are called to keep order on Drammat and throughout the galaxy. Defense students, your calling is to protect and preserve our beautiful utopia. And finally, Colonization students are called to expand the human family and ensure our eternal survival. No matter the specialty, all of us are responsible for using our knowledge to move the human family forward. The next four years will be a gauntlet of trials that will take you to the end of your endurance, but those who make it will mold the future. Look around you. These young men and women will be your classmates and your future colleagues. They are also your competition. Classes begin tomorrow, so take the afternoon to explore and prepare. Find your classrooms and get to know your roommates. You are dismissed."

The room erupted with excited chatter. Aria's strained smile remained as she faced her roommates, but beneath, a dozen different emotions warred for prominence. Fear, excitement, hope, embarrassment, and a dozen unnamable feelings. It was just like her dreams: foreign feelings that didn't make sense or correspond to her experiences. One of her therapists had once explained that her subconscious mind created Luca to give voice to the emotions she was unprepared to deal with from a more personal perspective. She had never bought into the idea, but what else could explain the sickening mix of feelings in the pit of her stomach?

"Are you guys hungry?" Gemma asked. Aria forced herself to pay attention. "We were so busy organizing and decorating our apartment that we didn't get lunch. I think my stomach is trying to eat itself."

"Starving!" Allison said. "Let's check out the food court first!

Jeslyn pulled up her neurolink screen, swiping at a map that was invisible to everyone else. "The food court is in the Student Engagement Building, across the courtyard. Come on."

Aria followed along quietly. The girls walked through the courtyard and skipped past a set of large sliding glass doors into a vast room full of first-year students. A glass wall let natural light spill into the room. Students sat at tables and bars set up around the space. Aria closed her eyes as she inhaled, letting the aroma of good food ground her. The girls strolled around the food court and eyed the various stations.

"Do you smell that?" Gemma said. "That's authentic Corbo curry. I would know it anywhere!"

The girls laughed as Gemma scuttered off toward the source of the smell. They continued browsing until they each found what they wanted. Aria chose a sushi roll and grabbed a bottle of water. Aria barely noted the receipt of credit transfer that flashed across the top left corner of her vision as she exited the market area. The girls aimlessly roamed through a maze of tables until Dima spotted Nick sitting with some of the guys in their cohort and waved.

"Hey!" Nick shouted. "Come sit with us."

The rest of the girls followed Dima as she weaved a path through the labyrinth of tables and took the seat next to Nick. Aria sat in front of him, and the other girls gathered around them.

"Hey," Dima said with a bright smile. "What are you boys doing later tonight?"

"Boys?" one of the other guys yelled from across the table. "I think you mean men!"

"Ummm, no," Dima said. "I mean boys."

Aria laughed with the rest of the table, a bit of her anxiety melting away.

"Aria," Dima said, "you're from around here. How should we celebrate our first night at the Academy?"

"Don't waste your time asking Wonder Geek," a brunette boy at the end of the table said, smiling smugly.

"Wonder Geek?" She turned to the rude boy. "Look. The only thing you need to know about me is that I'm just a smart kid like all of you. None of us would be here if we weren't brilliant and hard-working. One year younger is hardly anything, and in your case, I'd bet a thousand credits that your maturity level more closely resembles my ten-year-old cousin."

Many pairs of wide eyes stared back at her from around the table as several of the boys stifled laughs.

Aria rolled her eyes. "Alright. What about a beach party?"

"Yes!" Dima squealed. "I love it!"

Everyone at the table, other than the boy who called her a geek, agreed.

"Then it's settled," Aria said with a satisfied smile. "We'll tell the girls and be in charge of food. You can get the drinks and make sure the other guys get the message. Bring whatever games you can round up too. And don't do anything that could get us in trouble before our first day of classes."

Everyone agreed, and the conversation turned to party preparations. Aria sighed in relief as attention finally drew away from her. She'd never thrown a party, and somehow, this felt like her first test at the Academy.

When the girls finished eating, they set off to see their first-period classroom, if one could call it that. It looked like a giant outdoor dance floor with an expansive grass field and a track nearby. A well-worn trail led from the track into the foothills, where the peninsula met the mainland. The girls zigzagged across campus, running into other groups of students as they poked their heads into every room where at least one of the girls had a class. It was all state-of-the-art, as was to be expected. They even tried to enter the famed greenhouse maintained for practical Colonization labs, but it was locked. By the time they had exhausted their tour destinations, it was nearing dinner time, so they trekked across the campus to the Academy Train Station.

Five credits left her account as she stepped onto the outbound station, only a preview of the credits that would be subtracted at each station they passed. Tonight, they weren't going far. The sound of humming increased as the train pulled into the station. An Engineering student in the usual black T-shirt whistled in response to the train's lightning-fast approach. The sleek, silver machine shined in the dipping sun as it slowed to a stop. Aria ran her fingers along its side and stepped in to sit with her roommates. Something gradually shifted within her as the train pulled away from the station. For the first time all day, she almost felt alone in her own head.

Content to finally feel halfway normal, Aria dashed around Bridgewater with her roommates searching for food and decorations. They found everything they needed quickly and made it back to the station just in time for the six-thirty p.m. train. An annoying sensation niggled at the back of her mind. By the time they reached the end of the line, the anxiety was back in full force. What was wrong with her? She should be having fun! As she and Dima trekked down to the beach to set up, allowing the other girls to head to the apartment to get ready, she put on her best imitation of a smile. They found a dozen guys in bathing suits rather than uniforms, setting up games and a drink tent.

"Nice work, boys!" Dima said as she set down a heaping armful of decorations.

"You just wait and see," said a muscular boy with a playful grin.

"Did you guys invite everyone?" Dima asked.

"Sure did," Nick yelled from inside the tent. "Even the cohort leaders. Hopefully, they're cool."

"Great!" Dima said. "So did we. I'm sure they'll be fun."

The girls finished decorating and helped Nick choose the music before rushing back to the apartment. People would start showing up before nine, and it was already after eight-thirty. They burst into the front room and sprinted to their closets. When they finally finished, Aria looked down at her simple coral swimsuit and frowned. Her roommates all looked like goddesses. Gemma's powder blue swimsuit perfectly complemented her pale skin, dark eyes, and black hair, and accentuated her cute, boyish figure. Allison's bright pink suit highlighted the pink sections of her long braids and accented the richness of her dark skin. Jeslyn's gold suit on her tan skin and curvaceous body made her look like she belonged on a runway. Dima quickly changed into a simple green suit that mirrored the color of her eyes and showed off just how tall she was. She put a hand on Aria's shoulder when she finished.

"You look amazing! Something about your features is so exotic and unique!" she said. "No need to be nervous. It'll all be great. Let's just go have fun!"

Aria's insides coiled at what she was sure was meant as a compliment. She had been described as exotic more times than she could count, and it had always seemed to bother her mom. At least Dima seemed to truly think she was beautiful—that or she was a very good actress.

"Thanks, Dima," Aria said, smiling through the crippling anxiety. "Fun," she muttered, "Let's do this."

THREE

MUSIC BLARED from the beach and multicolored lights danced off the water like a million fireflies as Aria and her roommates left the Women's Boarding Hall. The beach was bursting with kids dancing, playing games, and flirting: every indication of a good party. But despite Aria's smile, the uneasy feeling from before was ever present in her belly. Something about it enthralled her attention. It was as if the source of her anxiety was somewhere in the crowd, drawing her deeper into the sensation as she neared the party.

"Sweet party, Aria!" a tall boy said.

"Yeah, great party!" the girl on his arm echoed.

"Thanks!" Aria said. "It was all of us."

She shook her head in frustration. Nothing was adding up. She genuinely wanted to relax and have a good time, but her mind was fighting it. Strong, conflicting emotions assaulted her from the inside. Suddenly, Dima pulled Aria to a stop and looked her squarely in the eyes.

"Aria, what's going on?" she whispered. "I know we've only known each other for like half a day, but you can trust me. I genuinely want to be your friend."

"I do trust you," Aria said. Wincing probably didn't help her case. "Look, you're right. Right now, all I wanna do is dance, swim, and talk to a cute guy. I promise I'll tell you tomorrow."

"Fine. But you're not getting out of it."

Dima hooked her arm through Aria's and tugged her toward the table where Nick was serving drinks. Dima and Nick's flirtations faded to the background as Aria used every mental trick her psychiatrists ever taught her to calm her mind. She felt her control slipping, and finally, an image of Luca tore through her mental wall. The blurry background of young people dancing near him was eerily similar to reality. He sat alone, leaning against a palm tree and staring into the night. A shadow of confusion flowed through her. She ordered Luca away, but her mantras and mind games did nothing now. For a brief second, she returned to reality.

"Aria!" Dima shouted. "Look at me! You—"

The vision slammed across her sight again, cutting Dima off. Some primal instinct propelled her to her feet. There was that feeling again, like a beacon somewhere in the crowd, calling her toward it. What was she doing? She dimly recognized Dima desperately trying to block her path, but Aria's curiosity had taken over. Intellectually, she knew that she needed to stop drawing attention to herself, but every instinct told her to run to the opposite side of the beach. She shuddered at the thought of everyone watching her make such a scene, but she had to understand what was wrong with her.

Aria both felt and saw Luca stand and start walking, and as he did, whatever power was pulling Aria strengthened. She stumbled through a crowd of dancing teenagers, elbowing her way through the sweaty bodies. The object of her hunt was close. She spun wildly, searching the crowd. A strong hand gently grasped her shoulder and the pulse of heat and electricity skittered across her skin, sinking pleasantly into her bones. The owner of the hand turned her around, and tears sprang to her eyes.

The boy was tall, so tall Aria had to tilt her head up to stare into his deep green, gold-flecked eyes. There was a steadiness there that she would recognize anywhere, but she didn't need the confirmation. The unmistakable sensation of his emotions flowing into her left no room for doubt; it was Luca, and Luca wasn't real. Devastation rolled over her. She really was as crazy as her parents had always feared. Worse, she may have exposed the secret she and her family had spent her entire life hiding—all for a figment of her imagination. Hot tears poured over her cheeks as she closed her eyes and repeated her mantras in her head, but someone touched her arm and she jumped. Dima walked between Aria and her ghost.

"I think I should get you home," she whispered, glancing over her shoulder. "Is this guy bothering you?"

"You...you can...see him?"

"Aria, you're scaring me. Please let me take you home."

"But you can see him? I don't...I can't..."

Aria's entire body trembled as she stared past Dima into the eyes of the lifelong villain of her story. What was going on? Why couldn't he stay in the dark hole in her mind where she had hidden him years ago? Her breaths came fast and shallow as she looked around at the many students watching the drama unfold. It was too much.

Aria nodded and Dima pulled her into her arms and slowly turned her around, half-carrying her up the beach toward the Women's Boarding Hall. Aria looked back at the impossibly real boy standing on the beach staring back at her. He looked just as scared and confused as she was, but she didn't need to see him to know that. She felt every flicker of hope and wave of confusion. More tears escaped as she started to sob.

"We're almost home," Dima said, hugging her tighter. "It's gonna be okay."

"You don't know that," Aria said through her tears.

"Let's just get back and get you in bed, okay?"

Aria nodded slowly and let Dima guide her to their room. She sat Aria down on the edge of her bed while she searched for her pajamas.

"Are these shorts and this T-shirt okay?" Dima asked.

Aria nodded again, not even looking at the selection. Dima helped her out of her swimsuit and into the clothes she had picked out for her. Aria might have been embarrassed, but in her current state, she was grateful for Dima's help.

She pulled a blanket over Aria and began to retreat.

"Thank you," Aria whispered.

Dima paused in the doorway. "That's what friends are for. Do you want to talk about it? I don't know what's going on, but it never helps to keep things locked inside. Not to mention you'll see that guy in our first class tomorrow."

"Great." Aria groaned, pulling her knees into her chest and burying her face in her hands. "I didn't even think about that. But I do want to tell you. I've never really been able to talk about it with anyone. I don't know how to start. And, I mean, I don't even know you."

Dima crossed the room and sat down on the bed next to Aria. "I know you don't have a reason to trust me yet, but I promise you can. Just start from the beginning. I won't judge you, whatever it is."

Aria's brain screamed at her not to do this, but some instinct told her she could trust Dima. Besides, everyone on the beach probably already thought she was crazy, so what did it matter? She sighed, consigning herself to whatever consequences came next. She was done being alone.

"As long as I can remember, I've had a boy named Luca in my head." The words spilled from her lips between bouts of sobbing. She told Dima about her imaginary friend and the way her parents changed when he stuck around too long. She told her of the psychiatrists, of the medications, and the years of isolation because she couldn't let anyone get close enough to see her illness. She told her about the boy who lived on a metal ship in her head, who never aged and was always sad. And she told her how the visions increased and the feeling grew stronger as Academy orientation loomed.

"Well, that explains a lot," Dima said. "But what does that have to do with what happened on the beach?"

"Tonight was the worst it's ever been. Something pulled me, and I couldn't help but follow it. The boy you saw me with touched my shoulder, and it was like our energy connected. It was him. Luca was right in front of me."

"You mean your vision overlaid reality or something? Like it made that guy look like the guy from your dreams?"

"No, Dima. I think that guy *was* Luca, the same Luca I've known in my dreams for my entire life. I know how that sounds, but I could feel that it was him."

"Wow," Dima said.

"You think I'm insane," Aria said, burying her face in her hands again. "I get it. I would too."

Dima studied Aria as a long silence passed. The corner of her mouth quirked upward, and she pressed a hand over her mouth as a loud snort escaped. After a brief and unsuccessful struggle, a full laugh burst through her fingers, and she gave in to hysterics. Aria scoffed and hit Dima on the shoulder.

"You said no judgment!"

"I'm sorry, Ar! I believe you. Or, at least, I believe that you're experiencing something the rest of us can't see." She wiped a mirthful tear from the corner of her eye as she composed herself. "Seriously, I'm sorry you've gone through this alone, but now you have something you never had before. You have me."

A reluctant smile broke over Aria's lips. "Thank you."

"So, here's the plan," Dima said as she stood and folded her arms. "You're gonna kick butt in all your classes and have the best year of your life with your new friends. If people are weird about tonight, I'll have your back, and it'll die down. When you feel a vision coming on, leave the room before it happens. And, for all Drammat, please don't go anywhere after one's already started."

"Okay," Aria said, running her fingers through her hair. "Thank you for being so cool about this."

"Of course, but I'm not finished. We need to find a real solution, starting with talking to that boy who looks like Luca, or is Luca, or whatever."

Aria groaned. "He probably thinks I'm a freak."

"You'll have to see him anyway because all first-years have Defense class together. It's better to address it before it gets weirder. Honestly though, to anyone who was paying attention, he was just as weird as you were."

Aria's eyes flashed to Dima's. "Weird? How?"

"He was stumbling around looking all wide-eyed and crazy, just like you were. When he saw you, it was like he saw a ghost. No, an angel! I can't describe it very well, okay? The point is that he might have answers. If he doesn't, maybe you can search for them together. He might know what you're going through in a way nobody else can. So, yes—you're talking to him. Now, get some sleep."

Aria threw a pillow at Dima as she walked out of the bedroom.

"Goodnight!" Dima yelled, dodging the pillow.

Panic crept up in Aria, but she quickly forced it down. Maybe he *wasn't* her Luca. Maybe she was crazy after all. Still, Dima's words tumbled around in her head as she drifted off to sleep. "He might have answers."

Aria woke to the sound of her alarm, feeling almost as exhausted as when she had fallen asleep. Her eyes felt puffy from the previous night's tears and her mind was hazy from her dreams. She had dreamt of Luca, as she did most nights, but that was the only thing that remained the same. Instead of the metal halls of the ship, he strode along a sandy beach. Instead of the tiny cot in the cabin he called home, he slept in a large, comfortable bunk bed. Most unsettling of all, her dreams consisted of watching Luca sleep for most of the night.

She rubbed the drowsiness from her eyes and tried not to feel like a freak. Today was the start of the rest of her life, and now she had way more to worry about than classes. She hopped up from Dima's precious bottom bunk by the window and saw her friend sleeping in her top bunk. What would she have done without Dima? Aria braced herself for the coming backlash; the rest of her classmates wouldn't be half as understanding about the scene she caused.

She rushed to the bathroom to get ready. Despite everything, pride flowed through her as she dawned the green T-shirt and jacket that signified so many years of hard work. When she finished, she walked into the kitchen where Jeslyn and Dima were eating breakfast.

"Hey Aria," Jeslyn said. "I hope you're doing okay after last night."

"I'm all good now, Jess. Thanks."

She cringed as she grabbed a breakfast bar and went back to her room to finish gathering her things. Once her bag was packed, she zipped it up and returned to the sitting room, desperately attempting to avoid her roommates' nervous gazes. She laced up her boots and threw her bag over her right shoulder with a deep breath.

"Alright ladies," Dima said. "Let's go kick butt and take names!"

Aria led the way out of the apartment, determined to appear confident despite her anxiety. If she could get through this first class, things would get better. As soon as the girls left the boarding hall, Aria could feel Luca nearby. With every step toward the Defense building, his pull increased. He was behind her, but she couldn't bring herself to look back and search for him. A vision of him walking along a gray pathway crossed in front of her sight. Based only on the blurry background, it could have been any path in the galaxy, but she felt his precise location. His feelings of anxiety and excitement overpowered her own, and she shivered at the combined severity. The girls arrived at the southern edge of the training floor outside the Defense building with five minutes to spare. The tension continued to rise as Aria felt Luca close the gap between them.

"I've got your back, Ar," Dima whispered, resting her arm on her shoulder.

"And so do we," Allison said as the other girls nodded and smiled. "We're here for you and happy to resort to violence if needed."

"Thanks, guys, but I don't think violence will be necessary. Let's just stick together today."

"Duh," Dima said. "But stop worrying. You're gonna be fine."

Aria ignored Dima as the protection of distance quickly diminished. Luca's presence was nearly on top of her when she looked to the horizon. Her breath caught as she spotted his tall frame walking toward her, surrounded by a group of young men in black T-shirts. There was a glow inside him that radiated out and warmed her, a glow she felt within her soul. In an instant, she was sure. He *was* Luca, not some doppelganger or lookalike, but her very own Luca. Both Luca's and

Aria's emotions were so similar that she struggled to untangle them. Anxiety, fear, wonder, joy, and confusion whirled between them. Unshed tears sat in Aria's eyes, watching Luca stare back at her as if it were a reunion he had waited for his whole life.

Aria finally built up the willpower to break eye contact and look at her friends. All four of them were staring with amused grins. She shifted her gaze to the groups directly behind her friends and found countless faces examining her and Luca with interest. Suddenly the reunion seemed more embarrassing than sacred. She shot a look back at Dima, silently pleading for help.

"Are you guys nervous about this class?" Dima asked loudly. "I, for one, am terrified. My parents said this class was one of the hardest they took at the Academy. Although my parents are nerds, and I'm a lot more athletic than they ever were, so..." Dima's chatter continued, spurring other conversations all around them.

"Thank you," Aria whispered to Dima once Gemma took over the conversation. "I think I'm gonna go talk to him."

Dima nudged her. "I don't think you have to. Great Explorer, he's cute."

The invisible bond alerted Aria that Luca was coming closer. She turned to face him, and her body swayed slightly toward him, almost against her will.

"Hi," Aria said, locking her bright eyes on his golden green ones.

"Hi," he said. "Your name is Aria." It wasn't a question.

"It is," she said, her mouth uncomfortably dry. "And you're Luca." She tried to speak with as much confidence as he had, but her voice came out small. She shifted as his intense gaze burrowed into her.

"Good morning, students!" a burly man in an instructor's uniform shouted. "All five hundred of you are here because the safety of our Academy students is paramount to advancing the human race."

His commanding tone cut off all idle conversation as everyone turned to get a better look at their instructor.

"This course will focus on self-defense and physical fitness. I'll do my best to prepare you for any situation, but your work and dedication will determine your safety in the field. We'll begin with some basic self-defense moves with a partner who you may choose. Partners are permanent, so please introduce yourselves and prepare to spar."

"Be my partner?" Luca asked, holding a hand out to her.

Heat rushed to Aria's cheeks. She may have been more intimately connected with him than any other person in the galaxy, but that didn't mean she wasn't nervous. She had always thought he was one of the most attractive guys she had ever seen. She nodded and took his hand.

"Listen," Luca whispered, leaning so close his lips grazed her ear.

An electric buzz sparked under her skin where his lips touched her skin, and some invisible force pulled them infinitesimally closer.

"I know we need to talk," he said. "But I don't think we can do that here. So let's just get through this class, and then we can decide when to meet up. Is that okay?"

"Okay," Aria said, focusing all her energy on defying the magnetic pull. "Just one class. How hard can it be?"

FOUR

VERY HARD. The answer was very hard. As the rest of the five hundred first-year students paired up and dissolved into the vast space, Aria moved away from Luca, stretching the electric pull between them. It was hard to tell which feelings belonged to her when she was close to him. Everything she felt was echoed by him and multiplied in intensity. Her heart raced as she led him into one of the squares painted on the far north side of the floor. It was far enough from the front not to be the center of attention, yet all eyes seemed to stray toward her and her partner.

"How's this?" Aria asked.

"It's perfect," Luca said. "Good choice."

He slowly walked toward her, strengthening his pull on her with every step. Aria's eyes darted downward, deliberately avoiding his intense gaze. The connection pulling them together only accentuated the growing awkwardness between them. Bradford was still helping straggling students find partners, so if there was ever a time to break the ice, it was now.

"How did you know my name?" Aria blurted.

"I heard your friends call you by it," he said. "You were all talking when I walked over."

"No, I don't think they did." She narrowed her eyes. "I wasn't even in the conversation."

"Well, it must have been at the party last night when your friend was helping you."

A flush rose to her cheeks. "Oh. Yeah, I guess that could've been it."

His lips curved into a friendly smile, but Aria's anxiety flared dangerously at his casual mention of the party. Maybe Dima was wrong; maybe this thing was totally one-sided.

"So about the party," she said, clenching her fists to stop them from shaking. "I'm sorry I was so weird."

"No," Luca said. "You don't need to apologize for that. It was a weird night."

"So you noticed." She grimaced.

"Oh yeah," he said through a dry laugh. "I noticed."

A burst of excitement overwhelmed her. It was so far from her own emotions that she flinched. She knew instinctively that it was Luca's emotion flowing into her. How was this connection even possible? It was one thing to experience it in her dreams of an imaginary perfect guy, but the man in front of her was one-hundred-percent real. And unlike the boys at the lunch table yesterday claiming to be men, Luca *was* one. It wasn't just his muscled body and the way he carried himself, but something internal that spoke of more real experiences than Aria or any of her peers had ever known.

"So, what exactly happened from your point of view?" she finally asked.

As Luca opened his mouth to answer, Instructor Bradford poked his head between them. "Are you two good to go?"

"All good here, Instructor," Luca said. "Thanks!"

"Aria, can I speak with you for a moment?" He didn't wait for her answer to start heading off to the side.

"What's up, Instructor?" Aria asked.

"You know, I was one of your dad's closest friends when we were at the Academy," he said, smiling. "I knew your mom too. Good people."

"Oh, I didn't know. But thank you. Yes, my parents are great."

"See, I have a favor to ask you," Bradford continued. "I know you're up to the task because I know your folks and I trust that they raised a good girl."

"Okay," Aria hedged. "What do you need me to do?"

"Oh, just keep an eye on your partner. I was happy to see that a trustworthy girl like you partnered with Luca. If you hear him speak about anything taboo or spout any lies about our government, I want you to let me or one of the other instructors know. Can you do that?"

"Sure," Aria said. "But why..."

"Just a precaution," Bradford interrupted. "I have to start the class, but feel free to come to my office any time."

Without another word, Bradford threw out a thumbs-up and walked to the front of the room, but not before glancing sidelong at Luca. Aria bit her lower lip as she walked back to her partner. What on Drammat was that about?

"Quiet down!" Bradford yelled. "There's a reason we require this class for every first-year. Those of you who make it to graduation will begin a life that may often take you into danger. I aim to make you capable fighters so you can defend yourselves and others. My aides and I will be observing and correcting your technique as needed, so feel free to ask any of us for help at any time. Let's begin."

Bradford gave instructions for the first exercise, a simple one Aria's father had taught her as a kid. Bradford instructed the smaller partner to be the perpetrator and the larger one to be the victim, which meant that Aria would have to grab Luca's wrist while he attempted to break free. Aria turned to

Luca and took a deep breath before she reached for his wrist. As the space between their hands shrunk, the electricity between them sparked, and a tingle raced across her skin. Warmth coursed from his skin and sunk into hers as her fingertips touched his wrist. Aria gasped and Luca stiffened at the touch.

They said nothing as they continued the exercise. Luca flipped his constrained hand over, raised his arm to jaw level, and brought his other arm up to grab her wrist. He turned, breaking her hold on him, and the electric warmth cut off as they let go of each other. They went through several exercises, the unsettling buzz returning at the slightest touch.

"For our last exercise today," Bradford yelled from the front of the class, "the smaller partner will be our victim and the larger will be the perpetrator. Perpetrator, wrap your arms around your partner, clasping your hands under their sternum as if you were trying to lock their arms down and lift them. Make it tight!"

Electricity sizzled in the air as Luca approached Aria from behind. Her lungs froze, and her heart raced when his breath tickled her ear. He pressed his chest to her back and folded his arms around her, hands clasped firmly over her chest. Aria's mind went blank. The only thing in the world was Luca's strong body at her back and his arms surrounding her. She glanced at Bradford, who was staring at her. How long had she been immobilized and disoriented? She shook her head and exhaled sharply. She performed the routine shakily, but she broke free quickly enough. Having a Defense chief for a father meant she had learned most of these basic exercises as a young child, but if she didn't get a hold of herself, even muscle memory couldn't save her. Thankfully, Bradford nodded, moving on to inspect another pair.

With only a few minutes left in class and having finished their work, Aria opted to look forward, avoiding eye contact with Luca. The electric hum pulling her toward him was becoming constant, putting her nerves on edge. Bradford returned to his place at the head of the class with a minute to spare.

"Good job today," he shouted. "We'll work on these exercises all week. Your first exam is on Friday, so find some time to practice with your partners. You're dismissed."

A collective sigh of relief went up from the class. Luca walked silently by Aria's side as she wandered away from the floor.

"What class do you have next?" he finally asked.

"Physics 108." She hated how breathless she sounded. "What about you?"

"Microbiology 134. I think that's in the same building. Can I walk with you?"

"Uh, okay. Just let me grab my bag."

Aria jogged toward her roommates, who were picking up their things. Their curious faces peered at her as she approached. She waved as she slowed to a stop, scooped up her bag, and shouldered it.

"You ready to go?" Jeslyn asked, looking past her to Luca with a poorly disguised smile.

"Actually," Aria mumbled as she felt Luca catching up, "umm..."

"Oh, that reminds me, Jes!" Dima interrupted, leading her away from Aria, "I forgot I had to show you guys something!"

All three of Aria's other roommates were immediately derailed by Dima's exuberant rant. Her ability to speak and be heard was almost a superpower.

"Bless that woman," Aria said.

She felt Luca arrive at her back. "You ready?" he asked.

She nodded and led the way toward the Math and Science Building. Because it was right across the courtyard, they wouldn't have a problem making it to class on time, even if they walked at a snail's pace.

"So, where are you from?" he asked, something strange about his tone.

"I'm from a small coastal town," Aria said, shrugging. "A suburb of Kan City."

"Really?" he asked, though he didn't feel surprised to her. "What's the city like? I'm not from around here, but I've been studying up on the local geography. I've read that it's one of the largest cities on Drammat and the most technologically advanced city in the galaxy."

"Yeah, I mean, it's cool. Honestly, I didn't get out to the city much because my parents are beyond strict, but the beach in my backyard is amazing! Although, now that I've seen the beaches here, it hardly seems special."

"I'm sure it's beautiful," he said. "I would bet that all of Drammat's beaches are beautiful."

He would bet? What a weird way to say that. She cocked her head slightly, but she didn't want to make him uncomfortable. Now that she thought of it, he did have a bit of an accent, one she had never heard from anyone else.

"Maybe I can take you sometime and you can see it in person," she said.

She flushed as soon as the words left her mouth. Did she seriously ask a stranger home to meet her parents? She winced and looked away, but it was too late to take it back.

"You know, I would love that," he said. "Thank you."

Aria ducked her head so he wouldn't see her blushing. "Okay...yeah. What about you? Where are you from?"

"Umm," he paused for a moment as if deciding what answer to give. Finally, he said softly, "Earth."

Aria laughed and raised her eyebrows at him. "Right. And I'm a unicorn," she said, still giggling more than the joke deserved, if she was being honest.

Luca stared back at her in silence, nervously chewing his cheek. Aria's smile faltered and her laugh died as she subconsciously stopped walking.

"What?" she hissed. "Why do you look serious?"

"Umm...'cause I am," he whispered. "I got here the morning of orientation; good thing too, because if I got here any later, I would have had to wait a year to enroll."

She opened her mouth, but nothing came out. Then, closing it, she turned and continued walking swiftly, Luca jogging behind her.

"Assuming you're not punking me and you're actually from Earth," she finally said as they neared the entrance, "how did you get here? Drammat hasn't allowed immigrants from other planets in decades, not even on education visas."

He sighed, and a feeling of weary grief overflowed from him. "It's kind of a long story," he finally said.

"We have time," Aria prompted as they came to the front of the Math and Science Building. "Class doesn't start for another ten minutes."

He glanced around at the other students entering the building. Finally, he threw his hands up and grunted, leaning close to Aria.

"My dad's parents were our only family members who stayed on Earth during the last great migration," he said softly but quickly. "They always thought they'd join the family on Drammat once their work contracts were over, but then the borders closed and they were stuck. They fell in love and had my dad. On Earth, families are only allowed one child, so it was just the three of them. My dad met my mom in college, and they got married and had me. My mom was an orphan, and my dad's parents died when I was a kid, so most of my life, it was Mom, Dad, and me. Then my mom died when I was eleven, and my dad wasn't the same without her. Six months ago, he passed too. Technically, he died over ten years ago, but it was just six months for me."

"What?" Aria asked as they walked through the front doors.

"You know, because of time dilation," he said. "The journey here was only about four months, but we traveled near lightspeed most of that time, so those four months for me were ten years for you and everyone else who wasn't moving at lightspeed. I just turned eighteen, but my Earth records state that I'm almost twenty-eight."

"Wow," Aria whispered. "That's right. I understand time dilation as a concept, but I've never imagined what it would be like to live it. At least, not so dramatically. So, everyone you knew is now ten years older? I'm so sorry."

"No, don't be." Luca shrugged. "I had some friends at school, but we were about to graduate and go our separate ways anyway. I just had to finish some work on the voyage to graduate before starting here."

"But that doesn't explain how you're allowed to be here," Aria said.

"Well, do you remember how I didn't have any relatives other than my Dad?"

"Sure."

"When he died, I was a minor with no living relatives on Earth, but I did have living relatives on Drammat—lots of them. So, it was either send me off to a group home for a few months and let me out on my own with no family or support system to speak of, or put me on a ship and send me off to relatives I'd never met who would age by ten years before I got to them. The courts decided this was a better option. It wasn't my choice, but I'm grateful."

Heat rose to Aria's cheeks as Luca's deep green eyes roved across her face. She stopped near the doorway to her physics classroom.

"I'm glad they decided to send you here too," she said. "But you're gonna be late. You should go."

"You promise we'll talk later?" Luca asked with a crooked smile.

"I promise!" She shoved him down the hall toward the biology wing, electricity sparking at the point of contact. "Get to class!"

"I'll find you tonight," he said, backpedaling through the hall.

She almost asked how, but she already knew.

The same way she could find him.

FIVE

ARIA ROLLED the revelations of the last hour over and over in her head. As illogical as it might be, there was only one explanation: this thing, whatever it was, went both ways. If she was right, Luca could feel her presence the way she experienced his: everyday moments, emotions, and the irresistible force pulling them together—he could feel it all. *Wait, everything?* Embarrassing moments began flashing through her mind. She slumped over at her desk, palming her face in self-loathing.

Some time later, her physics instructor introduced himself and began teaching, but every time Aria attempted to focus, her thoughts inevitably wandered back to Luca. She still had so many questions, but Luca had answered an important one. It had always been strange to her that Luca had aged normally when she was a child, only to stop aging altogether for ten years. She ran the numbers in her head, thanking her lucky stars that Drammat was the most similar inhabited planet to Earth in size, rotation, and orbit. Luca would have been almost twelve years old when Aria was born on Drammat and would have kept aging until he left for Drammat at age seventeen, nearly six years. For the next ten years, while Aria aged from six to sixteen, he was on a ship, living only four months of his life in ten years of hers. She made a face. How strange to think that, although she was born when Luca was twelve, they were now less than two years apart.

Aria jumped as students around her stood and gathered their belongings. Was the class already over? Familiar guilt bubbled up inside her. She wasn't thinking clearly; she had worked her entire life for this opportunity and couldn't allow anything to jeopardize that. And yet, the shade of pink Aria had worn on her cheeks for the last two and a half hours darkened when she thought of the figment-turned-real boy. There was something almost supernatural going on, and didn't she have a right to seek the answers to her questions?

"Hey!" a familiar voice said, a petite hand waving in front of Aria's face. "Drammat to Aria!"

"Huh?" Aria asked. She snapped back to reality to find Jeslyn's large brown eyes staring back at her suggestively.

"You have to tell us what happened with Mr. Dreamboat!" she squealed. "You were almost late to class after a fifteen-minute plus period to walk two hundred meters. What happened?"

"No way!" Aria said, picking her bag up and fleeing. "I'm *so* not talking about this here! I promise I'll tell you guys when we get back to the dorm, okay?"

Allison appeared behind Jeslyn. "Fine," she said. "But we want every detail!"

Aria and her friends went their separate ways for their following classes, Aria's being History of the Human Race. Unsurprisingly, it went by similarly to the last—either thinking about Luca, or explicitly trying not to think about Luca and failing. When the class was dismissed during another daydream, she growled inwardly. If she couldn't focus, her destiny would slip through her fingers. She was acting like a child. She needed to revert to the exemplary student she had always been, but until she got some answers, she would likely continue being a distracted airhead. She packed up her untouched instruments and headed to the Student Engagement Building for lunch. She was determined to make breakfasts and dinners at the apartment, but lunches were more convenient if she stayed in her classes' vicinity. She browsed the endless food options until she found a chicken salad that called to her. Twenty credits were subtracted from her account as she left the market area and sat down alone at a nearby table. It was one of the only empty tables since the first-years were no longer the only students on campus.

"Hey, Aria!" Nick yelled.

She looked up from her lunch, scanning the crowd. Nick was a few paces away with several friends, all walking toward her. She smiled and waved at him, which he took as an invitation. Aria smiled, but it didn't reach her eyes. She hadn't had the nerve to talk to anyone but her roommates and Luca since the incident at the party. She was probably about to get bullied to oblivion.

"Hey," Nick said. "How have your classes been so far? I saw you and that Engineering guy getting a little cozy during first period. Did you two already know each other?"

Aria's mouth fell open. "What do you mean? We were doing what we were told, just like the rest of you!"

"Right," he said with a grin. "Whatever you say."

He took the seat next to her, and his friends followed, including the rude one who had called her a geek the day before. The party was supposed to shut him up for good, but her pathetic meltdown probably did more damage. Yet the boys sat down as if nothing out of the ordinary had happened. They didn't seem the types to let such golden comedic material pass them by.

She leaned close to Nick's ear. "Why isn't anyone messing with me about last night?"

"What do you mean?" Nick asked through a bite of his burger. "That party was great!"

"You know what I mean," she said, lowering her voice even more. "When I had a mental breakdown in front of literally everyone?" Nick raised one eyebrow but said nothing, so she pushed. "Nick, I looked like a crazy person!"

"Aria, I swear," Nick said. "I don't know what you're talking about."

She sighed, rolling her eyes. "When I walked across the beach like a disoriented zombie and stared at Luca," she said, raising her voice. She took a deep breath and whispered, "That's the Engineering kid I sparred with this morning. I freaked out, and Dima had to take me back to our apartment. You can't tell me you didn't see any of that! I know you followed her after she followed me!"

"Well, yeah, but do you hear yourself? You walked across a beach and looked at a guy who looked back at you. Then Dima walked you back home. That's all that happened. Yeah, it was a little weird how intense you both were, but trust me when I tell you much weirder things have been known to happen at parties." He raised his voice so his friends could hear. "Like when Elio lost his trunks in front of those Medical girls last night, thanks to Milo. Now *that* was funny!"

The boy Aria guessed was Elio rammed his shoulder into the rude boy, who must have been Milo. The other guys laughed and taunted Elio. Aria tilted her head and stared at the rowdy group. They seemed genuinely unaware of her breakdown. A wave of relief replaced the tenseness she had been carrying all day, but a new worry gripped her.

"If you weren't talking about the awkwardness of last night, then what did you mean about Luca and me getting cozy in first period? Everyone was doing the same exercises!"

"Come on," he droned. "You know what I mean. The chemistry between you two was nuts! My partner and I could feel it on the opposite side of the floor!"

"Wait, you talked about this with your partner?" Aria asked, eyes widening in horror.

"We just made a little fun," he said, trying to hide a smile. "And so did just about everyone else."

"The entire class was talking about us? How do you even know that?"

"I told you. It was thick! Nobody could have missed it. It looked like you were both barely holding it together. I lost fifty credits betting you'd give in and start making out in the middle of class!"

"No," Aria whispered. She groaned and dropped her head into her hands. It was so much worse than she feared. Her face felt so hot she thought it might burst into flames.

"Aria, come on," Nick said. "It's great if you guys like each other. A little quick if you just met, but still cool. We're all headed to History of the Human Race, so we better get going, but do me a favor and stop worrying. You're killing the vibes around here." He stood from the table and the other guys followed. "I'll catch you later!"

"Later," she said, waving halfheartedly before dropping her head into her arms again.

So much for keeping a low profile. But she had to admit, a little gossip about a budding romance was much better than speculation about her mental fitness for the Academy.

Romance. She blushed. Was that what this was? As she peeled herself off of the table and made her way to the library, the corner of her mouth lifted just a little.

Aria had the fourth period off, so she wanted to catch up on what she missed in Physics and History. She sat at a secluded desk by the tall back window and absently scrolled through her Theoretical Quantum Physics class module on her neurolink screen. She tried to focus on the list of assignments, textbook passages, videos, and VR simulations as they overlaid her current surroundings. Still, her mind wandered back to Luca every time she made the tiniest hint of progress. Before she knew it, it was time for her next class, a Diplomacy course her mother had recommended, and all she had done was come up with more questions for Luca.

She arrived breathlessly and sat down at the closest desk to the door moments before class began. Instructor Nori was uncommonly young for an Academy teacher. She had thick, dark hair and a conventionally beautiful face, and her mannerisms, poise, and style reminded Aria of her mother, the perfect diplomat. Somehow, Aria made it through class without her thoughts wandering to Luca every few seconds, and after a morning like hers, that seemed like a colossal accomplishment. She even managed to take a few notes.

As the class closed, Aria scooped up her things, and a smile crept onto her face. Her last class of the day was Colonization 102, the introduction to her dream career. Everything in her life had led to this moment. Colonization was the bread and butter of modern humanity; she would be a part of it, discovering new habitable planets and turning them into beautiful homes for the human family. She felt almost giddy as she rushed to her final class. She had envisioned this moment millions of times, and nothing could distract her from it.

As she stepped into the classroom, Luca's presence slammed into her like a solid wall. How had she not registered his closeness? She glanced around the room to find him seated in the far row of desks, just as stunned as she was. Each desk had two chairs, but the seat next to Luca was already taken by a gorgeous brunette girl wearing Diplomacy purple. Any chance she had of focusing on the class died. It was probably for the best that the seat beside Luca was taken if she wanted to achieve any amount of concentration. Something about the girl's face was familiar, but Aria couldn't place how she knew her. An uncomfortable mix of relief and disappointment tightened in her chest as she scanned the room for an open seat, finding one near the back.

She glanced at Luca as she crossed the front of the classroom and stiffened as she saw him whisper into the beautiful girl's ear. A hot wave of jealousy rushed over her, and she clenched her jaw. The memory of his breath on her cheek and his lips on her ear shot through her. She knew she had no claim on Luca, but some crazy instinct screamed that he was hers.

Luca pulled back from the brunette's ear, and she stared at him, looking confused. She stood up, scooting the chair loudly across the glossy floor. Her face turned cold, and she snatched up her things and rushed to an empty desk farther back. Luca aimed a half-smile toward Aria and tilted his head in the direction of the now-empty chair.

Aria's pulse increased, and she pointed at the empty chair, mouthing, 'Now?'

He nodded and gave that crooked smile again.

Stunned, Aria let the electric pull between them guide her. She passed the girl Luca ejected from the seat and tried not to cringe at the death glare she was giving her. Guilt tugged at her, but she sat down anyway.

"You didn't have to make that girl leave," Aria whispered.

"I know," Luca said. "I didn't force her to leave, but I wasn't gonna pass up on the chance to sit with you if she was willing to go."

Aria blushed through a smile. Luckily, the class was interesting enough to keep her attention more easily, even when she was sitting right next to the source of her distraction. Still, every time their knees bumped or hands touched, her full attention returned to him. Several times, she caught him staring at her out of the corner of her eye and felt his nervous energy burning in her own chest. She forced her attention to remain forward, no matter what she saw or felt. The instructor dismissed them after what felt like an eternity, and Aria finally turned to Luca. He was smiling at her.

"What?" she asked with a laugh.

"You looked like you enjoyed that class."

"Well, it *is* my specialty. I'm surprised to find so many students of other specialties in this class."

"Colonization is a big part of the system. I guess they think we all need an intro because it was a required class for me too. It's different for you, though. You looked so in your element."

"I do love it," she said, blushing. "Thank you."

"I have an idea," Luca said. "Do you want to go on a hike with me? We can pack a picnic for dinner and hike a little way up that trail we saw during Self-Defense. What do you say?"

"It's the first day of classes! We can't just leave."

"That's why it's the perfect day. Do you have any home-work you have to get done before tomorrow?"

"Well, no, but..."

"But?" He smiled. "I don't want to take you away from your responsibilities, but is there any real reason we shouldn't go?"

That pesky, familiar guilt blossomed into full fruition, but Aria ruthlessly pushed it down. It might cause her to remain behind in her physics and history classes, but she felt she would never be able to focus until she got the answers she needed.

"I guess not," she said. "Okay. Let's do it."

"Perfect! I'll walk you to your apartment, then head over to mine so we can both get changed for a hike. Don't worry about the food. I've got it."

They sped down the peninsula, talking and laughing as

they went. Aria told Luca that her favorite kind of food was seafood, having grown up on the coast. She learned that he loved the water on Drammat because Earth's natural water sources were all polluted, so water had to be chemically purified. They talked about their classes and hopes for the semester, and before she knew it, Luca was dropping her off at the front door of the Women's Boarding Hall. He promised to be quick and sprinted off toward his apartment.

Aria sighed as she turned and walked through the sliding doors. Less than twenty-four hours prior, Luca had been a figment of her imagination. Now, he was a living, breathing person, as real as she was. More than that, everyone could see there was something happening between them.

She stopped just short of entering the apartment. It was always possible that this whole thing might be an impressively realistic psychotic episode. She shook her head and commenced walking. Everyone else seemed to agree that Luca was indeed a real person. A dopey smile crept across her face as the apartment door slid open, but the moment she stepped through, she regretted it. All four of her roommates had been waiting, and the questions came faster than she could answer.

"Woah!" she yelled, setting her bag on the bench by the door. "Slow down!"

"Me first!" Dima shouted, shutting the other girls up. "What happened this morning? Everyone is talking about it! You two looked like you were in your own little world!"

All four girls giggled uncontrollably. Aria kneaded her temples with both hands. "When you say everyone, you mean *everyone* everyone? The older students too, or just our class who saw it?"

"*Everyone* everyone," Dima said. "Word spreads fast, girl! I heard he kicked Celeste Brant out of the seat next to him so he could sit by you!"

Aria's eyes bugged and she nearly choked. "That was Vice President Brant's daughter? I knew she looked familiar."

"So it's true?" Gemma asked. "That's not good. With her connections, half the school's gonna do whatever she says."

"Well, I'm about to go on a date with Luca," Aria said, unable to hold back a smile. "So bring on the rumors."

"What?" all four of her roommates said in unison.

"What happened?" Allison asked. "Aria, come on! You *have* to give us some details!"

"If I do, I'll be late! I promise I'll tell you guys tonight! I'll have more to tell after our date anyway!"

Without waiting for her roommates' assent, Aria ran to her closet and threw on some light blue shorts and a gray tank top. She didn't bring her heavy-duty hiking boots with her to school, so she slipped on her favorite running shoes. She pulled her hair up in a high ponytail and rubbed on some sunscreen. As an afterthought, she brushed her teeth and put on some lip balm, just in case.

She stared at the clean tap water as she filled her water bottle, and Luca's comment about the polluted water on Earth swam uncomfortably through her mind. His life on Earth must have been so difficult; she had honestly never given much thought to the people still living on Earth. It wasn't something they were *supposed* to think about. She tightened the lid and left the apartment.

Aria waited for Luca at the front entrance, her anxiety building as the minutes passed. He was taking longer than she expected. She fiddled with the hem of her tank top and tapped her toes awkwardly as she waited. Finally, she felt Luca leaving his room and soon he appeared carrying a heavy pack, his muscular, tall frame accentuated by his athletic shorts and T-shirt. He wasn't overly bulky, like those men who thought that working out was their sole reason for existence, but he was in great shape.

"Sorry it took so long!" he said, holding up his pack. "I had to make our dinner!"

"No worries," she said as she threw her water bottle in her pack and slung it over her shoulder. "Let's go!"

Her anxiety was at peak level, but somehow it was overpowered by her need to know Luca. She hadn't just waited all day to have this conversation—she had waited her entire life.

SIX

THE UNSPOKEN ANTICIPATION between Aria and Luca built with each step toward the trailhead. They walked in tense silence as they passed students and faculty on the trek up the peninsula. When they finally reached the trailhead and began the ascent into the foothills of the Western Mountains, a hundred unspoken questions swirled through Aria's mind.

The trail was too narrow for them to walk side by side, so they attempted light conversation while Aria smiled over her shoulder at Luca climbing behind her. Occasionally, he said something that caught Aria off guard. Once he said he had never seen such a clear sky before coming to Drammat. Then, he casually mentioned that the ocean wasn't clean enough to swim in on Earth. Aria played off her shock each time, but a knot grew inside her stomach. Her leaders were responsible for barring immigration from other planets. Of course, there weren't enough resources on Drammat for the trillions of humans living on other planets, but if Earth was in such bad shape, surely they could find some way to help. That's what the Colonization field was for, yet billions were still suffering on Earth.

"Are you okay?" Luca asked.

"Sure," she said, startled. How long had it been since she stopped listening? "Why do you ask?"

"I can tell when something is bothering you," he finally said.

Aria stopped, making Luca run into the back of her. This was it, the make-it-or-break-it point for her theory. Great Explorer, she hoped he felt it too.

"When," she said. "You said *when* something's bothering me—not *that* something's bothering me. What's that supposed to mean?"

"I think you know what I mean." Luca crossed in front of her and started up the mountain, nervous energy flowing into her as he passed.

"Please tell me what you meant," Aria said, chasing after him. "I think I know, but if I'm wrong and say what I think, I'll sound crazy."

"It looks like we're at an impasse, then," he said. "I'm worried you won't want to hang out anymore if you think I'm nuts."

"What if I promise to hang out with you anyway?" Aria asked, running up beside him with a cheesy grin.

Luca stopped walking and turned to look at her. "If I tell you my secret and it's not the same as yours, will you still tell me?"

Aria bit her lip. "Only if you make the same promise," she finally said.

"Deal," Luca said. "But I don't want to do this without being able to see you while I talk to you. So let's find a place to sit and eat, and then I'll tell you."

"Okay," Aria said. "That's fair."

Minutes of anxious silence passed as they scaled the mountain. The incline was becoming steeper, making it challenging to speak even if they wanted to. Salty sweat dripped from Aria's upper lip into her dry mouth. She paused mid-stride as she turned a switchback and found herself in a beautiful meadow. The path diverged onto a patch of grass under a tall tree with blooming yellow flowers. The late afternoon sun was beginning to lower in the sky, spilling golden rays on the patch of grass and casting a haze over the mountains and sea. It was Aria's favorite time of day during summer, and she couldn't help but close her eyes as she inhaled the mountain air.

Luca went to the tree and squatted down to unclasp his pack's straps, swinging it to the ground. He unzipped the deepest pocket, pulled out a quilt, and laid it on the grass in the shade of the tree. As Aria set her pack on the ground beside his, reaching for her water bottle and taking a swig, Luca was already pulling out various items and placing them artfully on a wooden board when Aria sat next to him.

"A charcuterie board for a picnic?"

"What?" Luca asked. "Is it too much?"

She chuckled. "Yeah, a little, but it's beautiful. Thank you."

He smiled as he arranged a variety of cheeses, dried meats, crackers, fruits, and berries in a creative pattern. Everything looked delicious and perfectly placed.

"Where did you learn to do that?" she asked.

"My mom used to make them all the time," Luca said. "Of course, she mostly used canned foods and whatever stale bread she could scrounge up, but they were always beautiful. I think she did it because it helped her focus on what we had instead of what we didn't. She taught me, and ever since, it's been my personal mission to try to make one as beautiful as hers always were. I think this is the closest I've ever come.

Aria sensed deep sadness wash over Luca.

"What is this?" she asked, holding up a mysterious-looking piece of meat on a cracker.

"It's called *ceviche*. It's an Earth dish from the southern part of the American Empire. You don't have that here?"

"Maybe. What's it made of?"

"It's just white fish," Luca said. "This one is halibut. You just prepare the fish and soak it in citrus juice for a few hours. I did a few other things to mine to give it that awesome flavor, but that's the gist."

"You're telling me you had this super intricate dish lying around on your second day here?"

"My aunt and uncle came prepared when I landed yesterday morning," Luca said. "They don't really know me yet, so I think they were trying to compensate. They gave me enough food to stock the fridge for the whole dorm, but they made sure to add in a few special things just for me. I think they knew ceviche would remind me of home. My grandma was from the district of Peru, so it was a delicacy in our house whenever we managed to get fresh fish. All I did was add some seasoning."

"Thank you for sharing it with me," Aria said. "I won't pretend I know what Peru is, but it's cool that you know about your ancestors. Nobody here talks about where our ancestors came from. We kind of ignore that part of our past. The only time we mention Earth is to criticize it."

"That sucks." He looked thoughtful, eyes fixed on some faraway place. "But I think most people on Earth would give up the knowledge of their ancestors if it meant they got to live here."

Silence fell as a somber mood settled over them. Aria scrambled for something to say, but nothing seemed adequate. Every time she learned something fascinating about Earth, it came with a tragic side. She suddenly noticed that she had been rolling the soft fabric of the quilt between her fingers.

"Where did you get this quilt?" she finally asked, grasping for any reason to change the subject.

"My mom made it for me when I was a baby," Luca said, smiling at the old quilt as he ran his fingers over its frayed edges. "I couldn't bring much from home, but I would've smuggled this here if I had to."

A sudden urge to twine her fingers between Luca's overwhelmed Aria, but she pushed it down. "What was she like?"

He looked up with a sad smile. "My mom? She was the best. I don't remember much because I was pretty young when she died, but I remember that she was kind to everyone. She was my favorite playmate, and she always had so much energy—until she got sick, at least."

The sadness and anger that had grown in Aria all day on Luca's behalf suddenly swelled to a boiling point, and tears welled in her eyes. "Luca, I'm so sorry."

His brow drew together in confusion. "You, of all people, can't be sorry for that, Aria."

"Why not?" she asked. "My whole life, I've felt sorry for myself because of my strict parents who expected too much of me, while you were living on a dying planet with hardly any family to speak of, and the few you did have—" She shook her head as her voice cracked.

"That's not what I mean," he said.

"What, then?"

Luca gulped and fidgeted with his hands.

Aria could feel the anxiety expanding inside him, and the sudden rush of emotion overwhelmed her.

"I told you about when my mom died and everything that happened since then," he said, "But there was one significant part—or person—that I didn't tell you about."

Aria's heart jumped. This was it. "Okay..." she said, nudging him to continue.

"When my mom died, I was eleven," he said, staring through her to somewhere in his past. "I was so upset I couldn't even get out of bed. My dad was even worse than I was, so he couldn't help much. Then, one day, a few weeks after my mom died, something happened to make me feel like I wasn't alone anymore."

He paused, shifting his focus to Aria. The intensity in his gaze startled her, but she nodded.

"That night, I had the weirdest dream. Everything was dark except for a dim light dancing around. That sounds scary, but it wasn't. It felt warm and safe. The only sounds were muffled voices and two distinct pounding rhythms, one fast and the other slow. The same dream came every night for months, and it became my escape. I thought it was my mom trying to comfort me.

"After I'd been having the dream for about eight months, a few weeks after I turned twelve, something changed. I felt super anxious all night as I dreamt. The next day, that anxiety stuck with me even after I woke up, and the next night, the same anxious dream came, but it was so much worse. All night it got scarier and scarier until suddenly, everything turned bright white. It was blinding at first, but when it died down, I saw the most beautiful baby being wrapped in a blanket and placed in the arms of a blonde woman. I was so overwhelmed with love and concern for that baby, but I was so confused. Obviously, it wasn't my mom's spirit or anything. After that, the anxiety vanished, and all I felt was the purest joy. To this day, I've never been so happy as that moment."

Aria's eyebrows knit together. So far, his experience sounded nothing like hers, yet she was captivated by his every word.

"When I woke up the next morning, that joy stayed with me, and over the next six years, I saw that baby grow in my dreams to be a sweet, smart, feisty, six-year-old girl. Sometimes, I even saw her when I was wide awake. I never told anyone because I knew I was probably just crazy and that they would try to fix me. I didn't want the delusion to go away. I had this little light in my life, and even when I wasn't watching her grow during my dreams, I felt her presence in my life like a guardian angel. Sometimes she had tantrums, which was weird because I felt all those intense emotions too, but overall, she was a light in my very dark life."

Aria struggled for breath as her heart pounded violently in her chest. Whatever she was expecting, it wasn't this. She swallowed hard and waited for Luca to continue.

"When my dad died, her presence became even more important in my life," he said. "This imaginary child was all I had at that point. Then the courts decided to send me to Drammat, and things got crazy. One week into the voyage, I noticed that the little girl was aging more quickly. By the end of the first month, she seemed at least three years older than when I left, and by the time I landed on Drammat, she was a teenager. In just four months, I watched her grow from a sweet six-year-old to a capable young woman. When I got to Drammat, the connection I had always felt to her ramped up so high that I started having visions almost non-stop."

Aria's hands began to shake and she clenched her fists to try to calm them.

"I felt super weird at the party last night, but my roommates convinced me to stay. I spent most of the night sitting or leaning against a tree, trying to be present and have a good time. Eventually, I realized that wasn't gonna happen, so I stood up and started walking, but once I did, my legs had a mind of their own. I just followed where my feet led, and suddenly, I knew exactly where she was. When you turned around, I can't explain how surreal that was. The little girl who saved me from the darkness in my life had turned into an unbelievably gorgeous young woman, and she was real. All I could think was how lucky I was to meet her, even if only once."

Aria's eyes brimmed with tears. She covered her mouth

with trembling fingers, struggling to keep the tears from over-flowing. The lump in her throat made it nearly impossible to speak.

"I know this all might sound completely crazy," Luca said. "But whether you want to spend time with me or not, I'm so grateful I finally got to meet you in person."

"It does sound crazy," Aria said, her voice trembling. "To any sane person, it would, but to me, it sounds like the other half of a story I've been hiding my whole life."

"You mean…do you…" Luca faltered.

He didn't have to vocalize his question for Aria to know it. It was the same question that had tormented and distracted her all day.

"I experienced the same connection," she said, shaking. "Except I never lived without it. I didn't have the luxury of age and experience to know that telling people about you would land me in therapy. I spent years trying to get rid of you, because if any of my peers ever found out, I would be shunned. If my teachers and future employers found out, I wouldn't be taken seriously. My future would be over before it had the chance to start. You're the reason my parents kept me locked away in our house studying and practicing extracurriculars. They didn't trust me to be around kids my age without saying too much or screwing up. Of course, there are medical records, but my mom is really good at convincing people to keep her secrets. Thanks to her, none of my records expose the psychosis element of my disease. Since six years old, I've seen you as my arch-nemesis. But when I dreamed about you, it was completely opposite. I craved those dreams, and that made me feel guilty. It's all really messed up, so when I saw you, I froze. I'm sorry I left so soon. I just wasn't in a good headspace."

"I'm the one that should be sorry," Luca said.

"You?" Aria asked. "Why would you be sorry?"

"You were the best thing that ever happened to me, but it sounds like I was the worst thing that ever happened to you."

She shook her head, searching for the right words to explain, but he held a hand up to quiet her.

"You showed up right in the darkest time of my life, and you were the light I needed. You got me through it all. For you, I was a plague. You've never even known life without me, and my being in your life caused you pain and heartache. Where you were a light in my dark life, I was a darkness that sucked the light out of yours. I watched you go through your struggles, but it was different when I didn't see you as a real person."

"You were never dark," she said. "Don't ever say that. It's true you made my life more complicated, but when I was in the middle of a dream, there was nowhere I would rather have been. You were never dark. Your world was dark and I felt your grief, but you made me feel safe before they conditioned that response out of me."

"Really?" Luca asked.

"Of course! I only tried pushing you out because the professionals said you were what made me crazy. I would never have given in if I had known you were real."

"And now that you know?" Luca asked.

Aria turned toward the setting sun, which reflected off the water. "I don't know," she said. "It's gonna take some time to undo all the damage inside me. But I know I want you to be a part of my life."

He smiled, and Aria knew it was genuine. "So, did those shrinks ever give an explanation for why I was in your head? I rarely got to sit in on those sessions, and I don't remember ever hearing a specific diagnosis."

"None that ever felt right to me. We pretty much came to the consensus that I had a severe anxiety disorder and that you were a part of my subconscious that my brain used as a coping mechanism to disassociate when things were too stressful. The thing is, I'm high-strung, but I don't get as anxious as a lot of high achievers I know. It was always a weird diagnosis to me."

"That sucks. All of my theories that had to do with spirits and visions were immediately debunked when I learned that you were a living, breathing human."

Aria tried not to feel disappointed, but ever since Dima had planted the idea in her brain, she had pinned her hopes on the thought that Luca might have answers. They were silent for a while, basking in the rare knowledge that another person truly understood how they felt. Aria traced the angles and shadows of Luca's face. Somehow, they had moved so close that his shallow breaths warmed her cheek. Their pinkies intertwined over the quilt as their electric connection attempted to pull them together. Luca brushed a stray lock of hair out of her face and rested his hand on her cheek. Warmth rushed into her where his skin met hers. Her breath stopped as Luca's eyes left hers and landed on her lips. She bit her lip nervously and glanced at his. Luca froze, but Aria leaned in slowly. Luca brought his other hand to rest on her waist, and electricity shot through her entire body, scintillating in the air between them.

Wait, what were they doing? She had almost let her emotions run away with her, and she couldn't even trust that they were *her* emotions. How would a relationship between them even work? More importantly, what would it feel like if they broke up and they had a front-row seat to the other person's hard feelings for the rest of their lives? Aria stiffened, resting her hand on Luca's chest.

He froze again, so close she could feel his breath on her lips. After a moment of agony, he slowly backed away.

"I'm sorry," Aria said. "Trust me, I want to, but I don't think it's a good idea. Until last night, I thought you were a dangerous part of my subconscious, who I admittedly had the hots for. But you were imaginary then! I'm gonna need some time to figure out how I feel about Luca the person. I understand if you can't accept those terms."

"I would be an idiot not to accept that," Luca said. "I'm just happy to be with you at all. Friendship is all I wanted from you all these years. Honestly, the whole desire side of this relationship is new to me. I mean, four months ago, I saw you as a little sister or something. I didn't even start being attracted to you like that until about a week before I landed. Then, suddenly, I definitely was. Now, *that* was confusing."

Aria chuckled. "Thank you for understanding. So, friends for now?"

"Friends," he agreed. "Unless we decide we want something more. But I won't pretend you're not the most beautiful girl I've ever met. My acting skills aren't up to quite that big a challenge."

Aria smiled and wrapped her arms around him, electric warmth spreading through her entire body. He held her tightly against him and energy pulsed through them both.

"When you touch me," Aria said, "especially skin to skin, like our arms are now, do you feel…"

"Like a lightning storm is going on inside me, and we're both about to burst into flames?" he asked.

"We aren't exactly normal, are we?" she asked.

"Normal? Who wants normal when you can have this? Bring on the lightning, baby!" He hugged her tightly again before releasing her abruptly. "Can I still hug you and hold your hand if we're just friends?"

"I guess I can live with that," she said, glowing.

Luca whooped as he stood and lifted Aria in his arms to spin her around. He set her down and wrapped her in his arms for another long hug, both of them basking in the incredible sensation. He released her reluctantly, and when he looked at her, his expression was serious again.

"Let's make a pact. Just because the so-called experts couldn't come up with a reason doesn't mean that one doesn't exist. There has to be a scientific explanation for this connection, and we're the only ones with enough information to get to the core of it."

"So, research?" Aria asked.

"For a start. It might take our whole lives and endless experiments, but let's promise each other that we'll never stop searching for the answer."

Aria's smile brightened and she nodded. "I can definitely promise that."

"Perfect. We've already spent way too long up here," he said, hurrying to pack his things. "We're gonna have to run on the way down, or we won't make it back to campus by dark."

Aria joined him to finish packing up, and they headed down the mountain. The hike was faster on the way down, but they jogged anyway. By the time they reached the foothills near campus, they had to slow down to ensure their footing.

They finally made it back to the far end of campus by eight-thirty, and the path back to the boarding halls was well-lit, so they walked side by side without fear of tripping. Luca took Aria's hand in his, and they strolled in contented silence, not needing words to communicate their feelings. Her overwhelming joy and relief were magnified by his.

They slowed as they neared the Women's Boarding Hall and stopped at the front doors, struggling to let go of each other's hands. In all her sixteen years, Aria had never seen Luca so free from his demons. She wanted to bask in his joy, but they couldn't stand outside forever. She reluctantly pulled her hand out of his and wrapped her arms around him. Luca kissed the top of Aria's head and pulled away.

"That doesn't count, right?" he asked.

"I'll allow it," she said, smiling. "Goodnight, Luca. See you tomorrow."

Aria turned and practically floated through the front doors, up the elevator, and into her apartment. When the door slid open, all four of her nosy, wonderful roommates swarmed her.

"So?" Jeslyn asked. "What happened?"

Aria looked around at each of her friends' expectant eyes, and a huge smile broke over her face. Unable to contain herself any longer, she let out a high-pitched squeal and jumped in a circle. Within seconds, her new friends were screaming and jumping right along with her, flinging questions left and right. Her conversation with Luca had provided just as many questions as answers, but she could worry about that another day. For this moment, nothing could ruin her high.

SEVEN

ARIA SPENT over an hour explaining her complicated relationship with Luca to her roommates before the conversation evolved to cover other boys in their class. Naturally, she left out the part about the supernatural mind powers or whatever was going on between her and Luca. All her roommates cared about was the juicy stuff anyway. They were very disappointed not to hear about a kiss, but luckily, some of the other girls had significantly juicier news to spill.

When most of the girls finally succumbed to exhaustion around midnight, Aria told Dima the whole truth, but even loyal Dima eventually shut her eyes and left Aria alone with her thoughts. Although, she was beginning to think she was never truly alone. Aria could sense Luca's presence like a physical string holding them together, and she could tell he couldn't find sleep either. She wasn't sure who finally succeeded in falling unconscious first, but after her bout with insomnia and a painful awakening to her alarm, she ended up with less than three hours of rest. Her eyes drooped as she dressed in her usual green and black uniform, put on minimal makeup, and threw her hair in a loose braid to hide her bedhead. She bit into a shiny green apple and pulled on her pack as she stumbled out of the apartment.

Luca was nearby and getting closer. He whistled a song Aria didn't recognize as he walked along the path. She picked up her pace and jogged through the sliding doors with a tired smile. She found him walking toward her building with a grin.

"I just realized it's gonna be tough to surprise each other," Aria said.

"What's wrong with that?" Luca asked as he slipped his hand into hers.

"How are we supposed to keep things interesting?"

"You don't think empathic mind powers keep things interesting?" he whispered.

"You have a point."

"And besides," he continued, "there's more to surprising someone than just sneaking up behind them or planning a surprise party. We might not surprise each other in the traditional sense, but you've given me enough surprises for a lifetime."

"I'm still sad I can never throw you a surprise party." She pouted.

"It's a good thing I hate surprises, then," he said, smirking. "What's your schedule like today?"

She frowned but conceded to the change of subject. "I only have one class and one lab today. Mondays, Wednesdays, and Fridays are my tough days with five classes, but Tuesdays and Thursdays are easy."

"You're taking six classes and a lab your first semester in college, and at sixteen?" His dark eyes bulged. "What is that, like nineteen credits?"

"I'll be fine. I thrive on huge class loads. That's how I graduated high school a year early."

Luca shook his head at her, chuckling softly.

"What?" she laughed, pushing him playfully to cover the heat rising to her cheeks.

"You're the most intimidating girl I've ever met," he said, his intense gaze at odds with his playful smile. The heat in her cheeks rose to a full blush.

"Oh, shut up," Aria said. "I'm the *least* intimidating person on campus."

"Whatever you say, genius girl." He winked.

"Oh, not you too!"

"Hey, I'm honored to be friends with the Academy's geekiest geek. You know that's impressive, right? This school only admits geniuses, and you're a genius among us."

Aria rolled her eyes. "Okay, you of all people know that's a load of crap. I don't know where everyone is getting this genius stuff. I'm very normal—at least, by Academy standards."

"Oh, give yourself a little credit. Most eight-year-olds can't create a habitable biome for insects using only synthetic base elements. Or what about the time you got a hand-written letter from the president for winning Colonization Student of the Year when you were twelve, or the time when..."

"Whatever." She frowned. "Sometimes I don't like that you already know almost everything about me. Will I see you at lunch?"

Luca chuckled. "I would be honored to dine with you, Miss Aria." He spoke with a strange accent she didn't recognize, punctuated by a formal bow.

Aria cocked her head. "Earth thing?"

He frowned at her, and Aria felt loneliness bubbling up inside him.

"Yeah," he said with a forced smile. "I forget you don't know all my cultural references. I'm gonna be late for class, but I'll see you at lunch. Okay?"

She watched him walk away, the electric sensation from

Luca's hand in hers gradually disappearing as she entered the Language Building, the farthest building on campus from the Women's Boarding Hall. When she glided through the classroom door, she was the first student to arrive. A plain, middle-aged woman leaned against the instructor's desk at the front of the class. Her head shot up as Aria entered, and her vibrant smile reached her dark eyes.

"Welcome!" she said in a smooth, rich accent. "Please come in! What's your name?"

"I'm Aria Blake."

"Aira, good to meet you! My name is Instructor Rojas. Do you have any interest in languages?"

"No more than the average person, I guess. I've never seen much point in learning other languages since translation software has become so accurate. Plus, English is the universal language. What use would another language be?"

"That is precisely the question," Instructor Rojas said. "Why do you think the Academy requires a basic understanding of the most common languages in the galaxy before our students are allowed to travel to other worlds?"

"Honestly, I've never thought about it. Why do they?"

Two Medical students wearing red T-shirts walked through the door just as Rojas opened her mouth to answer. "Ah, welcome. Please, take a seat," she said to the newcomers before turning back to Aria. "If you can find the answer to that question by the end of class today, I'll tack a letter grade onto your first test."

"Are you serious?" Aria asked. "You're on!"

She scuttled to the middle seat in the front row of desks as more students streamed through the door and filled in the desks around her. She opened the class module on her neurolink screen and reviewed the syllabus and assignments. Dozens of conversations blurred together around her, but she remained focused. Yesterday she had a momentary lapse in character, but today she was back.

"Welcome, class!" Instructor Rojas said, instantly quieting the rowdy crowd. "Please take your seats and prepare to take notes. My name is Instructor Rojas. I was among the very last immigrants allowed onto Drammat before the planet was fully closed to immigration. I was only nine years old when my family made the journey, but I vividly remember my youth on Sratta. While many languages and dialects survive in small subcultures here on Drammat, there are worlds where English is *not* the primary language. Sratta is one such world. The original settlers of Sratta were part of a private space company from a country on Earth called Argentina, whose native language was Rioplatanese, a dialect of Spanish. Over time, the language evolved. Srattan Spanish is now the official dialect of Sratta. I became a linguist to help keep my native language alive here on Drammat. Since my time as an Academy student, I've worked with people from eight planets in ways few others could. As a result, I am the most qualified professional in language and translation you'll ever meet, and I am *here*, of all places, to teach you. I don't tell you this to brag. I simply want you all to understand the magnitude of this opportunity. What you learn in this class could lead you to a life of understanding and connection."

The hour passed in what felt like fifteen minutes, and Rojas had all fifty-some students in the palm of her hand the whole time. She had the class weeping, laughing, or utterly silent in suspense with each personal story or allegory she told. When Rojas dismissed the class, the students meandered out slowly, flooding the hallway.

"So, Aria," Rojas said as Aria stood up to follow her classmates. "Do I owe you extra credit?"

"I don't know, Instructor," Aria said. "I can give my best guess."

"Well, let's hear it."

"I think language study is required because language is about more than communication. It's also about culture, belonging, and a sense of self. Take you, for example. Even though you speak better English than most native speakers and rarely need to use Srattan Spanish anymore, you still speak it as often as you can. When you do, you connect with your roots and other people who share those roots. It's not quite the same when a foreigner speaks your language, but I imagine even knowing a little bit can build confidence and trust in a way that speaking English can't."

Instructor Rojas's eyes widened and her mouth curved into an impressed smile.

"I've made the same wager with dozens of students," she said, "and I've never given the extra credit. Ms. Blake, that was the most insightful answer a student has ever given to that question. I look forward to having you in class this semester. The letter grade is yours."

"Thank you," Aria said, shaking Rojas's hand. "I look forward to learning from you."

Aria left the classroom feeling unexpectedly inspired. She always thought math and science were the most essential aspects of Colonization, but she still had so much to learn. Even the talks she had with her mother growing up about the role of negotiation and politics in Colonization had never gotten to her the way Rojas had. The applications seemed endless, especially if she were to spend her career among peoples of all cultures as she hoped she would.

Lost in her thoughts, she suddenly found she was nearing the library. She passed through the security barrier and started up the stairs to the second floor. She had always adored libraries, but the Academy library was her new favorite. It was one of the only libraries on Drammat that lent out physical copies of books. Most originals were in museums or long gone from not having been stored correctly. Modern libraries were spacious rooms with comfortable seating and plenty of desks, but no books. When any desired information was accessible through the neurolink network, what was the point of wasting space on physical books? That was the argument, anyway.

But Drammat was built on the value of traditionalism, convinced that Earth's decline was due to their technology-induced greed. It was a big part of why Aria's ancestors left Earth, banned the use of artificial intelligence, hyper-realistic virtual reality, and other dangerous tech, and practically started civilization over. So, while some technological progress was inevitable, some silly preferences remained, like the love of holding a book in one's hand or the smell of old parchment. Aria was one of those silly people.

She strode through the towering rows of books, basking in the sunlight pouring in through large windows and skylights. Due to her attention crisis the previous day, she needed to catch up on notes from most of yesterday's classes. As she rounded a corner near the historical section, a boy's voice caught her attention.

"From Earth?" the voice whispered. "Really? That's not just a dumb rumor?"

Aria stopped dead and backed against a row of books, heart racing. Whoever had designed the library with transparent glass rows and shelves didn't have espionage in mind. She pulled the first familiar title she saw from the shelf and opened it, pretending to read as she leaned back on the shelves.

"I'm positive," a girl's voice whispered. "My dad doesn't usually talk about his work, but this was a huge deal. He stressed over it for months."

"How could they let him in, though? Didn't anyone object?"

"Tons of people did, including my dad. I guess everyone

who voted 'yes' thought it was a special case, but my dad saw it for what it was—Earth's attempt to weasel their way into our government. Now we have this liability walking around making friends with the future leaders of Drammat. It won't end here."

"I can't believe more people sided with the Earth kid than with our government."

"It was close," the girl said. "They only lost by two votes. I still can't believe they let him into the Academy. There's no way he's Academy material—no way an archaic place like Earth could produce someone like us."

"If he didn't get accepted on his merit, why would they let him in?" asked the boy.

"Keep your enemies close, right? My guess is they want to keep a close watch on him. Just wait until he starts spreading Earth propaganda."

"About what?" the boy whispered.

"Conspiracy theories, mostly. My dad says people from other planets, especially Earth, are known for spreading lies about Drammat. Earthers are crazy. You wait and see."

Who was this girl and what did her dad have to do with Luca?

"What about the genius kid?" the boy asked. "Do you know anything about her?"

Aria's stomach dropped. Didn't these people have anything better to do than sit around and gossip about first-years? She took a deep breath, steadying herself. She inched forward just enough to get a view of the pair through one eye. Her heart lurched as she recognized the beautiful, brunette girl as the one Luca ejected from the seat beside him in favor of Aria— Celeste Brant, the queen bee herself. The guy she was talking to was tall and muscular. His tan skin looked out of place against his curly platinum hair and crystal eyes, like he had spent too much time in the sun.

"Oh, please," Celeste said, rolling her eyes. "She's no genius. She's just your run-of-the-mill geek. If I had zero social life, I'm sure I would've gotten in early, too."

The lump in the pit of Aria's stomach tightened and she clenched her fists around the book in her hand, pressing permanent fingernail prints into the hardcover. Maybe it wouldn't hurt so much if it wasn't the truth. She slammed the book shut and stepped out from her hiding place.

"Hey," Aria said. "Sorry to eavesdrop, but I assume the genius girl you're referring to is me. You remember me from Colonization class, don't you?"

Celeste's cheeks reddened slightly as her body stiffened. "What are you talking about?" she asked. "Were you spying on us?"

"Let's just get one thing straight," Aria said as she closed the distance between her and Celeste. "If by 'geek' you mean the person with the highest standardized test scores in history, a perfect grade in every class since preschool, six first-place awards in the International Young Scientists Fair, and personal letters from the presidents of three different nations for my contributions to the scientific community, then yes—I guess I am a geek. But, don't get it twisted. I never claimed to be a genius. It's everyone else who keeps throwing that word around, and I'm sick of it."

Celeste's face burned bright red and her fists clenched at her sides. She opened her mouth to respond, but Aria cut her off before she could start.

"The biggest difference between you and me is that I don't waste time on frivolous things like gossip and character defamation. Maybe if you took a page from my book, you wouldn't feel the need to bolster yourself by insulting others."

Aria walked between Celeste and the curly-haired boy, roughly pushing past Celeste with her shoulder. She scanned the shelf for the book she was originally searching for. Celeste tried to speak again, but Aria cut her off before she could form a single syllable.

"And one more thing," she said, slipping the book off the shelf and into her arms. "That Earther boy is more civilized, intelligent, and genuine than the two of you combined, and he more than deserves to be here. If you're ignorant on a topic, I recommend you don't speak on it. Just a tip."

Aria stomped away from the pair, book in hand. She pushed through the small crowd gathered at the end of the row to witness the scene. She clenched her jaw, tightening her free fist until her knuckles turned white. She blew through the sliding doors, paying no attention to the media check-out record that popped open, floating at the corner of her vision. She plopped down in the grassy courtyard. How could any educated person honestly believe that Earthers were somehow inferior to Drammatans? She knew that Earth was dying, so the people there had fewer resources, but that didn't make them stupid or evil.

She violently opened her new book and absently flipped through the ancient pages. She read the first sentence ten times without comprehension before she closed the book and took a deep breath. The words she had overheard played over and over in her head as if they were on repeat. How much truth could there be to the gossip? Would Vice President Brant tell his daughter such sensitive information? How could one teenage boy spark so much controversy?

She looked down at her lap and cocked her head in surprise. There were two books there, not one. Apparently, she had never put her disguise prop back on the shelf, and now it was lying in her lap beneath a physics textbook. She had picked it up because she recognized the title, but she hadn't taken the time to analyze the cover. Now that she saw it clearly, she couldn't take her eyes off of it. It was so old the text on the outside was almost completely rubbed clean. She dusted off the old leather cover and flipped to the first page. *The Human Origin* was the title.

She wrote a report on the famous book in high school, but had only seen the digital copy. Back then, she had enjoyed the book but found several places in the digital copy that seemed to be cut off without a clear conclusion. One in particular had her stumped on the report, and she never figured it out. She also remembered several chapters about human evolution. Maybe there was something there that could point her in the right direction to begin her research with Luca. She still had the file, so she pulled it up on her neurolink screen, turned to the section she marked in high school, and found the hard copy's corresponding page. She combed through the paragraph in each of the two manuscripts, but found no additional information or contextual clues to clarify her question. She scanned the page again, and her breath caught as a tiny flaw jumped out at her—two page numbers were skipped. She examined the pages closer and found a tiny lip where an extra page used to be. She remembered another section that had seemed cut off and flipped to it after some searching. Four pages were missing from that section. She flipped to the beginning and searched for more missing sections. She opened her note app and jotted down the chapters, titles, and sections where pages were skipped.

Whole sections were missing from "Leaving Earth's Solar System", "The Great Explorer", "The Spread of the Human Family", and "Colonization: Our Savior". Aria stared through the transparent note page to the clouds above. Something was off. Colonization was Drammat's highest priority. They should have wanted to broadcast that message loud and proud, not cut information out. Had a student stolen the pages? But that would only account for the physical copy, not the digital one. A dark feeling stirred deep inside Aria's stomach, and she pressed her hand to her temple to curb a headrush. Someone had gone to extraordinary lengths to conceal this information.

In the last three days at the Academy, Aria had learned more than she could have imagined, but not the things she had come here to learn. She still hadn't learned how to rearrange the bonds in elements to alter planetary atmosphere or how to prepare a colonizing population to deal with differences in gravity and rotational and orbital length. Instead, she had learned that her parents and therapists were wrong about her entire existence, she actually wasn't crazy, her supposedly fair and benevolent government was neglecting billions of humans on Earth, and apparently, it was also altering its own history. She had no idea what or who to trust.

She was deep in the research rabbit hole of human evolution when she glanced at the time and jumped. It was already five minutes into her lunch hour, and Luca was probably waiting for her in the cafeteria. She shot to her feet, scooping up her pack and carefully placing the two books inside before sprinting off.

Out of breath, she blew through the cafeteria doors, dodging students in her path. A much-needed sense of calm washed over her as she felt Luca nearby. She turned toward the sensation and spotted him standing at a table across the vast room. His eyes held the worry she already sensed in him. They met in the middle of the room, and Luca wrapped his arms around her. As Aria buried her face in his chest, electricity pulsed through her body and calmed her reeling mind.

"What's wrong?" Luca asked. "I had a feeling you were really upset. I saw part of it; you were yelling. What happened?"

"You saw that?" Aria asked, wincing. "I heard some people talking about you in the library. They said some things about Earthers."

Luca's eyes dropped to the floor, and he grabbed Aria's

hands. "Thank you for defending me, but I don't want you doing that again. It's better if we both ignore them."

"I can't hear someone spreading lies about you and not put them in their place!"

"Aria," he said softly. "Please lower your voice. I'm not sure what they said, but there's a good chance it's truer than you think."

"There's no way—" Aria said.

"Let's just go get some food and sit down," he said, cutting her off as he glanced around the room. "We'll eat, and then we'll talk."

"Don't hide things from me," she seethed. "Do you know how annoying it is to know exactly how you're feeling but only get bits and pieces of what's actually going on?"

"If I tell you, you can *never* unhear it," he said. "Do you understand that? Never."

"My whole life has turned upside down in the last three days. There's already no chance of going back. I want to know, Luca. I *need* to know."

"You're impossible," he said, rubbing his forehead. "I don't want you to get involved in this, but I can see that you're never gonna let it go. You have to promise me that this stays between us, because it's information that could get us both killed."

EIGHT

ARIA SAT DOWN NEXT to Luca in a secluded corner booth. She picked at her food while she watched Luca dig into a mountain of nachos. He finally finished and leaned back, wiping cheese sauce from the corner of his mouth.

"So?" Aria asked, tapping the table with her fingertips as her patience wore thin.

"Tell me what they said about Earth," Luca said, "and I'll tell you what they got right."

"They said Earthers are inferior to us. Celeste said there's no way you could've gotten into the Academy unless it was some larger scheme to keep an eye on you."

"Oh," he said, shrugging. "Was that all?"

"Well, no," Aria admitted. "But the rest was beyond insane. She said you were here to sabotage Drammat by spreading Earther propaganda. I know that's ridiculous, but..."

"Stop, Aria," Luca whispered, cutting her off. "The part about Earthers being inferior is crap, but the part about me potentially spreading propaganda isn't out of the realm of possibility. I would be worried about me too if I were a Drammatan official."

Aria's mouth dropped open slightly and her brow furrowed. "I don't understand. Why would you do that?" Her voice sank to a harsh whisper. "Was everything you told me yesterday a lie?"

"No! Look, that's not why I'm here, but I understand why the government would be worried about that."

"You're right. I don't understand."

"It's not about me. They'd be afraid of any citizen from another planet, especially Earth. Drammatans are known for being ruthless, cold, and selfish. Most Earthers think you're all evil. Honestly, so did I, but I've realized it's not that simple. The people in charge are the problem, and their strategy is to keep their citizens in the dark. My being here and knowing the truth complicates that. But I'm no activist; I'm a kid, and I'm not even here by choice. I don't know why Drammat accepted the ruling when the courts on Earth chose to send me here, but here I am, and all I can do is try to survive. To do that, I need to keep my mouth shut."

"What could make them so afraid?" Aria asked.

"Seriously messed up things. Drammat controls everything. We're trying to take care of our planet and rehabilitate it, but Drammat won't let that happen. They control our resources and use them to benefit themselves instead of us. They take what they want and beat, rape, and kill our citizens. We can't say a word or we disappear. Yet we have to pay protection and maintenance taxes to those pigs."

"That can't be right," Aria said, shaking her head before he even finished. "That goes against everything we stand for."

"It goes against everything *you* stand for," Luca said, reaching for her hand. "Before I came here, I hated Drammat just like all Earthers. But, since I've been here, I've seen genuine goodness and acceptance in you and a few others. I understand that you're all just doing the best you can with the information you have."

Aria pressed a hand to her forehead as she took several deep breaths. How could Luca's version of events be accurate? Drammat was a beacon of prosperity and hope for humanity, not an evil overlord. Yet, how much did she really know about the other colonies around the galaxy? About Earth, she knew almost nothing. Was this the reason they weren't supposed to talk about Earth?

"I found something today," Aria whispered. "Some discrepancies in a history book. It seems like every copy is missing the same pages."

"I'm not surprised." Luca snorted. "For thousands of years on Earth, changing history was one of the staples of all tyrannical governments. From book burnings to banning opposing viewpoints, it's all about controlling the narrative."

Aria stared at Luca, her mouth hanging slightly open. He seemed so calm, like they were discussing the weather and not the total breakdown of her worldview.

"We have to do something," she whispered.

"No!" Luca whispered a bit too loudly. He leaned in and lowered his voice again. "I'm already a target, and we don't need you becoming one too. Promise me you'll keep this between us."

"But it's not right, Luca."

"No, it's not." He agreed. "But I'm not exaggerating when I say your life could be in danger if they knew I told you the truth. I only told you at all because I was afraid that you would do something stupid to figure it out. Promise me."

Aria's heart clenched. She couldn't possess this information and not do anything with it. Billions were suffering, and nobody knew. Yet, who would she tell? What could a teenage girl do? Aria's head began to pound as if the truth were fighting for space in her brain.

"You're right," she said, rubbing her temple. "I'm not thinking straight. But I'm not promising I'll leave it alone forever."

"I know," Luca said, smiling. "You wouldn't be you if you did. When we're older, we can make slow, safe changes. That's what the Academy is for, right? Creating the leaders of tomorrow." Luca stood and cleaned up the table. "You coming?" he asked, holding a hand out for her.

Aria took it and let him guide her out of the Student Engagement Building into the afternoon sun. She basked in the electric buzz of his touch. Having Luca by her side soothed her slightly, but her stomach was still tied in knots.

Over the following weeks, Aria settled into a comfortable rhythm. No new life-altering revelations threatened her pattern, and her classes kept her almost too busy to obsess over the bombs that had already been dropped. Her favorite courses were Self-Defense and Weapons with Instructor Bradford, Intro to Colonization with Instructor Croft, and Basic Languages with Instructor Rojas. She spent most of her time on Tuesdays and Thursdays studying and working on projects in the library. On those days, there inevitably came a time when she couldn't possibly study anymore, and when that happened, she could never stop herself from opening up *The Human Origin*. She uncovered eight more instances of missing pages. She found a similar pattern when she moved on to other old history books. The only thing the books seemed to have in common was their age: all were published at least a hundred and fifty years ago.

The mystery plagued her when she was alone, but for the first time in her life, she had friends to distract her from her studies. Aria, Luca, Dima, and Nick had become inseparable, hanging out in the common area nightly and going on all kinds of weekend adventures. Aria's other roommates and Nick's friends made up their larger friend group. Luca swore that he was making friends in his Engineering cohort as well, but he had yet to bring any of them around. Still, for the first time in Aria's life, she had an actual social life, and she loved every minute of it. Of course, Celeste and her loyal band of followers continued to stick their noses up at Aria and Luca, as well as their friends for associating with them, but Aria was surprised by how little she cared.

Aria had even begun to acclimate to the constant pull of Luca's presence, the electric warmth of his touch, and the random bits of his life that she got to see through her visions of him. As long as she didn't think about the absurdly intrusive nature of the connection and the fact that she never knew what Luca might see, she enjoyed the comfort Luca brought her.

Midterm week came quickly, and while Aria's above-the-table studies had her positioned for fantastic marks, her secret research was getting her nowhere. There had to be another way. Luca would freak out if he knew what she was planning, but she needed to talk to someone—someone she could trust.

Her second to last midterm exam before the Colonization Day break was in Basic Languages on Thursday. If there were ever a perfect time to corner Instructor Rojas, it would be after the midterm while many students were headed home for break.

She hurried through the test and was the second student to finish. Leaving the classroom, she sat down against the wall, waiting for her classmates to finish and leave Rojas alone at her large desk.

Aria twisted her hands in her lap, running through every possible reaction Rojas might have. The last student finally finished his test, submitted his work, and packed up his things. As he left the room, Aria stood from her seat on the floor and brushed off her pants. She slowly stepped back into the room, mild nausea rising. If Luca was right about the danger they were in, Rojas could be a part of the problem, but something instinctual told her she could trust her instructor. She cleared her throat and swallowed loudly.

"Instructor Rojas," she said, "is it okay if I ask you a question?"

"Oh," Rojas said, spinning around to face her. "Aria! Come in. Please, have a seat. What is it you need to ask me?"

She indicated the chair across from her, and Aria clumsily rushed to pull it out and sat on the edge. She clenched her fists, attempting to steady her shaking hands.

"Thank you, Instructor," Aria said, smiling awkwardly at her feet.

"As you know, Aria, I am an expert in communication. Communication goes far beyond words, so I'm sure you're aware that I can tell how nervous you are. Please, go on. There's no harm in asking."

"You say that now," Aria mumbled, her stomach churning. "I'll understand if you're worried about what I have to ask you, but I need you to answer honestly and know that this comes from a place of curiosity."

"Ask your question. I'm sure it's nothing I haven't heard before."

"Here goes nothing," she breathed. "What happened a century and a half ago that the government is covering up?"

Something in Rojas's eyes lurched at the question, though the rest of her face remained expressionless. She stared at Aria for a moment, searching her face.

"Can you elaborate?" she finally asked. "What evidence do you have that something happened?"

Aria's heart jumped into her throat. Could she have

misjudged Rojas? It was too late to bail now. She stood and linked her neurolink with that of her instructor. As Rojas accepted the connection, Aria pulled several old leather books from her bag. A glint of light sparked across Rojas's eyes as she watched Aria open *The Human Origin* to the first missing section.

"I've noticed that there are missing pages in all of the physical history books I can find that were published at least a hundred and fifty years ago," she said, running her index finger over the carefully cut remnants of pages. "That would be weird enough, but the same sections are also missing in the digital copies. It's like someone tried to erase some parts of our history. But if they did, why not publish new books altogether? Why leave the evidence?"

Rojas inhaled a shaky breath and let it out slowly. She leaned close to Aria as her eyes darted around the room.

"You have stumbled upon something hazardous," she finally whispered. "It is dangerous to your graduation, future career, and possibly your life. A few have made these observations, but as far as I know, you are the first Academy student to connect the dots. As for why they didn't reprint the books, I suppose it would be more suspicious if all of the literature from a certain period suddenly disappeared. Or maybe it was simply hubris. Regardless of their reasons, I came to the same conclusion in my third year as an instructor, though I'll admit I did not conduct such an extensive investigation as you seem to have done. I had already spent many years working in other government sectors, so I knew more about how the world works than you do. Therefore, I knew I had to ignore my findings."

"You're telling me to forget it?" Aria's spirit deflated. "That feels so wrong."

"I'm telling you to wait, Aria. That's all."

Aria huffed. First Luca and now Rojas? Everyone seemed

to think waiting was going to solve everything, but if everyone waited, no one would ever be the one to act.

"But for how long?" Aria asked, raising her voice.

"For as long as it takes," Rojas barked. Bringing her voice back down with an effort, she whispered, "There is a prophecy that brings hope to my people on Sratta."

"A prophecy?" Aria asked. "Like magic, wizard stuff?"

"Exactly what *is* magic?"

Aria shrugged. "It's an unnatural power to do impossible things, I guess."

"No, Aria. Magic is a word humans give to things that science cannot yet explain. Thousands of years ago, a human on Earth would have thought a spaceship could have only been magic. Even a drug that relieved pain or an antibiotic that healed infection would have been considered witchcraft. I believe there is no such thing as impossible. If we believe it to be impossible, we simply haven't figured it out yet. How does your definition hold up now?"

Aria thought for a moment. "Magic," she finally said, "is an excuse to remain ignorant rather than understand something new."

"Very good," Rojas said softly. "Many religious people call it the power of a higher being. Others see it as mystical. Whether you see it as magic or the power of some god, current science would tell us it is fake—an illusion. That is ignorance."

Aria sighed, confused by the turn the conversation had taken. "What does this prophecy have to do with missing pages?"

"The prophecy was made on Sratta about fifty years ago, but people all over the galaxy believe in it. It says that a savior, a woman of great influence, will unite many worlds against the great oppressor, leading them into battle and overthrowing the adversary. There is much more to it, but the point is that someone *will* come to help. Alone, you and I are just a couple of people who found corruption in a powerful government. Corruption is nothing new. It would be social and professional suicide to fight the system alone. We wait for the one who will unite trillions against the hand of oppression and injustice in the galaxy."

"Wait," Aria said. "You've been waiting your entire life for this chosen one? If this savior is so great, why hasn't she come already?"

"The point is that she *will* come," Rojas said in a soothing tone. "And when she does, you and I will be here to support her in her cause. She will need allies on this planet."

Aria stood up abruptly, stumbling backward as she bumped into her chair. Hundreds of new questions danced around her head. How many people had noticed what she had and brushed it off? If she had found the missing pages, but never knew Luca or learned of the atrocities of her own people, would she do anything about it? The answer was a resounding no. What were they talking about here? As far as Rojas knew, there was a bit of missing information in a few history books. But was that *all* Rojas knew? Why would the Srattan people need a prophecy to believe in if they weren't being oppressed? She nearly asked the question aloud, but the hard set to her instructor's eyes told her the conversation was over.

"Thank you for listening," Aria said. "You gave me more answers than I hoped for."

"You're welcome," Rojas said, her brow furrowed with concern. "Please be careful."

Aria waved goodbye as she stepped through the door into the long hallway. She glanced at the time, and fresh panic shot through her like hot lightning. She was already five minutes late for her lab. She took off at a run, aware of the strange looks she was inviting. She arrived at the door almost ten minutes after the test had begun, trying to peer around the room inconspicuously, but the automatic, transparent door gilded open, announcing her tardiness to the entire class.

"Decided to show up, after all, Ms. Blake?" Instructor Croft asked.

"So sorry!" Aria said, breathing heavily. "I was meeting with another instructor after my last midterm and lost track of time. It won't happen again."

She hurried to the empty seat next to Luca as Croft motioned for her to enter. Luca narrowed his eyes at her as she sat.

"How did your little talk go?" he whispered.

"What do you mean?" Aria asked, guilt rushing through her body.

"You know you can't lie to me, so I don't know why you try," he hissed. "I heard what you and that instructor were talking about."

Her throat tightened around her words. "You don't understand..."

"Don't I?" Luca whispered, cutting her off. "I could feel your guilt on the opposite side of campus, so don't act like I'm the one in the wrong here."

"Later, okay?" Aria asked. "Let's finish this test."

Luca turned his head away from her, returning to his work in silence. She dropped her head into her hands. A shadow of anger flooded Aria's system as it overflowed from Luca. The knuckles on his clenched fists were white as bone as they trembled slightly on the desk. Tears suddenly sprang to Aria's eyes. She had betrayed her promise, and Luca had seen it all.

NINE

DESPITE COLONIZATION BEING Aria's favorite class, the midterm was torturous as she battled with Luca's emotions for space in her brain. He was hurt, and he had every right to be. She couldn't deny that she was at fault, but it was also unfair of Luca to try to control her. The tension between them heightened as the exam wore on. Aria tried desperately to block out her connection to Luca as she rushed to complete the test, but his proximity made the invading hurt and rage all the more potent. Despite their distraction and late start, or maybe because of those factors, they were the first two students to finish the test and exit the room, Aria just minutes before Luca. The hallways were empty and silent as exams dragged on in the surrounding classrooms. Luca blew past her on his way out, but she jogged in a pathetic attempt to keep up with him.

"Luca, please slow down!" she yelled as they burst through the doors into the bright sun. "We need to talk!"

"Talk?" he asked, whirling around to face her. "You don't think you already did enough of that today?"

"Excuse me?"

"You promised me you would leave this alone!"

She considered apologizing for half a second, but the words she was dying to say exploded from her lips instead. "I tried, but I can't—not even for you. I appreciate that you want to keep me safe, but what about everyone else? According to you, there are billions of people suffering on Earth and who knows where else. What about them? Staying silent is wrong!"

Luca stopped and whirled to face her, moisture gathering in his eyes. "Keeping you alive isn't wrong," he said, voice cracking. "Why did you lie to me?"

"I'm sorry," Aira said softly, eyes dropping to her shoes. "It felt like you were trying to control me or change me."

"I would never want to change you. I love your passion and strong morals, but wasn't lying to me wrong?"

"It was," Aria said, finally looking at him. "And I'm sorry. I should have told you, but I can't apologize for the rest of it. I can't stand by and let people suffer."

Luca turned away from her, weaving his fingers through his thick curls as he paced the empty sidewalk. "You're right," he said. "There has to be something we can do."

"Wait, did I hear that correctly?" Aria asked. "You think I'm right?"

"Oh, shut up. You know you're right. If we don't do something to help, we're just as bad as them."

"Wait. Really?" Aria asked, eyes wide as she grabbed his upper arms and sent a jolt of electricity through them both.

"Yes," Luca said. "But we need to get something straight. Two kids aren't gonna make a difference. If we do this, we need to be smart about it. We need a strategy, and we need to be patient."

She rolled her eyes. Hadn't she heard this speech before?

"Okay." She sighed. "So what's our strategy?"

"I haven't gotten that far yet. All I know is we need more

help. From your conversation with Instructor Rojas, it sounds like there may be other people who are hoping for change. They're just waiting for the right leader to show them the way forward."

"But we don't have their precious savior," Aria said. "Are you suggesting we bluff?"

"No, nothing like that," Luca said, his eyes distant and calculating. "But if we can find enough help and resources around the galaxy, we might be able to move things in the right direction without the savior. We don't want war, anyway. That's not gonna help anybody."

"Okay," Aria said, pacing the grass in front of Luca. For the first time, the slow and steady route to change was starting to make sense. "So, what's our first play?"

"You had the right idea with the library, but we need more info than what we're legally allowed to have."

"Right. So, we need to find out what happened a century and a half ago on Drammat that prompted them to change history. If we find that, we can probably figure out how to fix it." A smile crept over her face. "So am I forgiven?"

"For lying to me?" he asked.

"Yes. And I promise, from here on out, there are no secrets between us. It was pretty stupid to even try, given our situation."

"Pretty stupid," he said with a small smile. "I forgive you. I'm sorry for being so overbearing about this. I just can't handle the thought of anything happening to you because of me."

"You were trying to protect me. But from now on, let's work together as equals, okay?"

He nodded. "I'm always on your team. What's important to you is important to me."

The intensity of his regret pierced her heart, but another feeling she couldn't quite place caught her attention and reflected in his eyes. It was something warm and inviting. She flung herself into his arms, and he stumbled back, barely catching himself before they both toppled over.

"So, you're still coming home with me for Colonization Day?" Aria asked into his chest, the smell of ocean and pine enveloping her.

"If I'm still welcome, there's nowhere I'd rather be." His strong arms wrapped firmly around her.

"I can't wait to show you everything!"

Aria pulled away slightly, blushing. Luca let go of her but kept one arm around her shoulders as they started back down the peninsula. By then, a few other students had finished their exams and were laughing and talking about their plans for the break as they passed by.

The Academy would become a ghost town in the next twenty-four hours as nearly everyone packed up and left for the holiday. Because Luca's aunt and uncle always used the holiday as an annual couple's trip, Luca would have been left with the handful of students staying on campus for break if he hadn't agreed to go to Miller Bay with Aria.

They strolled through the doors to the commons and found a few of their friends lounging around an unlit fire pit. Dima stood up from where she sat talking with Nick and his roommates and jogged over to meet Aria and Luca. She threw her arms around Aria dramatically.

"Are you ready for a whole week with Loverboy?" she whispered.

"Dima!" Aria hissed, attempting to wiggle out of her clutches. "He's coming with me as a friend!"

"Right," Dima said with a wink. "Come on! We're all hanging out for a while before everybody starts leaving for home!"

Aria let Dima drag her toward Nick by her wrist and grabbed Luca's hand to tow him behind her. She looked around to see who "all" included. Dima and Nick were talking with two of Nick's roommates, Brock and Finlay. Jeslyn and Allison sat nearby, flirting with a couple of guys from the Defense program. Gemma and some of the guys were missing, probably still taking midterms. Dima led the pair to an empty seat at her left.

"Yo Luca," Nick said. "Why don't we ever hang out with any of your Engineering buddies?"

"I only have a couple of friends in my program," Luca said, shrugging. "My closest friends are twins, so they spend most of their time together. I'm closer with you guys than anybody from Engineering."

"Does that bother you?" Dima asked.

"Not at all. Where I'm from, our colleges have tons of different programs, so if I had stayed, most of my friends and roommates wouldn't have been in my program. To me, this is just normal."

Everyone in the group knew about Luca's unorthodox background, but while they had all been welcoming and understanding, they usually chose not to talk openly about his origin. Whenever they did, they did so quietly.

"Really?" Nick whispered. "What about in high school? Was it that way too?"

"Don't tell me they make you specialize in high school," Luca said, eyebrows raising. "Do all schools do that here?"

"Well, yeah…" Aria said.

"Criminal, isn't it?" Dima asked, tossing her fiery hair over her shoulder with a pout. "When we're super little, like eleven, they make us take this test to tell them if we're better at analysis or creativity. Based on those results, we go into different middle schools for different paths. The same happens before high school, but they narrow it down to specific subjects like math, science, or language. After high school, our last exam tells us which specialty best suits our strengths.

When a class graduates, the system has hand-picked the next generation of workers. It's all just a giant assembly line."

"I think it makes a lot of sense," Nick said. "Without the help of the placement tests, a lot of people would waste time trying to decide which field they should choose. Otherwise, people could just change careers all the time. That's plain wasteful. This way, we milk the highest potential out of every Drammatan citizen."

Dima rolled her eyes. "And that right there is the eternal debate. Is freedom of choice or productivity more important? I guess it all comes down to your values. I, for one, value people as human beings rather than cogs in the machinery of our society, but I guess that's just me."

Luca raised his hands defensively. "Woah! I didn't mean to start a fight! I was just surprised."

"It's not your fault, man," Nick's roommate Finlay said. "This has been the biggest political disagreement on Drammat for as long as anyone can remember. A lot of people don't like the way we do it, but it's how it's always been."

"How do they do it...where you're from?" Dima asked.

"Every country does it a little differently," Luca said, lowering his voice even further. "Where I'm from, governments are independent, not just parts of one planetary government. My country's public schools don't make you choose a path until college. Even then, people can still change their minds. Some countries do something similar to what you guys do here, just less intense. They don't force anyone into a certain field. It's just sort of expected."

"Technically, nobody's forced here either," Nick said. "But if you do what the test advises, your education is paid for, and even after you graduate, you get aid from the government until you're making enough to sustain yourself and contribute to society. If you don't conform, well, it's not an easy life."

"I can see how that works," Luca said. "But my home country is very individualistic, so that wouldn't fly there. Sometimes it would take a few tries to get it right, and people would end up wasting money, so I can see Nick's point. He's right about people changing their careers a lot, too. I hardly knew anyone back home who stuck with one career their whole life."

A crowd of fifteen had gathered as the rest of their friends were drawn into the hushed conversation. The prospect of such a disorganized system made Aria's head hurt; it was no wonder Earth was a mess. Yet she couldn't deny that there was something compelling about the idea of choosing a life for herself. Wide eyes and intrigued whispers confirmed that the others felt similar shades of confusion—except Dima, of course. A shadow of anxiety flowed into Aria from Luca. Such an innocent topic should have been safe, but he had drawn too much attention.

"It's not necessarily a better way," Luca said hastily. "It's just different. We...I mean, *they* have different priorities and different experiences, so it's...different. No biggie."

Some faces among the small crowd relaxed, but a curious tension hung in the air. Dima winked at Aria. "If you ask me, they just know how to have more fun! Speaking of fun, what should we do tonight?" The tension immediately diffused as she turned the conversation to lighter topics. The unwanted attention passed, but the uneasy feeling remained.

Eventually, everyone decided to go into town for a nice dinner to celebrate the end of midterms. They sat talking and laughing for a long time after they finished the expensive meal. Finally, at the end of the night, they returned by train to prepare for the next day's travels. Aria and Luca had planned to leave right after breakfast, but Aria hadn't even begun packing. When they returned to Academy Station, Luca offered his hand and together, he and Aria sped past their friends. The night was the chilliest of the fall so far, and Luca's warm, electric presence drew Aria to his side.

"Thank you for inviting me to your family holiday," Luca said.

She smiled up at him. "You're welcome. But trust me, it was purely for selfish motives. A week with my parents will be less painful with you there."

"I'm happy to play my role, even if I'm just a buffer," he said, smiling back with a lazy wink. "Seriously, thank you. I haven't had a happy holiday in so long. The last truly happy day I can remember was Christmas when I was nine years old. That was before my mom got sick. We had Christmas Eve dinner with some of my parents' friends and their kids. There were lights and decorations everywhere. And the food. Oh man, the food! Each of us kids got to open a gift before we left, and everyone was so happy."

"I can't promise you something so meaningful," Aria said. "But there'll be lots of food and decorations because my mom goes way over the top. It's like her motto—do it extravagantly or don't bother to do it at all."

"I didn't mean that I wanted it to be exactly like that," Luca said. "I just want to be happy, and you've already made me happier in the last two months than I've ever been. I know it'll be perfect because I'll be hanging with you."

They arrived at the Women's Boarding Hall and stopped a few paces from the door, a blush creeping up Aria's neck at his words.

"I'm sorry you've had so many bad things happen to you," she said softly. "But I sincerely believe you're the amazing guy you are today because you've overcome those things."

Luca pulled Aria slightly closer. "I'm okay as long as I have you in my life," he whispered. "That's always been true."

The electric buzz under Aria's skin was like a magnet pulling her to Luca. He slid his hand around her back and pulled her the remaining distance into his arms. Her heartbeat quickened as the electricity sizzled under her skin. Luca's feelings were impossible to miss, pouring into her more clearly than ever—affection, joy, desire. He leaned in, touching his lips gently to her ear.

Aria swallowed as his breath danced across her skin. Over the last two months, they had done so well keeping things friendly, but every cell in Aria's body told her that now was *not* the time for friendship. She wanted to give in to her feelings and ask him to be hers forever. Instead, she struggled to hold on to the logical side of her brain. She wasn't yet seventeen years old, and there was no untangling herself from Luca if their relationship went bad. If she did choose him, the repercussions would be forever, good or bad. Besides, in their situation, how would she ever know if this was her choice or just something fate chose for her? She pushed back softly from his broad chest and peered up at him.

"You'll always have me as a friend," Aria said. Luca's disappointment immediately flowed through Aria, but she forged ahead. "And together, we can do anything."

"I'm pretty sure *you* can do anything. I'm here as your sidekick, or maybe just eye candy."

"Oh, definitely eye candy," Aria said through a crooked smile, unsuccessfully attempting to ignore the racing of her heart. "So, tomorrow morning, meet me in the commons at nine-thirty."

"Uh, perfect," Luca said, a little taken aback at the sudden switch in the topic. "I can't wait."

Aria gave Luca one final hug before bounding through the sliding doors and backing herself against the front wall. She closed her eyes and cringed. "Seriously?" she whispered to herself. Together they could do anything? He'd always have her as a friend? What was she doing? At this rate she wouldn't even convince herself, let alone Luca, that they were better off as friends.

His electrifying touch lingered on her skin; she could still feel where his lips grazed her ear and his arms encircled her. Suddenly, a part of her regretted asking Luca to spend the break with her. One week with him might be more than her waning self-control could take.

TEN

ARIA'S ALARM BLARED, and she threw off her covers. Despite having stayed up far too late talking with the girls, she was instantly alert. After two months away from home, today she was returning to her old haunts. On top of the stress of being with her parents again, Luca would be with her all week. It was both terrifying and exciting.

Aria hopped out of bed and bounded across the hall and into the shower. She had strategically planned today's outfit and set it out days ago, but her hair and makeup took almost an hour to complete. She hadn't worn a full face of makeup in months, but her mom would expect it the whole time Luca was around. She curled her long, caramel tresses and braided the top into an intricate crown. At last, and with all of her roommates still asleep, she stepped into view of the full-length mirror by her vanity.

Aria had always had a lean, toned body due to excelling in several sports, but the Self-Defense and Weapons class was no joke. She had gained impressive muscle mass, so her clothing was tighter now, showing off her newfound definition. Her black pants and beige high-heeled boots accentuated the length of her legs, and her shimmery, beige top flowed around her elegantly.

She didn't often wear jewelry, but today she wore a short gold chain with a small diamond and a matching set of earrings. Aria threw on a dressy white coat, shouldered her travel pack, and yelled goodbye to her roommates, who she could now hear chatting sleepily across the hall. She was running so late that she and Luca might need to catch the next train out.

She rushed outside and into the commons, frantically searching for Luca.

"I know! I know!" she yelled as she spotted him standing to greet her. "I was the one who said to be on time, but it took longer than expected to transform into a creature worthy of my mother's affection."

As she drew closer, she noticed the expression on Luca's face. His eyebrows were raised, and though his mouth was wide open, no words came out.

"Hello? Luca? Anyone home?"

"Sorry," he said, shaking himself. "You look..."

"I look . . . ?"

"I'm having trouble finding a word that accurately describes how stunning you are."

She raised her eyebrows at him, though she couldn't help the heat that rushed to her cheeks. "So because I got all dolled up, I'm stunning?" she asked, giving him a crooked smile.

"No!" he blurted out. "You're always stunning. You're stunning right now, but that doesn't make you less stunning at other times."

"Good save," she said, rolling her eyes as she led the way to the train station.

"I'm serious." Luca followed, running a hand through his thick curls nervously. "Like, when we went sailing a couple of weeks back, and a few of us went swimming out there. Remember that?"

"Sure," Aria said. "The water was gorgeous."

"Well, after you got back in the boat, you put on a big T-shirt, and your hair was a soaked mess. I'm pretty sure you didn't have any makeup on. That was just you, right? Nothing artificial?"

"Yes," she said dryly. "You've made it abundantly clear that I was a mess. That was me without any of this." She gestured to her whole outfit from head to toe.

"That's exactly my point," Luca said. "You were a self-proclaimed mess with none of the stuff you're wearing now, but you were more stunning than ever."

"Oh, whatever!"

"I'm not trying to flatter you! I had a hard time keeping my eyes off of you, and I wasn't the only one! You're always stunning, but that day, at that moment, you were completely breathtaking. Right now, like then, is one of those times when you catch me off guard."

The unmistakable sensation of desire seeped from Luca into Aria and her cheeks flushed brighter. She bit her lip, trying to hide her emerging smile as she hopelessly searched for a response.

"Thank you," she finally said.

The rest of the walk to the station was silent and Aria could feel Luca's embarrassment burning a hole through them both when they finally arrived at the station. She smiled at him and the sensation dissipated, but it remained a reminder of just how complicated a relationship between them would be.

They barely caught the nine-forty-five train, sliding into the nearest car just before the doors closed. They settled into the anticipation of the holiday over the hour train ride as Luca asked questions about her childhood and the towns they were passing.

When the train pulled into Miller Bay Station, a surprising wave of excitement filled Aria, accompanied by a dark shadow of anxiety. Aria whirled around to find Luca's face pale. She took his hand and guided him onto the arrival deck.

"It'll be great," she whispered.

"I know."

From across the station, Aria's dad waved and came hurrying toward them. "He's here!" Aria yelled. "Let's go!"

Luca struggled to keep up as Aria rushed past other travelers and fell into her dad's hug.

"Ari-bug!" he said. "How's my little girl?"

"Hey, Dad! Thank you for picking us up."

Finally noticing Luca standing awkwardly behind his daughter, he released Aria and turned toward Luca with an outstretched hand. "Luca, isn't it? Good to meet you, son. Let's get you two to the pod."

"Pleasure to meet you, Mr. Blake," Luca said as he took the massive hand. "Thank you for having me."

"Please call me Noah. You're Aria's friend and a guest in our home."

Aria smiled at the two men, surprised to see that Luca was only slightly smaller than her dad. The trio arrived at the pod and stowed the travel packs in the storage compartment. Aria's dad offered Luca the passenger seat, but Luca insisted on riding in the back so Aria could ride in the front with her father. He relented and fired up the pod. He spent the ten-minute flight telling Luca about the quaint town's history and his role in the community as head of the regional defense center. As the minutes passed, Aria paid close attention as Luca's feelings transformed from anxiety to excitement. Finally, Aria's dad pulled into the garage and turned off the pod, lowering it to rest on the floor.

"Home sweet home," he said as he opened the doors.

Luca and Aria both stepped out of the pod and went around back to grab their packs. They hauled the bags across the garage to the chrome-colored door that slid open as it registered Aria's bio-signature. She breathed in the scent of home as the door closed behind the group, sending a wave of nostalgia over her.

She glanced at Luca, who was standing wide-eyed, taking in every surface of her childhood home. It wasn't a mansion, at least, not by Drammatan standards. Aria was too young when Luca left Earth to remember what his own home was like, but compared to his bunk on the ship, Aria's house was the definition of luxury. Massive windows all over the building let natural light pour into the front room and make the expensive fabrics and metals glisten. The entire home was tastefully but thoroughly decorated in Colonization Day blue and gold, the way her mother always kept it this time of year. The walls were programmed a stark white in some places and a neutral gray-beige in others.

"Your home is beautiful," Luca said.

"Thank you, son," Aria's dad said, patting Luca firmly on the back. "My wife can take credit for that."

The woman in question walked into the front room from the kitchen wearing a full face of makeup, a sundress, and an elegant bun tied into her bright blonde hair.

"My darling girl!" she said, pressing Aria's face between her palms. "How was the trip? I am so happy to have you home! Clearly, you've been eating plenty."

A pang of disappointment stirred in Aria's stomach. What was that supposed to mean? Her mother had always been partial to a thinner aesthetic, but Aria was proud of her new muscles.

"Hi, Mom," Aria said with a weak smile. "This is Luca."

Her mom turned to Luca, and Aria suddenly became very

aware of his appearance. She had been so worried about her own attire that she hadn't even noticed what he was wearing until her mother's judgmental eye turned on him. Aria scanned Luca's outfit, searching for flaws her mother could use against him later. Thankfully, he looked incredible. Like Aria, the hours spent sparring and working out in Self-Defense class had a very positive effect on his physique. Her dad still had a few centimeters and dozens of kilos on him, but Luca looked like he could hold his own. His clothes looked new, the latest in Drammatan men's fashion. He had never worn them around Aria before. He also had a fresh haircut, making his dark curls even more captivating than usual. She hadn't been the only one to go to extraordinary lengths for this first impression.

"Luca," her mom said, putting her hand out for him to take. "It's so nice to finally meet you. Please, come set your things down and get situated in your room. Aria, can you show Luca his room? We'll have lunch out on the patio when you're both ready."

"We'll be quick!" Aria said. A relieved sigh escaped her lips as she snatched Luca's arm and dragged him up the stairs to the loft-style second floor. The stairs opened up to a living area at the top, where a large, blank space sprawled the back wall for connecting personal audio and video feeds with large groups. Several oversized bean bags and a large couch provided seating, with a plush rug laying in the middle of the floor. There was a counter on the back wall with food and drink dispensers.

"This is awesome," Luca said. "Somehow, this all seems bigger in person."

"It was my parents' attempt to keep me home more," Aria whispered. "But yeah. It's pretty cool."

On either side of the room was a single door. Aria walked over to the door on the left, which slid open for her.

"This is your room," she said as she passed through the door.

It was a simple, elegant bedroom that never got much use. The walls were white, but they could be programmed to whatever color a guest chose. The large bed was covered with a simple gray comforter, and throw pillows with different textures and patterns lined the headboard. There was a large, virtually empty closet, a small dresser, a full-length mirror, and two doors on the far side of the room. One of the doors was solid, but the other was transparent glass that showed off a balcony and an incredible ocean view.

"This is your closet," Aria said, pointing to the empty compartment. "You can unpack if you want. You can also use that dresser, but some of the drawers are full of extra blankets. This door is your bathroom. It's self-cleaning, so every morning when you go down for breakfast, remember to take out anything of yours, like clothes or whatever."

"Seriously?" Luca asked. "Your bathroom is self-cleaning?"

"Yeah. They all are. Even the half-bath downstairs, but that one isn't automatic. We have to enter the command manually when we want to clean it."

Luca chuckled. "It's funny that you don't realize how cool that is."

"Why? The bathrooms in our dorms at the Academy are self-cleaning."

"But that's the Academy! This is just a house!"

"Are Earth bathrooms not self-cleaning?" Aria asked.

Luca laughed. "Well, some are, but only wealthy people can afford that kind of thing. What other self-cleaning rooms do you have?"

"Only the bathrooms and certain parts of the kitchen," Aria shrugged. "Oh, and all the floors are self-vacuuming, but they're manual so we don't lose anything. We do clean a lot of things by hand, though. Some homes on Drammat have a lot more self-cleaning features!"

"I don't know how I never noticed that your life had a suspicious lack of brooms and mops," Luca said, still laughing.

"Lack of what? You know, never mind," Aria said, bumping Luca's arm with her shoulder. "Come check out the best part."

Luca followed as Aria walked to the transparent door and it slid open. What looked like a small balcony from inside the guest room was actually a massive deck that rimmed the entire back of the house and wrapped around the far corner.

"Tada!" Aria said, "This balcony goes all the way around to my room on the other side, so we share it. On that side, stairs lead down to the beach. I'll show you after lunch, but we'd better hurry. Unpack and meet me in the game room when you're ready!"

She rushed back into the guest room and disappeared through the door, skipping into her old bedroom and dumping the contents of her pack on the bed. As she stuffed her clothes into an empty drawer in her dresser, she paused in front of her floor-length mirror. She ran her fingers through her hair and smoothed her top. It was hard to tell whether or not her mom had approved of her appearance. The confidence that had filled her an hour before was gone. A quiet knock rattled her door, interrupting her musings. She unlocked and opened her door through her neurolink.

"You know you look amazing, right?" Luca said. "Whatever you were thinking, it's not true."

"You might think I look good, but I can guarantee my mom will find something to criticize. So I just want to minimize the number of flaws she can find."

"I can't tell you how awful it is that she does that to you," he whispered as he stepped into her room. "But you shouldn't care what she thinks. People who care so much about physical appearance are missing out on what's beneath that. Beneath your beauty, which I find astonishing, by the way, you're so much more than a pretty face."

Aria shrugged. "I know that, and I think she does too, but beauty is a bigger part of the equation than it is for most people. She cares about her appearance, but she seems to care even more about mine."

"Well, if she doesn't think you look incredible, she's blind, insane, or both," Luca said, holding his arm out for her to take. "Let's go show her how gorgeous you are."

Aria took the offered arm with a small but genuine smile, and they descended the stairs together. The scent of fresh seared fish made Aria's mouth water as they stepped through the dining room onto the back patio. There were tiny loaves of homemade bread in the center of the table, along with a platter of grilled cod and several bowls of fresh vegetables and sauces on either side. A place was set for each of them across from Aria's parents, who were already seated.

"Thank you," Luca said as they took their seats. "This looks incredible."

Aria's parents insisted that Luca begin first, but when he didn't know how to eat the foreign meal, Aria demonstrated. She opened one of the small loaves of bread with a knife, placed a thin layer of the grilled fish between the halves, scooped in vegetables, and drizzled the yellow sauce over the sandwich's contents. Luca followed her example and eventually had a messier-looking but still delicious sandwich. When everyone finished, Aria and Luca offered to clear the table.

"Do we have any plans for today, Mom?" Aria asked as she filled the sink with plates.

"Not today. We figured you two would be tired from traveling, so we thought we would stay home and hang out. Do you have anything in mind?"

"I just wanted to show Luca the beach. Can I do that now?"

"That sounds like a great idea. Just be back by five for dinner, okay?"

"We'll be back! Thanks, Mom!" Aria grabbed Luca's hand and dragged him out the back door and into the sand. She stopped as a thick shadow of hopelessness suddenly seized her heart.

"What's wrong?" she whispered, letting his hand drop.

"Oh, it's nothing," Luca said.

"Come on. Tell me."

"It's nothing important. I just realized that all parent-child relationships seem kinda harmful. It doesn't seem worth it to bring a kid into the world if you're just gonna mess them up."

"That's a little dark," Aria said. "What made you go there?"

They stripped off their boots and socks, leaving them in a heap by the door, and resumed walking. Aria relished the feeling of sand seeping between her toes.

"I used to be jealous of the relationship you have with your parents because they were so involved in your life," Luca finally said. "But then I realized the way your mom makes you feel about yourself is pretty messed up. Even the best parent-child relationships have issues."

"I see where you're coming from," she said. "But parents give a lot of good to their kids too. They're not perfect, but I think good parents try to give more good than bad."

"Do you want kids?" Luca asked.

Aria closed her eyes and opened her arms wide to take in the gentle sea breeze as they walked along the narrow, sandy beach. Her hair whipped around her face, and the sun warmed her skin.

"Of course," she answered. "Don't you?"

"I never thought I would," Luca said. "Home and family

haven't been happy things for me in a long time. I never saw a happy family as a possibility. Ideally, I'd want enough kids to form a basketball team and an awesome wife to help me raise them, but ideals and reality rarely match."

"What's basketball?" Aria asked.

Luca smacked his forehead. "Oh, right. I can't believe you don't have basketball here!"

"What is it?"

"Only one of the greatest games ever invented! I'll have to show you sometime. I still can't believe that golf made it here, but basketball didn't."

"I don't know about that," Aria said. "We'd play it here if it were that good."

"Them's fightin' words, right there," Luca said with a strange accent.

Aria's eyebrows knit together, but a smile lingered on her face. "I don't understand half of what you say sometimes."

A wave of loneliness flowed from Luca into Aria, and he shrugged halfheartedly.

"Doesn't matter," Aria finally said. "The important thing is that you keep your dream. You won't have a perfect family because nobody does, but you'll be a great father and husband one day if that's what you want."

She smiled and broke into a run. Luca immediately grinned and chased after her, tackling her onto the sand. They spent hours hand-in-hand along the beach, dipping their toes in the shallows, exploring coves, and telling stories. While the beaches at the Academy were sandy and resort-worthy, Aria's beach was rocky and perfect for exploration and childhood adventures. She had spent countless hours by the ocean with her parents, doing experiments and feeding her imagination. The nostalgia of the moment contrasted starkly with the newness of having Luca at her side. Everything felt so perfect here on her favorite beach with Luca holding her hand.

They turned around to walk back home for dinner, and Luca put his arm around her, sending a shockwave of electricity through her body. He smiled down at her and winked. She could kiss him. She wanted so desperately to kiss him. If only she could shut down the logical part of her brain for two minutes and just do what felt good. But she had always been logical, and she couldn't help running scenarios in her head. The only way to protect both of their hearts was to stay firmly in the friend zone. They were already riding that line too recklessly, and it was dangerously clear that neither of them wanted to stop.

ELEVEN

ARIA AND LUCA tracked sand up the patio stairs and into the guestroom as they returned from the beach, windblown and chilled from the autumn breeze. The smell of dinner wafted through the air. Aria ran to her room to freshen up. She brushed the sand off the bottoms of her pant legs, smoothed her hair, and even touched up her makeup in honor of her mother. Finally, she shrugged at her reflection in the mirror; it wasn't going to get any better. She found Luca sitting on a beanbag in the game room.

"You ready?" she asked.

He stood and held his arm out for her. She took it and, somehow, her confidence soared. From the aroma in the house, Aria could tell before they reached the ground floor that her mom had made one of Aria's favorites: grilled tilapia over wild grains, with a side salad made entirely from vegetables in her dad's garden. It would have made her mouth water at any time, but after having been out on the beach for hours, it was intoxicating. Aria's parents were setting the table when the kids entered the dining room, so Luca took the glasses from Aria's mom and turned to arrange them at every place setting. In her mother's usual way, everything was a bit over the top in formality. The four of them sat at the table and began dishing up their plates, insisting again that Luca go first. This time, at least, he didn't need instructions.

"This is amazing!" Luca said as he swallowed his first bite. "Thank you!"

"You're welcome." Aria's mom beamed. "You're too kind."

"Seriously. The freshness of everything is unreal."

"There's nothing like fresh food," Aria's dad agreed. "Most people choose to get their food from vendors, but out here in the country, we prefer to grow and gather what we can ourselves."

Luca's eyebrows raised. "You grow all this yourself?"

"You, son, are looking at a champion gardener." He waggled his eyebrows playfully. "My wife always says they got my placement wrong, that I should have been a farmer."

"Well, sir, it's the best produce I've ever tasted. I don't want you to think I'm flattering you. I really mean it."

"Thank you, son. We also catch our own fish daily, and when we want other meat, I have some friends who raise chickens, cows, and pigs, so we get that meat fresh as well."

"Not to mention," his wife cut in, "much of my husband's family lives up north and they're big hunters. When they visit, they bring frozen cuts of deer and elk. They freeze them the day of the kill, so they're also fairly fresh."

"Are Uncle Tony and Aunt Paige coming with the kids for Colonization Day this year?" Aria asked.

"They are. Even your cousin Cade will be coming. You haven't seen him in such a long time!"

"Not since he went to that boarding school," Aria's dad said. "He's supposed to be something special, you know. If all goes well this year, he'll certainly be at the Academy with you kids next year. Although, he'll be studying Engineering."

"I'm an Engineering student," Luca said.

"Oh?" Aria's mom asked. "Aria didn't tell us that. How did your exams go? Our nephew Cade is quite bright, so we don't expect he'll have any problems. Of course, he's not quite as bright as Aria."

"Mom!" Aria said, her face flushing. "Cade is brilliant. The difference is that he didn't graduate early because he actually had a life. I'm sure he'll do fine in the exams."

"Oh, Aria. There's nothing wrong with knowing your strengths. You're uncommonly adept at everything you try your hand at. It's not boasting to say so if it's true. Even as a baby, you did everything early, and then you went on to excel in nearly every activity your schools offered. You got your first taste of competition, and that was that. Anyway, we're being rude. Let's talk about our guest instead. Luca, where are you from?"

Luca hesitated but finally said softly, "I'm from Earth, ma'am."

The atmosphere in the room instantly darkened. The glass in Aria's mother's hand exploded in her vice-like grip, blood dripping from her palm. She grabbed her wrist with her uninjured hand, but her eyes never left Luca's. Aria glanced at her father in shock, but he stared unabashedly at Luca after he wrapped a towel around his wife's hand. Aria's mom wrenched the towel from her husband's grasp and finally broke her glare.

"Aria, come with me to the kitchen."

Aria stood and followed her mother, staring at her blood-stained impromptu bandage. The second the men were out of sight, her mom spun around with a threatening finger pointed between Aria's eyes. Her teeth showed in a grimace.

"What were you thinking, bringing that Earth rat into our home?"

Aria reared back. "Excuse me?"

"He is a filthy criminal, and you bring him here to eat at

our table, sleep in our home, be *alone* with you—" She threw her hands up, unable to continue.

"He's my friend," Aria said, just above a whisper. "And a criminal? He's here legally. He's a student at the Academy, a great student! What right do you have to call him a criminal?"

"You may not know the whole story," she hissed. "Your father and I have access to government information that Academy students do not. The courts may have voted in his favor, but did you know that the rat was just days from becoming an adult when he arrived here? If that isn't deceit, I don't know what is. An eighteen-year-old man doesn't need a guardian."

"If you have all the information, why didn't you recognize him when we showed up? Why didn't you know his name when I asked if he could come? I thought you already knew!"

Aria's mother glared at her. "Part of that ridiculous vote was regarding what protections he has a right to. All of my friends in the senate agreed that if he is allowed here at all, the public should be notified of his presence and the risk he poses. But apparently our councils are run by fools, because enough of them thought his life was worth more than our planetary security that they voted to keep his name and like-ness confidential until after he either fails or graduates from the Academy. Idiots. He came here to spread lies and Earther propaganda. Can't you see he's using you?"

Aria flinched at the venom in her mother's words. She had never heard her speak so hurtfully about anyone. She could be exacting and intense, but not bigoted.

"That isn't true," Aria whispered. "He doesn't have an agenda. I shouldn't even tell you this, but apparently, you need to hear it. He didn't have a single person in his life on Earth. If I lost you and Dad when I was seventeen, I would have tons of family to take me in and help me find my way. He lost everyone he loved on Earth, but he had extended family here. It wasn't his choice, anyway. The courts on Earth decided, and Drammat agreed."

"Regardless, you need to be careful. From the moment you told us his name, I didn't trust this boy. Are you sure that's even his real name? He could have found out about your illness and used the name to make you trust him!"

"Do you hear yourself? You sound insane! There are plenty of boys named Luca all over the galaxy. And how would he possibly find out about my illness? You've assured me that as long as I don't give anyone a reason to look too closely, no one will ever find out. I'm going back in there, and I'm going to finish my meal. You should probably go to the hospital. When you get back, I hope we can have a more civil conversation about this. Great Explorer, I never thought my own mother could be so hateful."

Aria turned and stomped back to her seat. Luca and Mr. Blake were sitting in tense silence, clearly having heard the entirety of the hissed conversation. A fire burned in Aria's eyes as she sat down next to Luca. She stared forward, evading her father's infuriating gaze. Finally, her mother rushed in and whispered something in her husband's ear. He nodded and stood.

"We're going to the hospital," he said. "With any luck, we'll be back shortly. You two can watch a movie or play games or something. Just please don't leave the house."

"Call if you need anything," Aria said. "I hope Mom is okay."

Aria's dad blundered through the door behind his fleeing wife, and they sped off to the hospital. Her mom's cuts hadn't seemed too serious, but there was a lot of blood, so it was impossible to be sure.

Aria buried her face in her hands and let her tears flow through her fingers. Luca wrapped his arm firmly around her and pulled her close. She resisted, wanting to revel in her pain, but finally gave in. She turned toward him and tucked her face into his chest. Her cracking worldview had shattered in the space of thirty seconds. It was one thing to hear Celeste Brant spouting her prejudicial lies, but hearing her mother use the exact words felt different. Aria's parents had always taught her to treat others with respect, no matter what. She always assumed that sentiment applied to those from other planets as well, but that was before she brought controversy into their home. Although, they had never been receptive to her questions about Earth or her ancestors. Maybe it had been there all along. Maybe that same prejudice existed in her as well, and only knowing Luca had changed her perspective.

Acid burned her throat as disgust set in.

Luca stood up, pulling Aria into his arms. He carried her up the stairs as she wrapped her arms around his neck and soaked his shirt with her tears. He sat down on the oversized couch in the game room, setting her on his lap and pulling her closer to him, where she cried into his chest until no tears were left. In time, her sobs became quieter and her breathing less desperate, and she eventually lifted her head to look at Luca. She knew her eyes were puffy and red, and she was sure her cheeks were streaked with the remnants of makeup.

"Thank you," she whispered.

"Always," Luca said with a weak smile.

"Did you hear what she said about you?"

"No. I heard a few scattered words, but I couldn't hear well enough to know what was said. I could sense how it made you feel, though. What happened?"

"You don't need to know," Aria said, shaking her head. "She talked about you and Earthers the same way Celeste did. I would never have guessed that my own mother could be so hateful and ignorant."

"I think she means well," he said.

"How could she mean well?" she snapped. "It's disgusting!"

"She's worried for you. She's wrong, but her reasons are good. She's a mother trying to protect her daughter."

"That's not good enough," Aria said, shaking her head more forcefully. "She taught me that every human being is equal. That applies everywhere and to everyone!"

Luca sighed, sounding exhausted. "Aria, the way you see Drammat isn't how the rest of the galaxy sees it. Where you see an advanced and civilized society that works for all humankind, the rest of us see an elite class filled with ruthless, brutal slave drivers who use their self-proclaimed superiority to justify horrific crimes. I was terrified to come here, but what I found was almost scarier than I expected—an entire planet that's been brainwashed to think they're the good guys."

"You're right. I feel like I don't even know who I am anymore. My whole identity was wrapped up in this idea that I would one day discover and prepare new planets to expand and save the human race. It's like being a god, isn't it? We play at gods and act like we're the benevolent, merciful sort when we're actually the power-hungry, vengeful kind. It's all a lie."

"Only extraordinary people can see past the lies," Luca said, pushing a stray lock of hair behind Aria's ear. "We're all seeing lies. On Earth, we only see the bad in Drammat, and on Drammat, you only see the good, but it's a lot grayer than any of us want to believe."

"It has to be possible to make them understand the truth," Aria said. "Right now, we're relying on your testimony alone. That's as good as fact for me, but everyone else is going to need hard evidence."

Luca opened his mouth to speak, but he faltered as his brow wrinkled. "Sorry, I'm getting a call."

"Right now? Who is it?"

There was genuine fear in Luca's eyes. "It's my legal representative. I've only ever met him through calls."

"Well, answer it, and let me hear."

Luca adjusted the settings on his neurolink to allow Aria to connect to the call as an observer rather than a participant, and accepted the call. The image of a man with a long, pointed face, pale skin, and a sour expression was projected directly into Aria's optical nerves, and when he spoke, the recorded sound reconstructed as speech in her brain.

"Good evening." The man had a nasally, high-pitched voice. "Are you well?"

"I'm well enough, sir. Thank you for asking. How are you?" Luca's nervous energy coiled around him and Aria alike.

"Fine enough. I have been tasked with delivering a summons for you tomorrow morning. You are expected at the Allied Nations Capitol Building, Suite 207 at nine o'clock sharp."

"The Capitol Building?" Luca asked. "Tomorrow? Why so sudden? Have I done anything wrong?"

"Yes, tomorrow," the lawyer said. "Is that going to be a problem for you?

"No! No, of course not. I'll make arrangements."

The call cut off abruptly and Luca turned with wide eyes to Aria. "That can't be good, right?"

"I'll go with you," Aria said.

"No way. You don't need any extra attention on you. In fact, I should have just stayed at the Academy. This is exactly why I didn't want to tell you."

"Are you under orders not to talk about your life on Earth?"

"Not in so many words, but it seemed like a pretty clear unspoken treaty."

"I'm not letting you go alone," Aria said. "But we can't let my parents know where we're going. I'll make something up and hopefully, they'll feel bad enough about tonight to let us go to the city."

"But you can't come in with me. There's no way they'd allow that."

"Unless they don't know I'm with you." A little of Aria's fire sparked back to life in her eyes. "Think about it, where better to learn government secrets than in the heart of government operations?"

Luca was shaking his head even before she finished. "Do you know how dangerous that would be? This isn't like sneaking into a party you weren't invited to."

"Obviously I get that. Heart of government operations, remember? But you're an engineer. Don't you have some hacking skills?"

"I can't believe you just asked me that." His face was turning pale. "I can hack a bit, but this is the height of security tech we're talking about!"

"Okay, so it's not your area of expertise. You don't know anyone who has the skills to get me in there?"

Luca stood and ran his hands through his hair as he began to pace the room. Aria watched him stress from her seat on the couch. She felt the exact moment when anxiety turned to hope.

"You know someone," Aria said.

"I think so," he said.

Aria launched to her feet in celebration.

"Wait, wait, wait." Luca's large hands gripped her shoulders. "She and her twin brother are my best friends in the Engineering program. They're good people, raised differently from most kids on Drammat because their grandparents were immigrants."

"And this girl has the skills we need?"

"Maybe. She's definitely the best hacker I've ever met, but

I don't know if my friendship is enough to convince her to help without any explanation. I'm going to give her a call. I'll be right back."

Luca stepped into the guest room and the door slid closed behind him. Aria willed a vision to allow her into the room, but it didn't seem to work on command. How very inconvenient. What use were supernatural powers if you couldn't count on them when it mattered? The two things that seemed constant were the invisible string that always showed her his location and her ability to sense his emotions. She followed that string through the closed door and felt how he paced the floor. His voice was muffled by the walls, but he sounded loud, either angry or excited. His emotions didn't offer up much in the way of deciphering his progress. He was definitely anxious, but there were undercurrents of excitement and terror. Humans were strange that way, always feeling so many things at once. Hearing thoughts on the other hand, now *that* would be a useful skill.

The door suddenly swung open and Aria jumped, feeling slightly guilty for trying to eavesdrop. Yet why would she feel guilty? They couldn't help but feel each other's every emotion. This was exactly why a relationship between them wouldn't work. The normal rules just didn't apply to them.

"What did she say?"

"She's going to help," Luca said. "But she said that it will work better if she's live on coms with you the whole time. I had to tell her what we're looking for."

Aria swallowed. "And?"

"Like I said, she's different. But she won't keep it from her brother, so we have two new lives on our hands if this goes sideways."

"Or two possible traitors."

"I trust them," Luca said. "And right now, that's all we've got."

TWELVE

ARIA WAS startled awake by the sound of footsteps downstairs. At some point, she and Luca had fallen asleep on the couch. She sat up, confused to find herself still fully clothed, hair matted and makeup smeared on her sleeve. Her eyes felt puffy and dry. If there was ever a time for her mother to criticize her appearance, it was now, but she scoffed at the thought. She couldn't care less about what that woman thought of her after her behavior tonight. Even if Aria were the ugliest girl on the planet, at least she was kind, which was more than her mother could say. Aria squirmed out of Luca's arms, leaving him dead asleep on the couch as she crept down the stairs, planning how she might confront her mother. She stopped halfway down the stairs when she heard her mother's shaky voice.

"I just worry for her, Noah," she said.

"I know you do," Aria's dad said. "But we can't control her entire life anymore."

"She's only sixteen. I think of the choices I made as a sixteen-year-old and cringe!"

"Hey, dating me was one of those choices!"

"No, I was almost eighteen then, and I probably made some bad decisions there too. I got lucky that you turned out to be a wonderful man. Aria doesn't even know this kid."

"Exactly. Kids are supposed to make mistakes. We have to hope she learns and grows as a result. Besides, we don't even know if they're in a relationship."

"Oh please, Noah. Just look at the way they ogle at each other. They may not have an official relationship, but Aria is in trouble with that boy."

"I still say she should make her own choices," he said. "Earther or not, he seems like a fine young man. We should give him a chance. If his only living family members are on Drammat, it makes sense for him to be here. And even if he chose to come here, who can fault the boy for wanting a better future for himself if the law allowed it? I admire that."

"I know there's some truth to that," she said. "But it's so suspicious. I want to trust Aria, but I can't trust that boy."

"Lori, if we don't trust her with this, all we'll do is push her away and right into his arms. I'm not saying we should trust an Earther. I just don't want to lose our daughter. I share your worries, but it may be time to loosen the reins, at least a little."

The fury that had driven Aria down the stairs in search of her mom simmered down as she let the overheard conversation sink in. She had been ready to scream and fight, which would have only escalated the situation. She and her mom were more alike than Aria cared to admit. Her dad, on the other hand, could be so sweet for such a large and intimidating man. Gratitude toward him filled her heart along with the seed of guilt that had begun to grow. She needed to make amends now, or she would never fall back asleep. She tiptoed down the rest of the stairs and shuffled into her parents' bedroom. Her mother's hand was bandaged, but it didn't look too serious.

"How's your hand, Mom?" she asked.

Her mom jumped and clutched her pearl necklace with her good hand. "Great Explorer! You scared me." She paused with a hand over her heart as she took in the sight of her daughter. Her lips curled in disgust and confusion.

"What on Drammat happened to you?"

Aria shifted. "Just crying and sleeping in my makeup, two things you always tell me not to do. I know I look like a trash bag, but can we focus on you for a sec?"

Her mom sighed and turned to face Aria more squarely. "My hand will be fine. All the injuries were minor cuts—other than my thumb, which will take a few weeks to heal. I'll need more of your help than usual with the Colonization Day dinner."

"I'll be happy to help, Mom," Aria said with a forced smile. "I know Luca's origin was a surprise, and I should have told you before that he was from Earth. I honestly didn't think that you guys knew anything about the kid from Earth. It's pretty hush-hush at school, and the friends who know are super cool about it. I thought it would be the same here, but I should've realized that your friends in Congress would tell you."

"You really should have told us, but I understand why you didn't. I'm the one who should be sorry for behaving so horribly. You know it's difficult for me to be seen by society in a negative light, and we've heard so many ugly things about this Earther boy. I should have known you wouldn't be the kind of girl to befriend a criminal."

"No, I'm not that kind of girl, and Luca most definitely isn't anything like what those people say. He's kind, genuine, bright, driven, loyal. And he definitely doesn't spout Earther propaganda. He does his best not to mention Earth at all."

"I believe you, but I'm going to keep worrying and hoping that you don't have this boy all wrong, because that's what mothers do."

She opened her arms wide, inviting Aria in. Aria collapsed into her mother's slender arms. Luca's theory about all parents messing up their children sprang to her mind; he was more on base than she first considered, but she also recognized that the love she felt for her parents and that she knew they felt for her was real. They would have her back above all else, even their loyalty to Drammat—at least, she hoped that was true. One day, she might have to put her theory to the test.

Aria straightened. "Thanks for not telling me how terrible I look. I haven't checked a mirror, but I think I would cry again."

"Honey, nobody needs to be told they look like a mess when they're as much a mess as you look right now." Her mom smiled, suppressing a chuckle.

Aria snorted as she tried to stifle a giggle. She decided not to hold it and burst into laughter, a nearly hysterical release of all her pent-up emotions. Her mom gave a rare, genuine smile before she burst out in laughter as well. They laughed until tears streamed down their faces and Aria's abdominal muscles ached. Her mother's arms pulled her into another hug, and she basked in it for a while before pulling away.

"Mom, Luca and I wanted to go to Kan City tomorrow so I can show him some of the museums. Would that be okay?"

"That would be...fine." Her jaw was visibly tight as she formed words that were clearly hard for her to say. "I'm sure he would love to learn more about his new home."

Aria tried to cover her surprise. She smiled, acknowledging her mom's effort.

"Thank you, Mom."

"In fact, I'll need you to pick up a few things in town for the festivities. I'll make a list."

"I would be happy to," Aria said. "I'm gonna go take a

shower and get to bed. I'm exhausted, and I bet you are too. Goodnight."

As she climbed the stairs, anxiety began to swell in her chest once again. She paused at the top of the ascent, staring at the incredibly handsome boy snoring quietly on the couch. She didn't know whether to be more afraid that they would find something important tomorrow or that they wouldn't. Maybe she should be most concerned that someone might discover her presence there. Her worries marinated as she quickly stripped, showered, and dressed before climbing greedily into her childhood bed. She lost consciousness before her head hit the pillow.

Aria opened her eyes to the warmth of sunlight through her window for the first time in months. The sounds of birds chirping and waves crashing on the sandy beach promised hope for a better day than the one before. Then she remembered her plans for the day, and a wave of anxiety washed over her. Or was it excitement? Either way, she needed to tell Luca about the story she fed her mom in the middle of the night. They needed to get their stories straight.

She stretched her arms above her head as she stumbled into the game room. Luca had disappeared from the couch where she had left him in the middle of the night, so she decided to get ready before finding him. She put on comfortable pants and a sweater, twisted her hair into a long braid down her back, and very purposefully skipped the makeup. From now on, she would wear makeup when and how she wanted to, not out of some sick sense of obedience.

She walked across the floor to the opposite side of the room and knocked on Luca's door. It unlocked and slid open as Luca stepped into the doorway, wearing nothing but a towel. Aria's jaw dropped slightly as he leaned against the doorframe, water droplets shimmering on his skin and dripping from his hair. She clamped her mouth shut and forced herself to look at his eyes.

"Good morning," he said.

"Oh, wow," Aria said. "I uh...yes, yeah. Good morning!" She touched her cheek as heat rushed to her face.

"Morning," he said, the corner of his mouth tilting up. "Just give me a minute to get dressed, and I'll be out."

"Okay. I'll wait out here, and we can go down to breakfast together."

Luca shut the door and reemerged from the guest room in business casual. He really had prepared to meet her family. Aria took his arm and they walked down to breakfast. The kitchen was empty.

"I think my parents are still sleeping," Aria said. "They got in pretty late last night."

"Was your mom's hand okay?"

"Yeah. She's gonna be fine. There was one deep cut that will need to be bandaged for a few weeks. They were able to heal the smaller cuts at the hospital."

"I'm glad she's all right. Did you guys talk when she came home?"

"We did. She's still worried you're using me and I'm still disgusted at her behavior, but we're gonna try to trust each other and keep things calm this week."

Luca smiled. "That's a start."

"I'm just worried that one day we'll have to do something my parents won't agree with, and they'll disown me or something."

"Your parents are good people. When it comes down to it, they'll do the right thing. We have a lot of work to do to show them and everyone else on Drammat what the right thing is."

"Speaking of, I asked my mom if we could hit up some museums in Kan City today, so we're good to go."

"And she said yes?" Luca's eyebrows nearly disappeared into his hairline. "I thought they never used to let you go out. Now they're gonna let you go out with me, the evil Earther?"

"I heard my parents talking last night. My dad thinks that they need to give me more freedom so I don't pull away from the family once I'm an adult."

Luca nodded almost absently. Aria pulled out two of her dad's homemade breakfast bars and handed one to Luca.

"Thanks," he said, breaking off a large chunk. "My friend will be calling you soon. She said that I should leave without you and that she would explain it all."

He stuffed a piece of breakfast bar into his mouth and moved to the front door where he shrugged his jacket on.

"Are you sure?" Aria asked. "I don't want you to go alone."

"I'll be fine. You should see the public transportation in my home city. This little train ride will be a piece of cake."

Aria only had time to nod her head before Luca slipped through the door, the brisk morning air sweeping in to fill the space he vacated. A chill overtook her body, whether from the cool morning or something more, she couldn't tell. Before she had time to panic, an image flickered in her vision and then came in clearly. A stunning girl with large brown eyes, deep brown skin, and close-cropped natural coils sat in an armchair with her feet propped up. Aria jumped and pressed a hand to her chest, feeling her rapid heartbeat.

"Luca's friend, I presume?"

The girl pressed a finger to her lips and began a series of quick movements in front of her face and chest. "All right," she said. "We can talk. My name's Alika. You're Aria."

It wasn't a question, but she answered anyway. "That's me. Thanks for your help."

"You know," Alika said, "for a genius girl, you're kind of stupid."

Aria's mouth snapped shut and her eyebrows drew together.

She didn't get a chance to respond before Alika continued, not that she would have known how to answer. "I mean, I get that our people as a whole are becoming more ignorant and subservient with each generation, but you'd think that a school for the most gifted young minds on our planet might boast a little more collective common sense between us."

"Hold up," Aria said.

But Alika cut her off again and Aria tried to hide a smile. "We're free to speak now, but I can't believe that you and Luca had so many sensitive conversations without any protection." She scoffed and shook her head. "He should have asked for my help weeks ago."

"First of all," Aria said, more loudly this time, "I fully reject the term 'genius'. I'm book-smart, but I'm realizing that there's a whole lot more to life than academic achievement. So, tell me, what exactly did we do wrong?"

The girl in the chair continued to swipe her fingers in all directions. "They're always listening. We know this. They can listen to our conversations, see through our eyes, and track our whereabouts. What on Drammat made you think they wouldn't be listening to *you*?"

"They can't listen to everyone at once, and they have no reason to…" Aria trailed off as the argument she had heard and then parroted countless times hit her differently. "Oh no."

She had never felt so stupid in her life. Frankly, she had never felt stupid at all. Two fundamental truths hit her at the exact same time. First, Drammat's system rewarded obedience, subservience, and blind loyalty. Second, she had always been the perfect Drammatan child, her insecurity over her supposed mental illness only serving to make her more devout in her service to the system. If it weren't for her supernatural connection to Luca, she probably would have spent her entire life happily living under Drammat's pretty lies. And because of her trust, she had believed the lie of privacy. Maybe some random teenage girl like Aria would be safe from spying, but of course the government would have Luca under surveillance at all times.

She tried to remember every conversation she and Luca had, what treason they may have committed. The floor suddenly seemed unstable beneath her feet.

"Well, there's nothing we can do about what's already happened," Alika said, roughly tearing her from her downward spiral. "Now we have to focus on damage control. It's time to follow Luca. Step outside."

Aria immediately obeyed, still jarred. The cold air slapped her in the face, but she hardly noticed it. Alika's image disappeared, but her voice still streamed directly into Aria's brain. When Alika told her to walk quickly and steadily to the station, she followed the instructions exactly. When she arrived at the mostly empty station and stepped through the train doors, Alika spoke again.

"Don't talk to anyone, don't touch anyone, and don't manipulate anything around you." Aria moved her mouth to ask why, but stopped herself at the last second.

"I've made you invisible," Alika said. "It's still very experimental, and I can't guarantee how well it will work, so you need to draw as little attention as possible."

Aria grasped a metal bar to hold herself stable as the train picked up speed. She itched to ask a thousand questions but clamped her lips together instead.

Talk about genius. Alika was the true genius of their generation.

"Obviously you're not actually invisible," Alika continued. Aria looked down at her fully opaque form and nodded.

"Instead, I've programmed your neurolink to recognize all other neurolinks within eyesight. Then, it manipulates the optical information they're taking in and deletes your body from the overall image. It's definitely not a precise science, so stay in the shadows as much as possible. I also used more traditional methods to shield your location. As far as official feeds show, you're at home having a lazy day inside waiting for Luca to return. They're watching a conglomeration of footage that I took from your neurolink archives and used AI to make it look just different enough."

Aria blanched. Unsanctioned use of artificial intelligence was illegal—very illegal. Then again, she didn't have much room to judge lately.

Towns passed until the spaces between them shrunk and the outskirts of Kan City streaked by. When the train stopped at Kan City Center Station, it was packed. Aria squeezed between groups of shoppers and weaved around morning commuters, careful not to touch anyone. She breathed a sigh of relief when she exited the station and took in the plaza.

The scent of quality food wafted from nearby restaurants and the sounds of city life buzzed in Aria's ears. Nostalgia assaulted her from every angle. Kan City was one of the largest cities on Drammat, with more history and pride than any other. Colonization Day decorations lined every building and post. The Capitol Building, the federal courthouse, and old churches, cathedrals, and temples from every major religion on Drammat were displayed in a glorious semicircle opposite the equally exquisite train station. In the middle of it all stood a large plaza with perfectly maintained grass, fruit trees, and flowers. Glittering pathways and benches cut through the grass, all leading to an enormous statue of Captain McCormack, the man who led the Great Explorer to humanity's new home. His statue sat atop a vast fountain where dozens of children were leaving flowers to float in the water, just as Aria had done countless times. The nostalgia of her childhood clashed with the growing feeling that she and her people were being lied to.

"Luca is in the waiting room of the Foreign Affairs Office," Alika said. "Cross the plaza now."

Aria walked carefully along the quakestone paths, sure to avoid puddles, grass, or anything else that might shift under her weight. She slipped through the grand doors to the Capitol Building behind another group. She barely refrained from whistling as she looked up at the galaxy mural on the domed ceiling, distinct shapes marking each of the inhabited planets.

"Keep it moving," Alika said. "Up the stairs to the second floor, take a left, then your next right."

She followed the directions and found herself tiptoeing over the wood floors and velvety carpets as she entered a large waiting room. Luca sat in the corner, completely alone. Fifty years ago, this room might have been packed with recent immigrants applying for planetary citizenship. Even twenty years ago it might have held a few Drammatans from other countries applying for visas to stay in the Allied Nations long-term. Nowadays, the other countries were little more than districts of Aria's home country. It was all one government now—the Drammatan government. She had always seen the unification of countries as a beautiful thing. Now, she couldn't help feeling uneasy that so much power rested on so few.

"Luca Cornelle," a saccharin sweet voice called from inside the office, the door sliding open to reveal a woman in a vibrant purple pantsuit sitting at a large wood-carved desk.

Luca stood and Aria felt the acute press of anxiety flowing into her. She followed closely behind him, careful not to bump any of the chairs on the back wall. It wasn't until she turned to survey the room that she noticed the bodies in those chairs. Her heart nearly jumped out of her chest when she recognized the two officials in the middle of the row. President Chen, a cold, middle-aged woman with straight, black hair falling in a sheet to her shoulders was joined at her right by Vice President Brant. Celeste's father was undeniably handsome, but with his mousey hair and brown eyes, it was clear that Celeste got her looks from her mother, Second Lady Maya Brant. Luca flinched at Aria's sudden reaction.

"Nervous, are we?" the woman at the desk said. "Frankly, you should be. Sit down, Mr. Cornelle. We have a lot to cover."

THIRTEEN

ARIA'S HEART raced as Luca lowered himself into the only empty chair in the office. He sat in the middle of the room, facing the lineup of government officials. He looked remarkably calm considering the vortex of terror and anxiety rolling off him.

The woman in purple stood from her place behind the desk and walked over to Luca, where she leaned down to the arm of his chair and changed several settings. Aria forced herself to breathe slowly and evenly, focusing on lowering her own stress level to help Luca.

"There. Now we can assure ourselves of your truthfulness." She moved back to her place behind the desk and steepled her fingers. "When the Earthen court system voted to send you here, had you previously had political backing or training?"

Luca blew out a breath. "Wow, we're really getting right into it, aren't we? No, I had no special training, political or otherwise."

"And yet you somehow secured one of only five hundred

coveted spots at the Grand Drammatan Academy. That seems to indicate training to me."

"My parents were both world-renowned scientists. You might say excellence runs in my blood."

"Hmm." President Chen stood, her tall form dominating the room, all sharp angles in a severe pantsuit. "I don't mean to be rude, but we didn't believe Earthers to be capable of the scores you exhibited on your entrance exam. How are we to know you didn't have help?"

Luca scoffed. His face was still controlled, though Aria could feel his anger rising. "Right," he said through gritted teeth. "That's not rude at all."

"Oh, please," the president said. "You can stop this charade. Your entrance scores were among the top one percent of applicants. Everything from your IQ to your physical fitness far exceeds the average scores for top collegiate graduates on Earth, and many of our own Academy students. Do you think we're stupid?"

Luca faltered as genuine confusion washed over him, tempered only by his defensive instinct. Aria too was confused by the turn the conversation had taken. Where was this going?

"I honestly don't know what you're talking about." No alarm sounded from the lie detector. "I was always top of my class, but I never even had so much as extra tutoring or a personal trainer. I didn't even know that I would be moving here until the week before I left."

President Chen seated herself back in the row of suits, crossing her arms as if to silently concede the floor to the next speaker.

"And you expect us to believe that your intimate knowledge of Miss Aria Blake's personal life comes from a magic connection?"

Aria's heart plummeted into her stomach. She couldn't tell

whose shock was more intense. Of all the things she had worried the government might have heard since Alika's revelation this morning, she had completely overlooked that one minor detail. She had been so preoccupied with the treasonous talk of Drammat's crimes that she had forgotten that Luca was the only person she had ever spoken freely with about her secret.

"We're friends, Madam President," Luca said. "Any knowledge I have of her she has shared freely with me."

"False," the chair screamed. Eyes narrowed on Luca as he visibly deflated. There was no way out of this.

"Did you honestly think that we would let you infiltrate our planet, our most hallowed ground, the place where our children are educated, and not watch your every move? You had the tracker and neurolink placed into your body the day you arrived. What did you think we would do with that information?"

"I never had any intention of sowing seeds of rebellion on your planet," Luca said, the desperation Aria felt finally showing through in his countenance. "I was terrified of Drammat, but a part of me hoped I would get to live in peace and have all the opportunities that my parents never had. When I met people who accepted me, people who weren't the monsters I expected, I let my guard down. I know that I put Aria at risk by sharing some of my experiences with her, but it wasn't my intention to incite her to action. I just didn't want to be alone."

"Aww," President Chen crooned. "So touching that I almost believe you. It takes a clever mind to speak around a lie without actually *telling* the lie."

"No, I swear…"

"Silence." The cold, harsh word came from Vice President Brant. He stood and paced toward Luca. "You will not disrespect us in our own governing seat. Please explain how you learned of Aria Blake's mental deficiency in order to earn her trust."

"If you've really heard everything we've ever said to each other, then you already know."

The older man's top lip curled in disgust. "Say it clearly," he seethed.

"I am connected to Aria Blake's mind through a supernatural bond. I told her the truth about my visions."

The vice president's face radiated smugness. When Luca repeated him word for word and the chair didn't protest, he sat down in a rage.

"I don't know how you're doing this, Mr. Cornelle," President Chen said, waving vaguely at the silent chair, "but you need to be aware that we are always watching. There is not one word, one stolen kiss, or one treacherous act that we will not see and hear through your neurolink. You won't be able to eat an apple without a member of your surveillance team tasting it through you. Do you understand what I'm saying?"

"To shut up and be a good boy," Luca guessed.

President Chen and Vice President Brant smiled. Chen stood first, followed by Brant, and finally, the rest of the officials in attendance.

"You're starting to get it," President Chen said. "It should help you remain vigilant to know that if you so much as breathe another word about Earth to Aria Blake or anyone else, we will not hesitate to remove you from the equation. You may have powerful enough friends to have gotten you here, but the law doesn't bar us from executing justice where treason is concerned."

The group filed out of the room, leaving Luca and the purple-clad woman alone, other than Aria's invisible form. She wondered if Alika had even tampered with Luca's perception of her. If she hadn't, Luca was a better actor than she knew.

Alika's slender face popped into view, closer to the lens this time. "Follow them," she said. "Don't worry, I'm with Luca too and I'll make sure he gets out okay."

Aria snatched up the opportunity without a second thought. She quietly ran through the hallway until she caught up with the group that had just vacated the Foreign Affairs Office. They turned several corners until they arrived at a second staircase leading to higher floors. The mood of the group was so completely different than it had been only seconds ago that she momentarily worried she was following the wrong group.

"No lunch with us today?" President Chen asked, turning to her vice president.

"Not today. Maya and Celeste are here, and I'm meant to take them out for lunch."

"No Celine this time?" one of the other men asked.

"Celine is busy with her internship on Sratta. She's really taken to her role there."

"It suits her," Chen said. "You've had jurisdiction over Sratta for longer than she's been alive. It's fitting that she would grow to love it after all the time you spent there with the girls during summers."

"Truthfully, I think it's the art of discipline that she loves rather than the planet itself."

The group reached the third fourth floor and paused.

"Well, then she takes after her father."

The group laughed and said their goodbyes. Aria hesitated as the president turned left and the vice president turned right. The president would probably have higher clearance and access to more secrets, wouldn't she? But she continued to watch Brant as he walked down the hall. She clenched her fists and made a snap decision. Was it her hatred of Celeste that propelled her down the hall toward the lesser of the two powerful officials? If so, it was too late to change her mind.

She raced down the hallway as quietly as possible, slipping through a door behind Brant as it slid shut. She fought to control her breathing as she found herself in a spacious office. The large windows offered a generous view of the elegant glass buildings and shimmering quakestone streets of upper Kan City, and two beautiful women stood facing it. Aria closed her eyes and checked in with Luca. The feelings coming from him somewhere deep in the Capitol Building were curious, not scared, so she focused on the family in front of her.

"My girls!" Vice President Brant said, holding his hands out wide. Celeste and her mother turned around, identical smiles spreading over their nearly identical faces. Celeste's black waves bounced as she fell into her father's embrace. Maya Brant came more slowly but with no less enthusiasm than her daughter. The vice president leaned down to kiss his wife.

"I was just telling Celeste what we talked about at the Order meeting last night," Maya Brant said.

"Oh good," her husband said, turning to their daughter with a smile. The familial affection was so unexpected that Aria couldn't help feeling off balance. "So, what do you think?"

"I'm honored," Celeste said. "I would still prefer to have more information about the goals of the Order so I can better help the cause, but Mom explained that the Order doesn't share most crucial information with recruits until well into adulthood. I understand and I'm willing to put in the work."

The vice president crushed his daughter to his side again. "Oh, cupcake, I know it's hard not having all the information, but that time will come when you're ready for it. After your first mission failed so quickly, I didn't think the Order would give you another chance for some time. Let's make the most of it."

"I still maintain that my so-called failure wasn't completely my fault. How was I supposed to get to know that filthy Earth rat when he's practically glued to another girl?"

"I know, baby," Maya Brant said, pushing her daughter's hair over her ear. "They just need to know that you're capable of greatness before they give you the Sratta job. I know that you won't let us down."

Aria's heart skipped a beat in her chest.

"Besides," the vice president said, "that little rat won't plague your school for long. I'm certain he'll make another mistake, and when he does, we'll deal with him."

"Thanks," Celeste said with a sweet smile, as if they weren't discussing casual murder. "Where are we eating?"

The family shifted into action, putting on coats and moving together toward the door. Aria scurried out of their way and followed closely behind. The last thing she needed was to be locked in the vice president's office. She allowed the family to pull farther and farther ahead of her as she turned around to take in the rest of the offices.

What was this Order? It didn't sound like a part of the government, but a separate organization. But what did Aria know? Maybe it was simply a term that the elite of her world had for themselves. And what was this about a Sratta plan? What could this Order possibly need a teenage girl for?

She pushed the questions from her mind and scanned the names on the glass office doors. So much from one overheard conversation. What other things might she overhear poking around up here? She walked toward the opposite end of the hall, but before she reached the glass to peer inside, she suddenly recognized fear in her body.

Luca. The adrenaline in her veins must have pushed his feelings to the background, because at some point, his curiosity was completely extinguished, and all that remained were terror and disgust. She turned and flew down the three flights of stairs to the main lobby, careful to steer as far clear of other bodies as possible. She swung her head around, seeing nothing out of the ordinary. No sirens or other evidence of a search. She closed her eyes and followed the ever-present string down below the floor. He was in the basement.

"Aria, stop," Alika said, but she was too panicked to listen.

She darted around the staircase and into several hallways before she found another staircase, one much narrower and less grand than the rest. Snippets of Luca's surroundings bombarded her mind, and with each snapshot, she descended further into panic. The image of a uniformed man standing threateningly over a cowering teenage girl. The footage of several men and women in uniform beating an elderly man. They came too quickly to digest, much less understand.

She descended, abandoning stealth in her desperation. She exploded into the basement, where the ornate architecture and detail work of the rest of the building were replaced by utilitarian sterility. She flew down a hallway and poked her head into several open doorways, only to find rows and rows of men and women, silently working at desks, swiping steadily in front of their faces.

Where was he? She caught a snippet of the white ceiling through their link, but it could have been anywhere in the whole basement. The string seemed to be leading her right where she stood. Aria turned in a circle and spotted a door emblazoned with the universal symbol for bathroom. She bypassed the women's bathroom and ran to the men's room. It opened for her despite her biosignature being blocked, and she silently thanked Alika with a thumbs up. All of the glass stalls were clear, indicating they were empty.

"Don't say anything," Alika said, appearing once again. "He's invisible and a little rattled, but I'll coax him out. He knows you're here. You both need to listen to everything I say, got it?"

Aria's brow scrunched, but she obeyed. The door opened again, and Aria waited until Alika told her to move. She walked quickly and steadily, following the voice in her head. When they emerged onto the main floor, Alika instructed Aria to wait by the front doors, away from foot traffic. Moments later, Luca walked out from the men's bathroom in the lobby and made his way to the exit. Aria followed him out. His face was composed, hiding his roiling emotions well.

"Be silent and follow three paces behind him," Alika said. "I think the program glitched for a second when Luca was in the basement. When you went upstairs, he went into the bathroom and came out invisible. The plan was to do some snooping, then get back in time to leave the bathroom visible. I shouldn't have pushed my program so hard on the first real trial. There were just so many people down there. I wasn't expecting that."

Aria screamed internally. She had probably never been silent for so long in her entire life, except in her sleep. She had so many questions and she had to wait for Alika to hopefully mention the answers. They couldn't get home fast enough.

Luca passed through the security and payment boundaries at the station without incident, and Aria followed with Alika's help. A train barreled into the station just as she stepped onto the platform. But as she waited for the masses of people to enter before she attempted to pass through unnoticed, a dark shape caught her eye. She turned to find a pair of defense officers staring right at her. Her heart jumped, though she was still invisible. They weren't staring *at* her, but *through* her. They were watching Luca.

She turned in a circle and found two other sets of defense officers in black uniforms. She scanned the crowd and noticed that more eyes were on him, civilian eyes. At least, that's what their clothing would suggest they were. But the menacing way that the dozen people converged on the train car told her they were anything but harmless observers.

Luca was being followed.

Aria's heart stuttered. The government wouldn't send someone to simply *watch* him. They were already planted in his nervous system. The only reason to employ physical force was to punish.

FOURTEEN

A BOLT of adrenaline shot through Aria's system. Maybe she was paranoid, but after everything she had learned in the last two months, and especially after the threats Luca received today, she fully believed that the men and women following Luca might have been sent to kill him. At the very least, they were meant to teach him a lesson.

Alika's face appeared once again over the backdrop of reality, her usual calm demeanor completely transformed. "I don't know what to do." Her voice shook with adrenaline and fear. "They wouldn't try anything in public, right?"

Aria wanted to comfort her with assurances, but at this point, she had no idea what her government would or wouldn't do. Not so long ago, she wouldn't have believed defense officers capable of assassination. Crime was virtually nonexistent, so their primary function was simply to maintain order. Although, if Luca's experiences were to be believed, Drammatan defense officers stationed on other planets had far darker roles. How much did she really know about the way her government functioned?

The sun had reached its zenith, and the station was packed

with travelers. Aria had no chance of sneaking in unnoticed, but she couldn't let Luca walk into a trap. She bounced on the balls of her feet and held her breath. This was such a bad idea. She slipped into the train, bumping passengers despite her best efforts to dodge the jostling bodies.

"No!" Alika screamed directly into her brain. "I can't protect you in there!"

Aria ignored the girl's protests and plunged deeper into the mass of travelers. The festive atmosphere in the train car was disorienting, at odds with the pounding of Aria's heart. More people filled the train, squishing the crowd closer together.

Aria spotted Luca standing near the front of the car, and she squeezed through the tightening aisle. As she brushed past several people, their heads turned to find no one. Finally, she reached Luca and pressed her body up against him, praying both that Alika had warned him of her approach and that her closeness to his visible body might repel others. Luca didn't react and Aria silently thanked her techy guardian angel. A glance back dispelled her relief. Several pairs of people, some uniformed and some in street clothes, stared at Luca between furtive glances around the crowded car.

Luca's heartbeat raced and Aria felt the pounding through his ribcage. His dominant emotion was panic, but he was good at masking it. Aria pressed her forehead to his back and breathed in his presence. A warm, inviting feeling swelled above the anxiety, and she closed her eyes for a precious moment. When her eyes snapped open, all her terror was replaced by desperate determination. She would do whatever it took to keep Luca safe.

She shimmied around his body until she was at his front, then tugged on his shirt until he got the message. He walked slowly behind her, as if they were one being rather than two separate people. The crowd was too tight to part for Luca as he walked to the nearest door, but he held his arms slightly raised to protect Aria from touching anyone. It didn't always work.

Luca opened the car door, and they walked through the transparent divider into the next car, the magnetic tracks flying past in a blur. The door shut behind them and they continued their slow walk toward the next car. Luca looked back and stiffened, his panic redoubling. Aria craned her neck to see behind Luca and she nearly stumbled. At least three pairs of their pursuers had followed them through the door, only one set in uniform, but all clearly following them. Aria and Luca instinctively picked up their pace, bumping into passengers at a terrifying rate. Aria looked back again. It was a bad idea—two of the pairs were quickly gaining on them.

"You're drawing too much attention," Alika said, voice shaking as she worked furiously on her end. "There are too many people looking at you. I don't know if my program will hold. You need to get out of there!"

The train began to slow as the next station was announced. It was in the Gov District, where most government officials and support workers lived. It would be nearly deserted today with it being the last day before the holiday officially started. The solitude might make them more vulnerable to attack, but they couldn't wait for another station. They had to go *now*.

People in the car were glancing curiously between Luca and the men and women pushing through the crowd. Then suddenly, their attention locked onto Luca. No, not Luca, but Aria. She turned to Luca and his eyes bulged in horror.

"It can't handle so many neurolinks at once!" Alika yelled. "My program is glitching!"

They abandoned any attempt at subtlety and pushed through gawking strangers to the exit as the doors slid open, surprised gasps in their wake. Luca grabbed Aria's hand and pulled her through the door, forcing her to keep up with his much longer legs as he flew across the platform.

"Don't look back," Luca said. "It'll only slow us down."

He released her hand as he jumped down from the platform onto the train tracks and kept running at top speed. He glanced over his shoulder, but Aria kept right on his tail. They cut across the tracks and darted into an alley. Just before they disappeared between two buildings, Aria looked back again.

"We've still got two on us," she said. "Twenty meters back."

"Are they in uniform?" Luca asked.

"No."

"Good. We'll get in less trouble for defending ourselves from civilians than resisting arrest."

"Defend ourselves?" Aria asked. "Are you crazy?"

"If that's the only way." He shrugged, out of breath. "But we'll try to avoid that if we can."

Suddenly, he darted into an alley to their left. Aria followed, looking back to see their pursuers make the same turn. They made several more sudden turns, but each time, the last partnership on their tail followed.

"We need to stop," Luca said, gasping for air. "We aren't gonna lose these guys and if we keep running, we'll be too tired to put up much of a fight."

Aria nodded once. They made a sharp right into another alleyway and slowed to a stop. A recycling collection shoot large enough for both of them to hide behind sat close to one of the buildings. She grabbed Luca's arm and pulled him to the ground beside her. A second after they hit the ground, both pursuers shot into the alleyway and slowed, searching for their missing targets.

"Where'd they go?" the burly man asked.

"We can't have lost them," his female partner said. "They're close."

Aria barely held back her tears, and Luca squeezed her hand. If these people were undercover defense officers, they would have much more experience and training in hand-to-hand combat than she and Luca had. Not to mention, they were both incredibly tall and heavily-built, so Aria and Luca didn't stand a chance of overpowering them. An idea popped into Aria's head. She turned to Luca, but even the smallest whisper could give them away.

"I know what to do!" Aria yelled in her mind, frustrated.

He turned to her, confusion and surprise evident on his face.

"Shh!" Aria heard in her head.

Her eyes widened. "Can he hear me?" she thought.

"Can you hear *me?*" the voice sounded in her head again as Luca's eyes grew even wider.

"No way," she thought. But her shock was instantly overwhelmed by the looming danger. Whatever was going on, they could figure it out later. Now, she would use it. "I have an idea."

"All ears," Luca thought. "Or brain, I guess."

Aria thought out her plan, and Luca somehow understood every unsaid word. He nodded in silent agreement.

Aria took off like a shot, sprinting as quickly as her legs could carry her, and both officers pursued her. The clatter of a small rock scuttling across the pavement echoed through the alley. She glanced behind her, just in time to see the woman stop dead and turn around. While the woman went to investigate, the huge man stuck on her tail. Why did it have to be the big guy?

Her muscles burned, but the excess of adrenaline in her body pushed her forward. Suddenly, the back of her shirt snagged on something, and she launched backward, her head whipping forward. Pain seared her head and back, and pulsing light clouded her vision. Her awareness returned as she lay on the hard ground, looking up at the terrifying man. His massive left hand pinned her to the ground by her neck while his right hand reached inside his jacket. A metallic sheen caught her eye as he pulled his hand back out. It was a gun, and by the look of the attached silencer, it undoubtedly was not a legal model. Panic raced through Aira's body as the man grinned and pointed the weapon at her head.

"Who do we have here?" he asked, searching her face with a greedy gleam in his eye that terrified her. "Traitorous little minx. What did the Earth rat promise you? Didn't know anyone might be dumb enough to throw their lot in with a dead man."

Aria tried to speak or even spit, but her airway was being crushed under the weight of the mountain of a man. She thrashed in his grip, hitting and scratching at his gigantic arms. Her vision blurred as her oxygen stores became depleted, and her eyes were suddenly so heavy she couldn't keep them open.

"Idiot girl," he scoffed, sounding strange and far away. "What a mess."

The cold barrel of the gun pressed against her temple. The air in her lungs was nearly gone now, and her body slumped. Panic coursed through her veins, the kind of panic she imagined only came to those at death's door. A dark figure flashed in front of her and the crushing weight of her captor suddenly released. Her airway opened enough to force breath into her burning lungs. She rolled to her side as her vision cleared and her breath returned. She coughed, searching for the source of the grunts sounding in her ears.

Luca had returned, but her relief was short-lived. He was two heads shorter than the man and much lighter, but for now, Luca was holding his own against the hulking beast. For every punch the monstrous man landed, Luca dealt one of his own, though Luca's fists did considerably less damage. The man connected with another right hook to Luca's jaw, sending him sprawling on the ground.

Aria scampered to her feet, still dizzy from lack of oxygen, and scanned the area for weapons. The man's firearm lay abandoned just a meter from her, but like most guns, it would only function when connected with its owner's neurolink. She hefted it and felt its weight before turning back to the fight. Luca was on the man's back, jabbing him in the side.

The mammoth finally got a grip on Luca and launched him into a wall. His body crashed against it with a sickening crack and crumpled to the ground. The torrent of Luca's emotions that always roiled inside of Aria ceased, and panic shot through her veins.

She could still feel the string. That had to be a good sign, right?

The oversized man sauntered toward Luca at a relaxed pace and crouched over his motionless body. Aria sprinted forward, lifted the enormous firearm high above her head, and smashed it into the man's right temple. Despite the blood now oozing from his hairline, the monster stood up and turned toward her. His eyes were confident and cold, but he staggered slightly. He threw another punch in Aria's direction, but she dodged the sloppy jab and smashed the butt of the gun into his scowling face. With the thud of metal on flesh, his eyes rolled back in his head, and he collapsed at her feet.

She kicked him lightly, but there was no response. Breathing erratically, she ran to Luca's side, hands shaking. She knelt over him and checked his pulse. It was strong, but he was still unconscious. She let out a breath she didn't realize she was holding as she shook him.

"Luca," she yelled. "Wake up. We need to go!"

His eyes fluttered open, and he pushed up on his elbow.

"Can you walk?" she asked.

He refused Aria's help and stood up on his own, wincing as he rubbed his neck. "Yeah, I think I can."

Aria immediately turned to lead the way, all of her senses on high alert. The other pursuers were still out there somewhere.

"What was that?" Alika reappeared in Aria's vision, this time with a boy who looked like the masculine version of herself.

"You're still here?" Luca asked. "Amare, what's up?"

The twins stared blankly, mouths hanging open.

"I *really* didn't understand what I was signing up for," Alika finally said.

"Neither did we." Aria gently touched the bruise forming on her neck.

"It's a good thing I'm as good as I am. I was able to keep basic protections in place, so they shouldn't have been able to see your identity, Aria. Unfortunately, when my invisibility program went down, it allowed security scanners access to your face."

"So they know it was me?" Aria asked.

"Unfortunately, probably. I've put the invisibility program back up for both of you, but I recommend walking as much as possible and only using public transit when there are fewer people on board with you."

Alika and her twin brother Amare stayed with them through the entirety of their trek home. They chose to walk through Kan City and only got on the train when they were well into the outskirts. They mostly kept silent, listening to Alika and Amare's many theories about all of the information Alika had seen throughout the day. When they finally made it to the suburbs, they slipped silently into the last train car and rode until they approached Miller Bay Station.

Aria was so exhausted that all she wanted to do was sleep, but so jumpy that she felt she might never sleep again. When they were finally alone, walking through the dark field near her parents' house, Amare and Alika finally said goodnight and lifted the invisibility. Aria had been ignoring her mom's and dad's many calls and messages for hours, but she couldn't put them off forever.

"What are we gonna tell my parents?" Aria asked, her voice raspy from the near-strangling.

Luca looked over at her and she winced at the pulp his face had become. "The truth."

"No way. It's too early for that!"

"How else are we going to explain *this?*" He gestured to their entire battered bodies.

"A fight with a rival from school." She shrugged. "You defended my honor."

He raised one eyebrow at her. "Have you ever been in a fight? Does that even happen here? It seems so...civilized. Outwardly, at least."

"Not often," she admitted. "But we don't have any evidence of the truth yet. My parents are loyal to the core. Especially if they're still worried about you putting crazy ideas in my head."

He nodded, mild annoyance transferring to Aria through their connection. "They're your parents. I'll follow your lead."

They finally stumbled up the Blake's front steps just after ten. The festive lights and decorations were painfully dissonant with the terror of their day. As the door slid open, they both staggered inside and collapsed onto the floor.

FIFTEEN

"ARIA?" her mom yelled, rushing in from the kitchen.

In the bright light of the front room, Aria got her first good look at Luca since the fight. Tears sprang to her eyes. To think she had wanted to hide the truth from her parents. There's no way they could have done it if they tried. Dark purple bruises were forming on Luca's face. From what she saw of the fight, though, the worst of his bruises would be on his back. Blood seeped from a cut above his left eyebrow, and the eye below was swollen shut. She probably looked just as battered as Luca. Her neck and throat throbbed, and several cuts on her face burned. It was impossible to tell if the blood on her knuckles and face was her own or someone else's.

Aria's dad rushed into the front room behind his wife. "Who did this?" he thundered, running to Aria's side.

"We were followed." Her voice was hardly more than a wheeze. "They attacked, and we fought back."

"Great Explorer, Aria!" Her mom's voice trembled as she ran back into the kitchen. "Who would attack children?"

A dozen scenarios played out in Aria's head as she considered how much she was willing to tell her parents. What could she admit without putting them in danger? Alika had shown Aria and Luca how to use her program to mask conversations, but even with that protection, she couldn't bring herself to tell them everything. Still, whatever lie she chose would have to be somewhat grounded in truth or they'd never believe it.

"We were snooping somewhere we shouldn't have been," Aria finally said.

Her mom returned with wet rags and first aid supplies in tow and started tending to their injuries.

"Where were you snooping that could have possibly resulted in all of this?"

"Luca had a meeting at the Foreign Affairs Office this morning. I didn't tell you because I thought you wouldn't want me going with him. We were going to go there first and then go to the museums, but I ruined everything."

"Well, you were right thinking we wouldn't want you going with him," her dad said. "What did the FAO want with Luca?"

"I'm the first immigrant to Drammat in four decades," Luca said. "I have check-ins to make sure that I'm behaving."

"That still doesn't explain...this," Aria's mom said, her voice breaking.

"It was my fault," Aria wheezed. "I wanted to poke around, and Luca didn't want to leave me alone, so he came along to try to keep me out of trouble. He's honestly much more sensible than I am." She turned to him and gave him a self-deprecating smile.

"This happened in the Capitol Building?" her dad asked.

"It happened after we left. We were using a program from a friend of ours at the Academy. It made us invisible. We poked into some things we probably shouldn't have, and I guess the program glitched, because we had defense officers on us shortly after leaving. We stayed invisible as long as possible, but eventually they caught us. We put up a good fight and got away, but not before one of the bigger officers got a hold of us."

Aria's mom finished applying bandages to Aria's split eyebrow with shaking hands and looked her daughter squarely in the eyes. "That still doesn't answer why this happened. What did you see that would warrant such a drastic response?"

"I really don't think it's smart for us to share that, Mrs. Blake." Both of Aria's parents turned to Luca with barely restrained panic. "If they were willing to do this to us just for seeing it, what would they do if we told someone about it?"

Aria's parents turned away from the children and began whispering. Aria's eyes automatically went to Luca's, and she focused her mind on transmitting her thoughts to him. No answering words appeared in her mind. Too bad. She'd give up sharing emotion for true telepathy any day. Still, Luca's uneasiness and the look on his face told her most of what she wanted to know. He was exhausted and afraid, but his concern was for her and her loved ones. Aria's parents turned back around and her dad spoke with an affected calm.

"I'm going to call the defense center in Kan City."

"No!" both Aria and Luca shouted in unison.

"I'll only ask for clarification on what crimes were committed to warrant such a harsh punishment. I'll tell them that you two were being very tight-lipped and that you clearly regret whatever mistake you made."

Aria tried to protest further, but her mom cut her off. "We need to head off any official reports or rumors. A scandal like this could get you both expelled. You wouldn't be looking at changing your career path. If it's as serious as you're letting on, you very well might end up without any prospects for work at all. If you became lost souls, we wouldn't have any power to help you."

Aria nodded, closing her eyes. When she opened them, her mother was staring daggers at Luca.

"It wasn't his fault," Aria said.

"I have a hard time believing that. My obedient, exceptionally mature daughter left for the Academy two months ago, and a wild, erratic thing I hardly recognize returned in her place. I'm not surprised that this is the consequence of becoming too close with an Earther."

Aria's chest swelled in anger as she prepared to defend Luca's honor once again to her mother.

"Lori," Aria's dad's voice cut through her indignant thoughts. "Enough. Aria's whole life changed from one day to the next and you think the only variable that might be at fault is Luca? I'm no more thrilled about our daughter growing up and making her own choices than you are, but cutting down someone she obviously cares about isn't going to help."

"Thank you, Dad," Aria whispered.

He turned his fierce glare on her. "That doesn't mean you're off the hook. We'll talk more about this once I've spoken with Kan City's defense center." He turned to his wife and continued. "I don't want to hear another word about Earthers. We'll all go to bed, and when we wake up in the morning, we'll start over. This week will be dedicated to fun and family. Is that understood?"

"Yes," everyone said in hushed unison.

"Get to bed, you two." Aria's dad threw his hands up in frustration as he walked away. "If anyone needs to go to the hospital, come get me."

His wife followed after him, fury in her eyes. Whether it was for her wayward daughter, the invading Earther, or her husband was anyone's guess. Aria and Luca limped up the stairs, each proceeding silently to their respective rooms to wash the blood off their bodies and collapse into bed.

Before Aria's shower, she cringed at the sight of the girl

staring back in the mirror. Her entire neck was already blue and purple. Each individual finger had left a clear outline. Other bruises and shallow cuts marked her face and body. Her bottom lip was severely swollen from where her teeth broke the skin, and blood was already seeping through the white cotton where her mom had bandaged a deep cut through her right eyebrow. Though her mom had tried to wipe it off, her skin was smeared with a mixture of blood and dirt.

The hot water soothed her aching body as she stepped into the shower. After summoning the willpower to leave the steamy bliss, she rebandaged her wounds, pulled on some comfy pants and a T-shirt, and crawled into bed.

After another night of blessed darkness, with no visions or dreams to speak of, Aria woke up to the same sights and sounds of the day before, yet everything seemed different. She tried to sit up, but her body protested as every muscle ached and her injuries throbbed. She felt Luca's grumpiness from across the loft. He was probably in just as much pain as she was.

When they finally pulled themselves out of bed, they spent the entire day playing games and watching movies in the game room, a silent tension between them. Their connection had transformed into a hurricane of emotions, and Aria couldn't be certain which ones belonged to her.

There was so much left unsaid between them with Aria's parents never letting them stray too far from earshot. She was desperate to talk about what she had overheard in Vice President Brant's office, and she still only had a vague idea of what Luca found in the basement of the Capitol Building. Aria repeatedly attempted to reconnect with Luca's mind as she had done the night before, but no response came. Whatever had happened, she couldn't do it on command.

The following morning, they both felt slightly better, though their bruises and scabs looked even worse. They spent the day in awkward tension as they helped Aria's parents prepare the meal and decorations for the following day when the family would arrive. The highlight came when Aria's dad pulled her aside with news about his call to the Capitol's defense center.

"Ari-bug," he said, a sure sign he was feeling emotional. "Can I have a second?"

"Of course. What's up?"

"I spoke with the chief of defense in Kan City and he was very apologetic about the whole affair." Aria's face crumpled into disbelief, but he continued. "They had received a tip that Earth was planning some kind of terror attack, so they were on the lookout for anything out of the ordinary. When security spotted Luca creeping around where he shouldn't be, they decided to question him. When he ran instead of complying, and then an accomplice appeared from thin air, they assumed you were dangerous too. They had no idea that you were a Drammatan citizen. They assure me that they never would have treated you that way otherwise."

"What about Luca?" Aria asked, harshness creeping into her tone.

"Well, honey, they're going to be monitoring him for a while, at least until he's proved himself loyal to Drammat."

Aria nodded. It wasn't anything she didn't already know. In fact, the lack of repercussions surprised her. She wanted to feel grateful that they had gotten off so easily, but a larger part of her knew that it was no accident. The authorities had let them go, but for what? Knowing that they were probably monitoring this very conversation sent her skin crawling. The best thing she could do was to act natural and stick to her routine.

Tuesday morning, Aria spent extra time caking on makeup to hide her injuries. She covered up her cuts and bruises, especially those ringing her neck, and filled in the part of her eyebrow that was split open. The injuries were still visible, but only from close up. Her voice had improved markedly as well.

Grandma and Grandpa Blake arrived first with a mountain of gifts in tow. Luca laughed as Grandma Blake pinched Aria's cheek, but he must have felt her annoyance because his laugh was cut short.

"Two of my cousins are younger than me," she said. "But everyone acts like I'm the baby of the family. Becca is only fourteen, but the adults treat her like she's twenty-five. I don't know how she does it. Maybe she'd give me lessons."

Luca laughed again, letting it ring out this time. "There's nothing wrong with being perceived as sweet and innocent."

She eyed him from the corner of her vision as her dad's oldest brother Eli and his wife Mara piled in with their two grown daughters and each of their families. Between the two of them, they had eight kids under seven and another two on the way. Aria could never remember whose were whose. It was hard to tell when they were always running around and screaming. Their arrival instantly transformed the house with energy and laughter.

Her father's sister Norina arrived with her husband and two grown children just before lunch. The two boys were twenty-three and twenty-five, and both worked in Defense like Aria's father, but neither had a wife or family of their own yet.

Aria's fingers tapped rhythmically on the windowsill as she watched for their final guests. Just before four o'clock, Uncle Tony and Aunt Paige's pod arrived outside, and Cade and Becca raced to the front door.

"Riri!" Cade yelled, scooping Aria up in a bear hug the moment he walked through the door.

"I've missed you so much!" she squealed through smashed cheeks.

"You're the one who's too busy to call me now that you're some Academy big shot!" He set her down lightly.

"I'm sorry, I've been so busy. You'll see what it's like next year. It's not *all* fun and games!"

"Hey," he whispered, lightly touching his fingertips to the makeup-covered cut on her eyebrow. "What's this?"

Aria winced at Cade's touch and covered the scar. "It's a long story," she whispered. "I got in a fight. Actually, Luca and I both got in a fight." She gestured toward Luca, who was standing a few paces behind her.

"Luca?" he whispered. "Wasn't that the name of...um...you know who?"

Cade was the only person Aria had always been completely honest with about her so-called imaginary friend. Explaining the truth would be painfully complicated, but he would understand better than anyone other than Luca.

"That's a long story," she said. "For now, all you need to know is that he's a good guy."

"Alright," he said, staring Luca down. "But if he hurts you..."

"I know you have my back. That's something you two have in common."

Cade nodded once and rested his arm over Aria's shoulders. He followed her to the kitchen, where Becca was dipping her finger in a bubbling sauce and wincing from the heat as she sucked it clean.

"Hey, troublemaker," Aria said, shrugging out from under Cade's arm to throw herself at Becca. "How's my favorite baby cousin?"

"Very funny," Becca said. "You call me that because you're projecting."

"You're not wrong, but I do have three years on you, even if you look like you're twenty-five."

"And you look like you're twelve."

Aria rolled her eyes. "When we're in our fifties and I look like I'm thirty, who's gonna be laughing then?"

"Yeah, whatever," Becca said. "So, who's the hottie, huh?"

"You mean Luca?" Aria asked. "It's complicated, okay? Play nice."

"So, you *aren't* together? Finally, some good news."

"Becca! Despite what you think, you're a kid, and he's literally an adult. Not gonna happen! Let's go help my mom set the table for dinner, like the kids we are."

She pouted but didn't protest. With so many tiny humans running around, dinner was a loud, messy affair. Aria tried to hold back laughter as her mom cringed at every smeared morsel of food and toppled glass. The Colonization Day meal commemorated the first settlers who landed on Drammat, so it only included simple dishes made from food initially grown on the Great Explorer. There wasn't any meat or fish, and not much flavor or extravagance of any kind. Afterward, they ate the traditional dessert of baked, mildly spiced apples. It wasn't an incredibly delicious meal, but that was the point. It was supposed to represent the sacrifice of their ancestors.

After dinner, the whole family retreated to the sitting room for the traditional telling of the Great Explorer's tale. Grandpa Blake always did the honor, and the littlest family members knelt at his feet while the adults sat on couches and chairs. Aria leaned against the back wall rather than subject herself to kneeling with the toddlers. Luca, Cade, and Becca took up places on the wall beside her.

Grandpa Blake told the story with the same colorful detail as always, but Aria's mind wandered to her and Luca's theories and the possibility of what Grandpa Blake might be leaving out.

"This is such crap," Becca mumbled under her breath, breaking Aria out of her distraction.

"Becca!" Cade whispered. "Enough with your conspiracy

theories!"

"Conspiracy theories?" Luca asked, looking at Becca.

"They aren't conspiracy theories," Becca whispered, glaring at Cade. "They're facts that anyone with half a brain can see are true."

"What about?" Aria asked.

"No, Becca," Cade warned.

"They wanna know," she said, turning to Aria and Luca. "There's a lost soul camp near our house."

"Lost soul camp?" Luca asked. "Your mom mentioned lost souls last night. Right, Aria? What's that about?"

"You don't know what lost souls are?" Becca asked. "Where'd you get this guy, Aria? Under a rock?"

"Earth, actually," Aria said.

Becca's mouth dropped open. "Are you serious?"

"Yeah," Aria said. "It's this whole thing, but I'll tell you later. What about the lost souls?"

"Well, Earth boy," she said, "lost souls are people who choose to defect from society rather than be owned. When you choose to reject the government's chosen path for you, you can't have access to anything the government provides, like healthcare, education, employment, property. Everything that makes life possible is taken from them, and they still choose that life over being enslaved."

"Great Explorer, Becca," Cade whispered. "You make it sound like we're under tyranny."

"We are, Cade," she whispered harshly. "It's just a kind of tyranny most people are fine with because it benefits them. What about people who are different? What if *I'm* different?"

"Becca, stop!" he said, a little too loudly. Several family members glanced back at them.

Aunt Paige shot a stern glare at her kids.

"You can't ruin your life like that," Cade whispered. "Nobody loves their job all the time, but you do what you're good at and what society needs you to do. You can use your free time for your passions, but choosing a life of crime and wandering isn't the way to go."

Becca crossed her arms and looked away. Aria raised her eyebrows at Cade, silently begging for more details. He leaned closer and whispered in her ear.

"She's been talking like this a lot recently. A huge lost soul camp moved in near our house and started stirring up trouble with the kids in town. They're living on protected wilderness land, so the police can't do anything but block access to food and potable water. I disagree with how the government is handling it, but I'm not willing to throw my life away over it. A lot of kids our age are protesting in the streets and some have disappeared. I just don't want Becca to get hurt."

"I'm sorry," Aria whispered. "I didn't know."

The four teens were silent for the rest of Grandpa Blake's story, but it was unlikely that any of them tuned back in. Luca's nervous energy and restlessness mingled with Aria's. She had always considered lost souls to be lawless vagrants who chose a life of idleness over a life of hard work. She was in third grade when she first learned about them. Her teacher called them traitors and said their punishment for treason was to live with nothing. In all her life, she had never questioned that judgment. Aria swallowed. Becca had said they chose a life of hunger and hardship over a life of slavery. Her parents seemed so happy, but suddenly it seemed possible that they, and everyone else she knew, were living a life of cloaked subjugation.

The story finally ended with an uproar of applause for Grandpa Blake, and the sudden eruption shook Aria from her trance.

With one day down in the Colonization Day marathon, they suspended tents in the air over the beach for much of the extended family to sleep in over the next several nights as

they didn't have enough guest rooms to accommodate everyone. Aria was grateful for the distraction their company
provided. Awkward tension weighed down the atmosphere
whenever Aria was near her mother, but with so much going
on, they both had too much on their minds to engage in verbal
warfare.

While Colonization Day was a sacred, historic day, the
days after were the opposite. They spent the next morning at
the annual Colonization Day parade in Miller Bay, then ate the
most outrageously delicious meal, and ended the day with
fireworks on the beach. The following day, they went to the
Miller Bay fair and ate more fried food than anyone should
before riding rides. On Friday, they spent the day seeing off
the extended family and cleaning up after the week-long party.
Beyond small talk, Aria and her parents didn't interact much
after everyone else had gone, and on Saturday morning, Aria's
mom joined her dad in the pod to take Aria and Luca to catch
the train. As they turned to enter the station, Aria's mom
grabbed her arm and pulled her close. She chewed on her
bottom lip, seeming unsure. It was an expression that seemed
fundamentally wrong on her mother. Finally, she opened her
mouth to speak.

"Please don't do anything that could get you hurt," she
begged, tears forming in her eyes. "I know some things about
life are unfair and you might want to change that, but you
need to learn your place in the world. I've been where you are,
but we have to accept our position in society."

"I'll be safe, Mom," Aria said, knowing in her heart that it
was a lie. She would probably never feel safe again. "I love
you," she said as she pulled away and joined Luca.

The tension that had built up between them over the days
since their attack was reaching a boiling point as they boarded
the train back to the Academy. They sat silently, side by side,
as the attendants finished final checks and gave the signal to

leave the station. As the train pulled out and picked up speed, Aria's foot tapped an anxious rhythm on the train floor.

"I can't wait any longer," she said, turning to face Luca.

"Wait," he whispered. He swiped at the air in front of his face and moved his fingers in a deliberate pattern. "There. Alika installed her program on my neurolink and showed me what to do. We can talk somewhat freely, but still keep it down."

Aria sighed as much of the tension in her shoulders melted away. "Finally. I've been dying to ask—what happened between us in the alley?"

"*That's* what you're worried about?" Luca whispered. "I'm more focused on the fact that someone tried to *kill* us!"

"Okay, maybe I buried the lead there, but you have to admit it was weirder than usual!"

"I'll give you that. But first, can we talk about how quickly the government went from vague threats to actually trying to kill us? The stakes are so much higher than we thought. Are you sure you want to keep pursuing this?"

"Of course, I do," Aria said. "Why would you ask that?"

"You have a wonderful life, Aria—just like almost everyone else on this planet. If Drammat's priority is protecting their people, they do a great job. I would understand if you didn't want to mess that up and put our lives and your family's lives at risk in the process."

A warm and familiar electricity seeped up her arm as she touched his hand. "Thank you for being so understanding, but nothing's changed for me. If anything, I'm more determined than ever. Now that my eyes are open, I couldn't shut them if I tried."

"If you're sure, I'm with you all the way," Luca said, squeezing her hand.

She smiled and turned to look out the window, leaning back on the seat. "Besides," she said, "lost souls are their people too, and they aren't doing a very good job of protecting them. My whole life, I thought lost souls were just lazy. Maybe there's more to it than that."

"I was thinking about that too," Luca whispered. "I wonder how many lost souls there are and how many people like Becca are protesting the government's treatment of them. Those are all people who might be on our side when it comes to that."

Aria whipped back around to face Luca. "No way," she said, shaking her head. "We can't involve kids in this. It's too dangerous!"

"Isn't that exactly what we're waiting for, though? We need the masses on our side, and the people most likely to accept and fight for change are young people. I mean, look at us. We're kids too."

Aria opened her mouth, but a response evaded her. She snapped her mouth shut and slumped in her seat. "Not yet," she finally said. "We still don't know what we're facing. We need more time before involving anyone else."

Luca was silent. Aria watched as he mentally battled himself. "Alright," he said. "But we'll need allies long before we decide to make a move. That's probably our next step."

Aria nodded and settled in for the rest of the uneventful train ride, a stark contrast to the hectic past week. She knew Luca was right; two kids without resources or connections couldn't do anything, but could Aria encourage others toward this path? Young, rebellious kids like Becca would gladly jump off a cliff if they thought it would make an impact, but they couldn't let children get hurt if they could help it. Before they involved anyone else, they needed to have a solid plan.

She rested her head on Luca's shoulder and dozed off to the humming of the train's motion. People were going to get hurt before this was over, but for now, she grounded herself in the constant electric warmth of Luca's presence.

SIXTEEN

THE SECOND HALF of the semester passed at a dizzying rate. When Aria and Luca had first shared with each other what they had each found in their search of the Capitol Building, the renewed fire of rage and mystery fueled their obsession. Luca refused to share much detail about his discovery. He only said that Alika helped him tap into the neurolink feeds of the rows and rows of workers, and that what he found had made him sick. The government employees were viewing and deleting videos found on Drammat's neurolink network. Luca watched less than a dozen videos before he fled to the bathroom, and from the few snatches Aria caught through their link, she suspected she would regret it if he expounded on the horrors he witnessed.

"They're covering up anything that could be seen as negative press for Drammat," he had said. "I've always thought it was weird that Drammat's history doesn't include anything bad. No wars, hardly any crime, no serial killers or child abusers. It's just too good to be true."

Aria had argued that point for a while, her deep loyalty to Drammat a difficult thing to unlearn. She had grown up with the absolute knowledge that her home planet was the moral authority of the universe and that she would grow up to be an integral part of that legacy. Now that the scales were falling from her eyes, she was forced to admit that her entire life's purpose and all her hard work were for nothing.

At first, Aria and Luca threw themselves into their research, using Alika's program to disguise their conversations as they scoured the dark side of the neurolink network for evidence of Drammat's crimes. Unfortunately, their classes became more intense as the semester wore on, requiring more time and energy to keep up. Their secret mission took a back seat due to a combination of frustration over being caught at a dead end and stress over their impending final exams, but no amount of distractions could reverse Aria's new perspective. Before the Academy, she had never doubted her teachers, but now she struggled to believe a word they said. She clashed most often with Instructor Nori in Diplomatic Negotiations. At least once in every class, Nori would reference the supremacy of Drammat, and each time Aria had to bite her lip and stare at her feet to avoid openly glaring.

The last day of classes before the final exams came faster than anyone wanted. Aria and Luca ate silently in the cafeteria with bags under their eyes, and the rest of the cafeteria's occupants were in a similar semi-comatose state. The excitement they felt just four months ago as they began their college education was now wholly extinguished by exhaustion and stress.

Aria jumped and dropped her fork as the girl at the table to their left gasped and covered her open mouth with her trembling hands. A second later, a boy across the room dropped his tray on the floor with a crash. More gasps followed from all over the cafeteria, and hushed conversations took over the previous near-silence. Suddenly, the entire cafeteria was alive with commotion. A girl at a table to their left clutched her shirt collar as tears streamed down her face and another girl clung to her. Several arguments had broken out across the cafeteria. An older student lunged at another boy at his table, knocking him to the floor. What was going on?

"Aria!" Dima shouted, waving her arm from the opposite end of the room. "Did you see it?" She dodged panicking and outraged students at every step as she ran toward their table, worry lines creasing her forehead. Aria clutched Luca's arm as she stood, pulling him up with her.

"How didn't you guys hear?" she asked breathlessly when she arrived at their usual table. "There's been a massacre."

"A what?" Aria asked as her heart leaped into her throat. "Where?"

"Some small town in the Northern Region. I think it's called Gavland or something."

Aria gasped, digging her fingernails further into Luca's Arm. She turned to him, eyes wide and brimmed with tears. "Cade and Becca live in Gavland."

"I'm sure they're fine," Luca said, wrapping an arm around her. He turned to Dima. "What happened?"

She swiped her finger in front of her face. A notification popped up on Aria and Luca's screens, and they opened it. A shaky video appeared with the sound of hundreds of people crying and yelling. Despite the poor video quality, Aria could make out three distinct groups: lost souls, the Allied Nations National Guard, and protestors. The lost souls were separated into two groups, men in one small circle and women and children in another. Several uniformed soldiers held guns to the men's heads and forced them to watch as their comrades brutally beat the women and children. Aria winced as she struggled not to close her eyes. Most of the protesters had discarded their signs on the muddy ground as they tried to fight past a wall of armored soldiers, but each new wave of protesters was beaten as brutally as the lost souls they were trying to protect. Guards arrested protestors and dragged them off-screen.

A sudden gunshot pierced the air, and the video became a blur of colors and shapes as the videographer took cover. More gunshots went off, competing in volume with hundreds of screaming people. The footage finally stabilized, half in the dirt and half viewing an upside-down image of the carnage. Dozens of motionless bodies lay in the mud created by their own blood.

Aria clamped her shaking hand over her mouth as a wave of nausea came over her. A single lost soul was still standing with a soldier's gun to his head. The soldier pulled the trigger, and the man fell, joining his loved ones on the blood-soaked ground. Aira closed her eyes, tears spilling down her cheeks.

"What happened?" she whispered.

"Nobody knows for sure," Dima said, voice shaky. "My guess is that the lost souls weren't complying with arrest."

The video cut off suddenly, replaced by a new message: "THIS POST HAS BEEN TAKEN DOWN DUE TO MISLEADING CONTENT."

"What could be misleading about our government massacring dozens of unarmed people?" Aria asked. "I don't care what so-called crimes they were committing! There were children!"

Her stomach twisted violently, threatening to expel her unfinished meal. Becca could have been in the crowd. She could have been hurt. It was just like Becca to throw herself in front of a threatened child. She might have been a handful, but her heart was pure. She sent a message to Becca asking if she was okay and got a near-immediate response.

"Mom and Dad didn't let me go," Becca's message said. "I'm OK."

"Becca wasn't there," Aria said, relief coloring her tone.

"She's safe. We can't let them take this down. Those people's lives matter."

"Don't worry," Dima said. "This wasn't the only video. There were dozens taken by different protestors, and they've all been copied over and over. They're trying to take down all the reposts, but it's impossible. It'll keep spreading like wildfire."

"Let's see them try to cover this up," Aria muttered to Luca.

"I'm sure they'll find a way," he said. "They've done it before."

"What do you mean?" Dima asked.

Aria chewed her bottom lip as she studied Dima. She had thought about telling her everything for weeks, but she could never bring herself to put her friend at risk. Dima was the kind of person who acted, no matter the consequences, and Aria couldn't be responsible for putting her best friend in danger. She stared at her loyal, passionate friend. It was time she knew. Aria glanced at Luca, and he nodded in agreement.

"There's something we should tell you," Aria whispered. "But we can't tell you here. Tonight, instead of going out with the other girls, we'll stay in, and I'll tell you."

Dima cocked her head and raised an eyebrow. "Okay? That's a little cryptic, but whatever. I can wait."

"Thank you, Dima. It's important."

Suddenly, a wave of campus defense officers spilled through the doors and stormed the cafeteria, trying desperately to calm the raging tempest of angry and crying students. Dozens were fighting back, completely taken over by the shock and rage that the video inspired.

Maybe there was hope for Drammat after all. Mere moments earlier, it seemed like she was the only Drammatan at the Academy who understood that things needed fixing, but now it was clear she wasn't alone.

"Stop!" said a calm, firm voice. President Gray walked through the main cafeteria doors and the cacophony was immediately silenced. The president of the Academy didn't often make appearances in the students' spaces. "I assume this idiocy is about the supposed massacre in the Northern Region. I am appalled at the lack of decorum and poise shown here today. These unsubstantiated reports, made public by unofficial means, have been greatly exaggerated and twisted to serve a criminal activist group's agenda. I understand that many of you have seen disturbing videos and images."

Aria's lips tightened into a thin line as she braced herself for disappointment.

"The Lost Souls camp from the circulating videos was one suspected of numerous illegal activities. The soldiers in question were sent to detain the community members to question and try them fairly for their crimes. The vagabonds resisted arrest by violence. What you saw was the unfortunate aftermath of a series of persistent attacks on our soldiers. While we understand that the footage and images were alarming, I urge you to remember that the government has our best interests at heart, including the lost souls of Drammat. It is unwise to question or criticize the actions and commands of our great leaders. There will be thorough investigations into the soldiers' conduct and decisions, and we can be sure that if there is justice to be had, our leaders will not fail us in providing that justice. We will not speak further about this incident. Your final exams should take precedence over all else at this time. That is all."

Gray turned on her heel and left the cafeteria with her chin tilted up, shoes clacking on the quakestone floor. Every cell in Aria's body heated as rage filled her. She had known for months now that Drammat was corrupt, but this was something she couldn't have imagined under the worst circumstances. Was this why Luca refused to share details about the videos he watched at the Capitol Building? Were they all like this? Or was the sickening inhumanity of this particular video what enabled it to go viral despite the government's best efforts? Regardless of the first sign of proof of Drammat's crimes, the cafeteria had calmed down remarkably quickly.

A wave of Luca's anger nearly overshadowed Aria's own, and even without a supernatural connection, she could feel Dima's rage radiating from her as well. This was the reason no one ever fought back. Drammat was too good at spinning lies and controlling the population. Aria and Luca might find sympathizers, but finding anyone willing to go directly against Drammat would be another story.

Though they were asked not to talk about the massacre, it was all anyone could whisper about for the rest of the day. Aria's thoughts were muddled by emotion, and nothing new entered her brain after lunch. One thing was on her mind: tell Dima everything. She wanted to wait until they knew what they were dealing with, but the government was forcing her hand. Soon they wouldn't have a choice but to fight back, and they would need allies when it came to that. When Aria's last class ended, she ran back to her apartment, exploded through the doorway, and threw down her pack. She jumped when she saw Dima sitting with the other girls in the front room.

"What's up, guys?" she asked, forcing a smile.

She looked around at each of her roommates, suddenly noticing how unwell they all looked. They each carried a unique brand of hopelessness in their slumped shoulders and puffy eyes.

"I think you should tell *all* of us what you know," Dima said, an apology in her eyes.

Aria opened her mouth to protest, but closed it as her roommates' tired, pleading faces stared up at her. Dima was right—they needed to know, and she needed to tell them. This wasn't about keeping people safe anymore. It was clear that no one was truly safe.

"Okay," Aria said, sitting down in front of the four girls. "But only if you're ready for everything you've ever known to come crashing down. If I tell you, there's no going back."

SEVENTEEN

ARIA BEGAN to carefully explain the mess that was her life over the last four months, but once she started, it all spilled out. From prying information out of Luca and Instructor Rojas to scouring the library for the tiniest of details, they listened silently. When she reached the attack in Kan City, her voice began to tremble and tears spilled over her face. It was the first time she allowed herself to relive the traumatic event. Her breathing became erratic as she struggled to get through the story, but the concern on her friends' faces encouraged her to go on.

Dima squeezed Aria's hand firmly as a tear slid down her own cheek.

"I thought we were looking at a few corrupt Drammatan officials stationed on other planets," Aria said through tears of anger. "But this goes so much deeper than I ever imagined. We're just cogs in the machine. When a cog fights back or thinks for itself, it gets destroyed and covered up so the rest of the cogs keep running. They were willing to kill two kids for the unlikely possibility that we had figured them out."

"That's so messed up," Dima whispered.

"So you believe me?" Aria asked, wiping the tears from her face. She was shocked by how much she craved their support. Suddenly, it seemed unlikely that all four girls would be on her side.

"I do," Dima said.

"So do I," Gemma said, reaching for Aria's hands as well.

Allison wiped the brimming tears from her eyes and placed her hand on the pile. "Me too," she said.

"And me," Jeslyn said, placing her hand on top of the others.

Aria's heart swelled and her chest quivered with emotion. She opened her mouth, but couldn't find the words to tell them how grateful she was.

"So what do we do?" Allison asked.

"That's the worst part," Aria said. "We still have basically no proof of any of this, so we can't do much yet. Just keep your eyes and ears open, and don't get killed. We can't afford to let any of our invisible enemies catch on to our goal, or it's game over before we've even started. We need more people on our side. Start bringing things up with the people you trust, but be very subtle. We now know for a fact that terrible things are happening on Drammat too, not just on other planets. Someone we know must have seen something."

"We can do that," Dima said.

The girls agreed to take it slowly and carefully, and over the course of the week, between studying and taking final exams, they talked to as many of their friends and classmates as they could about the massacre. Most refused to talk about it, per President Gray's command, but dozens confided in them about their fears and doubts. It seemed that at least thirty percent of their class was open to questioning the way things were, but they didn't dare bring anyone else into the circle yet. For now, they simply needed to sow seeds of doubt.

Between finals and their mission to gauge the student

body's reaction to the massacre, the last week of the semester flew by. Suddenly it was Friday, and the final exams were over. Aria and her roommates walked down from their apartment to the commons. Aria's stomach contorted and her heartbeat quickened as she headed into her first Cut Ceremony.

During the first year, thirty-two students would be cut from the class each semester. Every semester after that, thirty-one would be sent home until only the top half of the class remained at graduation. Today was the first of many Cut days that Aria and her friends would suffer through together—if they were lucky.

As they entered the commons, Luca and Nick forced smiles at the approaching girls.

"Hey," Luca said. "You guys nervous?"

"Nervous?" Dima offered a bright smile. "Us? I bet we all killed it!"

"Glad *you're* so confident," Gemma mumbled.

"We'll all be fine!" Dima said. "You'll see."

A bell rang through the commons, and a wide screen appeared in the middle of the spacious room. The five hundred scattered students immediately converged in the center of the room as tightly as possible. The students' collective anxiety was thick enough to choke on.

Aria tapped her foot absently as each student's neurolink synced together and a loading symbol lit up the screen. The sign disappeared, and the names of all five hundred first-year students and their ranks replaced it. The bottom of the list appeared first, slowly scrolling upward. A gut-wrenching cry came from a tall boy in a red Medical shirt near the front, followed by another girl in a purple Diplomacy shirt right next to Gemma. Dozens of other sounds of anguish and disbelief pierced Aria's ears as the thirty-two students learned their fate. They would leave behind friends, passions, and dreams. A girl in Colonization Green dropped to her knees and cried into her hands. Aria recognized her from Defense class. Several students stormed out as their names appeared at the bottom of the list while others were paralyzed. The list continued to scroll upward into the safe zone. Aria let out the breath she had been holding. Somehow, everyone most important to her had made it through the Cut.

"Oh no," Luca whispered. "Not David."

David was Gemma's new boyfriend and one of the only Engineering classmates Aria ever heard Luca talk about. She slipped her hand into his and squeezed. Since David and Gemma had started dating in the last few weeks, he had become a part of the group, and he and Luca had become close.

She glanced at Gemma. She was silent, holding one hand over her mouth to quiet her cries and the other on her chest as she struggled for air. The Cut was necessary, but Aria could never have imagined how painful this part would be. Not everyone felt the same, though. Some of her classmates were cheering and jeering at their peers' pain. Aria whirled around to see who the culprits were and rolled her eyes as they landed on the unnaturally pretty, dark-haired girl holding court among other important figures' children.

"Bye, losers," Celeste said, waving. "Enjoy whatever little service job they send you to."

Aria ground her teeth and forced herself to turn back to the screen, barely suppressing the urge to smash her overly-perfect nose. The list continued to scroll, but the anxiety of the moment was replaced by curiosity about her and her friends' class standings. As the halfway point came and went, and she still hadn't seen any of her close friends' names, a weight lifted off her chest.

She held her breath as more names scrolled by, hearing sighs of relief each time. She smiled at Dima when her name came up at number twenty-six. Luca came up a moment later at sixth place. She squeezed his hand, smiling up at him.

The list finally stopped when it reached the top and Aria scanned each name until her eyes met the first name on the list. Her stomach dropped as all eyes fell on her. She glanced around nervously. Some of the other girls in the Colonization program rolled their eyes and several unhappy faces whispered to their neighbors. Not only was she at the top of the class, but she was also the youngest student in history. Celeste's murderous face stuck out in her mind. She had ranked second, right behind Aria. Before the horror could overtake her, Aria's friends smashed into her and wrapped her in a group hug.

"Congrats, girl!" Dima yelled.

"I knew you'd be top of the class," Luca said from somewhere inside the group hug. He pushed through the small crowd and hugged her tightly. Electricity hummed between their bodies.

"Thank you," she said, pulling away to turn back to her other friends. "I'm so glad we all made it!"

She smiled apologetically at Gemma, whose eyes were puffy and red. As the unfortunate thirty-two left to pack their things, small groups formed once again and the conversation volume returned to near-deafening.

Gemma stood apart from the group, along with David. She hugged him tightly, burying her tear-streaked face in his chest. The same disappointment painted the faces of countless others.

Group by group, the students disappeared into their dorms or out onto the beach until the commons were nearly empty. Aria and her roommates walked back to their apartment in silence as they contemplated the upcoming Christmas break. When they returned, their classes would be entirely different. The second semester of each year was all about preparing for the end-of-the-year field trip. For first-years, that was a trip to Sratta.

She may have passed her first semester with flying colors, but everything was about to change. It was hours before she calmed her troubled mind enough to drift off to sleep.

Aria woke up early the next morning to transform into someone her mom could call her daughter. Despite her newfound independence, she had a hard time shaking off old habits. She dragged herself to the shower and tried to summon the motivation to do anything productive. A flashback to one of her mother's rants about appearance invaded her mind space.

"Never be caught in public looking anything less than perfect," she had said. "You control what others see and whether they respect you."

Aria curled her long, shiny tresses of caramel hair and threw the top portion into an elaborate bun before spending excessive time covering up the scar that cut through her eyebrow. It had been months, but the hair still hadn't grown back.

She squirmed into a tight, red dress and swiped on matching lipstick and gold eyeliner. It would be colder in Miller Bay, so she slipped some black boots over her feet and threw on a dressy coat. She took a last look in the mirror and spun around. She looked pretty good, but her mom would doubtless find something to critique. Not that she cared—or at least, that's what she told herself.

"Bye, guys!" Aria shouted into the busy apartment. "Love you! See you in two weeks!"

"Bye!" her roommates yelled back in unison. "Love you!"

A smile crept onto her face as she left the Academy behind once again. When she walked into the commons to find Luca waiting for her in an outfit worthy of a fashion icon, her eyes lit up. He learned since their last visit what it took to impress her mom and he had upped his game.

Aria raised her eyebrows at his dark pants, leather shoes, and deep green sweater. The other students in the commons were dressed for comfortable travel while she and Luca looked like they belonged on a runway.

"Wow," Luca said. "You look..."

"Not so bad yourself," Aria said.

A crisp breeze pushed Aria's hair back as they walked to Academy Station. Luca wrapped his free arm around her.

"Aren't you cold?" Aria asked.

"It's barely chilly," Luca said. "Where I'm from, it's usually snowing this time of year."

"Where are you from, exactly?"

"What do you know about Earth? Any places?"

"Well, I know of some countries. The American Empire, China, the European Alliance, Africa, New Paris, Las Vegas, places like that."

"Okay, well, some of those were cities, and one was an entire continent, but that was pretty good!" He coughed back a chuckle.

"Oh, shut up! How much did you know about Drammat before coming here?"

"I knew that the planet has two main continents and several island systems. The main continents are the Allied Nations, the larger of the two, and the Republic of Fara, the smaller one. I also knew about the Academy, although we always thought they brainwashed kids to become mindless killing machines, so maybe I was a little off."

"You may not have been too far off," Aria said bitterly. "Tell me about where you lived."

"It was in the American Empire—one of the oldest countries on Earth. Not as old as some countries, like China. That one's crazy old. But still, it's been around for almost a thousand years. I grew up in a city called Centennial. It was close to some huge mountains, and it snowed a lot there in the winter. Supposedly, it used to be a stunning city with lots to do outdoors, but by the time I was born, it was just dirty and dangerous."

"I can hardly imagine such an old country. Drammat didn't even have human beings on it until less than five hundred years ago. Even then, the Allied Nations weren't officially founded until about..." She paused to calculate. "A hundred and fifty years ago."

Luca and Aria both stopped walking.

"The Allied Nations weren't founded until a century and a half ago?" Luca asked.

"Yeah," Aria said, voice drawn out like she was thinking too hard to respond. "Before that, the continent was a bunch of smaller countries with their own governments. There was a big international conference between the leaders and they all decided to combine their resources for the good of the people. That's when everything got better for everyone. Just a few decades later, they started bringing countries from other continents to their alliance."

"That's what they're hiding," Luca said. "Whatever happened to bring the Allied Nations together, I'd bet all the credits I have it wasn't peaceful."

"What could be so bad that they had to hide the truth from everyone?"

"I think that's what we need to find out, but first, we need to catch the train." He grabbed her hand and gently tugged her along. "Come on, we better hurry or we'll miss it."

They barely made the early train out and spent the whole ride in whispered, cyclical conversation. They had made a habit of turning on Alika's defenses every time they were alone, but their experiences had only heightened their paranoia. The train arrived at Miller Bay Station just before noon, and they found Aria's dad waiting for them.

"Dad!" Aria shouted, hurrying into his hug.

"How are you?" he asked. "How did the Cut go last night?"

"We both made it close to the top of the class, so as long as we keep working hard, you're looking at two future Academy graduates!"

"That's great, kiddo!"

"That's technically true," Luca said, coming up behind Aria to shake her dad's hand. "But she's burying the lead. Aria ranked first in our class."

"Did you really?"

"Yeah, but it's not a big thing."

"It's a huge thing! Just wait till your mom hears! Come on."

He took her bag and wrapped his free arm around her.

A nostalgic smile crept onto Aria's face as they pulled up to her childhood home. The house was decorated to perfection, just like every Christmas she could remember. They stepped out of the pod and piled into the sitting room with their bags. Luca's eyes grew wide as he scanned the Christmas tree from the wide base to the towering top.

"Nice, huh?" she asked.

"Yeah! Is that a real tree? We haven't been able to use real Christmas trees on Earth for centuries! That's amazing! Wow, that smell!"

"There's nothing like a real tree," she said, greedily inhaling the fresh pine scent. "A lot of people here use faux or holographic projection trees, but that ruins the magic for me. Just wait until you see my grandparents' tree on Christmas Eve. They always get a huge one right from their backyard!"

"I'm going to go help your mother with lunch," Aria's dad

said. "Make yourself at home, Luca." He walked into the kitchen, leaving them alone in front of the glittering tree.

"You know, I wasn't sure what to expect," Luca said. "Everyone just kept referring to it as 'winter break', so I didn't know if there was a holiday associated with it or if it was just because the semester ended."

"You didn't know we were gonna celebrate Christmas?"

"Well, no. There are a lot of Earth holidays you don't have here. I didn't know if you would celebrate a holiday that was invented to honor a person who lived on Earth."

"You mean Jesus?" she asked.

"I know it's not only a religious holiday anymore, but…"

"No, you're right," Aria said, cutting Luca off. "Religious and ethnic holidays were the only ones that survived the move from Earth to Drammat. Hanukkah, Kwanzaa, Diwali, Easter. You get it."

"Why do you think that is?" he asked.

"I think it's because the other holidays had to do with countries on Earth and, as you put it, people who lived on Earth. Those things didn't mean much after a few centuries on a new planet. Our ancestors who came over on the Great Explorer couldn't bring much with them, but their beliefs and their heritage came for free."

"Are you and your family Christians, then?"

"I guess so. We don't go to church or anything, but we come from Christian ancestry, so it's at least an important part of our heritage."

"Do you believe in God?" he asked.

"Honestly, I don't know," she said, squirming a little. "What about you?"

"Definitely," he said.

"Really? If I had been through as much as you have, I don't think I would be able to believe in anything anymore."

"My life wasn't always great, but look at the good in it

now. If the horrible parts had to happen for me to be here with you, I wouldn't change it. It's hard to explain, but I feel like I was always meant to end up here. Whether it was to meet you or if it was so I could set change in motion, it was definitely meant to be."

Aria laughed. "That's very sweet, but you sound a little crazy."

"Whatever," he said, pushing her lightly. "I can believe in fate for the both of us."

EIGHTEEN

CHRISTMAS EVE always began with a two-hour pod flight to Aria's grandparents' house, but this time was different. This time, she was bringing Luca.

Aria's eyes fluttered open as the family pod came to a stop and lowered to the ground of her grandparents' long, secluded runway. She blinked the sleep from her eyes and lifted her head off Luca's shoulder. He was also squinting from the sunlight. As the doors glided open, Aria pulled herself out of the pod and stretched her stiff body. They had been flying for hours, and afternoon sun rays poked through holes in the thick forest, revealing specks of dirt and pollen floating in the air. Other familiar pods lined the driveway leading to the massive cabin. Luca ducked out of the pod and slowly walked toward her, taking in every particle of his new surroundings.

"Do you like it?" she asked.

"I've never seen so many trees," he whispered. A single tear escaped, and he wiped it away before it could reach his cheek. "It's like everything that was once good about Earth was transported here."

She took his hand and gently pulled him along the shimmering quakestone driveway, up the thick wooden stairs, and through the oversized door. The majority of the house was built out of trees from the very forest it sat in, and two expansive glass walls seemed to draw the wilderness inside. Family members swarmed Aria and Luca as they entered, smothering them both with hugs and prying questions.

"Luca, honey," Grandma Blake said, pulling him in for a hug. "Are you sure your aunt and uncle are okay with us keeping you away at Christmas?"

"Oh yeah. We honestly don't know each other well. They just want me safe, fed, and happy."

"Well, we can certainly handle that. Make yourself at home."

Luca forced an awkward smile through the rest of the greetings, but by the time everyone sat down at dinner, his smile was genuine. Joy swelled in Aria's heart.

Unable to get away to talk before dinner, Aria made sure to sit by her younger cousin. "Hey, Becs!"

"It's disgusting, isn't it?" asked Becca.

"What exactly?"

"All of this. While we sit here eating way too much of Grandpa Blake's insanely good food, others are starving to death."

Aria looked down at her heaping plate of food and rolled the vegetables around with her fork.

"Don't pretend you don't agree with me," Becca said. "I can see it in your eyes. You love all of this, but you feel guilty for having so much. I know because I feel the same."

"How did you first realize it?" Aria whispered. "That things weren't okay, I mean."

"I think I've always felt that way, but when I met some kids my age who were lost souls and saw that they were just like me, that's when it clicked. I can't just stand by anymore. What about you?"

Aria checked Alika's program and glanced around to make sure that none of the adults were listening in.

"When I met Luca, he would tell me things about his life on Earth, things that were normal to him but horrifying to me. I knew there was something wrong. Eventually, he told me about how Drammatan officials treat Earthers. I guess that was the last straw."

"It's so messed up that we can't do anything about it," Becca said. "Cade and my parents worry that I'm gonna drop out of school and run with the lost souls, but I'm too much of a wimp. Don't tell them, though. I like to keep them on their toes."

"Your secret's safe with me," Aria said, chuckling. "There might be something we can do in the future. We're both a little young to be starting a revolution right now, but hang tight and remember that your good heart is your best weapon."

"You sound like a lost soul," Becca said. "They have this prophecy or whatever about some woman from Drammat who's gonna unite the galaxy to fight for freedom."

From Drammat? She hadn't heard that part before, not that it changed anything. For all she knew, it was made up by Drammat to keep the Srattan population subservient.

"I've heard that prophecy too, but look. We don't need some mystical savior from a fake prophecy. We just need enough people fighting for good. Just don't get yourself into trouble, okay?"

Becca paused, honestly considering her answer. "I'll try," she finally said.

"I guess that's all I can ask. Now, finish your dinner so we can go whoop the guys' butts in all the games they think they're better at."

They both scarfed the rest of their meal and excused themselves from the dinner table. The adults were too engrossed in a debate over the best style of cheese dip to notice.

They climbed up to the loft, where Cade, Luca, and her two twenty-something cousins Ben and Jay were already setting up. As predicted, both of the girls slaughtered the boys in almost every arena. They even brought out some vintage video games from their grandparents' time.

"You guys want anything to drink?" Aria asked as she won a round and handed her vintage controller off to Ben. Everyone took her up on her offer. She descended the steep staircase and walked down the hallway toward the kitchen, repeating the drink orders in her head. The sound of laughter faded into the background as new voices came into focus.

"It's dangerous," someone whispered. "I worry for her."

"I worry about all of our children," whispered another voice. "Becca might be more vocal about it, but this whole generation is so easily deceived."

Aria stopped mid-stride and backed against a wall. She strained to make out what the hushed voices were saying.

"I remember having doubts when I was Aria's age," her mom whispered. "But our generation knew our place. I worry Aria's doubts will overtake her common sense."

"The problem is how spoiled these kids are," Uncle Tony said. "They haven't had to work for anything and they don't know what it's like to have nothing. They don't appreciate how good things are."

"Oh please, Tony," his wife Paige said. "As if you've ever known anything but comfort. The news is reporting on a famine killing thousands on Sratta, and you're here acting like we've known any hardship at all."

"More than our kids. Each year, our economy rises and with it, our personal credits. They certainly have more than we did. It's going to make them stupid and ignorant, and we're all going to suffer when the government has no choice but to resort to extremes to maintain order."

Noises of agreement sounded, and a stone settled in Aria's stomach as the words sunk in. She shook her head, unwilling to believe what she was hearing. These wonderful people, who she respected and loved, couldn't possibly know everything she had learned. Could they? What did it mean if they did? It was as if they believed that whatever the government did was justified to protect their way of life and best left unquestioned. She breathed in deeply, trying to regain her balance. She crept into the kitchen, opened the drink dispenser, and entered the six orders.

"It's hard to hear the truth, isn't it?" a smooth voice asked from behind her.

"Grandma!" Aria yelled, banging her head on the drink dispenser as she whirled to face her. "You scared me! I almost broke your dispenser!"

"Never mind that. I asked you if you found it difficult to hear the truth after so many years of lies."

Aria cocked her sore head. Could her grandma be implying what Aria thought she was? "What do you mean?"

"My grandmother, your great-great-grandmother, was one-hundred and eight years old when she passed on," she said as her eyes glossed over with distant memories. "When she was on her deathbed, she told me something dangerous, something I'm going to tell you."

Aria lowered her guard and rushed to the bar where her grandma was sitting, fidgeting mindlessly with a ring on her pointer finger. Aria sat on the stool next to her.

"Tell me," Aria pleaded.

"As long as I can remember, she told me stories about her childhood; stories of a time when the people could choose whatever path they wanted for their life. They sounded like fairy tales to me, but the night she died, while my parents were out of the room for a moment, she told me."

Aria clenched her fists to keep them from shaking. "You can tell me."

She looked up with glassy, faraway eyes. "There was a war, Aria, a bloody war that changed everything. My grandmother was only a teenager when the enemy attacked, but she and every other able-bodied person older than twelve had no choice but to fight. Many of her friends died, and she was severely wounded."

"Who attacked?" Aria asked. "And why?"

"They were the founders of the Allied Nations," Grandma Blake said. "I don't know why. She never told me. But they won, the old government was overthrown, and a new government was formed."

Aria's heart pounded wildly. Luca was right. "So there never was a peace treaty. Why do they teach us that in school?"

"Along with a new government, there came new laws. They took complete control over the lives of the citizens, forcing them into the jobs that needed to be filled, and yes, even banning talk of the war and everything that came before it."

"They made it illegal to talk about the war," Aria whispered. "But why did she tell you if it was illegal?"

"I think she just needed to tell *someone* before the end. What could they do to her if she was dying anyway? And she made sure I knew not to repeat it to anyone."

"But you *are* repeating it, Grandma—to me."

"And why do you think that is?"

Aria tensed. "I have no idea."

Her glassy look turned serious, boring into Aria. "I pay more attention than you think, dear. You've changed. Unlike most rebels, including Becca, you have the mind and the temperament to make a difference one day."

Aria shook her head slowly as she stood. "But why didn't you do something if it's so important?"

"I waited for the right moment for decades. It never came. The world is finally changing, but I'm an old woman now. I'll help you in any way I can, but you and your generation are the ones we need."

Aria glanced around and lowered her voice. "We? Who is we? And even if we're ready for change, how am I supposed to start a revolution? I'm sixteen."

She stood to meet Aria and reached for her hands. "We are humanity. You've always been a leader—someone who doesn't care what others think. That's what we need now. Those who seek to control us should be very afraid of Aria Blake. Now, get up there with your drinks. I'm sure they're all wondering where you ran off to by now."

Aria smiled feebly as Grandma Blake gave her a quick kiss on the cheek and piled the drinks into Aria's arms. She shuffled back down the hall in a daze. When Aria reappeared at the top of the stairs, she forced her fake smile again, passing out the drinks and slumping down next to Luca. Concern oozed from him, but she pretended not to notice. The small group spent the rest of the evening talking about the Academy and Ben and Jay's budding careers in Defense while Becca rolled her eyes at everything they said.

When they finally left the cabin and stumbled into the pod to go home, it was after midnight. Aria laid her head on Luca's shoulder and, despite the whirling thoughts in her head and the intense desire to tell Luca what she had learned, she eventually dozed off. When she stumbled into the house after her long nap on the flight, the only thing she wanted was her bed.

Because there weren't any little kids at the Blake house, there was no danger of being awakened at dawn to see what Santa brought on Christmas morning. Aria woke up shortly after eight and rubbed the sleep from her eyes. Sliding on some fuzzy slippers and wrapping herself in an oversized blanket, she basked in the luxurious warmth of her self-made cocoon. Cold weather was her favorite, precisely for moments like these. She shuffled to the bathroom to brush her teeth and tame her hair before descending to the tree. She left her room and hobbled down the stairs, wrapped like a burrito in layers of softness.

"Merry Christmas!" Luca said from the base of the tree. "That's you, right?"

"Haha. Very funny," Aria said through a tiny hole in her cozy cocoon. "Merry Christmas to you too!"

"Good morning, kids!" Aria's mom said as she and her husband entered the front room. "Merry Christmas! Who's ready for presents?"

"Luca," Aria's dad said, "as our guest, you open one first!"

"Oh no. I couldn't."

"You can and you will. Open this one!"

Luca hesitantly accepted the gift and turned it over in his hands. He unwrapped the scarlet paper and opened the box, finding a new pair of black work gloves.

"They're great!" he said. "Thank you so much. My gloves from home have holes in them, so I was worried about using them on our field trip next semester. These couldn't have been more perfect."

Aria's parents passed him and Aria gift after gift, smiling as they watched their grateful and excited reactions. They gave Luca several gift credits for restaurants, clothing stores, and game vendors, as well as an elaborate toolkit explicitly made for everyday engineering tasks. Aria felt his gratitude burn brighter with each gift, but she also felt his discomfort, presumably at receiving so much. They gave Aria several new sweaters, two pairs of shoes, an upgrade package for her neurolink screen, and a special Colonization field kit. Aria and Luca each gave small gifts to Aria's parents as well.

"Well," her mom said, standing up from the wrapping-covered floor. "We're going to make some breakfast."

"Thank you both so much," Luca said.

"Of course, son," Aria's dad said, following his wife to the kitchen.

Aria smiled at her father. It was the first time he had called Luca "son" after learning he was an Earther. Even her mother had come around and had been nothing but a generous host since they arrived. Aria bolted to her feet and ran after her mother, catching her by the arm and leaning close.

"Wait, Mom," she whispered. "Thank you for treating Luca like family. I know it must be hard sometimes."

Her mom sighed. "No. Thank *you* for teaching your father and me what's truly important." She smiled and pulled Aria in for a tight hug. "Now, go be with that sweet boy. You really should have put some make-up on before letting him see you, though."

Aria rolled her eyes playfully and let go of her mother. She skipped back to the tree where Luca still sat, gaping at his new gifts.

"I can't believe they got me all this," he said. "This must have been so expensive. I thought they didn't even like me!"

"That was before they got to know you," Aria said. "Plus, I think the whole fighting for my life thing helped a little—as soon as they realized you weren't the reason I almost died in the first place, that is."

"I guess that makes sense." He shrugged and started gathering his treasures.

"Wait!" Aria said. "I have something for you."

She ducked under the tree and probed around for the gift

she had hidden days ago. It was a small box, covered in deep green wrapping paper and accented by a golden ribbon tied in a bow. She emerged from under the tree, crossed her legs under her, and held the box out to Luca.

"You didn't need to get me anything," he said.

"Of course I did! It's your first Christmas on Drammat!"

Luca took the gift from Aria's hands and gently unwrapped it. Underneath the paper was an elegant, black box that opened like a clam. He ran his fingers over the velvety surface and hooked his thumb under the lip of the box. As it opened and Luca saw the gift, Aria sensed Luca's emotions shift rapidly from anticipation to surprise and finally, to something new. It was an emotion she didn't recognize—overwhelming but sweet like honey. It was terror and comfort, pain and pleasure, all rolled into one explosive sensation.

Luca lifted a dark, elegant, wide-banded bracelet from the box and ran his thumb over the emblem on the front. A world map covered the surface, but the left side of the map was a depiction of half of Earth and the right side was a similar depiction of half of Drammat. The two half-maps faded into each other, and golden flecks marked the American Empire and the Allied Nations.

"Aria, did you make this?" he asked.

"I designed it, but Amare helped me bring it to life. Finding a map of Earth was the hardest part. Do you like it?"

"Like it? I love it! Thank you!"

"Look on the inside."

She chewed her lip as he peered inside and squinted to read the engraved text. "The other half of each other's story." The same overwhelming feeling swelled even higher.

"I hope you don't think it's weird," Aria said.

"Are you kidding? You know how I feel about you."

Aria swallowed. She *did* know how he felt, and she knew he felt her apprehension. But that was the problem. The intenseness of his expression was nothing compared to the fire burning in his soul, spilling over into hers. How did *she* feel about him? Her heart pounded in her ears as Luca's eyes traced every curve of her face. She glanced at his slightly parted lips and forgot how to breathe. He was so close she could feel his breath on her face. He softly rested his hand on her cheek, fingertips winding in her hair.

She gasped, basking in the electric pull of his touch. She couldn't deny the attraction. But how could she ever know if that feeling was her own? And if she gave in and things ended badly, how could they exist in the same galaxy? Panic exploded within her. She backed away until his hand fell from her face and the passion in the air fractured. She pulled her hands through her hair, breathing rapidly.

"Sorry," she whispered.

"That's okay," Luca said. "No need to be sorry. It's time for your gift now."

"Gift?" she asked, still breathless. "I thought you said you didn't know if we were celebrating Christmas."

"I didn't, but I hoped we would. I would have given it to you anyway." He pulled something from his pocket, small enough to hide it in his fist. A dark blush tinted his cheeks. His fingers curled open to reveal a tiny, pearly white box. "Sorry, it's not wrapped. I'm not very fancy."

"I'm still shocked you got me anything at all!"

She tried to smile despite her thundering heart. Luca placed the box in her hands and she looked up at him, biting her lip anxiously. She rolled the tiny box around in her hands and lifted the top half from the bottom. Aria gasped. Inside the box was a gold necklace with an elegant, sun-shaped charm. A tiny star was etched into the metal. She turned the necklace over, and in tiny letters, it read, "You are my light".

"It's beautiful," she said, tears forming in her eyes. "Thank you."

"You see the little star on the front?" Luca asked.

"Yeah. Does that mean something?"

"It's me."

She cracked a smile as she laughed. "What do you mean?"

"The sun is your light. It's huge, and you share it with the world. You light up every life you touch. The world is better because you're in it. I'm that little star, just happy to bask in your light and warmth for as long as you'll let me. As long as you need me, whenever you need me, I'll be right there with you."

Aria's tear-filled eyes overflowed and she quickly wiped the moisture away, embarrassed. She took the necklace from the box, handed it to Luca, and lifted her hair. Still sitting on the floor, Luca scooted forward to lower the outstretched chain to Aria's chest. He pulled the two ends together, brushing her neck with his fingers. The electric buzz of his touch startled her for the first time in months. She felt his breath tickle her skin as he clasped the two ends together. He leaned in slowly and pressed his lips gently to her neck.

"So you like it, then?" he whispered.

Aria opened her mouth, but only the sound of her quickening breathing escaped. Her whole body buzzed from the electric current moving between their skin.

"I love it," she said, voice high and weak.

She turned around to face him and pulled him closer, their lips so close it felt like sparks were dancing between them. He was too good to be true. She could spend the rest of her life with him and it would never be long enough. And he was ready to be hers. She felt it more clearly than anything else. Luca loved her the way people dream of but most never find.

Yet, one singular emotion overruled even that. Her fear paralyzed her. It was the only thing she could be sure was her own, and it was screaming at her to use her brain. If she had to live feeling his pain, sharing her own but never able to untether herself from him, she didn't know if she would survive it.

"Aria! Luca!" her mom yelled.

Aria pushed off of Luca's chest, frantically putting space between them.

"I know I told you to take your time, but I'm about to put breakfast away. Come get some before we all have to get ready for dinner!"

"Sorry, Mom!" Aria yelled, her eyes focused on Luca's. "We'll be there in a sec!"

She turned and raced to the kitchen, leaving Luca to trail behind her. The tension in the atmosphere was suffocating as they ate. Aria wolfed down her food without so much as a glance in Luca's direction. When she stuffed the last bite of pancake in her mouth, she threw her dishes in the sink and flew up the stairs.

"Aria!" her mother yelled. "You know how I feel about you eating too fast! Where are you going?"

Ignoring her mother, she ran through her bedroom door and dove onto her bed, locking the door behind her. Her heart pounded erratically in her chest as she finally let the tears flow.

NINETEEN

ARIA AND LUCA spent the rest of Christmas break in a haze of dinner parties, family game nights, and secret, conspiratorial conversations on the beach. While they plotted and theorized, Aria constantly battled her rising feelings for Luca. He kept his word never to push her. He gave her the space she needed and acted as if what had almost happened on Christmas morning didn't change anything at all. Of course, their shared connection betrayed his confusion and hurt, but they never addressed it. Luca was consistently too good to be true. She knew she should explain her hesitation, but it baffled her that he seemed never to have considered the repercussions of a failed relationship between them. Either he was so sure that they would last forever that he was willing to risk it, or he didn't mind eternal torture. This wasn't the first time she wished he could hear her thoughts instead of feel her emotions, and it probably wouldn't be the last. She would eventually explain herself, but for now, it was easier to focus on the larger scale.

She didn't need to tell Luca about her conversation with her grandma after all. He had seen most of what happened, and she only needed to fill in details where the vision had faltered. With everything they had gathered, all they really knew was that Drammat was subjugating Earth and other planets while simultaneously oppressing lost souls and forcing their own citizens to live in ignorance of it all. They also knew that Celeste and her family were part of the Order, whatever that was, and that they had some kind of plan that Celeste was supposed to enact during the end-of-the-year field trip on Sratta. Maybe it was Aria's personal feelings toward the girl, but she was sure that whatever the Order was, it had to be sinister. Surely it was somehow related to governmental corruption. The vice president was a member, after all.

When the pair returned to the Academy, an anxious energy pervaded Aria's mood. On top of having finally found more substantial evidence for her and Luca's theories, everything about semester two would be a fresh start. They were no longer gaining theoretical knowledge. Instead, they would be learning through real-world experience as they spent the next three months preparing for the field trip to Sratta. The small planet was home to the supposed prophecy, so they were bound to have allies there, but they only had three months to figure out how to plant revolutionary seeds on their neighbor planet without acting suspiciously.

Aria stood in front of one of the many long mirrors in the powder room of her apartment and flexed her biceps. Though she wore the same uniform she had worn on her first day at the Academy, her body now filled it out differently. Months of strenuous training had paid off in transforming her physique. Even her face seemed thinner and stronger, maybe even older. Though her make-up hid the scars on her face well enough, they were glaringly obvious to her. She looked like a whole different person today, and the changes went beyond the surface. She *was* a different person. The old Aria was ignorant and unquestioningly loyal to Drammat and the Academy. Today, she couldn't claim either of those traits. She had come to the Academy with her whole life mapped out, but now she couldn't even imagine where she would be in five years.

She opened her new schedule while lacing up her boots. This semester, the entire first-year class only had three courses. The first was the same as last semester—Self-Defense and Weapons. The only difference would be the thirty-two missing students. The second class of the day was Mission Briefing. The final class was a practicum, a unique, program-specific course that focused on hands-on learning. Each period would be three hours long every day of the week, Monday through Friday. Last semester was intense, but this would be death.

As Aria left the Women's Boarding Hall, she sensed Luca nearby. She followed the connection with her gaze and her lips turned up as she saw his bright smile beaming back at her. She let him catch up and looped her arm through his. His new bracelet pressed against her skin and she couldn't resist a grin.

"Do you really like it?" Aria asked.

"What?" Luca asked, releasing her hand to hold it up. "Your gift? I love it."

"Were you honestly surprised?" Aria asked, narrowing her eyes at him. "You didn't see me making it? I can't hide anything from you, so how exactly did I hide the entire process of designing that watch?"

"Okay, you got me," he said, throwing his hands up defensively. "I knew you were designing *something* for me. I never saw much of it, though. I don't spy on you, and this seemed like something private. When it seems like there's something I shouldn't see, I tune it out."

"What do you mean?"

"Come on. I mean, haven't you ever seen any private moments in my life?"

"I guess so," Aria said, shrugging. "But I can honestly say I've never seen anything I didn't think I should. What things do you mean?"

He squirmed and looked at her apologetically. "Like when you're having a private conversation, or when you're taking a shower or getting dressed."

Aria stopped walking as she cringed. "I try really hard not to think about that."

"About what?" Luca asked.

"About the fact that I have zero privacy—that you've seen me in the shower and there's no way of knowing when you're watching and when you aren't."

"What? Like you haven't seen me naked?"

"That's different! Women *need* privacy." Aria's face flushed with heat, whether from embarrassment or rage, she couldn't decide. Throughout her life, she had thought of Luca as a part of her, and she didn't need privacy from herself. If she ever needed more evidence that a romantic relationship between them would be too complicated, this was it.

"Well, that's kind of a double standard," Luca said. "Don't you think?"

"I've never seen you totally naked, okay?" she whispered. "And if I did, I would block it out."

"That's what I've been trying to say. When I see something I know you wouldn't want me to, I block it out. I would never breach your trust."

"Oh, come on. Not even before you knew I was a real person?"

He shot a horrified look at her. "I think you're forgetting that in my timeline, until recently, you were a child. I'm not a creep."

Aria's face started to cool and the tension in her neck let

up. The unnatural connection between her and Luca wasn't his fault. He did the best he could to give her privacy and she trusted him, but something about knowing he could be watching at any moment still sent shivers up her spine. How could any relationship be built on a foundation of mistrust?

"How often does that happen?" she asked.

Luca looked down as they walked. "Well, you look at yourself in the mirror a lot more than the average person, so... often. I've gotten good at recognizing your patterns, so I can tune it out early."

"Are you kidding me?" Aria asked. She stopped again and let go of Luca's arm. "Now you're calling me vain?"

"No, Ar. That's not what I meant!"

"Yeah? What *did* you mean, then?

"It's just a fact," he said, taking her hands. "Not good or bad necessarily, but I understand why you do it."

"Oh, I can't wait to hear this," she said, rolling her eyes.

"You do it because your mom conditioned you to believe your worth comes from your appearance. You never like what you see, so you keep looking and criticizing."

She turned away from Luca. He was wrong. She was smart, hardworking, positive, loyal, determined. Her value came from so much more than her looks. Her conviction wavered as her mother's disapproving frown flashed in her mind. She sighed. Luca wasn't entirely off-base. Aria had spent her whole life trying to live up to her mother's impossible expectations, and maybe she was starting to internalize them.

"Hey," he said, lifting her chin so she met his gaze. "Two things. One. You're the most beautiful woman I've ever met, and I'm not exaggerating. Two. You are so much more than that. You're kind, smart, resourceful, passionate, terrifying—"

A snort escaped her. "Thank you?"

"You're welcome," he said, smiling. "One day you're not

gonna need me to tell you that anymore, but I'm always here when you need to hear it."

They started up the peninsula again, speed-walking to make up for their several stops on the way. They were one of the last pairs to arrive at Self-Defense class and take their place on the floor. Instructor Bradford yelled over the gathering crowd and students shuffled quickly to attention.

"This semester's going to be different," he shouted. "The class may have the same name, but that's where the similarities end. We'll push you to your limits, and when you reach those limits, we'll push you past them. We only have twelve weeks to prepare you for space and whatever emergencies you might encounter on Sratta. Looking at you now, I see we have a lot of work to do. When you're out in the field, you'll thank me for trying to kill you."

Dozens of voices grumbled in anticipation of the torture. Aria glanced around for her friends' familiar faces, and Dima nodded at her from across the floor. She, Nick, and the rest of the squad were spread across the space, though some of their partners had been dismissed during the Cut.

"Today, we're going to see just how many of you would die in a real fight," Bradford yelled. "This is war, kids. I already assigned your teams, so you'll find your assignment on the Academy app. Pick up some armor and a gun, and get dressed."

"I see how this makes sense for Defense students since they might end up in truly life-threatening situations," a girl in Diplomacy purple said. "But how does this apply to those of us who will be taking on less physical roles in society?"

"Don't make the mistake of thinking the only application for this exercise is physical," Bradford yelled, walking closer to the girl. "You'll learn to think on your feet, problem solve, and work as a team. If you also learn to defend yourself against an enemy, all the better. You never know what you'll run into on

Sratta and every other foreign planet you visit in your career. Now go!"

Bradford's scream set off a stampede of students trampling each other to reach the armor and weapons. Aria squeezed through the melee and snagged a small set of body armor for herself and a large one for Luca. She picked up two rifles and jumped at their unexpected lightness. She looked them over closely. They were fakes, just laser pointers that activated a light on the body armor. She crawled out of the fray with her spoils and handed Luca's equipment to him, already slipping into her own armor. She pressed the button in the center, connecting her armor to her neurolink. The light shone fluorescent blue, automatically opening a new app on her screen.

"Blue team," Aria said, reading the instructions on her screen. "What about you?"

"Let's see," he said, pressing the center button on his armor. The button lit up bright white. "Looks like I'm gonna have to kick your butt."

"Yeah right! See you on the battlefield!"

She turned and jogged toward her gathering team. Dima, Nick, Brock, and Jeslyn waved to her with blue lights on their chests. Unfortunately, Celeste and two of her followers stood behind them with chests lit up in the same color.

"We got Aria!" Nick yelled as she pulled into the blue camp.

"Those whites better watch their backs now!" Dima said.

A timer opened over Aria's vision, counting down from sixty. "Let's go!" she yelled. "We can't be out in the open!"

She took off at a sprint, barreling toward the foothills. With thirty seconds left, she cleared the first small hill with comrades to her left and right. At ten seconds, she chanced a glance over her shoulder. Most of her team was keeping up, but a dozen or so lagged behind. The white team's fastest runners were rapidly gaining on them.

Three, two, one.

Her screen lit up. "FIGHT" flashed in all capital, blood-red letters. The sound of gunfire shattered the air, sounding surprisingly realistic. She glanced back again. At least a dozen of her people now sported red lights where the blue ones once were. She cursed under her breath. So many out already?

"Stop at the next crest!" Aria screamed. "We need to make our stand! Don't let them pass!" Aria, along with another dozen teammates, crested the hill first. "Everyone spread out! We need to cover the others!"

She threw her body to the ground, bringing the rifle sight to her eye and taking aim at one of the fastest pursuers. She hit her target, instantly transforming his white light to red.

One down, two hundred and thirty-three to go.

Another of the biggest threats went down to his left, then another behind him. She lifted her head over the sight. White lights were turning red all over the front line, but they were losing blue lights too. The next blue-chested players to reach the top dove over the crest through the gaps in shooters.

"Get over here and help us!" Dima yelled.

Though out of breath, almost everyone obeyed, closing gaps in their defenses. Aria glanced back in disgust at Celeste, who was busy ordering her lackeys around like a war general while her own weapon sat idle in her hands.

Aria shook her head and turned back to the action. More blue lights crossed the threshold and joined the counterattack, but white players came closer to breaching the border as well.

Most of the blue lights had either been hit or had made it back to the line. Only a few were still running up the hill, while at least eighty white lights remained. Aria spotted Luca coming up fast on one of her slowest teammates left standing. She took aim, waited for her moment, and fired. He dodged, barely missing her laser, so she aimed and shot a second time, and again, he dodged it. She focused on connecting to his mind, and a brief vision of his perspective filled her mind's eye. When her vision returned, she retook aim, but it was too late. Luca took out her teammate and moved on to his next target.

"No!" Dima yelled. "Screw this!"

Aria turned toward Dima long enough to see her light turn red, then returned her attention to Luca. She shot another laser and missed again. Between shots, she turned back to Dima.

"How many do we have left?" Aria asked.

"Less than they do," Dima yelled over the chaos of battle. "Maybe two dozen. Yikes. Make that one dozen."

Aria turned back to her rifle. Could her connection to Luca allow him to dodge her fire? Her brief vision hadn't helped her in the slightest. She turned her rifle on another target and pulled the trigger—a direct hit. The light turned bright red, announcing her small victory. She found a new target and made the shot. She glanced back at Luca, who was still barreling up the hill. Someone else would have to take care of him. She found another two targets and downed them easily.

Luca was only fifty meters away now, coming directly for her, but she couldn't do anything about it. There were only four left on the white team, but she didn't know how many remained on hers. Aria frantically took aim and shot, then again and again, hoping desperately that someone else was left to pick Luca off. But no one ever did.

She turned to either side—all red lights. Only one blue light was left on the hill, and it was her own. She turned back to Luca, the last white player sprinting toward her. He scanned his surroundings and slowed to a jog. His feelings were mixed, but one thing Aria knew for sure was that he was hesitating. He came to a full stop, mere meters from her, and lowered his weapon.

"Finish it!" she yelled. Should she try to shoot him again? Why hadn't he tried to shoot her?

"I don't want to do that," he yelled back. "Can't we just call a truce?"

"No truces," Bradford's voice said through their neurolinks directly to their auditory nerves. "One's gotta go!"

Aria lifted her rifle again, finding Luca in her sight, and pulled the trigger. This time he didn't dodge her. It was her easiest shot all day, and he took it right in the chest. The last white light turned red, and a message appeared over Aria's vision, declaring Blue the winning team.

Luca walked closer to Aria and held out his hand. She didn't take it. A cheer broke out from her fallen comrades. Dima and Jeslyn ran to her and squished her between them in a sweaty, dirty hug.

"Why are you all cheering for her?" Celeste asked. "He *let* her win. Even her boyfriend knows she's nothing special."

Dima and Jeslyn stepped in front of Aria, coming between her and Celeste. Aria put her hand up to call them off and stepped forward.

"At least I fought," she said. "You sat back and commanded your minions around. You're right. I'm nothing special, but at least I'm not a coward."

She turned and stomped down the hill, leaving everyone in her dust. Luca ran after her and grabbed her arm.

"Let go of me!" she yelled. "You can't just let me win! You had a responsibility to your team and you let them down. Why?"

"I just couldn't do it. I know how much the Academy means to you."

"I don't want to be at the top of the class because you didn't take me seriously. I want to earn it. You should've had this one."

"Next time, I won't let you win. I promise."

Aria gave Luca an unyielding look and left him behind again. She ran to the locker room and drenched her sweaty, dust-covered body in the refreshing rain of a cold shower. If every day started this way, she would need to double her food intake to keep up. Aria let the cool water run over her skin and soothe her aching muscles. She put on her spare uniform, and when all her roommates were ready, they left the Defense Building and splintered off for their next classes. Her eyebrows drew together as she noticed a distinct absence in her mind. She could feel Luca's location, but she couldn't feel a single emotion radiating from him. As far as she remembered, that had never happened. She was tempted to panic, but another part of her decided to enjoy the sensation of being alone in her own head.

Mission Briefing was the only class of the semester where Aria and her roommates weren't all together, but Jeslyn and Gemma were in the same section as her. They shuffled to the History Building, muscles already stiffening from the exertion of the battle, and walked into a lecture room where long rows of desks were already filling with students from every program.

They chose three empty desks in the middle and sat down. Nick, Elio, and Brock joined them on Gemma's left. Her friends chatted carelessly while waiting for class to begin, but Aria sat in her own bubble, scanning the room. A tall, slim woman with big hair stood in the corner of the room, tapping feverishly on an unseen control system. She looked up from her work abruptly and stepped out from the corner.

"Welcome to Mission Briefing One," the woman said in a high-pitched voice. Dozens of overlapping conversations died down. "During the second semester of each year, you will take a mission briefing class, the purpose of which is to prepare you for your mission at the end of the semester. My name is Instructor Reed. We will use this time to learn our mission's purpose and better understand the history and customs of the planets we visit, including how they got themselves into the situation we're trying to fix. All of the information we speak of here is highly classified. Do not repeat it outside these walls."

Aria glanced at Dima, who grabbed her hand in return. An excited mutter traveled through the room like a human wave in a sports arena, but a bitter note tinged Aria's anticipation. She had waited and worked her whole life for this moment. It was supposed to be the first in a lifetime of missions, beginning an illustrious career in Colonization. Now, her future seemed so uncertain.

Instructor Reed paced the front of the classroom and stopped in the middle. "Millions of lives are at stake if we don't succeed in our mission," she said with a harsh tone, glaring at her wide-eyed students. "Listen carefully, and you might just save them."

TWENTY

THE LANKY, awkward woman glared intensely at the hundred silent students. If she didn't have their full attention before, she did now. The silence was so complete that Aria could hear her shallow breath rising and falling in her chest. Instructor Reed closed the gap between herself and the first row of students.

"We will be away from Drammat for a total of four weeks," Instructor Reed said. "The voyage itself will take one week each way. That means we have two weeks to ensure success— or millions of people will lose their lives. You may have heard on the news that a terrible famine has plagued Sratta for nearly two years, and thousands have already died despite their leaders' best efforts to solve the problem. Drammat has served as a protector of the galaxy for hundreds of years, which won't change now. We will find the cause of the famine and, if possible, a cure. Each of you will be a hero to the people of Sratta."

Aria's eyebrows drew together. She had come to expect the worst of the Academy, but there didn't seem to be any evil intentions or manipulative propaganda in Instructor Reed's words. If they could stop millions of Srattan citizens from dying of hunger, what could be nobler? There was no way she could find fault in that, yet there had to be more to it. Where did Celeste fit into this?

"Every person in this room will have a vital and unique role in our mission," Reed continued. "Over the next twelve weeks, each of you will learn the history of Sratta and begin your research on infectious crop disease. Today, we will review your competence. Your test has begun."

Aria's neurolink screen opened automatically to an old article. "Mysterious Mass Death of Northern Cattle Herd," it read. It was from almost fifty years ago.

"Cows?" she asked.

"What are you talking about?" Gemma whispered. "Your article is about cows?"

"What, yours isn't?"

"No. It's about some weird rice disease."

"Silence," Reed said. "This is an individual project."

Aria leaned back in her chair and scrolled through the text. She read the information once, then twice, marking essential clues. Something about the evidence—or rather, lack of evidence—wasn't adding up. Suddenly, the pieces clicked into place. She opened the neurolink network and did a few searches.

"That's it," she said. "Instructor Reed, I think I have it. How do you want us to present our results?"

Reed paused mid-step and turned a narrow gaze on Aria. "This isn't a joking matter, Miss Blake. You've only been at it for fifteen minutes."

"Well, I could be wrong, but I don't think so."

"Let's hear it, then. Stand up and present your findings to the class."

Aria looked around the room at the faces staring back at

her, most oozing with a combination of resentment and disbe-lief. She stood and cleared her throat.

"My article was about a herd of cattle that died of an unknown illness about fifty years ago in the Northern Region. At first, I looked for known viruses and bacteria that affect cattle, but I came up with nothing that applied in this scenario. Then, I looked for elements of human influence that could have negatively impacted the cattle, but still came up empty. The autopsies showed nothing out of the ordinary, so I thought a little bit out of the box."

"Of course she did," a familiar voice scoffed from some-where near the front of the class.

"Shut up, Celeste," Jeslyn hissed.

"Both of you, be quiet," Reed said. "Continue."

Aria swallowed hard. "I thought, how could an autopsy report come back normal if they died of an illness? It's possible if the disease was brought on by something they're exposed to regularly, something the examiner would expect to see in a healthy cow. So, I checked some online records and found out that the ranch had been buying tons of supplemen-tary copper, the kind you put in the soil. Cows need copper to live, but in extreme doses, they can get copper poisoning. With the amount the ranch bought, they could have easily killed all those cows over time with no trace. Whether it was malicious or a tragic accident is still a mystery."

Instructor Reed's expressionless face ticked slightly. There was more than surprise in that microexpression, but she was hard to read. Was it anger that flicked across her face?

"My my my," she said. "Have you heard of this problem from an older student?"

"No, I've never heard of it before."

Reed's expressionless face grew even colder. "Frankly," she said, "I don't believe you. No one has solved a case in this class as quickly as you solved this one. Even more suspiciously, no first-year student has *ever* solved this particular case."

Aria gazed up at the gaunt woman wordlessly. Her mouth twitched, but she couldn't make a sound.

"If anyone could do that, it would be Aria," Gemma said, raising her hand. "There's a reason she's the youngest Academy student ever."

"Well, aren't you little Miss Popular," Reed said. "Just like your mother."

"Not really, Instructor," Aria said. "But I am good at solving puzzles."

Reed's expression stiffened, and something in her eyes turned hard. She stared at Aria like a predator waiting for the perfect moment to pounce.

"Well then, it looks like you've done the impossible," she said. "But I'm not as easily impressed as your friends. I'll be watching you very closely, Miss Blake." She pivoted sharply, gliding to her position at the front of the classroom.

"It's about time," Celeste said to the girl sitting next to her. "At least one instructor sees her for the fake she is."

Aria tensed, hands instinctively pulled into fists. She had heard it all before. One didn't outperform so consistently and for so long without collecting more than a few enemies. But she didn't have time for the little games that people like Celeste insisted on playing, not when she had a galaxy to revolutionize in her free time. No more mind games. She beelined for Celeste's seat near the front of the room, gripped the corners of her desk, and bent down until they were eye to eye.

"Do you want to say that to my face?" Aria asked, a smile on her lips.

Celeste's eyes widened and she coughed out a short laugh. "Why not? Everyone knows it's true. Why do you think that little Earth rat boyfriend of yours let you win this morning?"

"Miss Blake," Reed hissed. "You already finished your assignment. You're done here."

"But, Instructor—"

"No," she interrupted. "Get out!"

Aria glanced back at her friends, whose jaws were on the floor. She lifted Celeste's desk slightly as she stood, dropping it as she turned away. Celeste lurched forward as it dropped, murder in her eyes as she tracked Aria across the room. Aria circled the room to her desk and snatched up her pack. Her face burned and her teeth ground together as she hoisted it onto her shoulder and stomped through the door. She had never been treated so coldly by a teacher. How dare she? What was her problem?

She burst through the front doors of the History Building with the strength of her pent-up fury. In the short time she had been inside, ominous gray clouds had rolled in, and the wind had picked up. A colossal raindrop splattered on her cheek as her hair whipped around her. As the cool air soothed her burning skin, embarrassment started to percolate in her conscience. Thunder rumbled in the distance as the rain started to pick up. Aria held her pack above her head and broke into a run. It would be lunchtime soon, but she didn't want to see anyone, especially those of her friends who had seen her outburst, so she picked up lunch on her way to the library.

She craved privacy, but the nagging feeling of being watched tugged at her. Could Luca see and feel her right now even though she barely felt his presence across campus? It seemed like his visions of her were much more frequent than hers were of him, which meant that she shared everything with him, whether she chose to or not. Right now, that bugged her.

She opened the study calendar on her neurolink screen, attempting to wash her mind of the unwanted thoughts. Aria decided to study and prepare for her next class, but flashbacks from the incident in Mission Briefing interrupted her focus. What had come over her? This wasn't her first rodeo when it came to being an insufferable overachiever. The key was to ignore the taunts and jealousy of others, not to give in to it. This just wasn't her.

An alarm buzzed in Aria's ears, startling her. Since meeting Luca, Aria had nearly been late to class more times than she could count, so her alarm would be her best friend this semester. Aria's last class was the Colonization Practicum, with all ninety-three remaining Colonization students. She took a deep breath and let it go with her anxiety. She had been waiting her whole life for this class, and an uncharacteristic reaction to a grumpy teacher and entitled classmate wasn't going to ruin it for her.

Aria struggled to keep her hair tame in the violent wind as she shuffled down the peninsula to the Colonization Building, sloshing through rainwater. The warmth of the interior enveloped her as the sliding doors closed behind her. She smoothed her windblown hair and shook the rainwater off her uniform and onto the mats. The doors opened behind her and familiar faces appeared.

"Great Explorer," Gemma said, rubbing her palms on her thighs. "It's freezing out there!"

"Please," Allison said. "If you think this is cold, you should spend five minutes in the Sonotch Islands during the winter."

"Aria!" Jeslyn yelled. "Are you okay? That was so dumb. I hate Reed already, and don't get me started on Celeste."

"What happened?" Dima asked.

"Our Mission Briefing instructor totally trashed Aria and made her leave class," Nick said. "And it was basically because she's too smart."

"What?" Dima asked. "What is wrong with her?"

"It's whatever," Aria lied, not wanting anyone to mention

the rest of the story. "Let's just get to class. At least we already know this teacher."

The reunited group piled through the classroom door into an overcrowded room. Instructor Croft was busily tinkering with a door at the back of the room. There were no chairs or desks, just a previously empty space now filled with students. Instructor Croft finally stood and turned to face the packed classroom with a broad smile.

"Welcome, class!" she said. "For the next three and a half years, this is your haven. It's your lab, classroom, and refuge. It's the place where you'll learn and grow into the people Drammat—and the galaxy—need you to be. This semester, we will conduct experiments to find the root of the Srattan famine, recreate it, and cure it. Then when the time comes, when your boots are on the frozen ground and it's all very real, you will be successful."

"Here?" a boy in the back asked. "This room's not even big enough for all of us!" He gestured to the open archway where dozens of students were attempting to peer over and around the others to get a better view.

"Oh ye of little faith," Croft said with a smile as she held her hand to a scanner next to the door.

The red light on the scanner turned green, and the lock disengaged. She gripped the handle and pushed the door outward. Bright yellow light like the golden rays on a sunny afternoon spilled in through the open door. Aria squinted against the brightness. Croft walked through the door and disappeared into the light.

"Well, don't just stand there!" she called. "Come on in!"

Aria looked around at her classmates, who were paralyzed in awe. She stepped forward and crossed the threshold, shading her eyes as they adjusted to the light and the room came into focus. Aria inhaled the humid air and closed her eyes to the sunshine on her face. She opened them as a colorful bird swooshed overhead. White sand covered Aria's boots, and green, lush vegetation sprouted up all around her. A pool of crystal water seemed to stretch on forever. It was a paradise in the middle of the school, and despite the storm outside, bright sunlight poured in from the clear sky above. A laugh escaped Aria's lips as she spun around in a circle, holding her arms out to her sides. Other students spilled through the door behind her.

"What's that?" Elio asked, pointing to the horizon, past the endless crystal pool.

Aria stopped spinning, fixing her gaze on the spot he was indicating. It looked like a typical blue sky, although there was something unnaturally perfect about it. She squinted harder until a thin, gray line appeared, then another, and another. It was a pattern, hexagons interlinking up the walls and ceiling.

"That's the veil," Croft said, walking out onto a shimmering quakestone path that cut through the sand. "There are over a hundred habitats and sub-habitats represented in our greenhouse, and as we explore new planets, it is ever-expanding."

"You have a full-scale replica of every known habitable area in the galaxy?" Nick asked.

"No," Croft said. "*We* do. The Greenhouse belongs to all of us. It's sacred for the Colonization specialty, and it plays an essential role in all of our missions."

"Does that mean we're going to a replica of the Srattan climates?" Aria asked.

"Excellent, Aria," Croft said.

The path ended at another door, which was made of the same material as the wall, contributing to the illusion of a never-ending rainforest. She opened the door, and Aria stepped through first again. Everything was sterile white. Students piled in behind her until Croft finally closed the door behind them and walked to another door across the white room. She scanned her hand again and the door slid open.

"Students," Croft said with a dramatic flourish of her hand, "welcome to the high tundra of the Mojare district of Sratta."

The pure white door opened and the room's warmth was immediately sucked out, replaced by icy, dry air. Aria stepped through the door, white powder squeaking under the weight of her body. The frigid air bit at her nose and fingers as her breath became visible. White crystals floated gently down from the illusion sky. Everything was pure white, except the mouth of a dark cave a few paces away. Croft stood on a heated path, which offered an easier route to the cave than through the deep snow. The only sound was the soft patter of feet on wet quakestone as Croft led the way. She ducked through the mouth of the cave, turning on the light embedded in the neurolink hub above her right ear. Aria followed her lead, turning on her own light, and made her way farther into the dark, seemingly endless cave. Not even ninety-four bright lights could reach the back of it. Stalagmites and stalactites jutted out from the stone in every direction.

"This is where we'll spend at least half our class time," Croft said. "We'll spend the other half in a controlled environment where we can test the samples you grow and extract here. Currently, healthy tupins are growing in the air pockets in the stone."

"What are tupins?" Brock asked.

"A rare type of tuber, similar to sweet potato. As far as we know, they're only native to the intricate limestone cave systems on Sratta. They grow in the vents and pores of the rock, and not only make up an important part of the cave ecosystem but also over thirty percent of Sratta's food crops."

"So, we're gonna try to recreate the disease on these

healthy tupins and reverse it, so we can replicate the process on Sratta?" Nick asked.

"Exactly!" Croft said, pointing a skinny finger at Nick. "But first, we need to understand what makes up a healthy environment for tupins, so we'll start there. Everyone pair up, choose one of the sectioned-off squares, and begin your research."

Nervous energy filled Aria's body. She swiveled her head, searching for her friends. She locked eyes with Dima, who winked and ran over. They perused the dimly lit cave until they came to a section that included a square meter of the cave floor and was about two meters high from floor to ceiling, including long columns of stalactites and stalagmites. Aria pulled on the gloves from her pack and ran her hand along the cave floor. Every detail was perfect.

They spent the next hour and a half carefully digging into pores and extracting samples to store in the lab. With each passing minute, it became more difficult as their fingers stiffened in the cold. The cave interior was much warmer than the icebox outside, but the chill set into their bones over time. When class finally ended, their lips were blue, and their bodies shivered uncontrollably.

"Better get used to this," Croft said, as she sealed the final door to the greenhouse and the whole group returned to the school. "Sratta is a mostly-frozen planet, after all."

"I'm a little nervous about that," Jeslyn said. "Isn't Sratta too dangerous for us?"

"Only if you break protocol," Croft said. "We'll take good care of you kids."

The class passed in a whirlwind, and the rain clouds had given way to the afternoon sunshine when the group spilled out of the Colonization Building. The warm rays thawed their stiff bodies on the walk back to the boarding hall. As Aria massaged her sore neck, a familiar feeling crept in. Just like that, the chaos of two people's diverging feelings was back. Luca was more nervous than anything, but not hurt. Still, Aria's stomach clenched at the prospect of apologizing for her overreaction to his self-sacrifice in Defense class. But something else had to take precedence right now, and Luca would understand. He could wait.

She walked through the apartment door behind her room-mates and took a deep breath. Turning on the program that Alika had built and supplied for her and Luca, she used four of the five available remote access links to hijack her friends' neurolink feeds. Hopefully, Alika would notice what she was doing and help make the footage convincing. Without her direct help, the program could only replay innocuous conversations from the last several weeks.

"I learned something over break," she said quietly.

All four heads snapped around. "What is it?" Gemma asked.

Aria kicked the wet boots off her feet and set down her pack before following the others to the sitting room. She leaned against the armrest of the couch, too exhausted to stand without support. Her friends sat down around her, looking just as drained as she felt.

Aria quickly broke the news to her friends that the old peace treaty that founded the Allied Nations was actually a bloody war. She told her friends of her great-great-grandmother's involvement in the war over a century ago, and of her grandmother's hope that Aria's generation would be the one to right the wrongs of the past.

"Why wouldn't your great grandma be allowed to talk about a war she fought in?" Allison asked.

"Because her side lost the war, right?" Dima asked.

"Exactly," Aria said. "The way Drammat controls everyone wasn't always like that. That all started after the war."

"Why did your grandma tell you this?" Gemma asked.

"I overheard my parents and aunts and uncles talking

about everything going on with the lost souls and how they wished my rebellious cousin would just go with it like everybody else. I guess she noticed how disgusted I was by their attitude."

"And that's all she said?" Dima asked. "That's not a lot to go on."

"Basically," Aria shrugged. "But she did say that things are changing and the time is soon."

"No pressure, right?" Gemma said.

"I think she's right," Allison said. "A lot of my family members feel the same way we do. They're just afraid to make waves. If we pave the way, I think a lot of people will support us."

"It was the same with my friends from home," Dima said. "My parents wouldn't hear it because they're worried I'm gonna get in trouble, but I think they'd support us too if they thought victory could be possible."

"Not mine," Gemma said. "Mine are loyal to Drammat all the way."

"My family is never afraid to talk about that kind of thing in our own home," Jeslyn said. "So I've always known how they feel about the government. They know a lot of things are suspicious, and they're willing to fight if someone shows them the way forward."

"So, what do we know?" Aria asked. "Over five hundred years ago, our ancestors came from Earth, and almost everything we know about life between then and a century and a half ago is probably a lie. After the war, the Drammat we know today was born, and some terrible things started happening. Or maybe they always were happening. If we talk about it or try to learn what they're hiding from us, they'll have us killed. Did I miss anything?"

"Just that, according to your grandma, we're somehow

supposed to save the galaxy," Allison said. "Even though we're just a bunch of kids."

"And that's the problem we keep running into," Aria said. "I need to call Luca. For now, just keep quiet and keep safe."

"Go," Gemma said. "I'll make dinner so you don't have to worry about it when you're done."

Aria smiled weakly. "Thanks, Gem. I'll be back soon."

Aria pushed off the armrest, her muscles protesting the sudden movement. The physical, mental, and emotional stress of the day was catching up to her, but if she didn't talk to Luca, she wouldn't be able to sleep. She awkwardly battled her sore muscles as she climbed into her top bunk and slipped under the covers. She tried one more time to push through the mental wall and speak directly to his mind. She waited several moments, then relented. She gave the mental command to her neurolink interface, and a second later, Luca's voice came in clearly.

"Hello?" he answered.

Aria laughed. "You really need to stop answering like that."

"Fine. Speak! That just seems so rude!"

"It's direct! I can't believe that 'Hello' is how Earthers answer calls!"

"I mean, it is pretty weird," he said. "That's not really a thing we say in normal conversation, but it's traditional. Never mind. What's up?"

"First of all, I'm sorry for blowing up at you. I understand that you were trying to help, but I don't need you to do that for me. Okay?"

"I'm sorry too. I realize now that I embarrassed you more than I would have if I had beaten you. Besides, you don't need my help."

"Thank you, but that's not true. I need your help with a lot of things, and I like to think you need mine too. That's the other reason I called. I just told the girls what my grandma told me on Christmas Eve. Most of them said their friends and family would be on board with a revolution if it came to that. That's a lot more than I hoped for."

"Well, that's good. Isn't it?"

"In theory," Aria said. "I still hope we can change things peacefully, but I don't see how. If we succeed in exposing Drammat's lies and building resistance, war seems inevitable. How do we know that this is the right decision?"

"If it comes to war, a lot of people are gonna die," Luca said. "And we might die right along with them. But if we want to change anything, we have to come to terms with that."

"I don't know if I'm ready for that."

"That's okay," he whispered. "We're just kids. We have a lot to do before anyone ever needs to go to war."

Aria looked up, blinking back the tears forming in her eyes. "Did you hear what our mission is about?" she whispered, remembering Instructor Croft's threat.

"Stop the Srattan famine, right?"

"Yep. Save millions of lives. If we overthrow the government, who's gonna help in times like that? What if we do more harm than good? And where does Celeste fit into all of this? She has some secret mission on Sratta. The only thing I can think to do is spy on her until we figure out what it is."

"We can definitely keep an eye on her, but maybe this is a sign that her mission isn't as sinister as we thought. For now, we might as well enjoy getting to do something worthwhile. We have plenty of time for a revolution. It doesn't have to happen on this trip."

"Sometimes I wanna just forget it all," she said. "Or at the very least, let someone more qualified figure it out."

"Do you see anyone else stepping up? You're a born leader, so like it or not, people are gonna follow you."

"My grandma said something similar, but I don't see it."

"She was right," Luca said. "You're gonna change the world, just maybe not at sixteen."

"Almost seventeen," Aria corrected. "But I know what you mean."

Luca laughed softly and she closed her eyes to the sound. If her destiny was to be the leader of a revolution, Luca's was to lift that burden with her. She could never be strong enough on her own, but with Luca fighting at her side, she could do whatever it took. He was right. For now, they could focus on helping the starving people of Sratta.

TWENTY-ONE

AS THE SEMESTER WORE ON, and the novelty of new classes combined with the thrill of spying on Celeste eventually faded, Aria settled into a monotonous rhythm. Every weekday, she woke up before the sun rose and got ready for Defense class, where a new form of torture unfailingly waited. They didn't always play war games. Some days they ran until several kids threw up. Other days, they lifted weights, continued their grappling drills from the previous semester, or learned to operate various lethal and non-lethal weapons. Aria's muscles were in a constant state of decay and regrowth, never resting from the intense workouts. She learned never to bother showering in the mornings.

Of the three classes, Mission Briefing would have been her easiest if Instructor Reed didn't have it out for her. She always assigned Aria the most complicated projects, and when she finished too quickly, Reed never failed to find a way to punish or embarrass her. Aria would have preferred struggling through Luca's advanced Engineering classes to spending one more second with Reed making her life miserable. It didn't help that Reed seemed to have a soft spot for Celeste.

As Aria began to pay more attention to the obnoxious girl, she grudgingly accepted that Celeste was capable, intelligent, a natural leader, and generally likable—so long as you weren't the target of her catty streak. Neither had Aria caught her doing anything abnormal. She was just a popular girl going about her life, and nothing could have annoyed Aria more.

At first, the Colonization practicum was a reprieve from the torture, but after weeks of failure, even that class started draining her, and she wasn't the only one struggling. No one had made any progress in finding a possible cause of the famine—let alone a solution. Scientists from all over Drammat had already been camped out on Sratta for months trying to solve the problem, and they were bringing in the new blood of the Academy students as a last-ditch effort.

Aria spent every evening in the library, poring over literature about Sratta, agriculture, and disease. When she noticed that Celeste had a similar routine, Aria moved her study location to a place where she remained out of Celeste's sight but within earshot. Unfortunately, the only lead she had gathered from weeks of eavesdropping was an upcoming meeting between Celeste and her mother sometime during the week before finals. They were set to meet in the library after hours. That's all Aria had gleaned from Celeste's side of the conversation, but it sounded suspicious enough to be significant in Aria's mind. She had made a habit of staying as late as possible once she had overheard that gem of information.

Every night, she stumbled into the dorm red-eyed and dejected. By the weekend, all she wanted to do was wrap herself in blankets and hibernate, but she didn't have that kind of time to waste. Gone were the days of lounging on the beach and hiking with friends. Now she spent the weekends in the library with Luca, ripping her hair out over their lack of progress.

If it weren't for Dima making a surprise breakfast, Aria would have forgotten about her seventeenth birthday amid the madness. Dima, Luca, and the rest of Aria's friends brought her treats and gifts, but they were so busy that a party was out of the question. Everything fun and light-hearted about the first semester at the Academy now seemed a lifetime ago. At least she was able to keep her grades up, even with an evil instructor trying to ruin her life.

By the time finals week rolled around, Aria was a walking zombie, but the overachiever in her wouldn't rest until she knew her final test results. Even on the last Friday night before testing began, while her friends were all asleep, she was alone in the library.

Aria's eyelids threatened to close as she studied the last of the material for her Mission Briefing final. As her eyes blinked slowly and her attention drifted, a barely perceptible noise came from somewhere deep in the library. She forced her eyes open but saw no one. The dim light of the moon cast eerie shadows across the floor. Another noise echoed through the vast room, and Aria shot up, silently pushing her chair back. It was a whisper coming from somewhere so far off that she couldn't make out what the voice was saying.

She took a step, silently pressing her toes to the floor before following with the other foot. She slipped into a dark corner and activated Alika's program. She successfully started the main function which hid her location and ID, but when she tried to turn on the invisibility feature, an error message streaked across her vision. She cursed inwardly. Alika must have to do something from her end for the more complicated directive. She couldn't miss this chance, though. She'd have to do this the old-fashioned way. She pulled her jacket over her head to cover her face. She looked ridiculous, but facial recognition wouldn't be as grave an issue.

The sound of someone else's careful footsteps reverberated off the high ceiling. Aria stepped back into view and crept between the aisles of books, following the voice. As she neared the far corner of the library, she could make out two separate voices, both female. Her stomach fluttered in both excitement and fear. She was getting closer to the two women, but she still couldn't make out what they were saying. Suddenly, there was a click, and the voices reverberated as if in an amphitheater. Aria picked up her pace, turned a corner, and screeched to a stop.

In the back corner of the second floor was a door that always remained locked, restricted for library workers and other Academy employees. Right now, it was wide open. Through it, fluorescent lights lit a long, narrow hallway, and distant voices echoed. It was open now, but it wouldn't stay open for long. A bolt of adrenaline spurred Aria through the doorway just as it sealed behind her. The two women were nowhere in sight, but their voices carried from nearby.

Her back to the wall, Aria crept down the hall as silently as she could, passing doors and hallways on both sides. The two voices came into focus, no longer bothering to whisper.

"Do you think you can do that?" asked the older woman in a powerful tone Aria would recognize anywhere, despite having only heard it once in person.

"I think so," a younger voice said—a voice that had plagued her life from her first day at the Academy.

Aria's insides clenched at hearing Celeste's voice sound so small, her ego diminished in her mother's presence. Aria peaked around the corner she was using for cover. The mother and daughter stood mere paces from her hiding spot. She dropped onto her hands and knees and poked her head around the corner, just far enough to get a better look. There was no mistaking the raven-haired beauties for anyone else. Relief flowed through her at knowing she hadn't missed the meeting, which was immediately swallowed up by the anxiety of being somewhere she wasn't meant to be. A nagging terror ate at her insides, but she was pretty sure that was coming from Luca, not her. She pushed it out of her mind.

"We'll do the hard part," the older woman crooned. "Your job is easy. Just follow our instructions, and you'll get credit for creating the cure."

"I'm not a Colonization student," Celeste said. "How am I supposed to do this without them wondering why I'm not doing my actual job with the other Diplomacy students? I can't just wander around the Colonization projects."

The older woman's motherly tone dropped away as she straightened. "We're not having this discussion again. That's your problem to solve. It's about time you took some initiative. You're not a child anymore, Celeste."

Celeste looked down. "Okay. I'll make sure no one else figures it out before I do."

"You don't need to worry about that. It's not discoverable. Only you will be able to find the solution because only you know how the disease was engineered."

Aria bit down hard on her knuckle just in time to cut off her gasp. The second lady's head turned toward the corner where Aria was kneeling, and she ducked back behind the wall, heart pounding.

"Did you hear that?"

"Hear what?" Celeste asked.

Aria's heart launched into her throat, beating out of control.

"Never mind. We can't meet here again. I'll be busy with our preparations all week. If you need my help once you're on Sratta, call me."

"Can you please tell me what your part of the mission is? Why will you be on Sratta in the first place?"

"Baby, you know that's classified. Don't ask again. You do your part, and I'll do mine. I know you'll make us proud."

Celeste nodded silently as the older woman dropped her arms from Celeste's shoulders and turned toward Aria. The Second Lady's high heels clicked on the glossy quakestone floor, moving closer.

Aria bolted upright, adrenaline shooting through her body. In seconds, they would be right on top of her. The door to the library loomed at the end of the hall, and it was the only way out. She booked it down the hallway, worrying more about speed than stealth, but when she reached the door, it was as good as a solid quakestone wall. Panic rushed through her, and she looked back. The second lady turned the corner but was looking back at her daughter. The moment she looked forward, it would all be over. Aria's breathing became erratic as possible fates flashed through her mind.

"Aria," a familiar voice said. "Go to your left."

Luca. Relief rushed through her so powerfully that tears sprang to her eyes. Aria lunged to her left, just as the older woman's head turned and Celeste came into view. Her relief only lasted a millisecond before realization set in. They were still walking toward her, and in seconds they would overtake her again.

"Keep going. There's an archway at the end of this hall. Do you see it?"

Aria squinted. There it was, so dark that it blended into the wall.

"I see it!"

"Good. Run!"

She obeyed, propelling herself off the wall. She sprinted down the hall, keeping her steps as quiet as her desperation would allow. The footsteps of Celeste and her mother echoed louder as they drew closer. They were almost to the exit. Aria nearly slammed into the wall as she scrambled through the archway and out of sight when the women came into view at the end of the hall.

She watched from the shadows as the second lady punched numbers into an old-fashioned dual-authenticator lock, and the door slid open. Celeste passed into the library first, her mother tailing behind her.

"Move!" Luca said. But he didn't have to. Aria had already flung herself down the dark hallway toward the well-lit main door. She was almost there, but it was closing faster than she could run. She dove and stretched, sliding on the glossy floor until her hand slipped between the doorframe and the closing door. She exhaled sharply as the skin on two of her fingers split open. Wincing as her DNA spilled from her fingers and stained the scene, she pulled the door as hard as she could. It opened, probably a safety feature, so she stood and peeked through the opening. No one was there. Using her shirt hem, she wiped up the drops of blood on the floor and the smear on the door. She slipped through the open doorway and waited a moment for the door to close. It didn't.

"Hold on. The sensor says the door didn't shut," the older woman said.

"I'll go make sure nothing's wrong," Celeste said.

Another burst of panic shot through Aria. She was almost surprised her body had any adrenaline left to push. She hit the floor and scooted under the nearest row of books. The small space was barely large enough for her to squeeze into. Only the fear of death kept her in her hiding place despite the encroaching sensation of claustrophobia. Two sets of feet came into view as Aria struggled to take in enough breath to remain conscious.

"It's stuck," Celeste said.

"That's strange," her mom said. "Let me try this." The door slid shut a moment later. "There we go. Let's get you back to your dorm."

The sound of their footsteps retreated until only silence was left behind. Aria stood her ground as long as she could, but her lungs burned and her head spun. She was on the verge of unconsciousness when she finally squeezed out of the tight space and rolled over on her back.

"Luca?" she thought, grateful not to need her voice as her lungs heaved. "Are you still there?"

"Listening," he said softly.

"Listening?" Aria asked. "Is that another way Earthers answer calls?"

"No, but I don't like 'Speak' and you don't like 'Hello', so I figured we could have our own thing. What do you think?"

She smiled, her breathing slowly returning to normal as she lay on the library floor. If anyone had ever truly listened to her, it was Luca.

"I love it," she said. "Listening."

"So, are you gonna tell me what you were doing to get yourself into trouble tonight?"

"Just seemed like a fun thing to do on a Friday night." Aria shrugged, unsure of whether Luca could see her or not. "Thanks for showing up when I needed you."

"I always will, but it seems like this telepathy thing only happens when we're in massive trouble, so let's try not to make it a habit."

"Unfortunately, I don't think that's an option. We're in this now, and we need to see it through. How much of that did you hear and see?

"Everything after the sneaking started. That's how I knew how to get you out. I felt your fear, and suddenly I was there. Frankly, you're not great at self-preservation, so while you were focused on Celeste and her creepy mom, I was making escape plans."

"At least we know the famine will end," Aria said. "Even

though all our work was for nothing and the whole thing was manufactured."

"Why would they do something like that?"

Aria could sense his disgust. "I have no idea. What reason could they possibly have to justify killing so many innocent people? Even by Drammatan standards, this just seems like a waste."

"So what should we do?" Luca asked.

"Get through finals and go to Sratta. Once we're there, we do whatever we can to find out what the real mission is and get some evidence. While Celeste is busy fixing the problem they started, her mom is going to be there too, and not even Celeste knows why."

She waited a moment, but Luca didn't respond.

"Luca? Are you still there?"

There was no answer. She stood up and dusted herself off before making her way back to her dorm.

The six days following Celeste's secret rendezvous in the library were the most difficult of the semester. Aria struggled to stay focused on her final exams while the ever-growing sensation of impending disaster robbed her attention. Something big was coming, and she had no idea what it was or how to stop it. Luckily, her extreme focus over the previous eleven weeks prepared her better than any last-minute cramming could have. Despite her wandering, anxious thoughts, she was ready. Now that she knew the famine was an artificially made disease designed for Drammat's evil ends, the pressure to solve the fake mystery lifted. Her anger boiled higher as she thought of the thousands of lives that had already been lost to the famine. Whoever was responsible deserved to pay for the deaths they had caused.

One disturbing thought was stuck on repeat—Celeste was a part of this. Obviously, she didn't know everything yet, but if she was the kind of person who believed the lies about

Earthers, maybe she was also the kind of person who would do anything to protect Drammat's so-called utopia. But stopping Celeste from doing her job on Sratta was out of the question. She was the only one who could save the millions who would otherwise starve this winter. All they could do was watch Celeste's every move.

TWENTY-TWO

WHEN FRIDAY FINALLY CAME, Aria woke up before her alarm, her senses buzzing with anticipation. Today was the Defense final, the last battle. This time, Aria would win on her own merit. Her mother's words rang in her mind as she prepared for the fight: "The way you look has power over your allies but also your enemies."

She swiped thick black eyeliner over her eyelids, painted her lips deep red, and completed the look with two messy, black smears across her cheekbones. She pulled her hair into a tight, high ponytail and frowned in the mirror. She would sweat it all off during the battle and wash whatever remained off in the shower, but it was worth it. She wouldn't want to face herself looking like that. She didn't think this was what her mother had meant, but she liked it.

Just like every morning before, she and Luca walked up the peninsula together, but unlike their usual morning commute, neither spoke a word. Luca was nervous. He didn't even seem to notice her war paint. A shadow of his anxiety crept into Aria's soul, magnifying her own nerves. Anyone else would have seen deadly confidence and coolness in both of their faces, but they knew better. The silent walk ended as they stepped onto the practice floor. Even though it was still early, almost everyone was already there, while only a few other students shuffled in behind them. Aria's roommates and some of their guy friends were already suiting up with their armor and guns. Alika and Amare, who usually kept to themselves, came and greeted them with a smile. As she waved, Aria's screen suddenly popped open with her assignment.

"I'm Team White this time," she said. "What about you?"

"Nah," Luca said. "Now I'm Blue."

"Dang. Well, remember what I told you."

"I know, I know. Don't let you win."

They collected their gear and moved to their separate sides as the rest of their classmates finished strapping on their gear. She scanned the crowd with blue lights on their chests but stopped when her eyes found the one person she had hoped would be there. Celeste glared back at her with her lips turned up in a self-assured grin. It was the first time they wouldn't be on the same team in a battle, and it would make the game that much sweeter.

"Okay, students," Instructor Bradford shouted. "This test is simple. You know the rules. Almost everything about this battle is the same as every other time we played, but there is one major difference. Before, your armored vests were only there to indicate a hit by changing color, but they're capable of so much more. We're turning up the stakes. Now, when hit, you will receive an electric shock."

"What?" a girl in the front screeched. "You can't be serious! That's child abuse!"

"Do you see any children here?" Bradford asked. Aria refrained from mentioning that *she* technically *was* a child. "You're all adults, and you wouldn't be here if you couldn't handle it. In the real world, you may need to defend yourself or others, and no one is going to have a harmless laser gun.

The vests are designed to deliver a shock that corresponds with the location of the hit."

"What does that mean, exactly?" Nick asked.

"It means if you get hit in the shoulder, you'll get a shock, but it won't drop you," Bradford said. "But if you get hit near a vital organ, you'll get a wallop. If you get hit directly over the heart, you'll get maximum power. Your light won't turn red until your body hits the dirt."

"So even after we get hit, we can still keep going until we fall?" Nick asked.

"That's right, but good luck staying up through a fatal blow. Any other questions?"

The students answered with stunned silence.

"Good," he said. "You have three minutes to make a plan and get in position. Go!"

Adrenaline coursed through Aria's veins as students scrambled around her with genuine terror on their faces. The short window allotted for planning was already running down, so Aria scanned the area. Unlike the first battle but similarly to the many practice battles that followed, temporary walls were sporadically strewn around the field.

"Back behind the wall," she yelled at the top of her lungs. "If you're dying to fight, you're on the front line with me!"

The mob of frantic students obeyed her command, falling back to the wall, leaving just over two dozen white lights remaining by her side.

"Brock," she said, "we need your leadership and strategy skills with the second wave behind those walls. Otherwise, they'll run around like headless chickens."

"Got it," Brock said. "We'll cover you."

Aria turned back to the remaining force as Brock retreated to lead the second line of defense. Those still standing by her were some of the strongest and bravest in the class. She smiled as they crowded around her. They mapped out a hasty strategy and the huddle broke as the alarm blared, commencing the battle.

Aria dove behind a short wall sticking out of the damp ground. Consistent spring storms had turned their battle-ground into a slippery mess. Elio, Jeslyn, and Nick followed her, while other groups set up behind nearby walls.

"Jes, you're the best shot here," Nick said.

"I've got you guys," Jeslyn said, already placing the sight to her eye. "Go!"

Aria pushed off the ground and sprinted around the wall, awkwardly crouching as she ran. Nick and Elio followed a pace behind to either side. A scream came from behind. It could have been anyone, and there wasn't time to waste searching for the casualty. She dove the last stretch to the next wall, rolling to a stop. She propped herself against the stone wall and readied her weapon. Aria gripped her gun against her body as Nick and Elio dove to safety behind her.

Nick screamed wildly as he hit the muddy ground. He rolled to a stop, face contorted in pain.

"Nick!" Aria yelled. "Where were you hit?"

He winced as he clutched his side. "Just the right shoulder. I'll be fine for a while, but not long. Bradford forgot to mention that the electric shock isn't just a one-time thing. It won't stop!"

"Can you still shoot?" Aria asked.

"I think so. Unfortunately, it's my trigger arm, but I think I can cover you with my left."

"Good," Aria said. "We need to get to the next wall."

"Go!" Nick said, resting the barrel of his gun on the top of the wall with a grimace.

Aria and Elio peeled off from either side of the wall. Blue soldiers were already infiltrating their territory, and their allies were dropping faster than Aria could count. Screams rang up from every corner of the battlefield. Some pushed on through the pain, while others fell on impact. Bodies littered the ground on both sides, and with all of them donning the same red lights, it was impossible to tell which team they belonged to.

A blue soldier set her sights on Aria and pulled the trigger. She dodged to the side just as her attacker let out an unholy scream, and her body stiffened. The girl's light turned red as she shook with pain and finally collapsed on the muddy ground, her rifle falling from her limp hand. Aria backed away from the unconscious girl's body and took cover.

"That must have been a direct hit," Elio said breathlessly.

"That looked intense," Aria said.

"We'll be okay, Ar. We've got each other's backs."

"But that means we have to do that to other people," she said, grimacing. "This shouldn't be legal."

She flipped around, peeking over the wall. They were right in the center of the action, where blue and white players clashed all around them. There were already more red lights than white and blue combined. A scream came from behind them, and Aria turned her weapon toward the noise. One of her teammates was hit in the back but remained on her feet. The perpetrator was right on her tail. He drew his closed fist back and connected squarely with the girl's jaw, sending her reeling backward.

Aria jumped, aiming her gun sloppily with shaking hands. What was getting into everyone? They had never resorted to true violence in one of these simulations before. There was no way that Bradford would allow this. Yet he wasn't stopping them.

Aria was mere meters from the boy. If she pulled the trigger, she would knock him out instantly. She hesitated as the image of the girl who she watched take a direct hit flashed through her mind.

Her fallen teammate steadied herself and lunged forward,

knocking her attacker to the ground. She buried her fist in his face, and her other fist followed. He caught the second blow at the wrist and yanked the girl onto the ground, kneeling over her. He wound up to bash her bloody, swollen face again.

Panic pushed Aria to act. She exhaled slowly and pulled the trigger. She hit his shoulder squarely, sending him reeling backward in pain. He caught himself and turned back to the girl, eyes crazed. He wouldn't stop—she had to do it. She aimed again, directly at the blue light over his heart, and pulled the trigger. The hulking boy flew backward, seizing as the veins on his face and arms bulged. By the time his body hit the ground, he was out cold.

A wave of nausea washed over Aria, and she squeezed her eyes shut to block out what she had just done. She turned back to Elio's spot beside her, but he was gone. She crept above the wall, scanning the battlefield. It was littered with her unconscious classmates and friends. Her eyes stopped on Elio, out cold like the guy she had just taken out. She shivered as a drop of cool rain hit her hand. The first wave of her eager fighters was almost completely gone. Only four others remained awake, shooting recklessly at the oncoming enemy.

"Line two!" Aria yelled at the top of her lungs. Her vocal cords burned from the strain.

"Go, go, go!" Brock screamed.

A battle cry rose in the distance, gaining volume with every second. Thunder cracked overhead, and the scattered raindrops turned into sheets. Aria wiped the water from her eyes. A separate battle cry sounded as a line of blue dots appeared through the rain. They were gaining ground, both lines racing toward each other at dangerous speeds. Water rushed around Aria's feet, filling up the pit where she stood. She climbed out from behind the wall, searching for blue lights emerging from other walls, but the rain blocked her view. In seconds, the lines would clash. The white line rushed past her, and a moment later, several dropped to the mud, screaming over the sound of the worsening torrent.

Aria raced toward one of her fallen teammates, who was face down in the mud, water rushing around his head. The situation had moved from unethical to unsafe. She knelt and flipped him over, immediately leaving him to search for others in similarly dangerous situations. At least those who were unconscious were considered dead, and the electricity had stopped pulsing through their bodies. Another girl to her right was face-down, and another boy behind her. She ran from one body to the next, hauling them over and checking their pulses. At least no one had died yet. The screams continued, and there was no way she could check hundreds of fallen soldiers by herself. Her only option was to finish the game. Once the battle was won, Bradford would have to help.

Aria stood, gun in hand. The battle raged in the center of the field. Only a few dozen remained on each team, and most were rolling in the mud, locked in hand-to-hand combat. There was only one fast solution, and she hated it. She sprinted forward until her view was clear and squatted down to steady her shot. She aimed her weapon at the first blue light she saw and squeezed the trigger. As the scream confirmed a direct hit, she looked away, searching for her next target as she blinked tears from her eyes. She clenched her jaw and shot again.

One target after another, she turned blue lights red. She ran forward to join the teammates she had just saved. Only twenty or so blue lights remained through the thickening rain.

The girl to her right suddenly screamed out, falling to her knees and toppling over into the mud. Aria whipped her head from side to side, but saw no one who could have been the shooter. The boy to her left dropped to his knees as his light turned red as well. Some hidden enemy was taking out her teammates one by one. Only a few blue lights remained, and her last teammates had them pinned.

Pain exploded at Aria's side. She screamed, falling to her knees. Three blue lights appeared from behind a wall, walking toward her slowly. Searing pain pulsed through her body with the electric current. She strained to lift her gun to the new threat.

Only one other white light remained on the field, and he pointed his weapon at the trio and fired. One of the blue lights turned red at the same instant that a scream shook the air. One of the two left standing turned to Aria's last remaining teammate. His white light turned blood red just as he got off one final shot. The blue shooter fell a second later, and suddenly it was one-on-one.

Aria strained again to lift her gun, but the pain in her side radiated outward, pushing her down on her hands and knees. She couldn't move—the pain was too much. It was over. The last blue light steadily grew closer as the rain poured over Aria's eyes. The face of her opponent finally came into view.

"You've gotta be kidding me," Aria said, laughing painfully. "Still as big a coward as ever, aren't you, Celeste?"

"Shut up, Blake. Fighting smart isn't cowardice."

Other than being soaked by rain, Celeste bore no evidence from the fight—no mud, no torn clothing.

"You mean fighting lazy?" Aria asked.

Celeste brought the rifle at her side up to Aria's chest and pressed the barrel to her white light. "Any last words?"

"Actually, yeah," she said through gritted teeth. "You better watch yourself on Sratta because I'll certainly be watching you."

Celeste's jaw tightened and her lip twitched. As she opened her mouth to speak, her body jolted backward. She screamed, shaking in pain. The blue light on her chest turned bright red as her eyes rolled back and her body went limp. A blue light registered in Aria's peripheral vision, and she turned toward it. She pushed up on her knees and finally succeeded in pulling her gun up to defend herself, despite her uncontrollable shaking. There had to be another white light left somewhere on the battlefield; someone had saved her. But the only light left was blue. A stone dropped into her stomach.

"Aria, it's okay," her last opponent said. "You can shoot."

"Luca?" she whispered. "What are you doing?"

"I can't shoot you, Aria. Please just do it."

"But your team will lose! You won fair and square. I can barely move."

"Please. This pain is real. Don't make me do that to you."

"I can handle myself, Luca." Her voice trembled with pain. "We talked about this. Don't treat me like I need saving."

"I'm sorry, Aria, but I won't shoot you." He raised his gun and pointed the barrel at his chest.

"Wait," Aria yelled. "No!"

He pulled the trigger and his body shook violently as his light turned red. He went limp, falling in an unconscious heap to the muddy ground.

"Luca!" Aria screamed, pain still shooting through her body. "No!"

TWENTY-THREE

MUDDY WATER RUSHED around Luca's limp body, and Aria's gun fell from her shaking hands as she dropped to her knees beside him. She strained to turn him over but winced at the searing pain in her side. The same alarm that had started the battle blared again and with it, her pain was immediately gone. Fallen bodies all around her began stirring. Luca opened his eyes as she helped him to his feet.

"Congratulations, Miss Aria Blake!" Instructor Bradford yelled. "You earned your team an extra two percent on your final grades, and an extra five percent for yourself."

Students from all over the battlefield were gathering in the center, most of them helping each other to walk. The students who were downed by electrocution were the lucky ones. Those who fought hand-to-hand didn't get the same relief from their pain. Even with medical care, theirs would persist for days, even weeks by the look of the bruises and cuts on some of their faces.

"Luca," Bradford said, "for self-sabotage, you have taken half a percent from your teammates' final grades, and two percent from your own."

Aria's face contorted as she glanced back and forth between Bradford and Luca. Her instructor was acting as though forcing kids to brutally attack each other was a perfectly normal occurrence for a final exam. She let go of Luca's arm and stomped up to Bradford, halting mere centimeters from his face.

"What is wrong with you?" she screamed. "How could you put students through this kind of pain? And on top of that, let them beat each other half to death, not to mention the rain! Do you have any idea how many people I pulled out of the mud so they wouldn't drown?"

"Aria!" Bradford said. "Stand down! This is why you sign waivers before you're ever allowed on this field or, for that matter, at the Academy. We train for the real world here. You'll thank me the first time you're in an actual life-or-death situation."

"But putting our lives in danger?"

"No. I would never put a student in real danger. Your vests monitor your vital signs throughout the battle. If anything were wrong, we would have paused the game to administer aid. Don't ever accuse me of endangering my students again. Now, get in line before I take back your reward!"

Aria's face softened and her anger, though still strong, lost its edge.

"Yes, Instructor," she said through gritted teeth. "It won't happen again."

"All of you get to the showers," Bradford yelled. "You're a mess!"

The hundreds of soaked, battered students scattered as quickly as their injuries would allow. Aria bolted away from the battlefield, ignoring her friends' pleas for her to slow down. Someone grabbed her hand and she whirled around to scream at whoever it was. Her eyebrows drew together as she recognized his face.

"Luca?" she asked. How had she not known it was him? All at once, it hit her. She hadn't felt him since the battle began. Not his presence, not his emotions, nothing.

"Aria, are you okay?" he asked.

"No, Luca. I'm not. I told you not to treat me like I'm some damsel in distress!"

"That's not what I was doing."

"No," she said, cutting him off. "You don't get to do that. I don't forgive you."

Some of their friends had formed a semicircle around them.

"Aria, come on," Dima said, putting a hand on her arm. "You just need some time to cool off."

"No, I don't!" she yelled, throwing Dima's hand off. Her entire body shook as if finally letting all her fears and doubts come to the surface. "Luca, you can't control me! I get that you care about me, maybe a little bit too much sometimes, but I don't need you to protect me! I can handle myself without you taking every choice away from me!"

"I'm sorry," Luca said, taking her hand.

She wrenched out of his grip and turned back toward the Defense Building.

"I don't wanna hear it," she yelled as she took off at a run, leaving Luca and all their friends behind. She had to get through two more finals, and luckily Luca wouldn't be present for either of them. She couldn't stand to think about him, let alone see his face.

Aria stumbled through a foggy haze of anger and stress. Only the hundreds of hours spent studying over the semester saved her from a meltdown. She blocked out everything but the tests, and once she finished the last one, she shut down entirely. Her friends' voices melted into the background as she tore through campus. She ignored Dima's persistent pleas to slow down until she finally climbed into her bed and pulled the covers over her head, blocking herself off from the world as she let the tears lull her to sleep.

Aria's eyes fluttered open to the sight of her dark room. Slow breathing came from the beds around her. She checked the time—already a quarter to five in the morning. Her eyes felt raw and heavy from the excessive tears of the previous night. She had slept like the dead for more than thirteen hours straight, and in just over an hour, her alarm would inform her that it was time to depart on a trip she still hadn't packed for. She pulled the covers off and jumped down from her bunk, stumbling to the bathroom in the dark. She turned on the light and squinted at the startlingly bright image of herself in the mirror. She was a mess. Her face was so puffy that her eyes couldn't open entirely, and her hair was a wild nest of tangles. The quick shower she took after the battle hadn't gotten nearly as much mud out of her hair as she had hoped, and the scrapes on her knees and elbows were proof of the dive and roll maneuvers she pulled during the battle.

Beyond the physical, there was something uglier about her reflection. Memories of the battle and its aftermath flooded back to her groggy mind. She dropped her head into her hands and moaned desperately.

She hadn't meant to say any of it. Of course, Luca hadn't wanted to shoot her. She didn't want to shoot him either. He was doing what any good friend would do. He had kept his word to never let her win all semester. It was the severity of the pain that had put him over the edge. Aria wasn't mad at Luca, she was mad at the system—one that would put a bunch of teenagers through excruciating pain to make them desperate enough to fight each other like animals. At this rate, by year four, they would have to slaughter a band of lost souls for a final exam.

She had played right into their game, shooting down dozens of her classmates despite the gut-wrenching torment that accompanied each kill. Luca was the only one who ever questioned it, and she had punished him for that.

Still, there was truth to the words she let out in her rage, and that scared her most of all. Luca's connection to her seemed so much stronger than hers was to him. Even now, she couldn't feel a thing from him. That might have been refreshing, but she had no idea if he still felt her. He could be watching her every move right now. It should have been comforting to know he was always there, but there was something unfair about it. She hadn't chosen him. Her whole life, he had always been there, never changing or leaving. He had already chosen her, and she would need to choose him back if she were going to make a relationship work between them, but Luca had the advantage. He had known a life without her in it. Aria had rarely known a single moment without the repercussions of having him in hers.

She turned on the shower, wishing the water would wash her down the drain with the grime. She finally got most of the residual mud out of her hair and the blood off her body before dressing in her uniform and recklessly packing her bags. They were only allowed three extra extreme-weather uniforms, a few essential toiletries, and the tools they would need to accomplish their mission. Her pack was refreshingly light when she threw it over her shoulder. The other girls were up now, but she wasn't ready to talk about what had happened. She grabbed breakfast from their shared kitchen and flew out the door before anyone could stop her.

"Aria!" Dima yelled. "Wait for us!"

But she ignored her. Lengthening her stride and picking up her pace, she just barely held back from breaking into a full-blown sprint. She burst through the front doors and sped across the peninsula to the campus launch site, nestled between the foothills to the north and the Academy Train Station to the south.

Aria inhaled the sea air, which was growing warmer as summer approached. She stopped to remove her jacket when beads of sweat started forming on the back of her neck. The new uniform was made specifically for extremely cold environments. They weren't much thicker than the standard uniforms, but they supported a new thermal technology that was supposed to work down to negative fifty degrees Celsius. It was way too much warmth for spring on the peninsula.

Tying the jacket off around her hips, she hoisted the bag back onto her shoulders and took in her last sight of Drammat from the surface. The morning sun cast a golden orange glow over the dips and high points in the land.

Transfixed by the picturesque dawn, Aria let the peace swallow up her anguish. A cool breeze lightly tossed her long locks so the tips tickled the backs of her arms. She took in every sensation, from the sun on her skin to the smell of the budding flowers. Despite the perfect morning, an uneasy emptiness nagged at her. Without Luca's presence as a guiding star and his emotions filling the empty places in her soul, she hardly felt like herself.

Other students were gaining on her from the direction of the Boarding Halls, so she pressed forward toward the site. As she crested a small hill, her mouth dropped wide open. Luca hadn't shut up about the launch site all semester, but she never could have imagined the impressive reality of what he had been working so hard on. Four massive ships sat side by side on gigantic landing pads attached to runways. The fourth-year Engineering students had designed the sleek, silver ships, and the second and third-years built them. Luca and his classmates were simply observing the process and training to operate the colossal thing.

All four sites were bustling with movement as Engineering students prepared for four different class missions. They were in charge of take-off, navigation, landing, and any tech or navigation problems on the way. Despite the cocky Colonization attitude, the Engineering students were the real all-stars this time. Without them, the Colonization students wouldn't even make it to Sratta.

A twinge of regret sent a shiver up Aria's spine. She focused her mind on finding Luca, but she felt nothing at all. Just yesterday, she had wished their connection away, and today, her wish was granted. Tears welled up in her eyes, threatening to spill over. She looked up at the sky and blinked them back as she arrived at the Colonization boarding gate, marked with a green glowing arch. Other than the Engineering students, who had worked through the early morning hours to prepare the ship for launch, she was one of the first students to arrive.

"Aria!" a familiar voice shouted from behind her.

She turned around slowly, a grimace on her face. "Hey, Dima."

"Are you done yet?" Dima asked. "You're acting like a twelve-year-old."

"I'm just a helpless child, remember?" She hardened her face in one final rebellious glare, but she felt her anger melting away.

"And you're acting like it. What on Drammat is wrong?"

"I'm sorry. I'm not sure what's going on with me. Can we talk tonight?"

Dima stared Aria down, narrowing her eyes. "Fine. Whatever it is, I expect full detail. Like more than usual full detail."

"They aren't those kinds of details, Dima. They aren't fun, gossipy things. But fine. You can have all the weird details about how messed up I am if that's what you want."

"Perfect!" Dima said with a self-satisfied smile. She looped her arm through Aria's as if they hadn't just argued and led her toward the boarding gate. "Great Explorer. It's amazing, isn't it?"

"It's a beauty," Aria said, craning her neck to see the top of the ship.

"Yo!" Nick yelled, waving with Brock, Milo, Elio, and Finlay as they came over the hill. "You guys excited?"

"I could throw up," Aria said.

Dima wrinkled her nose. "Do you barf when you get nervous?"

"I'm not nervous, just excited in a terrifying way."

"That's like the definition of nervous, hon." Dima patted her head.

Aria shrugged Dima's hand off as all three boys laughed. A whistle rang out from somewhere near the gate, immediately hushing the excited conversations from the growing number of Colonization students under the green arch. They stood in their matching uniforms with bags strewn around their feet, like a bunch of kids headed to summer camp.

"First-years, listen up!" yelled Rhen. "Our official job doesn't begin until we get to Sratta, but that doesn't mean we're gonna sit on our butts this week."

"That's right," Jake said, stepping in front of his fellow second-year. "As your cohort leaders, Rhen and I will be monitoring your preparation for the mission. Our designated faculty members are Instructor Croft and Instructor Reed. We're all here to help you be successful."

Rhen crossed her arms and stepped in front of Jake. "In a few minutes, we'll go in and set up our quarters. Work fast; takeoff is in an hour."

The material that formed the ship's outer shell seemed to be forged of a single, seamless piece of metal and polished to perfection, but as a whoosh of air sounded, a crack appeared in the surface, below the glow of the green arch. The newly revealed door sank inside the ship and slid up out of view, revealing a simple, metal hallway. More than fifteen students could fit through the door shoulder to shoulder and even more through the hallway. Rhen and Jake led the way.

Aria ran her hand along the cold surface of the wall as she entered the ship. Everything was state-of-the-art and made to perfection. She would never have guessed college students built it. Aria's hand came to a metal box, forcing her to lift her fingers from the wall they traced. It was an old dual-authenticator lock with a password pad, just like the one Celeste and her mom used to enter the restricted area in the Library. She cocked her head at the antiquated technology. Such tech could often be found in old buildings, but what was something so outdated doing on a brand-new ship? She stared at the scanner until the group rounded the corner into an open room filled with plush rugs, pillows, and chairs.

"This is our common room," Rhen said. "It's where we'll eat and hang out on our limited time off."

"See that door?" Jake asked, pointing to a large door across the room. "Through there is a smaller version of the tupin environment in the Greenhouse. There's also a lab where you can take your specimens. We'll resume our work immediately after takeoff."

"Your room is through the door on the left," Rhen said. "Yes, you heard that right. You will all be sharing one room, but before you get too excited, there are separate locker rooms for men and women, and we are always watching. Don't try anything stupid. We're here to get a job done." Stifled snickers passed through the crowd. "I'm looking at you, Nick."

Nick threw his hands up. "What? I'm respectful! Tell her, guys! Aria, Dima, I'm respectful, right?"

"Whatever you say, Nick," Rhen said. "Everybody, go in and secure your stuff so it doesn't get thrown around during takeoff. Then get back here and line up. We're headed out in ten minutes."

Aria followed the crowd of Colonization students into the

cramped room, packed with rows of bunk beds firmly bolted to the floor. The doors, bed frames, and floors were made of the same cold, shiny metal as the outside of the ship, but the bed looked plenty comfortable and warm, with thick green blankets and black sheets covering the plush mattresses and pillows.

"They didn't say anything about assigned bunks," Nick said. "Do we get to choose?"

"I think so," Dima guessed.

"Then we can all sleep together!" Nick said.

"Ew," Dima yelled, smacking his chest with the back of her hand.

"Not like that! Jeez! I just mean it would be cool to all be near each other so we can talk and stuff, like a slumber party or whatever you girls call it."

"Cool," Aria said. "But I get that bottom bunk in the corner!" She broke into a sprint and her friends stampeded behind her, colliding with each other as they dove for the best bunks. Aria stashed her bags in one of the two compartments under her bed and strapped them down as Dima plopped down face-first on Aria's bed. She rested her chin in her hands, kicking her legs back and forth through the air.

"So, you gonna tell me about Luca yet?"

"Come on, Dima. We have two minutes to get back out there."

"Ugh, fine." Dima rolled over and pulled herself up by the bars of the top bunk. "But I'm not gonna stop asking until you tell me, 'cause I'm worried about you."

"It's nothing to be worried about, Dima." She looped her arm through her friend's and led her back through the door.

"Four lines," Jake yelled. "Let's go!"

The girls stumbled into line behind their friends just in time to join the march. The hollow sounds of hundreds of footsteps on the cold metal floor reverberated through the ship. They weren't the only cohort on the move. The noise increased with each step forward until they spilled into an enormous room meant for passengers and crew alike. Hundreds of cushioned passenger seats lined the bottom floor. Where a ceiling should have been, there was open space, as if a hole had been cut through two floors in the middle of the ship. Only a short safety railing separated the crew from a long fall into the passenger pit.

Engineering students in all-black ran around the second-floor balcony that circumnavigated the entire room, dodging and weaving around each other as they hurried to prepare for take-off. A door toward the bow read "Pilot's Cabin". The only non-student crew members would be seated through that door. In eerie contrast to the rest of the room, the third-floor balcony was nearly dead. Only a few Engineering instructors stood at the rails, silently observing their students. Aria searched for Luca and even Alika and Amare, but it was point-less in the pre-flight chaos. She dug inward for the string that tethered her to Luca, but she again came up short.

"Our cohort will sit off the starboard bow each time we launch or land the ship," Rhen said, gesturing to the seats in front of them.

"What does that mean?" Dima whispered.

"This corner," Aria said. "That's starboard, and that's the bow," she said, pointing to the front and right of their seats. "You're gonna need to learn ship directions."

"Why do you know them? It's not exactly common knowledge."

"It is when you grow up on the coast."

Among the last in line, they shuffled through the aisle, climbing over long legs and overhanging elbows. Finally, they found enough empty seats for everyone near the back of their section, and all ten of them sat down and fastened their safety harnesses. Aria grabbed Dima's hand on her left and Allison's hand on her right, squeezing for reassurance. They would assume Aria was nervous about takeoff, but that couldn't have been further from the truth. The knot in her stomach tightened. Was it possible that Luca wasn't here at all? Had something happened to him?

Anguish shot through her at the thought of never being with him again. All this time, she had blamed their connection for taking her choices away from her. She hadn't considered how much it would hurt to lose it. She quickly wiped away a single fallen tear as her heart called out in silent apology.

A warm concern filled her. It was faint, hardly there at all, but after the silence inside of her, it was unmistakable. More tears welled in her eyes as she scanned the upper deck again, following the faint pull of the delicate string. A set of dark, tight curls caught her eye. He was turned away from her, working at the controls near the pilot's cabin. Her heart rate increased, and her stomach lurched. Suddenly he straightened, pausing his work. Slowly, he turned his body to face her, and his dark eyes caught hold of hers. She opened her mouth to speak, but nothing came out.

What was the point when they were so far apart? He wouldn't have heard her regardless.

Luca looked down, tinkering with something in his hands, and glanced up at her again. She could see the hurt on his face, and a shadow of pain filled her. Tears pooled in Aria's eyes. She looked down at her shaking hands and jumped as she saw two other hands there, crushed in her vice-like grip.

"I'm so sorry!" she gasped, dropping her friends' hands as if they had burned her.

"That's fine," Allison said, rubbing her crushed hand. "But for real, I think we need to talk about Luca."

Aria opened her mouth to try to put words to her feelings, but a voice came over the loudspeaker, cutting her off.

"This is your captain. We'll be taking off in approximately five minutes. I'll begin making our way to the launch runway now. Please fasten your harnesses and enjoy the ride. Take off is the hardest part, but once we overcome Drammat's gravitational pull and we're in free space, it'll be smooth sailing to Sratta."

The ship hummed as it crept forward. Dozens of harnesses clicked as the second-floor Engineering students strapped themselves into standing restraints. Luca tightened his harness and immediately went back to work. The students swayed in inertia's pull as the captain took a wide turn and finally straightened out. Silence settled over the whole ship in anticipation, as even the Engineering students paused their work.

Suddenly, the ship shot forward. The back of Aria's head smashed into her cushioned seat back and stuck there. She glanced around with her eyes, unable to lift her head. Allison's eyes were pinched shut, and her face was scrunched. Dima's were wide, but her smile was even wider.

"Woohoo!" Dima yelled. "Yeah!"

The ship tilted further upward, putting the passengers nearly flat on their backs as another jolt rocketed them faster and farther into the atmosphere. Aria glanced over at Allison, whose limp body was plastered to her seat, seemingly unconscious. Dima, along with a few other crazy souls on the ship, were still screaming as if they were on a ride at an amusement park. Someone wretched across the room, followed by the splatter of vomit and disgusted cries.

The ship jolted forward one more time, pushing the air out of Aria's lungs. The yelling stopped immediately, replaced by miserable groans. Aria's head pounded and her lungs fought for air but failed to expand. Aria looked forward, straining to see Luca in her hazy vision. He was there, working hard at something. Darkness encroached from her peripherals, threatening her sight and consciousness. She blinked, suddenly very sleepy. The ship jolted violently again and quickly slowed. The force holding Aria's body down lifted, and suddenly she was free.

Aria stretched her neck in a circle, fighting the urge to lose her breakfast. She looked around the cabin. Allison and Brock were both passed out, limbs hanging limply. Nick looked like he would join that other poor soul in throwing up all over himself. Gemma, Milo, and Elio were slightly green but seemed fine, and Jeslyn had tears running down her expressionless face as a pale-looking Finlay tried to comfort her.

"Congratulations, kids," the captain said over the speaker. "You've just survived your first space launch. Stay in your seats until we stabilize our speed for optimal gravity levels."

Several anxious minutes later, the pilot came back on. "Artificial gravity is now at full capacity. Once you're up to it, feel free to unbuckle your harnesses and make your way back to your common rooms."

Aria closed her eyes and breathed slowly for several minutes. When her head stopped spinning, she pressed the button to retract her harness. It flew back into the seat, and she stood slowly, one hand still on the headrest for balance. She took one step and smiled. While the motion of the ship created enough gravitational pull to keep everyone's feet on the ground, it was much less than the level they were used to on Drammat. She took another step and laughed. She paced the aisle and jumped up and down.

"This is so cool," she said.

"That wouldn't be my word for it," Allison muttered, rubbing her head with both palms as she came to.

"Allison!" Aria shouted. "Are you okay?"

"I can't tell yet. Just help me up."

Aria slipped both arms under Allison's armpits and hoisted her to her feet. Everyone held on to someone else for support as they stumbled down the aisle. They shuffled out of the massive room, but Aria glanced over her shoulder one last time. Luca was still working at the controls on the second-level balcony with his back turned to her. He paused and stiffened as if debating with himself whether he should turn to her. Logic won and he resumed his task, never looking back. Deep lines creased Aria's face as she frowned. She glanced around the balcony at the dozens of kids working tirelessly to get them safely to Sratta.

It really was a shame that the whole mission was a hoax. Celeste would take credit for solving the mystery, and her associates, likely the Drammatan government itself, would use the trip as a cover for whatever they were planning. When she had told her friends about the hoax, they had been equally enraged. It was difficult to keep up appearances in Mission Briefing and the Colonization practicum, knowing it was all a scam, but they did their best to act appropriately invested. She scanned the crowd of Diplomacy students for Celeste but something unexpected caught Aria's eye on the third floor. A different Brant with sleek raven hair stood gracefully near the balcony.

"No way," she whispered. "On *our* ship?"

"What?" Dima asked from behind her, where she and Nick were helping each other stay upright.

"Maya Brant," Aria said. "She's here!"

"What?" Dima asked. "The second lady? I wonder if her skin is really as perfect in person as it is during her husband's addresses."

"Really, Dima?"

"It's a valid question," Dima hissed.

"Actually, it *is* pretty perfect," Aria murmured. "But focus! Here, Nick. Take Allison. We're going info hunting."

"Sure," Nick said, reluctantly detaching himself from Dima and putting his arm around Allison's shoulders.

As soon as their friends had slipped into the hallway, Aria yanked Dima's arm, pulling her down into the shadow of a control panel near the exit.

"Look," Aria said, pointing up to the third-floor balcony. "I didn't expect her to be so open about her involvement. We need to get closer and see what she's doing."

Dima pointed upward. "She's talking to someone."

Aria squinted, straining to see. Dima was right. The other person's arm was waving around frantically, coming in and out of view. It was covered in a long purple sleeve, a standard Diplomacy student uniform.

"She's talking to Celeste out in the open," Aria said.

"She *is* her daughter, so it's not that weird, but I wonder what her cover is for being here."

"Does it matter? She and her people have all the power they need to do whatever they want when they want."

"So what do we do?" Dima asked.

"We follow her and get some proof."

TWENTY-FOUR

CELESTE TRAILED behind her mother as she glided across the highest balcony. They walked confidently below the bright glow of the ship's overhead lights, not attempting to hide their faces. Aria followed their trajectory, though she was two floors below them. She vaulted up the nearest flight of stairs to the second-floor balcony, trusting that Dima would follow. The Engineering students were bustling around and didn't pay them any attention.

The second lady led the way around the back of the ship, and as she came to a corner, she and Celeste turned out of sight. Aria searched for any sign of a ladder or elevator, but there was nothing. The third floor seemed to be completely cut off from the rest of the ship. Footsteps rattled the balcony above their heads.

"We're gonna lose them!" Dima whispered.

"No, we're not," Aria said. Crouching down below the railing, she scampered back around to the opposite side of the ship. Celeste's purple shirt came into view, but the older woman was nowhere to be seen. Celeste disappeared through a dark doorway.

"There has to be a way up," Aria said. "We need to see what's up there."

A hand clamped down on the back of Aria's neck, sending a jolt of pain through her spine.

"Ow!" Dima yelled. "What the—?"

"What are you two doing here?" hissed a gruff male voice.

The man released his death grip on their necks and pulled them upright to face him. He wasn't very tall, shorter than Dima and just taller than Aria, but he was strong. The deep lines on his comparatively young features told of many years in stressful positions.

"Why aren't you with your cohort?" he asked.

"We're sorry!" Dima said. "We just thought all this stuff was so cool that we had to take a look!"

"What you had to do was your assignment."

Digging his knobby fingers into their arms, he walked them back down the stairs, through the exit, and toward the Colonization common room. All the while, he ranted from his soapbox.

"Every person on this ship has a job to do," he repeated for the fifth time, "and you two are neglecting yours. You're distracting my students, which could endanger the entire ship."

Aria winced as he pushed them through the door to the Colonization common room. Dima tripped over a rug and crashed onto the floor with a yelp. Aria helped Dima to her feet as the sixty-one faces of their cohort members and leaders turned toward the commotion.

"I found these delinquents trying to skip out on their responsibilities and disrupt my students," the man said.

Rhen pushed past the gawking students and stood in front of Aria and Dima.

"Instructor Jorah," she said, "I'm sure this was just a

misunderstanding. These are two of our brightest, most well-behaved students."

"Then I'd hate to meet the rest of them!" he barked. He turned and stomped back into the hallway.

"What happened?" Jake said, coming to stand next to Rhen. "Where were you two?"

"We didn't leave the cabin," Aria said. "We just went to the second level to see what was up there and...we're sorry."

"Great Explorer." He rolled his eyes, as if to lament ever applying to be a cohort leader. "At least you won't have time to make any other stupid decisions. You're already late. Don't skip out on your duties again. Every second we spend slacking off is a second wasted when thousands of lives are at stake."

Dima opened her mouth, but Aria put a restraining hand on her back and she shut it reluctantly.

"We're sorry, and it won't happen again," Aria said. "Can we find our assignments in the greenhouse?"

Rhen smiled at the girls and showed them to the habitat. "This is where you'll spend every day until we land. You'll be doing the same thing you did on Drammat, and when you get to Sratta, you'll do the same thing there. We still need to find the cause before we can find a cure, so focus on that. If you need Instructor Croft, she'll be in the lab with the other group. Never leave our designated area unless we tell you to."

Aria smiled silently at Rhen and walked through the door as the frigid air swallowed her. The room was already nearly packed to capacity with over three dozen of their classmates. Aria and Dima pulled on their gloves and found an open dig site. The greenhouse at the Academy was much colder, but the chilled room was still uncomfortable. Several of their friends were also assigned to the greenhouse and nodded in greeting as they got to work.

"We need to see what's behind that door," Aria whispered, trying to keep her lips still.

"We'll figure something out," Dima said through her teeth. "For now, just work."

At the end of the day, they finished their work with stiff hands, blue lips, and no results. It was silly, but Aria held out hope that she or her friends would find the answer before Celeste got a chance to take the credit. Knowing it was manmade gave them all an advantage, at least.

They shivered as they stood in the dinner line. The aroma of the spicy soup filled the air, and the warmth of the bowl stung Aria's frozen hands as she sat down at a corner table with her friends. Silent stares replaced the laughter and jokes that typically dominated their conversations.

"Can somebody tell me what's going on?" Aria asked.

Finlay put a silencing finger to his lips and glanced around. "When you guys were gone, things got kinda weird," he whispered.

"Weird how?" Dima asked.

"Jake got a call," Jeslyn said. "Whoever was on the other side of that conversation wasn't happy you two were missing."

"We were gone less than five minutes," Aria said.

"He got the call before we even got back to the common room," Jeslyn said. "What were you guys doing?"

Aria looked over her shoulder. Their table was secluded enough that no one would likely overhear them, but it was still risky. She verified that Alika's program was still running.

"You know how Celeste met with her mom in the library last week?" she whispered, barely audibly. "She's here on the ship and openly walking around with Celeste."

"Hiding in plain sight," Nick said. "Did you see anything?"

"Not before that jerk, Jorah, caught us," Dima said. "But we did see them go into a room on the third floor of the main cabin. Our only leads are that room and Celeste herself, but trailing Celeste would require sneaking into the Diplomacy wing, so I think that's out of the question."

"The security around here is nuts," Elio said. "Plus, Rhen and Jake are gonna be watching us like hawks."

"Even those two overachievers have to sleep," Allison whispered, looking over Aria's shoulder. "We just have to wait for the right moment."

That moment proved difficult to find. Every day, the Colonization students woke up early, ate a nutritious breakfast, and went to work for the next ten hours, with just an hour for lunch to break up the day. When they finally finished their work, they ate dinner and went to bed. All the talking and laughing they imagined they would do when they chose their bunks never lasted longer than a minute or two before they were all out cold. And all the while, Aria spent pretty much every second of every day trying to make her thoughts reach Luca. His presence had increased to its previous level, and she felt occasional bursts of emotion from him, but being forced to remain separate from the other cohorts was driving her crazy. She wanted to sneak into the main cabin to see him even more than she wanted to spy on Celeste, but every moment of their day was planned, and someone was always watching.

On the night before landing, Aria lay awake in her bed shortly before lights out, her stomach tying itself in knots. They were running out of time. If their movements were so restricted on the ship, what were the odds that they would be any freer to roam around on base? She had been so sure they would find a way to escape that she and her friends had secretly stripped their beds of sheets and tied them together under their covers, just in case they needed a rope to reach the third floor. At this point, all Aria wanted was for someone to hold her and tell her that everything would work out.

She missed Luca so much it hurt. She wasn't sure of anything anymore—not where their connection was concerned. She had tried to call him through her neurolink, but every time, he sent back a message saying that he was busy. She soon discovered that she was usually on shift during his time off, and vice versa. Despite the emotional distance, tonight, she seemed to feel his presence nearer than she had over the whole trip.

Aria's friends spoke in hushed tones around her and she had been successfully tuning them out until a new voice caught her attention, a voice she hadn't heard in almost two weeks. Her head popped up from her pillow and she looked toward the source. Her heart jumped as she saw Rhen speaking with someone through the door frame.

"What's the problem?" she asked.

Luca's voice rang clearly into the room. "One of the sensors in the girls' changing room is saying there might be an issue."

"What, like a plumbing issue?"

"There's an important bit of machinery under the floor in there, so I just need to check that everything is fine. If not, I'll need to repair the part."

"Go on in, then." She waved him into the room and Aria's heart leaped as his eyes found hers and he winked.

She glanced at her friends, whose eyes were all locked on Luca as he walked toward them.

"Hey, guys," he said, stopping to lean against one of the bedposts. "How's it going?"

"Move along, Luca," Rhen said. "My cohort needs to get some sleep."

His eyes lingered on Aria's as he lifted a hand to salute Rhen. He turned and walked into the changing room and Aria's heart pounded. Both anxiety and excitement rolled off of him. It was the strongest emotion she had felt from him in weeks. This was more than a casual visit, yet Aria couldn't suppress the need to apologize and explain her actions to him. She pulled her blankets over her head and checked her settings on Alika's program. To her surprise, Alika's image appeared over her vision for the first time on the voyage. She held a finger to her lips and Aria noted students in black uniforms bustling around in the background. She was still on shift. Aria raised her eyebrows and Alika tilted her head in the direction of the dressing room. When Aria hesitated, Alika waved her hand in front of her face and mouthed 'invisible'.

Aria slinked out of her bed and placed her pillow where her body should have been. Her friends did their best to feign sleep, but many of their eyes bulged at the sight of the pillow moving on its own. Aria tiptoed on bare feet as she followed Luca through the door. Her head swiveled around the dark room and Alika let her invisibility drop. Luca stood at the back of the room near the last changing booth, a radiant smile on his face. Joy and uncertainty overlayed his nerves, but Aria's dominant emotion was relief. She ran across the room and leaped into his arms.

"It's so good to see you," he whispered.

"I'm so sorry," Aria whispered, tears springing to her eyes.

"What for?" He set her down and looked at her with confused eyes shadowed by his furrowed brow.

"For overreacting after the last battle. It was stupid. I realized that I wasn't actually mad about the game, but there *are* things we need to talk about." The words spilled out of her like water. "You've been so patient with me, but I think I need more than time. I need to feel like I have a choice in my fate. And beyond that, I need to know that this is going to work out between us before we take this somewhere we can't come back from."

Luca gripped her shoulders and looked into her eyes, gold flecks dancing in his. "Thank you for telling me. I really want to have this conversation, but right now isn't the best time."

Aria deflated slightly, but Luca spoke again.

"Please don't be sad. This is important. Today, I saw

Celeste with her mom and overheard them talking about a meeting tonight." Aria's disappointment immediately sank to the back of her mind, and his excitement and anxiety suddenly made perfect sense. "Celeste was upset that she didn't get to go with her mom. I told the twins and we kept watch all day. Alika is on duty right now and she told me that the second lady is in the captain's cockpit with a bunch of official-looking people. Right now, it seems casual, but they're still talking about an appointment tonight, so it hasn't happened yet. My best guess is that room they all keep going into on the third floor. You know the one, right? The one Celeste and her mom went into when you got nabbed by my professor?"

How did he know so much when she knew so little of him? Dozens of questions flitted through her mind, but she pushed them away.

"Let's go," she whispered, turning to leave.

Luca grabbed her arm and tugged her back. "I can't go. My shift is about to start, and you saw how strict Jorah is. Amare starts with me, and Alika will be off shortly after we start, but she'll be too late. Take a couple of our other friends and get to that door as fast as you can. Alika will be watching. If they go anywhere unexpected, she'll direct you."

"Okay. Thank you."

Luca's arms came around Aria one more time and a bit of her stress melted away. Luca pulled back and placed something small into her hand.

"A master key," he whispered. "It'll unlock most common locks."

He placed his hand on her back and urged her back into the main room. Alika appeared once more and made the hand signal that Aria was starting to recognize meant she was invisible. Aria hurried to her bunk and crawled in.

"Something's going down," she whispered. "And Alika is gonna help us get out."

"We get to be invisible?" Nick asked.

"Sounds like it."

"Count me in." He shifted in his bunk and Aria shushed him.

"Not yet. Alika has to link your neurolink to hers so she can manipulate what everyone else's neurolinks transmit to their brain."

"So cool," Dima whispered. "Can I come too?"

"Yes, but no more. We need stealth more than numbers."

After a moment of tense silence, Nick and Dima both gasped in unison. Alika was in. Aria placed her pillow where her body should have been once more and saw as her two friends' beds shift as well. As they stuffed their homemade rope into a backpack, Aria hoped that Alika's program was smart enough to include items they picked up after her modification. They were about to find out. Aria took a step toward the exit but bumped into someone.

"Sorry," Dima hissed. "You take the lead. I'll hang onto your shirt. Nick, you do the same with me."

Aria stepped forward again, and this time, resistance tugged at her shirt.

They paused at the door while Jake passed them by on the last check of his sector before lights out. Luckily, Rhen had already checked their side. They tried not to breathe until Jake turned the corner at the end of the room. Aria pressed the tiny chip to the control panel next to the door. The lock shifted and the door slid open, letting them slip out into the empty common room.

The stillness of the night would have been peaceful under normal circumstances, but with everything on the line, it was unnervingly quiet as they emerged into the ship. They tiptoed with bare, silent feet through the long hallway to the main cabin. The room was mostly dark, other than small lights on the controls where a half dozen Engineering students were assigned overnight duty. The only light and sound emanated from the pilot's cockpit. A hushed conversation drifted down to them, and Aria increased the volume on her neurolink, but they were too far to make anything out. Luca was up there too. She could feel their invisible string leading her straight to the place where he stood near the pilot's cockpit.

Having fantasized about this moment for weeks, Aria and her two friends didn't need to speak to know the rough plan. They crept up the stairs on their toes, barely breathing. If anyone caught them now, there was no chance of lying their way out, and Alika would likely be implicated too. Although, maybe not. That girl was slippery. The trio inched their way across the balcony on tiptoe.

Aria stopped and whispered. "The door's right above us."

She knelt, carefully shrugged the pack off her shoulders, and untied the knots she used to jimmy rig it closed. The sound of a zipper would have been too loud. She pulled the black wad of cloth from the bag and unraveled it.

"This better work," Dima murmured.

"It's the oldest trick in the book," Nick whispered. "It'll work."

"You mean it's the oldest *cliche* in the book," Dima said. "Do you know anyone who's successfully used a bedsheet rope? Because I don't!"

"Shhh," Aria whispered. "This is the best we've got, and we're running out of time."

Nick took the end of the sheet rope from Aria and tied a loop in it. Aria tied her backpack shut again and threw it over her shoulder while Nick practiced taking his shot. The girls stood back as he let the looped end fly. It soared halfway up to the third-floor balcony and fell back down. Nick caught it and immediately wound up to throw it again.

Aria winced. They may be invisible, but their rope wasn't, and any noise would bring unwanted attention their way.

Nick grunted as he strained to reach the top. The rope flew to the perfect height, but Nick's aim was off, and when it reached its peak, it fell back down into his hands. He wound up again and exhaled sharply as he launched the rope a third time. It flew up over the railing and landed firmly on the third balcony with a thud that echoed through the vast cabin.

Aria winced and dropped to her stomach. She had warned her friends that too many eyes on them might override Alika's program as it had for her in Kan City. Dima and Nick followed her lead, the other end of the rope still in Nick's hand. They had made the rope for strength, not silence, and now they were paying for their oversight.

"Did you hear that?" one of the Engineering students asked.

"I didn't hear anything," another said.

"I'm gonna go check it out."

Aria turned to watch as a tall, lanky boy in all black stood up and ambled toward them. If he got too close, he would see the rope dangling conspicuously from the third balcony. Countless bad ideas churned in Aria's mind as the footsteps grew closer. The only thing they could do was retreat, but even pulling down the rope would draw too much attention. Another set of footsteps came from behind the boy, this pair running.

"Hey, wait!" Luca's voice rang through the cabin from far away. "I'm gonna go with you, just in case."

"Luca's stalling for us," Aria whispered. "Nick, go!"

Nick stood back up and looked over his shoulder at Luca and the other boy. He turned around with the rope in his hand and made a waving motion over his head. The wave moved up the makeshift rope and shifted the looped end toward the edge of the balcony. He flung it again, over and over, and each time the looped end inched closer to the edge.

"Hurry up, man," the tall boy said. "Or I'll just go without you. I'm sure it's nothing."

"Hey. You're boot is untied," Luca said. "Let me help you with that."

The tall boy squatted out of sight as Nick flung the rope harder. The loop finally tipped over the edge and fell into his hands. Any second now, the boy would stand up and see them. Nick frantically put the loose end of the rope through the loop and pulled arm over arm until it tightened around the railing.

"I'll hold it steady," Nick whispered, pushing Dima to the rope. "Then I'll pull myself up." He flexed one of his biceps.

"Now is *so* not the time for your ego," Dima whispered as she grabbed the rope.

She sped up the rope using her hands and feet. Reaching the top, she pulled herself over the edge.

"Now, you, Ar." Nick said. "Come on."

Aria grabbed the first knot in the rope and pulled herself up to the next. The footsteps resumed, growing louder as they approached the corner.

"You're right," Luca said. "I bet it's nothing. We're not Defense students. We should be doing our job, not somebody else's."

Aria pulled herself over the ledge and let her muscles sag on the cold floor. Nick pulled the rope tight and reached for the knot above his head. He pulled his body up the rope hand over hand as Luca and the tall boy rounded the corner.

TWENTY-FIVE

PANIC COURSED through Aria's veins and a secondary wave assailed her from Luca. Aria motioned for Nick to pause his rapid ascent up the homemade rope. The lanky boy with Luca wouldn't see Nick, but he would see a rope swinging wildly beneath him.

The boy turned to face Luca. "What are you tryna pull, Earth rat? You know what they say about Earthers. I'll never trust you. Just leave me alone so I can do my job."

The second the intruder's back was turned, Nick hurried up the rope and pulled his body over the ledge. The makeshift rope flipped in every direction as he pulled it out of view. The end of the rope slithered onto the balcony at the same instant as the tall boy turned back to where the rope had been visible moments before.

Luca followed right on his tail. Nick, Aria, and Dima pressed their gear to the floor and tried not to breathe. The rope was still attached to the top of the balcony—any noise would draw attention to it. The footsteps drew closer until they were right below them.

"See?" Luca asked. "I told you it was nothing. You don't

have to trust me. You just have to do your job instead of pretending you're some kind of soldier or something. Let's go before there's a real problem and we're not there to fix it."

Instead of answering, the boy turned around and stomped back down the balcony toward the controls. Luca's relief doubled her own. When he and the other boy had resumed their work across the ship, Aria popped up and helped Nick stuff the rope into her pack. They tiptoed to the door to join Dima.

"Can you open it?" she asked Aria.

"I doubt it. Luca said it can only open simple, low-security locks. That thing looks like something you'd find in a government building."

"You're right," a voice cut into their conversation, and they all jumped.

Aria pressed a hand to her heart. "Alika, you can talk now?"

"Sorry for the scare. I just got off my shift and I found a supply closet to squat in for a few minutes. I'll need to get back to my common room, but I wanted to pop in and see if I can help."

"We're gonna try to find another way into this room," Aria said. "You happen to have blueprints for the ship?"

A knock sounded and Alika looked up, startled. "Closet," she whispered. "Air vent. I'll try to help when I can."

The audio feed suddenly cut off and they were left in silence.

"Closet, air vents?" Dima asked. "Can't get much more vague than that."

Aria stood up and digested the scene. Unlike the second floor, the third floor had endless hallways shooting off from the main cabin. She slipped into the hallway directly to the right of the door and Nick and Dima followed her into the corridor. They passed several doors with high-security locks until they came to a custodial closet.

"It's gotta be this one," Aria said, placing the chip Luca gave her near the scanner. After several seconds, presumably while Alika did her work, the door slid open to reveal excess cleaning supplies and a variety of tools.

"Okay," Nick said. "Now what?"

Aria scanned the walls and ceilings.

"Bingo," she said, putting one foot high on a shelf and pushing herself toward the ceiling. "Air vent." She slipped her fingers into the vent on the ceiling and popped off the covering.

"Atta girl!" Dima said, hoisting her into the vent by her feet. "Check if it's stable enough for all of us."

"Oh yeah. You're good. Come on up!"

She reached one arm down through the open vent and took Dima's hand. Nick grabbed her legs, and together, they boosted her up. Nick climbed the shelves, and the girls pulled him up when his hands reached theirs. Several vents shot off in different directions, so Aria took the one toward the main cabin. The narrow duct hugged Aria's shoulders and hips as she scooted through the passageway. She wondered how Nick was faring with his significantly broader shoulders.

Faint light showed through slats in the metal when they passed over rooms. Sweat dripped from Aria's forehead onto the metal surface as she dragged her body forward.

"There were three doors between the closet and the room we want," Aria said as they came to the fourth vent cover. "This is it."

She peered through the slats and frowned. She didn't know what she expected, but a boring, generic board room wasn't it. No one was inside and the lights were off, other than a strip of dim light around the base of the walls.

"No one's here," Aria whispered.

"Maybe we got the wrong room or they were going somewhere else all along," Nick said. "Or maybe it's just too early."

They waited in silence for several minutes, but nothing changed, and Aria was beginning to feel claustrophobic.

"Should we check this room out while we're here?" she asked. "We came all this way."

"Can you pop the vent cover out?" Dima asked from behind.

"I think so. Let me see."

Aria wedged her thumb under one of the slats and pushed down. One corner of the vent cover popped out.

"Wait," Nick whispered from behind Dima. "Do you hear that? The voices are getting louder."

Aria lifted her hand off the cover. Nick was right; several pairs of footsteps and hushed voices resonated from somewhere nearby, much nearer than the captain's cockpit. A loud beep sounded from the hallway, and the door to the room they hovered over slid open.

Aria held her breath. A tall, fiercely blonde woman wearing a designer suit entered the room, flanked by a man and woman holding massive guns. Her impressive entourage continued to pile into the room. Aria pressed a hand over her mouth to stifle any sounds as Maya Brant entered last. Strangely, the blonde woman's face was covered by a golden mask, though no other attendees concealed their faces. The conference room was furnished with a long metal table running the room's length and a large, blank space for group viewing at the front. The first woman left her bodyguards at either side of the long table and stepped in front of the screen. Unfortunately, it was blank for anyone not linked in the meeting.

"Please, take a seat," she said. Her voice rang with the clarity and power of a born and practiced leader. "I'll make this meeting short. I simply need to verify that everything is prepared and in order. Bordo, how did transport go? Any bumps?"

"Not at all, ma'am," a short, stocky man said. "All units executed the extraction seamlessly. Cargo is stable and ready for transfer tomorrow."

"Seamlessly? Is that what you call the incident in the Northern Region?"

"No, ma'am," the stocky man stammered under her masked gaze. "But you already knew about that. I didn't feel the need to rehash old failures."

"No?" she asked, slowly walking closer to where the man was seated. "What makes you think others won't rise up?" She put her hands on the table and leaned down to his eye level. "Every day, we see more evidence of insurrection. We can't treat the rebellion that led to the massacre in the Northern Region as an isolated incident. It was a preview of what's to come if we can't get a handle on the masses."

"I still believe the people would understand if they knew the truth," a man at the end of the table said.

"What gives you such faith in our people?" the woman asked, turning toward the man who had spoken against her. "Our ancestors tried the truth, and how well did that work for them? What makes you think it would be any different now?"

"I'm sorry, Madam President. Forgive me."

Dima tapped Aria's foot. "President?" she whispered. "Of where?"

It was a good question. She wasn't the president of any country on Drammat. Aria didn't think she was the president of any of the other human colonies either.

"You're forgiven," she said coldly, returning to her place at the front of the room. "Second Lady Brant, please update us on the situation with the students' mission."

"Everything is running smoothly, Ma'am," Brant said. "Celeste and Instructor Reed are filled in on their orders and prepared to solve the problem discreetly." Aria nearly bit through her lip. Instructor Reed was a part of this? That explained a lot. "None of the Colonization students have come close to discovering the actual cause, and I doubt they'll get any closer before my daughter steps in."

"Good," the president said. "When you're done with the kids, I have a few more jobs for you before we head home. I'll let you know if I need your help with Morales. Despite being our most loyal buyer, he sometimes needs to be reminded of where he'd be without us."

Aria's eyebrows drew together as another bead of sweat dripped into her eye. Buyer? What were they selling?

"Of course. I'm happy to help in any way I can."

"We land tomorrow," the President said. "That's when the real work begins. If there's no other business and everyone knows their orders, I propose we all get some rest."

The dozen men and women sitting at the long table stood and shuffled through the door. Only the President, her body-guards, and Second Lady Brant remained. Brant walked around the table to where the President stood.

"Celeste has been asking questions. I'm worried she won't be able to handle the burden of the truth once she's fully initiated."

"Dear friend," the intimidating blonde woman said, grasping Brant's forearms, "this is why we wait. No one Celeste's age is ready to bear this burden. Stay strong. One day, she'll be ready, but until then, she's just one more life we're responsible for. Remember that *we* bear the burden so *they* don't have to."

"I've always known the weight of the burden is worth it so my children can remain innocent," Brant said. "But every time I bring Celeste into Order business, she's that much closer to bearing it with us."

"Celeste is a strong girl, Maya," the President said. "She'll handle it better than us all, I'm sure. In the meantime, spare her a while longer."

Brant smiled weakly and turned away. They both exited the conference room, flanked by the president's bodyguards, and the door locked behind them. Aria let out a long breath after barely taking in air for the duration of the meeting. Sweat pooled below her body and her face stuck uncomfortably to the metal. They waited until total silence had returned. Nick backed out through the vent system, creating room for Dima and Aria to do the same. Aria finally slipped through the opening and back into the custodial closet with the help of her friends, their faces also dripping with sweat.

"What are they transporting?" Dima whispered.

"Something they're selling," Nick said.

"What does that have to do with the lost souls' massacre in the Northern Region?" Aria asked. "That president-lady acted like the protest was a blow to business."

"President, the Order," Dima said, brow furrowed. "It's like they were speaking a different language. I mean, what did we even learn from all that?"

"We know Vice President Brant's wife is in on whatever this is, so he probably is too," Nick said. "Who knows? Maybe President Chen is the one who sent Brant on this assignment."

"We still need proof," Aria said.

"And we'll get it," Nick said. "But right now, we need to get back before the bed checks in ten minutes."

Nick cracked open the door slowly and let the girls out. The only sound was the faint chatter of the Engineering students on the night shift. She thought she heard Amare's laugh and it made her smile. At least Luca had a friend or two by his side.

They ran to the end of the hallway and peered out onto the

balcony. Nick wrapped the rope in an intricate knot around the bottom rail.

"You first, Aria," he said.

He lowered her over the edge, and when she landed on the second level, they both helped Dima down. Once both girls were down, Nick untied the rope and slipped it around the bar with one side in each hand. He lowered himself down until the halved rope came to an end five feet in the air.

"You need to help me down," he whispered.

Each girl grabbed one of his feet and strained to hold him upright as he pulled the rope down. They squatted down to let him dismount and stuff the sheet rope in Aria's pack. They tiptoed along the balcony and down the stairs.

"Three minutes until Jake and Rhen wake up for bed checks," Dima whispered.

They ran through the hallway back to the common room, much less concerned with being heard now that time was running out. Aria returned the chip to the scanner and unlocked the door. As they tiptoed inside, movement caught Aria's eye in the corner of the room.

"We're too late," she whispered. "They already started."

"We can still make it," Dima whispered. They sped up, their corner of the sleeping quarters coming into sight. When they reached their beds and pulled back the covers, Allison poked her head out from her blanket and shook her head. Rhen came around the corner, centimeters from Aria. Allison jumped out of bed.

"Hey Rhen," she said, staggering side to side. "I don't feel very well. I might—" She made a gagging sound. "Can you help me to the bathroom?"

"Are you okay?" Rhen asked, rushing to help her. "Did you eat anything the rest of us didn't?"

Rhen held Allison up as she escorted her to the bathroom. Jake was still on the opposite side of the room. The three rogue students shrugged off their packs and jackets, threw all evidence of their night walk in the storage cubbies under their bunks, and slipped under the covers.

"Did you do it?" Elio whispered. Their friends were still awake, wide eyes peeking out from under their blankets.

"Oh, we did it," Aria said. "I don't even know where to start."

TWENTY-SIX

MORNING CAME TOO SOON after a night spent sneaking around the ship. Aria dragged herself out of bed with heavy eyes as her alarm blared. Today was the day she would finally set foot on Sratta. Aria had dreamt of this moment her entire life, but now that it was here, she was too exhausted and disillusioned to care.

The landing was scheduled just an hour after the wake-up call, and everyone was busy packing up their things. Aria watched bitterly as her classmates ran around laughing and talking about what the next two weeks would bring. If she had never met Luca, she would be just like the rest of them, ignorantly playing into the system that kept so many others suffering. A tiny part of her longed to go back and feel that lightness again, but she knew it was better to know the truth. Something the mysterious blonde president said the night before played over and over in her mind: "We bear the burden so they don't have to." She made it sound so noble and selfless, as if the protestors were the true villains in their story.

Aria absently moved into the line behind Dima as they followed Jake and Rhen to the main cabin. Everything looked the same as the first time they saw it, but somehow it felt different—darker. They strapped into their seats and prepared for landing. Excited chatter buzzed around Aria as the ship's velocity diminished rapidly, throwing the students against their restraints. The commotion and excitement blurred into the background as Aria searched for any sign of Maya Brant or the blonde woman who she assumed must be the president of the mysterious Order. Neither were present.

The ship jolted harshly, whipping Aria's head back into the headrest and breaking her focus. The ship's speed dropped rapidly and turbulence shook the cabin. Aria gripped her harness, digging her nails into the coarse fabric. Suddenly, the ship lurched upward and began the descent. They rocked back and forth as the ship touched the ground and finally shut down.

"Welcome to Sratta, ladies and gentlemen," the captain said. "Please follow your cohort leaders to the designated exits."

Aria loosened her grip on the harness and pressed the button to release her from it. She stood up, feeling infinitely better than she had after takeoff. There was no puke on the floor and everyone appeared fully conscious, but their movements were strange and sluggish in the lesser gravity of the small planet. Aria followed the lines of Colonization students through the hallway to retrieve their belongings and exit the ship, the awkwardness of their comparatively lighter bodies causing them to half-float.

Despite her disillusionment of this entire ridiculous farce, an old spark ignited inside her as the door cracked open and the frigid outside air rushed in. The door slid upward, letting in the blinding sunlight. Aria opened her eyes as they adjusted to the brightness and stepped outside.

The cool air engulfed her and bit at her exposed skin, but the sun warmed her face. The ship had set down on a quakestone pad right on top of an enormous mountain, unlike anything on Drammat. The vast mountain range stretched out in every direction, with rocky cliffs, cascading waterfalls, and frozen lakes dotting the valleys. Every semi-smooth surface on the mountain was coated in massive pine trees and frosted with thick, powdery snow that sparkled in the sunlight.

A city rested in the valley below, on the edge of a wide, frozen lake and under the protection of a tall cliff face. Most of the city consisted of tiny, colorful homes built on top of each other, but one section near the frozen beach boasted beautiful, modern buildings. Aria inhaled the strong scent of pine and closed her eyes to the cold breeze on her skin.

"You see that ridge?" Jake asked, pointing to the top of the cliff that sheltered the city. "Our camp is on the other side of it, and we need to get there fast. This time of year, getting caught outside after dark is a death sentence."

"After dark?" Finlay asked. "It looks like early afternoon."

"Honestly," Rhen said, rolling her eyes. "Did anyone pay attention in Mission Briefing? Sratta is much smaller than Drammat, and its rotation is much faster. This time of year, they get about three hours of sunlight during their six-hour day, and we're less than an hour away from the next sunset. So let's get hiking. Put on your gravity simulation boots and line up so we can head out."

The group rushed to swap their typical uniform boots for the new pair, gaining back most of their speed and control. When they were all ready, they took off at a breakneck pace, plowing through half a meter of snow in most places. Aria noticed three other cohorts following in their wake, none of them Engineering. Hopefully, they were right on their tail. The sun was already dropping rapidly, and with it, the temperature plummeted. Despite the bitter cold, the sounds of the forest seemed to warm Aria. A waterfall cascaded over boulders somewhere in the distance. Birds sang and chirped as they dove through the air, and small woodland animals scurried around the forest floor. Some of the animals were familiar, but others were as foreign as the ground beneath her feet. As the seconds turned into minutes, not even her wonder and curiosity could stem off the cold.

Twenty excruciating minutes later, Aria stumbled into camp, her joints stiff and her nose running uncontrollably. A cloud of steam obscured her vision with every labored breath of the thin mountain air. The sun was beginning to paint the sky orange and purple as Aria crossed the barrier to the heated facility known simply as "camp". The heat of the building almost burned as it flowed over Aria's freezing skin. She rubbed her gloved hands over her legs in a desperate effort to squeeze blood flow back into her limbs. Her friends stumbled in beside her, looking as miserable as she felt. As she took stock of the shivering students, panic shot through her. Not a single Engineering student stood among the frozen crowd.

"What about the Engineering students?" Aria asked, her voice high-pitched. "Are they still out there?"

"Calm down, Blake," Rhen said. "The Engineering students still have a lot of work to do on the ship. They'll make it down to camp eventually, but the majority of their responsibilities have to do with the ship, so they'll be there most of the time."

"Oh," she said, relief and disappointment warring inside her. At least Luca was safe. Surely, they wouldn't be stuck in the ship for long.

"See, he'll be fine!" Dima said as their cohort followed Rhen and Jake further into the so-called camp.

It was more of a luxury cabin than a true camp. The massive quakestone and wood building with huge glass walls and ceilings showcased the forest's majestic beauty. The snow on the ground ran up the glass walls with snow drifts three meters high in some areas.

"This is your home for the next two weeks!" Rhen said, opening her arms wide to present the space. "This is the common area. Unlike the ship, you won't be separated by cohort for meals, so you can eat with your friends from other programs as long as you're on the same meal schedules. Through that door are our sleeping quarters—same arrangements as the ship. Get unpacked and get back out here in ten minutes. We start work immediately."

The Colonization cohort moved into their new quarters with plenty of time to spare. The room's configuration was exactly like the ship, so there was no need for haggling over preferred bunks. Aria and her friends took their seats at a corner table in the common room.

"Now that we're all here," Jake said, "let's go over some ground rules."

"Yay, rules," Dima muttered under her breath. "My favorite."

"Your schedules and assignments are the same as they were on the ship. We will not tolerate the waste of our precious time. The only time you have for socializing is during meals, so use it wisely. This is the big one: do not, under any circumstances, attempt to leave camp. You'd likely die a cold and lonely death, so it's not worth a fifty-credit bet or trying to impress your crush. This is the only time I'll say it. Now, for those of you who are on lab duty, Rhen will show you the lab now. I'll show the rest of you to the cave."

They separated into teams, and Dima, Jeslyn, Nick, Elio, and Finlay joined Aria and the other thirty-nine students on cave duty. Jake led the group through the maze-like building, passing labs, medical bays, and other cohorts' sleeping quarters. The farther they walked, the more walls and ceilings were made of glass, showcasing the enormous cliff face towering above them. Suddenly, the floor beneath their feet transformed as well. Aria trod lightly as she crossed the glass tube over the vast ice gorge beneath them. The sky bridge dumped them out at the cliff face, where a glass door sealed the cave system off from the building. A supply closet and mudroom welcomed them into the mountain.

"Grab your equipment and get to work," Jake said. "You'll find your assigned area and partner on the mission control app ."

Aria opened the app to find her assignment in red letters— "PARTNER: NICK PORTO, SECTION: 12A".

"Looks like you're with me, Goldilocks," Nick said. "Come on. Let's go pretend to work."

With equipment in their gloved hands, they descended into the dark, damp cave. It was even colder than the one in the Academy greenhouse. After just a few minutes of chipping away at the stone, Aria's hands were already stiff with cold. Without the thermal tech in their clothes, gloves, and hats, they wouldn't have survived long. Nick finally broke through the surface into an air pocket and pulled something out. The slimy, brown, and black mass was shriveled and oozing a greenish, sticky liquid. The moment it popped out of its hole with a sucking noise, Aria gagged.

"What is that?" she asked, covering her mouth and nose with her dirty glove. No dirt could be worse than the smell emitting from the gooey mass.

"A tupin, I guess," Nick said, muffled by his hand.

Dima gagged from across the cave at her station with another boy from their cohort. "That's nasty! How much of the tupin crop looks this bad?"

"This is the epicenter of the disease," Jake said. "Nearly the entire mountain is diseased, but not all of it is past saving. We're here because it gives us the best chance of finding the cause, so get to work."

Jake began his rounds, checking on each pairing in turn throughout their first five-hour shift in the cave. The heat from their thermal clothing staved off hypothermia and frost-bite, but it didn't make them warm by any means. When the mercy of their lunch break arrived, Aria's hands were so stiff she almost couldn't take her dripping gloves off. Even if they didn't have to endure the frigid environment, the smell would have been torturous enough. Every time someone opened up a new pore, another dose of the vomit-inducing stench was added to the noxious air.

When she eventually peeled the sticky gloves from her frozen hands and walked through the door to the sky bridge, the sun was rising over the mountain for the second time that day. For every day on Drammat, Sratta rotated four times, meaning four sunrises and four sunsets. That was going to take some getting used to.

Aria sat down at a table with her friends and pushed the large meal of soup, bread, and vegetables away from her. If she ever ate anything again, it would be a miracle. She at least needed to let the nausea subside before she would risk a bite. Her body shook from the cold that still pooled in her bones. She looked around at the drawn faces surrounding her.

"I can't take this," Dima whispered. "We're stuck freezing half to death to dig up rotting food for no reason. We should be spying on Celeste."

"Quiet, Dima," Aria whispered. "We don't know who's with them."

"Fine," she hissed. "But it's true."

"I know it's true, but what are we supposed to do about it? When we're not stuck on cave duty, we're sleeping or eating. We're always being watched."

"Celeste could say the same thing," Finlay whispered. "But somehow, she's planning on taking credit for solving the tupin problem."

"She'll need to get away from her Diplomacy duties," Brock said. "And if she can do it, so can we."

"Does anyone know what the Diplomacy kids are supposed to be doing?" Finlay asked.

Brock laughed. "Those softies are probably rehearsing cryptic answers to the Srattan officials about our research and projected timelines for the cure. I don't get why they're even here."

"Well, they are," Jeslyn said. "And one of those Diplomacy students is doing some shady stuff. I don't see how we can get away without alerting the defense officers."

"We did it on the ship," Nick said. "We just have to do the same thing here."

"On the ship, we got lucky," Aria said. "Luca's not here to overhear important conversations."

"So we need to be out of bed every night," Dima said. "And skip out on meals. We'll take turns covering for each other."

"You don't think that'll be a little suspicious?" Jeslyn asked.

"We don't have another option. If we're gonna have any shot at figuring out what's going on, we have to go where we're not supposed to be."

"Fine," Aria said. "We start tonight. I'll take the first shift. I'll see if Alika is available to help out."

Alika *was* available, and so were Luca and Amare—at least the first time. After the first call, it was hit or miss. But despite the new strategy and the sheer number of square meters they had searched, the following two days passed without a single clue or whiff of something strange afoot. At each meal, two of the friends scarfed down a few bites of food and left the cafeteria to sneak around in search of Celeste, her mother, or anything out of the ordinary, no matter how insignificant. At night, another pair would sneak out of the common room to do the same, then return halfway through the night for another pair to take the next shift. But Celeste and the Order seemed to be using the same strategy. Celeste always seemed to be right where she was supposed to be. The only exceptions were mealtimes when she was nowhere to be found and all night long when she was absent from the Diplomacy common room.

After another mind-numbing, body-chilling ten hours in the cave on day three, Aria and her friends from the cave group shivered through the dinner line and sat down with their meals. Aria had finally learned to disassociate her meals from the rotting tupins they spent their days harvesting. The rest of their friends in the lab group had meals an hour before they did, so Milo and Allison had just completed a shift and reported nothing new. Now it was Aria and Nick's turn to scour the halls. Celeste was absent, as was usual at dinner. Aria gulped down her soup and stuffed a few bites of bread and vegetables into her mouth.

"Wish us luck," she said through a mouthful of bread.

Nick chugged the rest of his soup and stood to follow her. They walked out of the common room and turned the corner. They had mapped out what they could of the facility and were searching sector by sector. Today's shift would take them into the far reaches of the Colonization wing that was used by full-time government employees rather than students. Alika answered when Aria called and Luca stood beside her.

"Hey," Aria whispered. "Are you guys almost done up there?"

"We still have a few things to prepare for takeoff, but it looks like we'll be done in the next couple of days."

"I can't wait. Will this be a little vacation for you?"

"I'm sure they'll have us fixing something down there," Alika said.

Aria and Nick walked into their corresponding bathrooms and fell silent as Alika activated their invisibility. This sneaking around business went so much more smoothly when Alika was around. They emerged into the hallway and followed Alika's instructions to find each other. Arm in arm, they tread lightly through the corridors. They passed their own sleeping area, the lab where the other half of their cohort spent their time, and several conference rooms before they heard voices emanating from the far wing. They crept past dozens of private bedrooms, some with doors wide open and their occupants entertaining company inside. They found another lab, and peered in. There were far more people in the lab than anywhere else in the wing. Aria scanned the groups of scientists until her eyes locked onto one partnership near the back. Celeste and Instructor Reed sat hunched over a microscope, a container of rotten tupins on one side and one filled with healthy tupins on the other. Celeste's hands cradled a vial filled with clear liquid. Of course Celeste would be here. They had started their search in the Diplomacy wing, but they should have known that she would be with Reed. Aria stepped into the lab, Nick following close behind her. They dodged scientists as they moved from one table to another, and eventually, they made their way to the back corner, in earshot of Celeste and their instructor.

"It seems to be working," Celeste said. "I just don't know what excuse I can make to explain how a Diplomacy student discovered it."

"Give me a day or two to come up with a solution," Reed said. "I'm sure I can vouch for you and say that I gave you a chance to help in my research. Let me work out the details first."

"Thank you. I'm meeting my mother soon, so I need to take off early today. Is that okay?"

"Certainly. Give my regards to your mother, dear."

Celeste nodded and smiled, walking around the room and hanging up a green lab coat at the door. She walked quickly and with purpose, unknowingly making Aria and Nick scramble to keep up with her. They turned so many times that

Aria no longer knew where they were in the facility when Celeste finally came to a stop at the juncture of two hallways. One of the two corridors ended at a circular door that led to the outside world. Footsteps echoed from behind Aria and she turned to find Maya Brant on a collision course with her. She pressed herself against the wall and held her breath. The second lady passed her and embraced her daughter.

"Hi, baby. How is your mission going?"

"It's going," Celeste said.

"You still haven't gained access to the students' lab, have you?"

"I will. I'm just being cautious. If I walk around like I own the place while everyone else is under strict rules, someone's gonna suspect something."

"Smart girl. I know you'll make your father and me proud —make the Order proud. I don't think I need to remind you of what will happen if you fail."

"No!" Celeste shouted, almost hysterically. She reined in her emotions with a visible struggle and spoke again, more calmly. "Of course not. I'll figure something out. You can count on me, okay?"

"Good," Brant said, resting a hand on her daughter's cheek. "I wanted to check on you, but I have to go now. I have an assignment that can't wait, and I'm not sure when I'll be back—maybe two days."

"Good luck," Celeste said. "Be safe."

The mother and daughter hugged, then went their separate ways. Celeste retreated further into the building while her mother opened the huge, vault-style door and left the warmth of the inside for the frozen world outdoors.

"We have to follow her," Aria said.

"I'll send Dima a message to let the others know what happened," Nick said.

"I'm going out."

Luca appeared at Alika's side over Aria's vision. "Aria, no. It's way too cold out there. She could have a pod out there and be half-way across the city by now."

"I have to try."

Heavy footfalls echoed through the hallway again, this time a whole group of them. Aria's nerves buzzed as she imagined Brant getting farther and farther away. Dima, Jeslyn, Elio, Finlay, and Brock appeared at the end of the hall.

"Dima," Nick said, "tell Aria she can't just follow that woman outside!"

"Right now?" Dima asked as they caught up to them at the exit door. "Aria, you could die! You heard Jake—we can't leave!"

"The sun just rose a little while ago," Aria said. "So I have at least another hour before I need to be indoors."

"Aria," Jeslyn said, grabbing her shoulders. "Think about this."

"I am. I have to do this. Celeste's mission is only one tiny part of whatever is going on. We need to know what the real mission is. Something terrible is going on. I can feel it."

Dima sighed and set her jaw. "Fine. But if you're risking your life, so am I."

Aria blanched. "No, Dima. Only one person needs to take this risk."

"Fine," Dima said. "Then it's gonna be me."

"No, that's not..." She fell silent and rubbed her head.

"When are you gonna understand that we're equally invested in this?" Elio asked, pushing past Dima. "I'm going too, and there's nothing you can say to stop me."

"Me too," Jeslyn said. "I can't let you idiots die without me."

"I'm always up for a little trouble," Brock said, stepping forward.

"Besides," Finlay said, "if we make it back by sunset, there's minimal risk."

"I can't believe we're doing this," Nick said, stepping in front of all of them. "They're gonna know we left."

"We'll have to figure out our cover story on the way back," Aria said. She stepped to the door and raised the chip from Luca to the control panel. "We'll lose her if we don't go now."

After a moment while they waited for Alika to do her work, the doors slid open, and Aria burst out into the cold, her friends in her wake. The frigid wind immediately burned the exposed skin on her face and hands and burrowed deep into her bones. She pulled out her thermal gloves and tugged the hood of her jacket over her head as she surveyed the landscape. The whole world was white from the recent snow, but Brant was nowhere in sight. A bolt of terror went through her body, but it wasn't her own.

"Please be careful," Luca said, standing at Alika's side. Aria nodded once and stepped into the frozen world.

TWENTY-SEVEN

"LOOK," Jeslyn said, pointing to the snow at her feet. "Footprints."

"Those have to be hers," Finlay said. "This is fresh snow, and nobody else would have been out here since this morning."

Aria knelt and examined the prints. The deep snow went almost up to her knees, so Second Lady Brant must have had to drag her legs through the snow. It looked more like a plowed path than footprints. Aria traced the messy path across the icy landscape. It cut right to the cliff face and followed the rock's curve until it disappeared around a bend. She stood up and faced her friends.

"I only said it would be safe so you'd let me go, but the truth is, I know this is really stupid. At the very least, I could lose my spot at the Academy."

"We're with you," Dima said. "Let's go catch up to her."

Nagging guilt coiled in Aria's stomach. What had possessed her to involve her friends in this controversy in the first place? Whatever her initial reasons, it was clear that there was no shaking her friends' determination to follow her. They might launch themselves over a cliff if she did it first, and the realization made her skin crawl. Shaking her head, she turned to leave, and the entire group trailed behind her.

They trudged through the fresh, light powder covering tightly packed older snow, sending icy plumes into the air with every movement. Aria stopped at the bend in the cliff face and peeked around the edge. Only snow, rock, and ice waited for them there. She turned back to the faces of her unfalteringly loyal friends. They had no idea what they were walking into, but they wouldn't listen to reason.

In their defense, neither would she.

"Clear," she said, waving her friends onward. She tried to run as she turned the corner, but the snow caking her boots tripped her with each stride. The effort required to take a single step, combined with the thin mountain air, had them all exhausted only minutes into the trek. The sun was past its apex and steadily setting. They would have to turn back if they didn't make it to some form of shelter soon. Dima, who was now in front, turned the next corner and suddenly stopped. Aria slammed into her back.

"Ouch! What—"

"Shhh," Dima whispered, pointing forward into the distance.

Aria squinted. The light had diminished somewhat, but something was still visible through the grove of trees that rested between their group and the massive stone wall. They were only paces away from the base of the monstrous cliff, where a dark figure stood, pressing a hand to the face of the stone. A beeping noise echoed through the grove, and a whoosh of warm air permeated the clearing as a hidden door slid away.

"Something tells me we don't have access to that door," Aria said. "We can't let it close."

"I have an idea," Elio said. "Just be ready to move."

Second Lady Brant stepped through the doorframe and into the dimly lit hallway beyond. The door immediately began sliding shut behind her. Hot panic shot through Aria's body. If they didn't make it inside, they would likely die of hypothermia. An alarm blared from inside the mountain and Aria jumped back behind the relative safety of the natural wall.

"I'm gonna need some help at the East door," Brant said.

Her words trailed off as she walked further into the mountain. Aria peaked out to find the door jammed open.

"What did you do?" she whispered to Elio.

"I just stuck one of those huge pine cones between the door and the cliff to jam it," Elio said with a crooked smile. "It's gonna suck trying to get that out."

Nick smacked Elio on the back. "Atta boy! Let's go before that backup comes to find your pinecone."

The sun was already behind the mountain as they ran through the open door. They were safe—at least from freezing to death. Alika's voice cut into their thoughts as she took over their neurolink systems.

"You're all invisible to anyone with a neurolink system implanted in their nervous system. Most of Sratta's population isn't connected, so I can't guarantee it'll work on everyone you come across in there. But I can trick most surveillance systems as well, and I can guarantee that your locations and neurolink surveillance feeds are showing that you're back at camp preparing for bed."

"That won't do us much good when eyewitnesses will be able to refute the information," Aria said. "Still, at least they can't track us. Thank you, Alika."

The long corridor was bare and the only way in was straight, so the group proceeded into the narrow space two by two. Faint evidence of life came into hearing—a man and a woman talking nearby, children crying, miserable groans and cries, and the clinking of metal on metal. The hair on Aria's neck stood on end and a shiver ran from her head to her feet. The deeper into the mountain they plunged, the louder the tortured sounds grew. Aria's stomach lurched at the sound of a particularly young cry. The knot in her stomach tightened, and she clutched her abdomen. The hallway finally came to a bend, and Dima checked for danger beyond the turn before the rest followed. The end of the hallway came shortly, marked by a yellow light spilling into the narrow space.

Aria reached the end of the hallway first, pressing herself up to the wall and peeking around the corner into a massive courtyard. The room was reminiscent of the ship they traveled to Sratta on, but with five levels of wraparound balconies rather than three. The biggest difference was the darkness. Where the ship was bright and modern, the monstrosity looming over them was dark, illuminated only by dim yellow lights bolted to the walls. Aria fought back nausea as her nostrils burned with the stench of human waste. She plugged her nose and surveyed the room. Something was strange about the balconies.

She squinted, trying to put a finger on what was bothering her. As the reality of what she was seeing sunk in, she gasped and reeled backward. Faces, hundreds of *human* faces, stared blankly through iron bars. Some faces were old, others as young as toddlers, all with widely varying features. The one thing they all had in common was the vacancy in their eyes, as if they were already dead. The cries of a baby picked up again, echoing from somewhere in the cavernous room. Aria's dinner threatened to return and her knees buckled, forcing her to lean against the wall for support.

"What is it?" Nick asked.

"Cages," Aria breathed, her voice trembling. "Full of...people."

"Cages?" Nick asked. "Like a prison?"

"I don't think so," Aria stammered. "Can you hear the kids crying? We need to get closer, find out what's going on."

"We aren't armed," Dima said. "We can't just stroll in and save the day."

"Good thing we're here on a recon mission, not a rescue mission," Aria said. "We just need a way to prove that Drammat's government is behind all of this."

"What's that?" Elio pointed across the courtyard to the far corner of the second level, the same level where they now stood.

Nestled in the corner was a group of people dressed in colorful, formal gowns and suits, all sitting at a long table. A colossal feast overflowed from the table, and the guests gluttonously ate and drank between their laughter and conversation. Candlelight danced off the jewels and expensive fabrics adorning their bodies. Classical music played, probably in an attempt to drown out the sounds of agony all around them. The man at the head of the table was welcoming a newcomer who stood out from the rest. Rather than fine clothing, she wore a sturdy outdoor suit in all black.

"Brant," Aria said, her voice cold.

"Who are those people?" Finlay asked. "Royalty?"

Aria shook her head. "Sratta doesn't have any countries with nobility."

"Maybe they're just rich," Dima said. "I say we go see what they're talking about."

Aria was already shaking her head. "The prisoners will give us away."

"We'll tell them we're here to free them!" Dima said. She darted past Aria onto the second-floor balcony.

"Dima!" Aria gasped. She followed her out onto the balcony where her impulsive friend was crouched down at the first cell. "Dima, what did you say to them?"

She stood from the cage. By the way the eyes of the young

women in the cage bulged as they looked from Dima to Aria, it was immediately clear that they did not have neurolink systems for Alika to toy with.

"I told them we're here to make things right, and we need their help to get around unseen and unheard."

"And?" Aria asked, knowing that there had to be more.

"And I said we'd try to free as many of them as possible."

Aria's eyes bugged and her stomach dropped. "We can't just promise something like that, Dima!"

"I'm sorry, but I can't just leave kids in cages!"

Panic swelled in Aria's chest and pushed out to her fingertips. What was Dima doing promising something like that? Hadn't she just said that this was a recon mission? Yet even as she thought it, the cries and tortured moans of children rang in her ears. How could they leave this place without trying to help? Aria raked her fingers violently through her hair as she paced. This was suicide. They were just kids, not soldiers, not law enforcement.

"Even if we get them out, where are they supposed to go?" Aria asked. "It's a frozen wasteland out there. If the sun is down, they'll die almost immediately."

She gestured to the half-naked, starving women in the cell in front of them.

"You," Dima said, pointing to a girl who couldn't have been older than fifteen. "Are there shelters in Mojari? Resources for people who need help?"

"Yes," she said in a thick accent. "There are some homeless shelters, but they do not have the money to take care of us all. We are too many."

"Then we'll donate all our credits and send more when we get back to Drammat," Dima said, looking around at her friends for confirmation.

Everyone nodded.

"Okay, that's settled. What about a place for orphans?"

The girl stared back at her blankly.

"A place for children without parents?"

Recognition showed on the women's faces, and another teen girl spoke up. "Yes, there are those places as well, but like the shelters, they are very poor."

"We'll have to make it work," Aria said. "For now, we need to get you free and then get you to a warm place with food."

She couldn't believe what she was saying. There was no way any of this would work. But if they didn't have the prisoners' cooperation, they'd never get the proof they needed without being discovered. Her conscience burned a little hotter with each lie that left her lips.

"Let's split up to cover more ground," she said. "I'll start with one of the servants. Elio, you're with me. Everyone else, take the prisoners. Half this way, half that way. We need information about what they're doing here and who's in charge."

Silent nods confirmed her friends' agreement as all but Elio left her. Word of an impending rescue got around so efficiently that by the time they were halfway down the first wall of cells, the prisoners were silently smiling at them as they passed. The first few cells were packed with young women, followed by young men, some as young as twelve or thirteen. Despite the new spark of life in the prisoners' eyes, sadness and pain reflected there. Bruises and dirt obscured their faces, and their ragged clothes hung loosely on their rail-thin bodies.

As they turned the corner toward the dining area overlooking the courtyard, the demographic of the prisoners changed again. Children, some so small they couldn't yet walk, pressed their dirt-covered, tear-stained faces between the metal bars. They were packed in so tightly they had to walk and crawl all over each other to reach the front. The smell of urine, feces, and vomit was so strong it burned. Some of the older girls held infants on their tiny frames.

Aria choked back the cry that threatened to give up their

position as tears spilled onto her cheeks. She clenched the fabric of her shirt as she stumbled along the balcony. Nearing collapse, she leaned against the railing, staring into the faces of the children in the nearest cell.

"Aria," Elio whispered, breaking her from her dark thoughts. "We need to keep going, or we'll be seen. Babies can't understand to not make noise."

Aria shook herself. Elio's hand was on her back, and his eyes pleaded with her to follow him. Tears streaked his cheeks. She looked around the massive room with water blurring her vision. If every cell was as full as the ones they passed, there had to be thousands of men, women, and children locked up in the facility. Elio was right—they needed to move.

She turned back to the dinner party that continued as if everything was completely normal. Rage rushed through her veins. Someone would pay for hurting these innocent children.

They crept past the last cell filled with young girls and crouched behind a stone pillar. Aria scanned the servants attending to the guests. One girl stood out from the other servants. She was the most beautiful person Aria had ever seen, but the pain in her face told of a tragic life. Her eyes were like pools of grief that she could see from across the room.

"I'm taking the pretty servant girl," Aria said.

"I've got that shy-looking guy in the back."

Elio darted to the far side of the room as Aria crawled on the floor to the opposite end of the overhang. When she entered the dining room, the smell of human waste was drowned out by food and perfume. A narrow hallway opened up to the main dining area, where servants went in with empty platters and bottles and came out with full ones. She crouched low and ran through the hallway, emerging into a well-lit kitchen. A lip in the wall jutted out between the hall and the ovens. As footsteps approached from behind, she darted behind it and flattened herself against the wall. She held her breath as a butler entered with two empty wine bottles, tossed them in a pile with the others, and grabbed a full one. He popped the cork as he walked back out to the feast. A shaky sigh rattled in Aria's chest as she closed her eyes.

Footsteps echoed in the small hallway again, but not the same ones as before. They were feminine, the light clicking of high heels. A woman with rich, dark hair that fell below the waistline of an expensively embroidered mauve dress entered the kitchen. Her deep brown eyes and flawless almond-colored skin were revealed as she turned to pick up another platter of meat. The beautiful servant girl hefted the tray and turned to leave. Panicking, Aria frantically lifted a plate from the storage shelf to her left and cringed as she dropped it to the floor with a crash. The servant girl jumped as the plate shattered. She dropped the overflowing platter and squinted toward Aria's dark hiding place. Slowly, she followed the sound of the crash to the lip in the wall. As the stunning girl's face peeked into the corner, her concerned eyes widened and she gasped.

"Shh," Aria whispered, pressing a hand over the girl's mouth.

One of Instructor Rojas's lessons from her first-semester language class resonated in her mind. "If you want someone to trust you," she had said, "start by using their native language".

"I want to help you!" Aria whispered in unsteady Srattan Spanish. "Please, don't scream!" Slowly, she released the girl. "I want to help you. My name is Aria. What's yours?"

The girl responded in English with a thick, smooth accent.

"My name is Marisol, but most call me Sol. You say you can help me. How?"

Relieved to be speaking English again, Aria whispered, "I need to know some things, so I can help the people in those cages out there—and you, if you want. Can I ask you some questions?"

Marisol nodded, so Aria continued despite her budding guilt at insinuating that she might be able to save this girl. It wasn't a total lie. Hopefully, the information would help law-enforcement save them soon enough. That's what she told herself, at least.

"Thank you. Who's in charge here?"

"Mr. Morales," Marisol said, her voice trembling. The name tickled a memory in Aria's mind. Hadn't the mysterious Order President mentioned a Mr. Morales? "He is the man at the head of the table, wearing the finest suit."

"What does he do?"

"He is a businessman. And that is a business dinner."

"Okay," Aria said, losing patience. "What does he sell?"

Marisol dropped her head, staring at the floor. Frustration bloomed in Aria's stomach. She had to bite her lip to keep from grasping the girl's shoulders and shaking her. Surely they didn't have much time before someone noticed that Marisol was missing.

"What does he do with the people in the cages?" she asked.

Marisol fidgeted with her hands, refusing to look up at Aria. "They are one of his income sources," she finally said through building tears. "But you cannot free them. If you are caught, he will kill you. And if he learns I betrayed him, he will kill me as well." Her hands began to shake, almost imperceptibly, and a single tear streaked down her face and stained her dress.

"He sells people?" Aria asked, the words tasting like acid in her mouth. "Where does he get them?"

"He buys them, just like his other assets, like technology or medicine. Sometimes they are given to him as gifts by other powerful people."

She was looking around as if she expected someone to discover and punish her at any moment.

"Did he buy you as well?" Aria asked, taking the girl's nervous hands in her own.

"Yes, but I do not remember. He bought me when I was very young. I am one of the lucky ones."

Her eyes darted around the room, never settling on Aria. A sickening feeling settled over Aria, and she feared she knew exactly what was going on here.

"Are you more than just his servant?" Aria asked.

Marisol bit her bottom lip and violently clamped her eyelids shut, sending rivers of tears streaming down her face.

"Sol, you can tell me," Aria said. "I need to know what kind of man I'm dealing with here. Let me help you."

"Yes," she whispered after a long, agonizing moment. "I am a member of his household—one of his mistresses. I should not betray his trust by speaking with you. He is very kind to me. He tells me he loves me and showers me with gifts, and I have never been locked in a cage or beaten like the others. I am fortunate."

Bile rose in Aria's throat as she tried to speak. "What do you mean you're fortunate?" she choked out.

"Most people in my position do not have someone to love and take care of them. Some things about my life are difficult, but I am grateful that I did not end up with a worse family."

Aria's skin crawled and a cold shiver ran up her spine.

"Sol, this is not a family. You don't need to feel lucky because others have it worse than you—your happiness matters. You deserve the freedom to choose your own life, to choose who you want to be with and who you don't. You're worthy of more."

"Sol," a gruff voice yelled in Srattan Spanish. "Did you break something? Hurry up with the pork!"

"Go!" Aria said, letting Marisol's hands drop. "Then come back."

Marisol scooped up the platter she had dropped, repositioned the fallen meat, and shuffled out to the dining room. Aria clutched her abdomen and covered her mouth as she forced herself not to wretch.

"Idiot girl," the same voice said. That had to be Morales. "I swear, she's cost me more than she's worth."

"I'll take her off your hands," another man said with a serpent-like edge to his voice.

"No," Morales said. "She's not for sale. I made a promise, so I'm stuck with her. Besides, she has other skills."

Morales and his guests burst into laughter as the tapping footsteps returned, echoing through the hallway. Marisol rushed into the kitchen and turned to find Aria in her hiding place. Her lip quivered as tears pooled in her eyes again.

"Who buys the people?" Aria asked, voice cracking as she fought back tears.

"Many people," Marisol said. "They all go to different homes."

"Okay, but typically, where do they go? Is it in this country? Is it even on this planet? On another planet?"

"Clients come from all over the galaxy," Marisol said. "But generally, the age and sex of the assets determines what they are used for and how much they cost."

"What do you mean?" Aria asked.

"The older assets, both men and women, are generally people who have been trafficked by their families and were sold to Mr. Morales because they stopped being profitable. Mr.

Morales usually sells them to workhouses who cannot afford the more expensive young men."

"Wait. Hold it. Their own families sold them? How could anyone do that?" Aria's nausea continued to intensify. If she didn't get herself under control, she would lose her meager last meal on the kitchen floor.

"Sratta is one of the poorest planets in the galaxy," Marisol said. "People do what they must to survive."

"But that's horrible."

"It is the way things are. It is more common on Sratta because of our traditions and poverty, but it happens everywhere."

"Not on Drammat," Aria said.

"Drammat is Mr. Morales's best supplier," Marisol said. "Just two days ago, they sold him over five hundred new assets."

"People," she said, almost to herself. "They're selling people. That can't be right. How would they even do that?"

Even as she said it, the leaked footage of the lost souls massacre surfaced in her mind. The old-fashioned scanners on doors to cargo holds on the ship. The assets the Order President kept referring to during the overheard meeting. Suddenly, it all made a sick kind of sense. The only question left was why they would start a famine. If human trafficking was their game, wouldn't they want a higher population to allow them to exploit a larger number of people?

"Not all people are meant to be free," Marisol said. "Slavery has and always will exist. Mr. Morales has simply made the process more efficient. When your planet needs to get rid of so many people at once, it makes more sense to use his service than try to sell them individually."

"Even children?" Aria whispered, more to herself than Marisol.

"Yes. They are the most expensive. Especially the pretty ones."

Aria closed her eyes and breathed deeply, gripping the storage shelf behind her. Her entire body was shaking now, her mind reeling. Marisol talked about the most horrifying things as if they were discussing the weather. She had been abused and brainwashed for so long that to her, they *were* normal.

"Now you see why I say that I am lucky," Marisol said. "When other women who look like me would be sold for a high price, only to be abused by countless strangers, I am here. I am at the mercy of only one man, and he shows me kindness. I am very, very lucky."

Tears streamed down Aria's face. It was worse than she ever could have imagined. Dima was right. They couldn't leave these poor people here a day longer. Who knew how long they had? If they left the prisoners here and took back information for law enforcement to use, it might be too late for the current prisoners by the time they did anything about it—if they did anything at all. Frankly, Aria didn't trust any part of the system anymore.

"How can we free you?" Aria asked, pulling back to look into Marisol's deep brown eyes. "All of you."

"I still fear you will be killed if you try."

"We need to try, Sol. Please."

This time, Aria meant it, and Marisol seemed to sense her determination. After a long moment of hesitation, she spoke softly.

"You must go to the first floor where the controls are," she whispered, her entire body shuddering now. "From there, you can open all of the cells and the outer doors. I don't know how to operate it. I only see the guards opening cells when assets are bought or sold. But there are guards all around. It is impossible."

"Thank you. Now, forget you ever saw me. Stay calm and act like everything is normal. We'll get you out of here—I promise."

"Good luck," Marisol said, returning to her native language. "Please be careful."

"Thank you," Aria whispered. She ran through the kitchen to the hallway on the opposite end and peeked around the wall.

Marisol had rejoined the guests, and everyone was busy listening to a very charismatic Mr. Morales tell a story. From her new vantage point, she saw that Maya Brant sat in the middle of the long table, taking part in the feast. Aria slipped out of the kitchen and snuck back through the dining room. All five of her friends were waiting in the hallway.

"Jeez! Took you long enough!" Nick said. "We were worried you got caught!"

"Sorry, but I got a lot of info. Let's go back to the doorway so we can talk."

Her friends nodded their agreement, and they set off toward their original hiding place. A little girl, who couldn't be older than two, stuck her hand through the bars and touched Aria's leg as she passed by. Aria paused and crouched down to look at the little girl. Her hopeless, lightless eyes glistened with moisture. Aria held her tiny hand and squeezed gently. She stood again, wiping tears from her eyes as she caught up to her friends. They finally made it back to the doorway and ducked inside the hall.

"I think I'll have nightmares about this place for the rest of my life," Dima whispered.

"Tell me about it," Nick said. "Can you imagine what these poor people have gone through?"

"What did you all find out?" Aria asked.

Her friends relayed the stories of several prisoners and Aria's heart only broke into smaller pieces. The people languishing in cells all around her had experienced everything from homelessness and drug addiction to sex trafficking at the hands of their desperate parents. Whatever their route to Morales, at some point, they had all become worth less than the survival their life could buy the people who were supposed to love them.

"So how does Drammat fit into all this?" Dima asked. "We saw Brant come in here."

"That's the worst part," Aria said. "Marisol told me that Drammat is one of Morales's suppliers."

"Suppliers?" Jeslyn asked, horrified. "So, Drammat is selling people to this Morales guy? How? People don't just go missing anymore."

"Lost souls," Finlay said, his eyes wide. "That's how they're keeping it quiet."

Aria nodded as disgust flowed from Luca to double her own revulsion. She suddenly realized that neither Alika or Luca had spoken in some time. They must be back on shift, though Luca was clearly catching glimpses. Aria cursed inwardly. They would have to gather evidence without Alika's help.

"Sol said Drammat just dropped off five hundred lost souls," Aria said. "I think Drammat or the Order must have piggybacked off our field trip. Whether or not they're already here, we need to free these people, just like you said, Dima. They may not have another day."

"Any ideas?" Jeslyn asked.

"The bottom floor is where the controls for the whole facility are," Aria said, pointing over the railing to where a security desk stood guard over dozens of cubicles of working men and women—probably salespeople. "If we get down there and create a distraction big enough to leave those controls unguarded, we can open all of the cells and the outer doors."

"How do we get past the guards?" Dima asked.

"We tell the adult prisoners to stage a fight," Finlay said. "The guards will be distracted."

"What about when they're free?" Nick asked.

"We gamble," Aria said as she clenched her jaw. "Thousands of people will be flooding out of this place. We'll try to keep the guards confused as long as possible. Eventually, we'll need to fight so the last of them can get out."

"And when they're all gone, how do we get out?" Brock asked.

A long silence hung in the air.

"If we die, won't the truth die with us?" Elio asked. "Alika isn't around to broadcast our neurolink feeds to the public."

"We can't wait," Aria said. "Every moment we're here is another chance to get caught. Keep an open link to Alika and make sure your neurolink is set to record. As long as Alika has the footage, she and Luca will make sure that everyone on Drammat sees it.

Heads nodded around the circle and Dima thrust her hand into the middle.

"I'm in," she said.

Nick laid his hand on Dima's with a smile. Jeslyn, Elio, and Finlay each followed. Aria put her hand on top of the stack and looked around at her friends with a subdued smile. How had she gone from her lonely existence to having so many incredible people for friends? At least if she died, she would die among heroes.

TWENTY-EIGHT

RAGE PROPELLED Aria through the hallway, her friends following closely behind. Dima caught up to the group and nodded once at Aria. So, the prisoners had agreed to the plan —good. The news would soon reach the designated prisoners and a fight would break out. Aria's eyes burned with emotion as she backtracked to a bend in the hall, where a narrow doorway opened to a dimly lit staircase. Her face was raw from shed tears, but none fell now. She was certain she would fall apart later, but for the moment, her mind was hyper-fixated on releasing Sol and every other person in this abhorrent place. She crept down the stairs and peeked into the second-floor hallway. A lone guard paced at the balcony entrance. A steady stream of worry filtered into her from Luca, but he and Alika still hadn't reappeared.

"One guard," she whispered. "It hasn't started yet."

She turned the corner onto the last flight of stairs and tiptoed to the first floor. Aria peeked out into the hallway again and immediately fell back. One guard was positioned on either side of the archway at the end of the hall that led into the courtyard. Someone shouted from deep inside the vast room. Another voice yelled back. Suddenly, dozens of voices rose as a loud bang echoed through the hallway. The guards yelled back in their native language, and Aria stuck her head out again to find only one guard left in sight. The screams and sounds of fist hitting flesh intensified and the last guard standing in their way sprinted into the fray.

"They're gone," Aria said. "Let's move!"

She bolted out into the hallway, her friends on her heels as they barrelled toward the opening. They halted at the threshold and Aria pressed herself against the wall to sneak a glance into the courtyard. The only guards in view were busy breaking up fights between prisoners at the back of the vast building. The employees in the cubicles covering half of the courtyard floor popped out from behind their secluded bubbles to watch the action. On the other side of the court-yard, even the control desk, usually teeming with guards, was empty. The massive screen above the desk displayed security footage from all over the facility, but no one was monitoring it.

"We'd better get this done before one of the guards comes back to the control desk," Nick said.

"Wait," Aria said. "Isn't it weird that they left our path completely unobstructed?"

"It's total chaos in there," Elio said. "This has probably never happened before. The prisoners are risking a lot, all so we can get over there."

"Something just feels wrong," Aria said. "Even with Alika's help, I have a hard time believing that we've never been seen with so many cameras on us."

"Look," Nick said. "We don't have time for this. We have to move now!"

Aria's stomach turned over. The guards' one job was to handle threats. It couldn't be so easy to outsmart them. Could Alika, a kid still in her training, really have outsmarted such an advanced security system? Despite the merit of her worries, Nick and Elio were right, too. If they didn't move now, they might never get another chance.

"Fine," she huffed. "Four go to the controls and hide out under the table until we're sure the coast is clear. Two stay here to keep watch and signal us if anything goes wrong."

"Works for me," Dima said. "You, me, Elio, and Nick to the table. Jes and Fin keep watch?"

Jeslyn and Finlay positioned themselves on the wall and peered into the courtyard. They nodded, and the other four sprung from behind their cover at a full sprint. If Morales and his guests were still in the dining room, or if a single guard looked back, they would be completely exposed.

Aria felt utterly naked as she sprinted across the open floor. Adrenaline pumped through her veins as they reached the desk and slid underneath. She glanced at her friends under the desk and back at those who remained in the hallway. Aria's heart stuttered as she saw Jeslyn's expression. Her eyes were wide in warning as she held up one hand. Finlay wasn't with her anymore. Aria's heart pounded violently. She scanned the floor for any sign of him.

"There," Dima whispered, pointing across the floor.

A burly guard held Finlay up to a wall by his jacket, balled up in the massive fist of the towering man. Aria's stomach clenched as regret immediately seized her. If she hadn't been so afraid to move, they could have been in and out before Finlay was seen. Jeslyn frantically motioned for them to stay put, but if one guard already caught Finlay, it was only a matter of time before the rest started looking for accomplices. Aria took a deep breath, steeled her nerves, and stood up at the control panel. The computer's language was set to Srattan Spanish, and she only recognized a handful of the words on the desk. Panic welled up in her. She scanned the long desk again, searching for familiar words. "Open" was a good place to start.

The fighting behind her increased in volume. Movement caught her eye from under the table, and she did a double-take. It was empty. Where were her friends? She spun around to find that all five were clashing with a hoard of uniformed guards. An overwhelming desire to help threatened to break her, but she forced herself to turn back around. Open, open, open—it had to be somewhere. A large, red button with the Spanish word for "open" caught her eye. Relief rippled through her body. It was accompanied by a word she didn't understand, but she would have to take the risk.

"Aria!" Dima screamed.

Aria's guilt deepened as she ignored Dima's cry. Whatever was wrong would have to wait. She reached for the button as the bang of a gun echoed from somewhere behind her. Searing pain shot up her arm as something solid slammed into her hand, throwing it off course. A distant cry rang in her ears as she fell to her knees. Something told her that the primal, echoing cry was her own.

She looked down at the injured hand with blurred vision. Blood poured from a gaping hole in her hand and soaked her clothes as her body trembled.

She peered back at her friends. They were captured, already being restrained. Four guards were sprinting toward her, but none was close enough to reach her.

She pressed her injured hand between her legs, gritting her teeth as consciousness waned, and pulled herself up on the desk. For her and her friends, it was over, but it didn't have to be for the rest of the prisoners. She reached across the desk again and stretched her uninjured arm out to hit the red button.

Just as her finger grazed the surface of the button, something attached to her hair, brutally pulling her backward until her neck popped loudly. The vice-like grip reversed the motion, smashing her face into the desk. Intense pain shot through her head and into her spine. Her attacker released her, and she collapsed on the floor.

A blurry figure stood above her, a woman with silky, raven hair. Blackness crept in from the edges of her vision until the figure above her disappeared, and with it, so did the pain.

Aria gasped as she sat up. Throbbing pain boomed in her head, and intense heat radiated from her right hand. She cried out and immediately regretted moving so quickly. *What happened?* She lay back down on the hard floor beneath her and tried to make out her surroundings. Her friends were there and no one else looked seriously injured, but a row of bars separated them from the balcony outside. Memories of children in cages and gunfire rushed into her conscious mind, and she almost cried out. They were on one of the upper levels with a cell all to themselves.

"Aria!" Dima gasped, her voice hoarse, presumably from crying or maybe screaming. She threw her arms around Aria's neck and cried into her hair.

Aria winced, flinching out of Dima's clutch.

"Oh, sorry! Great Explorer, Aria! We didn't think you'd wake up."

"What happened?" Aria whispered, pressing her left hand to her forehead. On closer inspection, her friends *were* injured. Each one of them had a thin river of dried blood running down the right side of their face.

"We don't know," Finlay said. "From what we could tell, they knew we were here the whole time."

"Aria, I'm so sorry," Nick interrupted. "This is all my fault.

You knew something was off and I didn't trust your judgment."

"No," Aria said, grunting as she pushed herself up onto her left elbow. "I was the one who brought you all here without an actual plan. What you said made sense. The truth is that we never had a chance. I'm responsible for what happens to us."

"That's not true," Dima said. "We followed you here because what Drammat is doing is wrong. We didn't even know the half of it until we got here, but now that we do, I know we did the right thing."

Aria nodded, her eyes focused on a point in the distance. "At least Luca, Alika, and Amare have our footage, and the rest of our friends are still free. They'll make sure everyone sees the proof. It won't have been for nothing."

Her friends' silence dragged on long enough for Aria to look up at them with dread curling in her stomach. "What?"

Dima gestured to the dried blood on her face, her eyes welling with unshed tears. "They took our main memory hubs and disconnected the whole neurolink system. We have no idea what got through to Alika—if anything."

The shred of hope that Aria had been clinging to evaporated. That couldn't be right. Surely Alika had received something, maybe a little would be enough to start a fire that would lead to change. Her brain wouldn't let her believe anything else. Her life couldn't end this way, only for corruption and evil to win again.

Aria's eyes swam with tears and she didn't bother to hold them back. She could barely separate her anguish from the sorrow and terror that Luca projected into her. Where was Luca now? Would he be punished for his small part in this?

Aria was beginning to descend into her grief when the familiar click of high heels accompanied by the faint sound of boots on the stone floor floated through the courtyard, gradually growing louder. A memory flashed into Aria's mind, the image of a tall, black-haired woman standing above her with a chunk of Aria's hair in her fist. She instinctively reached for the back of her head and clamped her teary eyes shut as her fingers felt the bare, blood-crusted skin. The very woman from her flashback stepped into view in front of the bars as the clicking came to a stop.

"Look who we have here," Second Lady Brant crooned. "The prodigy who befriended the Earth rat."

Aria struggled to focus her blurry vision on the sickeningly beautiful woman.

"Brant," she said through clenched teeth. She tried to sit up straighter but winced from the effort. Dima and Nick ran to her aid, pulling her up by both armpits to a standing position. They stayed by her side, she imagined, for moral support as much as physical. "So, Drammat's behind all this?"

"Of course," she said matter-of-factly, a glint of humor in her eyes. "Now, can we talk about this sad excuse for a plan? I expected more from you, but you insisted on believing you could outsmart an organization of the most intelligent, well-connected, and powerful people in the galaxy. We flagged you as soon as you started hanging out with the Earth rat, and our interest only increased when you began obsessively researching questionable material. We've monitored your conversations, your whereabouts, everything. That boy has filled all your heads so full of lies that we can never allow you back into society. I'm sorry it had to come to this, but there's really no way around it."

"Why?" Aria asked. "Why cause the tupin blight?" Brant's eyes widened a fraction, but she quickly regained her perfect composure. "Why kill so many people? It makes even less sense now that I know you just sell people when it suits you. Why waste so many lives?"

Brant shook her head and sighed. "Honestly, child. We aren't monsters."

A bitter laugh escaped from Dima at Aria's side as she rolled her eyes.

"The numbers are greatly inflated." Brant waved her hand as if the matter were inconsequential. "Occasional threats are necessary to maintain order. Some starved, but not nearly as many as our reports would suggest."

Bile choked Aria as she stared at the elegant woman. Clearly, a sense of morality wouldn't sway her. Maybe appealing to her selfishness would.

"What if Celeste were with us?" Aria asked, staring into the second lady's cold eyes. "Would you imprison her too?"

"Don't you dare say her name!" Brant yelled, composure suddenly gone. She inhaled deeply and regained her precious control. "I wish it could be different, but we do what's necessary to protect our people and our way of life. I hope it brings you solace to know your sacrifice is for the greater good. Your delusions have put you in this situation, but you can rest knowing that we will continue to protect Drammat."

"What are you gonna do with us?" Aria asked. "Kill us? Sell us?"

"That's up to my friend, Mr. Morales." She turned and walked back down the balcony, her last words trailing off to the beat of her clicking heels. "If I were you, I'd pray for death, but Morales isn't usually one to squander a profitable opportunity."

Perfectly on cue, Mr. Morales stepped into view with two bodyguards at his back. He couldn't have been older than forty. His skin was nearly flawless, and his hair was still dark and thick. His expensive suit fit him perfectly, clearly designed for him.

"Morales," Aria said. "The monster himself."

A charming smile graced his handsome face. "I see my reputation precedes me," he said in his native tongue.

"No," Aria said in shaky Srattan Spanish. "I'd never heard of you before a few hours ago. Now that I have, I wish I hadn't."

"Do I scare you, child?" he asked, switching to perfect English.

"Scare me? No. You *disgust* me."

His cocky smile transformed into a scowl. "How dare you?" he hissed. "You know nothing of me or my business. I was a street child, then a drug addict before I built my empire. My people eat because of the work I do."

"And the people you sell?" she asked. "Many of them are your people too. Why don't you care about them?"

"Of course, I care about them. Is this an unsavory business? Certainly, but so is war. If I am to believe Mrs. Brant's intel, your father was an Army man and now works in law enforcement. Has he taken lives? Who can say which is the better of us?"

Aria shook with anger. "Don't talk about my father! You'll never be half the man he is!"

"I would not be so sure, Miss Blake," he said with a greasy smile. "Life is not black and white. Take you, for example. You came here thinking it was a noble choice, but you will have caused your friends to suffer in the end. Do you know how much I will get for eight Academy students? Especially a young girl as beautiful as yourself?"

Aria squirmed as she watched him undress her with his eyes and appraise her value. She couldn't keep her contempt in. She tried for the sake of her friends, but it was useless. She spat in his face.

"You're a disgusting, sad excuse for a man!" She shook with the cocktail of rage and terror that she and Luca were both creating. Was he seeing this moment play out, or simply experiencing her torrent of emotions? Morales's gleeful, power-hungry expression changed to one of fury as he wiped Aria's spit from his forehead with the back of his suit sleeve.

"Me?" he asked, eyebrows raising as his voice grew dangerous. "*You* are the disgusting one among us. Not many people would turn a good girl against her master, knowing it would get her killed. Marisol told you of our agreement, did she not?"

Aria clamped her jaw shut. She wouldn't put Marisol in any more danger than she already had.

"We only spoke to your prisoners," Aria lied. "I don't know who this Mari-whatever is."

"You are a good liar, Miss Blake. I would almost believe you if I did not have proof. Let me help you understand why I would spend my valuable time speaking to a stupid little girl like you. I promised Marisol's mother I would always keep her in my home, safe and loved. And she promised that her daughter would be a good, loyal friend to me. Until now, Marisol and I have both kept our promises. Now, because of you, she and I will both break our promises today."

Morales snapped his fingers, and one of the bodyguards disappeared. He returned, hauling a battered woman behind him. Her wrists were bound in handcuffs, and her mouth was gagged with a piece of dirty mauve fabric, ripped from her dress, which now exposed her legs through a long tear up one side of the skirt. Both the dress and her skin were smeared with dirt and blood, and her previously exquisite hair was a tangled mess. Fresh bruises covered her face, arms, and chest, and tears streaked clean pathways over her dirty skin.

"No!" Aria screamed, breaking free of Dima and Nick's hold on her. She stumbled forward and fell to the floor as the pain of her injuries returned. Grabbing the cell bars for support, she pulled herself up. "Sol, I'm so sorry!"

"It is too late for apologies, girl," Morales seethed. "Just look at what you have done to our family. I have kept this girl safe and loved in my home for nearly twenty years. In the space of fifteen minutes, you ruined her life."

"What will you do to her?" Aria's voice cracked. "She doesn't deserve this. I forced her to talk! I threatened her!"

Morales took Marisol's arm and yanked her in front of him. "I have to do to her exactly what I must do to all traitors. Though I regret losing my dear companion and friend, *you* chose this. Her blood is on your hands."

"No, please!" Aria screamed, reaching desperately through the bars. "I'll do anything! Take me instead!"

"I already have you!" Morales laughed. "Now watch as your actions take this poor girl's life. You owe her that much for what you have done to her and our family."

A reflection of the dim light glinted off a metal surface as Morales removed something small from inside his suit coat pocket. He pulled the blade to Marisol's neck and pressed it to her skin. A single drop of blood collected on the tip.

"Please!" Aria begged. "Please don't! Sol, I'm so sorry!" Tears burned Aria's cheeks.

Marisol's dark eyes glistened as tears streamed down her face and seeped into her dress. Her whole body trembled. Aria's friends ran to the bars of the cell, pleading for mercy beside her, but nothing they said made a difference.

Morales clenched his jaw as he burrowed into Aria's soul with his dark, lifeless eyes. In one fluid motion, he pulled the knife across Marisol's neck.

"No!" Aria screamed.

Marisol choked as blood poured from the wide gash and soaked the front of her dress.

Morales released his grip on her and pushed her forward. She collapsed on the floor, lifeless eyes staring into the cell.

Aria fell to her knees as a pool of blood seeped under the bars and soaked her jacket. Tears rolled down her face as an animalistic cry burst out of her. She backed away from Marisol's body and brought her knees to her chest, unable to take in air.

"Remember, Miss Blake," Morales said. "You did this. She would have lived a long and happy life if you had not been so selfish and naive. Let this be your lesson not to meddle in things you do not understand."

Morales turned and walked away from the body, his bodyguards trailing behind him. Aria rocked back and forth on the cell floor, trying to remember how to breathe. Marisol was dead, and it was truly Aria's fault. Sol said it herself—she was lucky. She begged Aria not to make things worse, and that's precisely what she did. Now, Aria and her friends would be sold to the highest bidders, split up, and subjected to unspeakable abuse. It was possible that no one would ever learn what they discovered, and Drammat would continue destroying lives in the name of order.

She stared at her blood-stained hands as they shook uncontrollably. It was all too much, too many feelings, too much pain. She couldn't do this. Without thought, she reached for her chest and clutched the tiny sun charm of Luca's necklace like a lifeline. His dominant emotion was easy to pick out now. It was a kind of desperate terror that she had never felt before. What would Luca's life consist of for the rest of her miserable existence? Forget the lifelong pain of a breakup. This would be infinitely worse for him. She felt her consciousness fleeing, and with the last ounce of resolve she clung to, she willed her words into his mind.

"I love you, and I'm sorry."

Aria's trauma-riddled mind fell back into darkness—its vain attempt to protect her. The effort couldn't be more pointless. She would never feel safe again.

TWENTY-NINE

ARIA AWOKE to the sound of jumbled whispers. She opened her eyes to a dark, blurry view of her cell floor, where Marisol's stiff, lifeless body still lay in a pool of her own blood. Red streaks traced a line from where Aria first fell to where she now lay at the back of the cell, as if someone had dragged her backward while she was unconscious.

Fresh grief overwhelmed her as the memories of the past twenty-four hours flooded back. The throbbing in her head was substantially improved, but the burning pain in her right hand felt like fire in her veins. A long strip of green fabric was wrapped tightly around the gunshot wound, but blood was already soaking through the makeshift bandage. Luca's terror hadn't lifted in the slightest. As for herself, she just felt bitter.

She sat up slowly, leaning on her uninjured arm, and searched for the source of the whispers that had woken her. She winced as she turned her head to see Dima and Jeslyn sitting silently in the far corner. Dima's T-shirt was ripped into a ragged crop top.

"Aria!" Nick whispered from behind her. "Guys! Aria's awake!"

Dima and Jeslyn stood and rushed to her side. "Aria!" Dima said. "How are you feeling?"

"Like I got shot," Aria said hoarsely. "Thanks for the bandage."

"Of course. You've been unconscious for almost ten hours. We were so worried."

"Ten hours?" Aria asked. "There's probably a search for us by now—too bad they'll never find us."

"Don't say that," Jeslyn said. "It's not over yet."

"Not over?" Aria asked. "We're stuck in a cage, about to be sold into slavery. We'd be better off dead, and it's my fault. I'm so sorry." Tears welled up in her eyes, and she dropped her head.

"This isn't on you," Elio said. "It's on Morales and Brant and all the other awful people involved in this scheme. We chose to come because you helped us believe our people could do better."

"You still believe that?" Aria scoffed.

"Yes," Elio said. "We're all proof that not everyone on Drammat is warped. I'd rather follow you to my death doing the right thing than live long enough to end up like Brant."

Everyone crouched down to Aria's level.

"We're proud to have fought by your side," Dima said.

Aria wiped away a tear as it fell. Wasn't she supposed to feel buoyed up by her friends' support? She couldn't feel anything but shame and so much pain. What had she been thinking? Did she honestly think she could just waltz in here and fix everything? Perhaps her fatal flaw had always been overconfidence. Even with the loneliness that came with her secret, never in her life had she truly struggled to come out on top. Somehow, though she had known the odds, it never occurred to her that she might fail in this. Now she understood all too well that she had seriously miscalculated. She was nothing, worse than nothing. She was the arrogant moron that got her friends sold into slavery.

"What's our play?" Jeslyn asked.

Aria barely glanced at her friend as she continued to berate herself inwardly.

"We wait until we get another chance to fight," Brock said.

"Or we wait for the savior to fight for us, like the rest of the prisoners," Finlay said, chuckling darkly.

"The savior?" Dima asked. "What are you talking about?"

"It's a fairy tale or prophecy some of the prisoners told me. They asked if we were here to liberate them with the savior." He framed 'savior' in air quotes.

Aria straightened up a little. For the first time, the idea of someone else coming to fix everything she had broken sounded incredibly freeing. "What did they say about the prophecy?"

"They said they were waiting for this savior to free the galaxy from Drammat's rule," Finlay said, waving a hand dismissively. "If you ask me, it sounds like a cop-out, but maybe they just need someone to believe in."

Aria nodded. As freeing as it would be to believe that someone else already had human liberation covered, the prophecy was no truer today than it was yesterday.

"Instructor Rojas told me about that last semester," she said. "I bet some Drammatan politician made it up to keep the Srattan people compliant."

A slit in the back wall opened, and six trays slid into the cell. Everyone but Aria rose to retrieve the trays. Elio came back with two and handed her one. A dry biscuit and a bowl of broth stared back at her. Despite the sad portion, Aria's stomach rumbled at the sight of her first meal in over twenty-four hours. She hadn't even finished her last meal because it had been her turn to spy on Celeste. She ate greedily and ran out too quickly. The slit in the wall shut as the six empty trays were returned. Aria lay back down on the hard floor, and no one else spoke a word. She listened as her friends drifted off to sleep one by one, but she couldn't persuade her body to sleep.

The heat in her hand radiated up her arm and shot daggers through her whole body. She shivered uncontrollably in the cold cell, yet sweat beaded on her forehead. She looked down at her bound hand. She might not make it long enough to be sold if she didn't get medical attention. Death by infection was certainly a better fate than a lifetime of slavery, wasn't it? Would it be better for Luca too? Would it hurt more to feel their connection snap or to watch and feel from afar as she lived a life of slavery?

She lay down, exhausted in a way that was new to her. Her possible future flashed through her mind, and suddenly, tears streamed from her eyes and pooled under her temple on the stone floor. She'd never see her parents again, never graduate from the Academy, never get to tell Luca how she really felt or see what a future between them might hold. An annoying grain of hope throbbed in her chest, and she couldn't help but try again.

"I'm sorry, Luca," she said in her mind as she drifted off to sleep again. "Now you get to have all the fun saving the galaxy without me."

Aria stirred awake to a dull ache in her head. She rubbed her raw eyes and looked around the dark cell, her brain foggy. Her friends were sleeping in heaps on the floor around her. Deep breathing and Finlay's light snoring were the only noises in her immediate area. Dima shifted and turned onto her side, settling back to sleep with her lips parted. There were no windows in their cell, and therefore no way to tell how much time had passed during her nap. Aria stretched her arms over her head, but a sharp bolt of pain through her arm stopped her. She winced and brought the injured hand to her chest. The pain radiating up her arm was only spreading and increasing with time. She awkwardly pulled off her jacket and T-shirt, trying not to wake her friends. She ripped the shirt and tied a sling out of it, securing her arm close to her chest. Maybe infection wasn't the way to go, after all.

She closed her eyes and focused her mind. Something had woken her, but the prison was quiet. The only sounds from beyond their cell were the soft footsteps of the guards on duty, the heavy breathing of sleeping prisoners, and occasional sounds of agony. Nothing had changed for hours. She focused on the sounds around her, squeezing her eyes tighter. Renewed anguish wrung Aria's heart as the soft sound of a child's cry registered. She inhaled slowly and refocused her thoughts.

Something tingled at the edge of awareness—not a noise, but a feeling. She felt so numb that she had almost missed it. She followed the emotion through her mind until it engulfed her. It was fear, but not the paralyzing kind. It was the kind of fear that made people do crazy things—the fear of losing someone you love. But that wasn't all. Luca felt much nearer than he should be. That tiny, pesky spark of hope jumped inside her.

"Luca?" she asked silently, focusing every piece of her shattered soul on reaching him. "Am I going crazy, or are you there?"

The silence in her mind mocked her brief hope. She smiled sadly and rolled over to find her place on the hard floor.

"Aria?" a faint voice resonated in her mind.

She sat up, searching for the source of the voice. Her friends still slept silently.

"Luca?" she called out desperately in her mind. "Is that you?"

"Aria, I'm here. I'm gonna get you out."

Aria gasped and pressed her good hand to her lips, stifling a relieved laugh. "Here? Where? In the prison?"

"We're almost there."

"Did you bring Alika?" she asked.

"She's the only person who could get me in here. I brought Amare too."

Joyful tears immediately sprung to her eyes and streamed down her face. "Thank you, Luca. And thank them too."

"You can thank them yourself when we get you out," he said. "Just hold on."

"Luca, we need to open the rest of the cells and help everyone else escape. We can't just leave them here."

"I know. I didn't see everything—it was a little patchy—but I saw enough to know this Morales guy deserves to be locked up for the rest of his life. We'll get everyone out. We have weapons, and I think we can pull this off. Just sit tight."

"Can I do anything from here?" she asked.

"Just be ready when we get there. Focus on keeping your mind open. I'm using our connection to find you."

"I can do that. But Luca?"

"Yeah?" he asked.

"Be careful."

Aria opened her eyes and strained to keep her connection complete and open, becoming a beacon for Luca to follow. She tiptoed to Dima's side and crouched down by her face.

"Dima," she whispered. "Wake up. We're getting out of here."

"What?" Dima asked, rolling over to look at Aria as she rubbed the sleep from her eyes.

"Luca's here, outside. He's coming to rescue us."

"Are you feeling okay? How's your hand?"

"I'm not hallucinating, Dima. He's coming, and we need to be ready. Help me wake everyone up, but keep quiet."

Her face took on a seriousness that was uncharacteristic of Dima. She nodded and turned to Jeslyn, who was sleeping beside her. Aria stood and tiptoed to the other corner where Finlay and Nick were sleeping. She stooped down and touched their shoulders. "Wake up. We're getting out of here."

The boys stirred and looked at Aria.

"Did you hear me?" she asked. "Luca's here. Be quiet and get ready to go."

Nick yawned wide. "What?"

"Shh!" she said, turning to him. "Luca's gonna get us out, and then we're gonna set everyone else free."

"That didn't exactly work out the last time," Jeslyn said, yawning.

"They brought weapons," Aria said. "We have to try."

Aria stood in front of her friends. Her recklessness had put all of their lives in danger, and now she had to make sure they made it out alive. Luca's voice rang in her mind again, and she turned away from the group to focus.

"Alika has the entire surveillance system on lockdown. We'll bypass all cameras and sensors. What else should we know about the inside?"

"There are guards, at least a few dozen but maybe more. Some are monitoring the cells, and a few are at the control desk on the bottom floor. I don't know how many are in the hallways and stairwells."

No response came, but a blurry vision of Luca filled her view. Amare and Alika, tall, dark, and beautiful, like a matching set in their Academy-issue jackets, followed behind him. All three hefted massive guns in their hands. They ran through a familiar hallway, and then the vision left as quickly as it appeared. A faint shuffling entered her ears, and her eyes shot open.

"They're here," she whispered. Her friends stepped closer to her, tightening ranks.

A muffled cry came from the right, followed by a thud. The shuffling grew louder, getting closer by the second. Three heavily armed people in all black screeched to a stop in front of their cell, nearly tripping over Marisol's body.

"Luca!" Aria whispered. She ran to the cell bars and stretched her hand out toward him.

"Aria!" Tears welled in Luca's eyes as he reached through the bars to touch her face, smooth electricity warming her cheek where his fingers touched her skin. "Are you okay?"

She pulled Luca's head toward her until their foreheads touched through the bars. The most exquisite joy filled her heart—love filled her heart. She still couldn't untangle the two separate sets of emotions, but did it matter? For the first time, the fear of losing what she had with Luca was outweighed by the fear of never knowing what they *could* have.

"Thank you," Aria whispered. "I can't believe you're here."

Luca pulled back and pushed a stray lock of hair over her ear. "As long as I'm alive, I'll be right where you need me."

"Alright, you two," Alika said. "Enough of this mushy crap. Let's go be heroes."

They laughed through their tears and let go of each other.

Alika, in all her tall, willowy grace, was working on the scanner at the side of the cell with a drive like the one Luca had given Aria on the ship. She typed furiously in the air in front of her, beads of nervous sweat dripping into her eyes.

"Amare brought us some toys," Luca said. "He designed and built almost everything we stole from the armory on the ship."

Amare knelt and slipped his huge pack onto the floor. He opened the bag, exposing dozens of weapons.

"Everybody, take one of each," he said. "We aren't gonna use deadly force unless we have to. We're in plenty of trouble as it is. So far, we've knocked out and restrained seven guards on our way here with these bad boys."

He pulled out a handful of gloves. Each featured a tiny, metal half-sphere secured to the rubber palm.

"What are they?" Finlay asked, pulling a stretchy glove onto his hand.

"Don't have a name for them yet," he said. "Put them on your non-dominant hand."

Aria inspected the strange device embedded in the rubber.

"When you're fighting someone within reach, press it to naked skin, and push down until you hear a click. It'll electrocute them, but it isn't deadly. Everyone reacts differently, but they should be out cold for at least five minutes. Once they're down, you can give them a nice wallop on the head for additional time."

"Sweet," Nick said, staring at the weapon.

"Everybody, take one of these," Luca said, handing six long tubes through the bars. "Amare's still testing them, so they're a little less predictable. They do the same thing as the tiny ones on the gloves but on a larger scale."

"How large are we talking?" Dima asked, running her fingers over the gleaming surface.

"It'll knock out everyone within ten meters, as long as they're within ninety degrees on either side of the cylinder," Amare said. "Just don't shoot it if any of us are near that range."

"Got it!" Alika said, pulling the drive from the scanner and securing it in her pack.

A low tone hummed, and metal clanked inside the cell door before it glided open. As soon as there was enough room, Luca squeezed through the opening door and rushed to embrace Aria. She melted into him as the familiar buzz of his touch enveloped her. Her wounds still throbbed, but her hope had returned.

"These are just for emergencies," Alika said, pulling firearms from her pack and handing one to each of them. "Typical handguns, and unlike my pacifist brother's weapons, they're very deadly. I have extra ammo if you need it. Try not to need it."

Aria hesitantly pulled away from Luca and picked up her weapons. Amare helped her wrap the glove around her forearm, just under the elbow. She would need her good hand for the other weapons. She stuffed the handgun in her pocket and gripped the silver cylinder in her left hand.

"Let's go," Aria said.

They strode lightly across the balcony, trying not to wake any of the prisoners.

"Hey!" a thin girl whispered, waking some of her cellmates. "Where are you going?"

"How did you get out?" another woman asked. Several women who were still sleeping in the surrounding cells tossed and turned.

"Shh!" Aria whispered. "We're here to save you! I'm gonna set you free or die trying, but we need your help. Stay silent!"

Dread hung over Aria as she thought of their half-baked plan. It was risky at best, a mass execution at worst. They had no way of transporting prisoners to the shelters they had been promised. They didn't even know where to look. But if they didn't act, thousands would be sold into slavery and lost forever.

"Luca," Aria said, "did you pass the city on your way here?"

"We did. The entrance we came through is in an abandoned building on the edge of downtown."

Aria turned to the girl who had first spoken to them in English. "Please spread the word for everyone to act like everything's normal. When the cells open, we need the locals to show everyone else the way to the nearest shelters. You'll come out near downtown. Can you do that?"

The teen girl and several of the other women in her cell nodded. Aria clenched her jaw and started back down the corridor, passing cell after cell of sleeping prisoners. Luca ran to catch up with her.

"What happened to your arm?" he asked, eyeing her hand-made sling.

"You didn't see that part? I got shot. I don't think it was too bad."

"Lying to me doesn't work, remember? How bad is it really?"

"I don't think it took too much of the hand off, but I'm worried it's infected," she whispered. "It's hurting pretty badly, but there's nothing we can do about it here."

"The second we're out of here, we'll get you to a medic."

He picked up his pace, increasing it for the whole group. Aria wouldn't argue with that plan. Her entire arm burned like it was covered in hot tar, and the heat that radiated through it hours ago now engulfed her whole body. She wiped her forehead with the back of her hand, mopping away the stinging sweat that dripped into her eyes. The only thing keeping her standing was a renewed overdose of adrenaline.

The group tried to keep their footsteps as light as possible, but the unknown of what would happen next pushed them to prioritize speed over stealth. Aria peeked over the balcony. Their cell was on the top floor in the farthest corner of the building, so they had a lot of ground to cover. They turned into the hallway and barreled toward the doorway that led to the staircase. Aria slipped as she changed direction to descend the stairs and banged her new weapon on the doorway. The metallic boom echoed through the corridor.

"Hey!" a gruff voice yelled from behind them. Aria whirled around, wincing. A burly, bearded man in a black guard's uniform sprinted toward them. Jeslyn, who was the last in line on the stairs, turned and intercepted him. She fell to the ground under his weight, and both rolled down the stairs in a tangle of limbs. The others jumped to dodge the human bowling ball, and Jeslyn and the guard rolled to a stop on the next landing. The man wrapped his arm around Jeslyn's neck and clamped down. Her eyes bulged as she fought for air and grabbed the back of the guard's neck.

"Don't touch him with your skin!" Amare yelled as the group ran down the stairs after her. "Only the device!"

A vein pulsed in her forehead as her skin reddened. She pulled her legs into her chest, dug her feet into the guard's stomach, and pushed with the last of her strength. The guard released her as he flew across the landing. She jumped up and pinned the man's head to the wall with the device between his forehead and her palm. A flicker lit his skin as he convulsed under the shock. Jeslyn dropped her hand, and the man's body fell limp.

"Why didn't you tell us that detail before?" Jeslyn asked, out of breath. "I could have died!"

"Sorry," Amare said. "You wouldn't have died, though. We just would have had to carry you for a few minutes. Let's go. There's no way nobody heard all that."

Jeslyn looked Amare over and gave a curt nod, as if he had passed her inspection. She turned to run down the next flight of stairs and the group followed.

"Remind me to ask that girl on a date if we make it out of this alive," Amare whispered to Luca as they descended behind Jeslyn.

They piled up in the doorway of the third-story hallway. Dima peaked around the corner. She signaled for the group to move to the next stairway, so they rounded the corner and bounded down the stairs.

As Dima and Aria made it to the second-story landing, two

guards rounded the corner and nearly smacked right into them. The tall female guard smashed the hilt of her gun into Dima's temple before she could get in a hit of her own. Dima staggered backward, momentarily dazed, but still conscious. Her frown hardened, and she threw her body into the guard. The others jumped down to help, but the other guard, a short, stocky one already had Aria in an arm lock against the wall with his gun to her friends.

They froze.

Dima and the tall woman grappled hit for hit until Dima finally got a hold of the guard's face. She kicked off the ground and went into a one-armed handstand, using her momentum to push down on the device. The woman's body convulsed as Dima struggled to land far away from the thrashing body. Finally free of her opponent, Dima kicked the gun from the male guard's hand. It landed with a crash and slid across the floor.

Finlay dove to retrieve it.

Aria twisted out of the stalky man's grip, spun around him, and smashed the device on her elbow over the side of his face. He convulsed on contact with the tiny device and finally collapsed on the landing. The friends rounded the corner and pushed toward the last flight of stairs.

"Wait!" Alika whispered, holding her arm out. "A dozen guards, heavily armed. We learned from the last guy they won't hesitate to shoot."

"That just means we have to take them by surprise," Amare said. "Luca, cover us with your handgun from here."

"Got it," Luca pulled it from its holster. "Aria, you should stay here with me."

Aria shot a glare in his direction. "I'm helping," she said. "I got us into this mess, and I need to help get us out."

"Aria, please," he begged, but she glared until he gave in. "Fine. But if you die—"

"I'll be fine, Luca."

He pressed himself against the doorframe and pointed his firearm toward the guards at the end of the hall.

"Go!"

The others exploded from the doorway and raced up the hall toward the group of guards. Aria lagged behind as her energy waned. One of the guards spun around to see Nick throw himself into the guard next to him.

"Hey!" he yelled, pressing something on a device in his hand. "Hallway four, code..."

Brock's boot slammed into his jaw, knocking him to the floor and cutting him off. He scrambled to his feet, but Brock palmed his face and pressed down. He convulsed and collapsed unconscious on the floor. The rest of his comrades rushed her friends, locking them each in one-on-one scuffles. Amare and Alika were equally targeted.

So it was true—the guards didn't have neurolinks, and even Luca and the twins wouldn't be invisible in this place. So much for that advantage. When Aria finally caught up, the remaining four guards had their weapons trained on her chest. She held her hands up in surrender and slowly walked closer.

Chaos spun around her and the four guards as Aria's friends traded blows. A flash of light to the left meant that at least one of them had finally stunned their opponent. One of the guards pointing a gun at Aria glanced toward the light. In the split-second when his attention was averted, she dropped to the floor and swept out his legs with her foot. He landed hard on his back, knocking the air from his lungs. She knelt over the man and drove her elbow into his neck. He convulsed to the rhythm of the flashing light under her weight and finally went still as she let up. She shuddered as his body went limp beneath her, but she stood, searching for a new target. Unconscious bodies were strewn along the hallway, and her friends were now ganging up on the remaining two guards.

"Aria!" Luca yelled.

She turned to find him in the stairwell, her heart pounding with a fresh burst of adrenaline. "What's wrong?"

"Look out!" he yelled, pointing his handgun right at her.

Movement registered in the corner of Aria's eye. She turned her head to trace it and found herself staring down the barrel of a gun. Another shot of adrenaline pumped through Aria's body. She jumped out of the way, knowing her odds of survival were almost zero at such close range. The boom of a gun rang in her ears as she flew through the air. She hit the floor with a painful thud, rolling to her side.

The initial pain of the impact dissipated, and she looked down at herself. Nothing was there—no blood, no hole in her jacket, nothing. She looked up at her shooter, standing with a hand over her ribs. The gun fell from the guard's other hand and crashed against the floor. A wet stain appeared through her fingers and spread across the front of her uniform. She fell to her knees, eyes glazed over, and toppled onto the floor. Aria scurried back from the lifeless body and turned to Luca. His hands trembled slightly, but his body remained stiff in his shooting stance. His eyes locked onto hers, and for a brief moment, they were the only two people in the fortress.

A burst of Luca's horror flowed through Aria, stronger than any feeling she had ever sensed in him. It was deep, soul-wrenching guilt, more potent than the anguish of losing his parents or the love she knew he felt for her. And yet, his relief somehow overshadowed his guilt. Her heart ached for him and what he had done for her.

Dima touched Aria's arm, breaking through the moment. "Aria, we need to go," she said. "After that shot, the whole prison knows we're here."

Luca clenched his fists to fight the shaking as he took one last look at the woman he had killed before following Nick down the last flight of stairs. Aria and Dima brought up the rear as everyone paused at the bottom. A group of guards raced toward them. More would be waiting for them in the courtyard, but they had no choice but to run right into the trap. Amare stepped out first, pointing his silver rod in the direction of the oncoming guards.

"Moment of truth, baby," he said.

He pressed the trigger down, and a high-pitched whistle rang through the air until it ended in a loud boom. An invisible wave rippled through the hallway, knocking half a dozen guards off their feet. They fell where they stood, heaped on top of each other. The smell of burning hair floated toward Aria.

"Are you sure these are non-lethal?" Dima asked, inspecting the cylinder in her hand.

"Pretty sure," Amare said. "I just finished the first model this week, so I don't know. Just don't point them at any of us."

"Agreed."

They turned toward the courtyard and sprinted to the entrance. Aria fell behind the group, unable to push through the pain as she had been doing. Luca looked back at her and stopped running.

"You okay?" he asked as she caught up to him. "I don't know how you're still standing."

"I'll be fine once we get these people freed."

The world around her began to tilt. Luca put an arm around her and helped her to the entrance. They stopped behind their friends, lining the walls by the opening, some holding metal cylinders and others holding handguns. Aria stretched her neck out to see into the room.

"There's gotta be three dozen security guards in there!" she said. "Where do they keep coming from?"

"There could be hundreds more, for all we know," Nick said.

"My cylinders can take out at least ten at a time, as long as they're close together," Amare said. "The only problem is that they're shooting to kill, and we can't knock them all out without going out in the open."

"Alika, can you somehow hack in from here?" Luca asked.

"I already tried that when we first got inside," she said. "Their security is state of the art. I need to physically plug in."

"Then we need to get you to the control desk and cover you while you work," Luca said, "But once the prisoners are released, we'll have to take out enough guards to make their escape possible."

Aria's vision went in and out as her body threatened to lose consciousness. She shook herself. "The longer we wait, the lower our chance of success. We need to make our move now."

"Yeah, but not you," Luca said. "You're not okay."

She put one hand on Luca's cheek. "I'll be fine, but I need to do this."

His anguish became visible as he fought an inner battle. He swallowed hard and finally nodded once. "I promise," he said. "I won't let anything happen to you."

THIRTY

THE SOUND of Aria's ragged breaths blared in her ears. Her body weighed a thousand kilos, and her eyelids ached. The adrenaline that had kept her going for the last two days was used up. She would have to run on pure willpower. She pushed herself off the wall and stepped in front of Alika.

"Now!" she yelled.

Aria stepped out from the shelter of the hallway, exposing herself to the first wave of bullets. Thirty-some guards waited for the kids with huge guns trained on them. If they won this fight, it would be all thanks to Amare's genius. Bullets sprayed the stone and metal around her as she ducked. One caught her pant leg, barely grazing the skin. Before her friends could step out behind her, she pointed her silver cylinder toward the guards who stood between them and the control desk and pressed the trigger down.

A high-pitched squeal was the only evidence that it worked until suddenly a deafening boom sounded and seven guards fell to the floor, convulsing violently. Aria turned toward the next wave of guards and aimed her weapon. Terror filled the eyes of the men and women facing her as they dove in every direction to avoid the foreign weapon.

Amare jumped into the courtyard, firing his cylinder to cover Aria's back. They were still surrounded, but their weapons had done their job. From their perspective, Aria and Amare had just killed over a dozen of their comrades in the space of a breath. Reluctant gunfire resumed and a bullet whizzed past Aria's ear and ricocheted off a cell bar. The prisoners on the first floor were in the direct line of fire, and children and adults alike screamed as they ducked for cover. It was hard to tell if anyone had been hit amid the chaos. Dima ran to Aria's side and shot another shock wave at Aria's attackers. Four guards collapsed, but another two dozen circled from behind their fallen comrades. Aria dropped to the floor again, bullets whizzing past over head.

"Everyone from Dima down, cover our backs!" Amare yelled.

Dima, Nick, Finlay, and Jeslyn curled around to face the new attackers. Nick fired his cylinder, and more bodies dropped. Luca fired toward the control desk, dropping another half dozen. Only four guards remained standing between them and the controls.

Luca, Aria, Amare, Alika, and Elio broke from their positions and sprinted for the desk. Bullets hurdled by, putting holes in the infrastructure around them.

Aria's heartbeat felt unnatural and erratic. She fell behind as they raced toward the last line of guards standing in their way.

Elio fired a shock wave in their direction, but they dove out of the way, rolling on the floor. Elio, Luca, and Amare lunged after the escaped guards.

Alika dodged the fourth guard and picked up her pace. She was only two meters from the desk when a hand reached out and caught her ankle—one of the first guards they hit had woken up and didn't waste any time. Alika's momentum carried her forward and she crashed on the stone floor. The monstrous man stood over her, the pain of electrocution still etched into his features. He pressed his boot to her face and pulled his weapon on her.

"No!" Aria screamed.

She couldn't use the cylinder or she would knock Alika out too, and Alika was the only one who could open the cells. In the half-second before the guard ended Alika's life, Aria slipped the non-lethal weapon into her empty pocket and reached across her body to pull the handgun from the other. It had to be a kill shot, or Alika wouldn't have a chance. She aimed for the man's chest and pulled the trigger. The force of the blast startled her as the man reeled back. She had shot firearms countless times before, but never *at* someone. A red stain appeared on the guard's shirt, and he fell to the ground. She fixed her aim on another large man who was waking up and shot again, this time to wound. The boys had stunned their targets and joined Aria's renewed sprint toward the desk. Another two dozen guards exploded from the doorway behind the control desk, guns trained on them. They slid to safety under the desk, pulling Alika with them.

"What do you need, Alika?" Aria screamed, her voice barely audible over the cacophony of battle.

"I just need to find the right port without getting my head blown off!" she yelled.

"Do you know where to look?"

"I think so."

"Then we'll cover you. Don't worry about anything except getting that thing plugged in!"

Aria stood, aiming her cylinder at the oncoming guards, and fired. Four convulsed on impact and dropped to the floor. They had to have taken out almost a hundred guards already, but more kept replacing the fallen. Aria stepped back to let Elio have a shot at the rapidly multiplying guards.

Luca and Amare stunned the first wave of guards back to sleep as small batches came to. Bullets were still flying but with less frequency. Aria glanced to her right, where Alika was scouring the control desk for the port. The memory of her previous attempt at opening the doors flashed in her memory. She shuddered, catching herself on the desk with her one good arm. Her body trembled with pain and fatigue. She ignored her shaking legs and foggy mind as she pulled herself back up to shoot another shock wave.

"Got it!" Alika shouted. "Now I just have to override the commands, and—"

A blood-chilling scream escaped her mouth and she dropped to her knees. Aria lunged to catch her as she fell. Blood poured from a hole in her shirt.

"No!" Amare cried. He collapsed and pulled his twin sister into his arms. "Alika, no! Stay with me!"

Alika ignored her brother and began tapping and swiping at the air in front of her with a trembling hand.

"Alika, stop!" he yelled. "We need to get you out of here!"

"I'm fine!" she said through clenched teeth. "You keep pressure on it while I work."

Amare reached for his sister's side with a trembling hand and pressed down. She winced but didn't pause her work. Luca tore a piece of his shirt from his body and offered it to Amare. A filthy piece of cloth wasn't ideal, but it might stop her from bleeding out. Aria stood back up, turning her attention to protecting Alika from the hordes of guards.

"There," Alika said weakly. "The first cells are opening. First floor, eastern wing."

"We need to get them moving toward the city," Aria said. "Which door did you guys come in from?"

"That one," Luca said, pointing to the northeast corner.

Every door on the far east side of the first floor slid open in unison, and the women and men inside poured out, but the battle was still raging. Dima and the others held off the rest of the guards, but their bullets sprayed the courtyard. A young woman cried out and collapsed as a stray bullet pierced her side. The mass of fleeing prisoners trampled her body and Aria looked away. Screams choked the air from every direction. No one would make it out in such chaos. Aria ducked down and ran to the front of the stampede.

"Hey!" she screamed with all the volume she could muster. "One at a time, and we'll all make it out alive! Follow me!"

Aria ran ahead, showing the way to salvation. Thanks to Alika, the northeastern exit was already wide open, and after leading a line of prisoners through a short hallway, Aria and the masses poured into a small, empty building. Icy air enveloped Aria as she exited the abandoned building to the view of thousands of tiny, colorful homes clinging to the mountainside. The sun was still in the sky, but well past its zenith. A shiver ran up her spine as she turned to the prisoners. Most wore thin rags, and many were barefoot. Frostbite was surely already setting in. Based on the dim light in the sky, it was either just after sunset or just before sunrise. Aria sent up a desperate prayer that it was the latter.

Prisoners were already fleeing up the mountainside. Aria only hoped that the instructions to follow locals to shelter had gotten to everyone. She raised her voice to address the hundreds of men, women, and children now flowing into the deadly cold.

"Everyone, follow the crowd to find shelter! If you have family or someone you trust in Mojare, go there instead!"

She couldn't wait around to see whether the prisoners would take her advice. She turned and stumbled back into the fortress. A steady stream of prisoners had developed along the walls of the massive room as Alika systematically opened section after section.

Aria's friends were still fighting, except for Alika and Amare, who hid under the cover of the control desk. At least a hundred and fifty limp bodies in guards' uniforms were strewn around the floor. Some were waking up to fight again, but some never would. The cells on the bottom floor were empty, and Alika was working on the second floor.

Hordes of malnourished, terrified children poured out of the stairwells toward the exit. Aria winced as she saw their bare feet and heard their fearful cries. An echoing scream caught Aria's attention, and her stomach dropped—it was a baby. Panic set in as she searched for the nearest stairwell.

She pulled herself up the stairs and into the first cell on the second floor. Three babies lay helpless on the ground, screaming so hard their faces were purple. Nearby, two toddler girls sat in a corner with their knees pulled tight to their chests. There had to be dozens if not hundreds of infants and toddlers. She wasn't sure she could carry *one* in her condition, but every instinct told her to try. She lifted the youngest infant in her good arm and winced. She pushed off the cell wall and stumbled to the closest unopened cell. A dozen scared teenage girls stared back at her through the bars.

"There are children—babies who can't walk yet," Aria said. "They need your help! If you help me carry them to a safe place, I'll make sure you all get out. Deal?" The girls stared back at her silently. "Anyone?"

The cell door opened, along with the rest on the second level. The girls pushed past each other to exit the cell, slamming Aria against the railing. Hundreds of prisoners rushed to the stairwell.

"Please!" Aria screamed. "Take the little ones!"

Someone tapped Aria on the shoulder through the crowd. She turned toward a wrinkled face and gray beard. The old man took the infant from her arms and smiled. The crowd died down, and he crossed the balcony to the nearest cell, scooping up a toddler in his free arm.

"Thank you," Aria said, her voice breaking.

He smiled again and followed the rest of the crowd. Two babies would make it out, but there were still countless others. She turned to retrieve another baby but was startled to see a woman in the cell. The woman helped the second toddler onto her back and hoisted an infant onto her hip. A young man entered behind her with a toddler on his back and pulled the remaining infant into his arms. A teenage girl passed by the cell with an infant in her arms and a little girl holding her hand. Aria spun around to see several others coming out of cells with infants and toddlers in tow. Tears of gratitude sprung to her eyes. Aria grabbed the arm of a child-less teenage boy as he passed.

"Hey," she said. "What's your name?"

"Matias," he said.

"Can you help me, Matias?"

"Of course, Savior. What do you need?"

She blanched at the use of the title, but there wasn't time for questions. "I need you to walk around the whole second floor and make sure there aren't any babies or wounded people left here. Can you do that?"

"Anything," he said, dropping to one knee.

"Thank you. Find others to help you if you can. And when you're done, follow me to the third floor to do the same there. We need to check all five."

She left Matias and hurried to the stairwell. Her lungs heaved as she stopped at the first step. Her body was giving out. She lifted her foot onto the step and pulled herself up, focusing on putting one foot in front of the other. The stair-well shook as the first wave of prisoners from the third floor poured down the staircase. Aria braced herself against the wall as bodies slammed into her on the way down.

When the first wave ebbed, she pulled herself up the rest of the stairs to find more volunteers. She continued to the fourth floor and then the fifth, trusting Matias to sweep the floors on his way up. The last of the cells opened, and the freed prisoners swept through the building. Aria began scanning the cells on level five for anyone left behind. As she exited one on the back wall, she slammed into Matias.

"Sorry, Savior!" he said, steadying her with his hands on her shoulders. "Everyone is out from here down to level two. Did you check the rest here?"

"All clear. Now we need to check level one."

Aria stumbled as she stepped onto the stairs, and Matias caught her. "Savior, you're hurt. Let me help." He hoisted her into his thin arms and resumed the descent.

"Why do you keep calling me that?" she asked, blinking excessively to make up for the haziness overcoming her.

He looked down at her as he rounded the corner on the second floor. "What?"

"Savior. Why do you keep calling me Savior?"

"Are you not our promised Savior? You have already fulfilled the first part of the prophecy."

"I don't know much about the prophecy," she said, her words beginning to slur together.

They reached the first floor, and Matias set her down at the courtyard entrance.

"I will tell you about it after we have saved the rest," he said. "Can you walk?"

Aria tested her weight and nodded. "We'll start here and work our way around to meet in the middle," she said. "Be safe."

She stumbled through the doorway and into the first open cell to her left. It was empty, so she pushed onto the next and the next after that. Bullets still ricocheted off the bars as the battle raged around her. The five-minute revival rate on their weapons put them at a decided disadvantage. The fight seemed unwinnable unless they were willing to massacre more than two hundred unconscious guards. She ducked into the sixth cell and stumbled over a motionless body.

"No," she whispered.

She pressed her fingers to the fallen woman's neck and shook her head when she felt no pulse. She steeled her frazzled nerves as she abandoned the body and went on to the next cell. By the time she checked her half of the cells, she had found twelve other lifeless bodies, ten adults and two children. She had lost what little food remained in her stomach when she came across the two lifeless toddlers. As she checked the last cell, two more bodies lay huddled on the floor. She squatted over the teenage girls and pressed her fingers to one of their necks. A weak heartbeat pulsed against her fingers as Matias ran into the cell behind her.

"This girl is alive," she said, checking the other girl's pulse. "And this one too!"

Matias raced to Aria's side and flipped the first girl on her side, exposing a bullet wound in her thigh. Aria pulled the other girl to a sitting position. Blood stained her shirt from a bullet hole in her side. It didn't seem to have pierced anything vital.

"I can pull one out, but you're too weak," Matias said.

"I'll figure something out," Aria said. "Thank you, Matias. Save this girl, and then save yourself."

He hesitated.

"Go! That's an order!"

He hoisted the girl over his shoulder and fled. Aria emerged empty-handed from the cell. Her friends were fighting hand-to-hand with the same guards over and over, as more woke up every minute. They were exhausted, and the blood and bruises from the fight were visible from across the room. They wouldn't last much longer.

She aimed her cylinder at the guards but couldn't get a clear shot. She considered knocking them all out and dragging her friends to safety, but in her condition, that was out of the question. She snuck behind the abandoned cubicles, inching closer to the battle. When she was near enough, she stumbled out into the open and screamed. "Retreat!"

Dima glanced at her in confusion. "What?" she yelled as she hit her opponent again.

"Now!" Aria screamed.

"Retreat!" Dima repeated. She threw one last high kick, crashing into her opponent's face and sending him reeling backward. "Go, go go!"

Everyone still in the battle abandoned the fight and followed Dima's lead. Aria stepped out farther, aiming her cylinder through her oncoming friends. As the last passed her, she pressed the trigger. A shock wave blew five guards to the ground, convulsing. She aimed her weapon again and shot, dropping another four.

"Now!" she yelled.

Dima ran to her side and stepped one pace in front of her, shooting down another half dozen guards. Luca stepped beyond Dima and took out another five. One after another, they took out the remaining guards.

"There's a badly injured girl in that back cell," Aria said, pointing to the cell where she left the girl. "Finlay and Jeslyn, can you get her out?"

"We're on it," Finlay said, taking Jeslyn's hand.

"Brock, can you help Amare with Alika? I don't know if she made it, but either way, we're getting her out."

"Of course." He took off toward the control desk where Amare still held his sister in his arms.

"The rest of us will stay to stun the guards as they wake up until you're all safely out with the injured. Go!"

Brock, Amare, Jeslyn, and Finlay carried Alika and the unconscious girl through the exit while Aria and the others followed with their weapons raised. They hit another dozen guards just as they started stirring and finally retreated behind their friends.

The cold night air hit Aria like a solid wall as she stepped through the door and closed it behind her. Finlay and Brock slid a heavy beam in front of the door, locking the guards inside. Her jaw dropped as she turned to the city. Rivers of people flowed up the mountainside as thousands of malnourished and abused prisoners trekked through the frozen streets. Their diverging paths looked like a tree trunk running into branches, which eventually split off into smaller twigs. Blood stained the snowy trail in their wake.

So much still needed to be done to help the survivors find refuge and treat the wounded. Even if they all lived, they may never fully heal the invisible wounds left by Morales and his greed.

But it wasn't just Morales, and it wasn't just Sratta. The plague of greed was everywhere, and Drammat was the epicenter of the disease.

Aria stumbled up the hill behind her friends. Pain coursed through her body with every step and every breath. Her vision went in and out as consciousness started to fade.

"You!" screamed a voice from somewhere up ahead.

Aria lifted her head weakly to find the source of the voice, but it was no use. It was a miracle she was still standing. The blurry shapes and colors around her were all running into each other, and she could barely make out the distinct figures of her friends. Suddenly, a gunshot ripped through the air. She thought she felt a brand new sting of pain rip through her abdomen, but her whole body was so wracked with agony that it was hard to tell. She fell to the icy ground and lifted her head. Everyone in the clearing had ducked, all except one group at the far side of the clearing. She squinted hard as she tried to focus on them. They wore all black and held weapons. As they closed in, one face came nearly into focus. Mr. Morales himself was at the head of the group with a gun in his hand.

"How dare you?" he seethed, stepping over her friends to point his weapon at her face. "You, a naïve, ridiculous child, have destroyed a multi-trillion credit company that kept this entire planet alive! You have forced thousands of people out into the cold from a safe, warm place. All you have done is destroy our economy and my business, and for what? They will all die, and their blood will be on your hands. You are no better than I am."

"You're wrong," she yelled hoarsely, pushing herself up to stand with the last bit of her strength. "You're not the problem. Don't get me wrong, you're disgusting, but you're just a product of the problem. Now that I know the truth, trust me, this is just the beginning."

She raised her cylinder to meet his glare, but he stooped down, grabbed a little girl who was cowering on the ground by the back of her neck, and put her between himself and Aria's weapon.

"I know people like you," he said, pressing his gun to the girl's temple. "You won't use that thing on me as long as you might hurt this child."

Her lip curled in disdain. The girl couldn't have been older than five, and they had no way of knowing how the shock of their experimental weapons would affect such a tiny, frail body. Morales was right; she wouldn't risk hurting the girl. There was no other option. She slowly moved her right hand out of its sling under the cover of her jacket. She only had one shot, and she had no idea if her injured hand would have the strength needed. She slipped it through the bottom of her jacket and onto the hilt of her handgun, struggling to keep the pain from showing on her face as she gripped it. In one fluid movement, she dropped the cylinder from her right hand, wrapped her injured hand around the handle of her handgun, and lifted the weapon to her eye level. With both hands on the gun, she pulled the trigger.

Morales jerked back, his firearm falling to the ground as blood dripped from a hole in his forehead. The girl in his grip cried out and fell to her knees as he released her. Morales staggered backward and crumpled to the frozen ground, his blood staining the ice. Satisfaction flowed through Aria's veins. This pig would never again hurt another innocent person. She felt no remorse as she stared at the corpse.

Suddenly, as if the trauma of the last day caught up to her all at once, fatigue rushed through her body. Her handgun fell to the frozen earth, and she collapsed to her knees. She could hardly feel the pain anymore. All she wanted was to lie down and sleep, but she knew it would be her death sentence. She blinked hard, trying to retain her vision as darkness seeped in around her. She attempted standing, but her strength gave out completely, and she fell forward onto the packed snow. Black boots rushed to her side as darkness enveloped her.

THIRTY-ONE

A SWIRL of light and color danced around Aria's head as the darkness receded. She blinked, squinting at the blinding light. Her vision slowly came into focus, revealing a white medical room. Luca was hunched over, asleep in a chair in the corner. A nurse was working at a standing desk across the room.

Aria cleared her throat. "What...what happened?" Her voice was raspy and quiet. She tried again, a little louder. "What happened to me?"

The nurse jumped, rushing to her side. "You're awake!" she said. "That's good! You've had a traumatic few weeks. You should rest some more while I get your doctor."

"Weeks?" Aria asked. "I've been out for weeks? How did this..."

She cut herself off mid-sentence as a storm of memories rushed back. The iron scent of blood stung her nostrils and the sound of battle echoed through her ears. A machine beside her suddenly blared as her heart rate increased, and the nurse rushed to calm her. The faces of Morales and the guards she had killed flashed through her mind, followed by a carousel of broken bodies on cell floors. She reached for her chest with both hands, but the crumpled fabric tickled the palm of only her left hand.

She froze as the memory of her injury collided with reality. She held her breath as she looked down at the hands on her chest. A lump of gauze and a tight bandage covered the space where her left hand used to meet her wrist. An involuntary cry burst from her throat as she brought her remaining hand to her lips.

Luca flinched and sprung out of his chair. He ran to her side, wrapping his arms around her and resting his face softly on her head.

"I know," he whispered. "I'm so sorry."

His love immediately flowed through her like a river, comforting and steady. The door slid open, and a woman in a red jacket entered the room. She waited as Luca pulled back and wrapped Aria's remaining hand in his.

"Miss Blake," the short, thin woman said. "How are you feeling?"

"I...don't know," she muttered, looking into the distance, rather than at her doctor. "In shock, I guess. I don't know what happened."

"That makes two of us," she said, moving closer. "You had very serious injuries, Miss Blake. Bleeding in the brain from moderate trauma, severe fatigue and dehydration, various lacerations and contusions all over the body, a gunshot wound to the lower abdomen, and of course, the injury to your hand and subsequent infection. Unfortunately, we couldn't save the hand, but prosthetics today are almost indistinguishable from legitimate body parts. Your body still needs rest, but shortly, you'll be able to choose a new hand."

"Why do I feel like it's still there?" Aria asked, staring in horror at the missing limb.

"That's quite common in amputees," the woman said matter-of-factly. "You may even feel phantom pain where your hand should be. It's nothing we can't handle with the right treatment plan. For now, get some rest. I'll have them call your parents up from the cafeteria."

"Thank you, doctor," Aria said.

The doctor and nurse exited the room, leaving her alone with Luca.

"What happened after I shot Morales?" she whispered. "I can't remember anything after that."

"I picked you up and brought you straight to the ship, along with Alika and the two unconscious prisoner girls. Dima and the others did what they could to make sure everyone got somewhere safe."

Aria gasped. "Alika!"

"She's fine. She was discharged a few days ago. Honestly, we were most worried about you. You were touch and go for a while. They tried to keep your hand but finally had to take it to save your life. After that, you got better every day. They transferred you here when we landed on Drammat, and your parents and I have been taking shifts ever since."

"Thank you," she said, tears brimming her eyelids. "What about the other girls? And the donations for the shelters on Sratta?"

Luca's face hardened as a rush of anger flowed through him and into her. "Look," he said, looking down. "There are things we need to talk about."

"What do you mean?" she asked, sitting up straighter.

"We're in a lot of trouble for what we did, and they're not telling the truth about what happened. They separated us from the girls we saved and won't tell us what happened to them, and they've barred us from sending or receiving money outside of Drammat's economy. Not just those of us that were involved, but all of our friends. The news is calling it a terrorist attack, saying a local terrorist organization misled and used us."

"No," Aria breathed. "We can't just abandon the survivors. They have nothing, and that's our fault! It's *my* fault. We have to do something!"

"I know. We're gonna figure this out, but we can't do anything if we're in jail."

"What about the famine?"

"Everything seems to have gone according to plan," Luca said. "Celeste is being lauded as a hero."

Aria nodded. At least some suffering would end.

The door opened as Aria's parents burst in. Their expressions struggled between relief and disappointment. Her mother slowly stepped forward, taking her hand from Luca.

"Aria, honey," she said, her voice tight. "We're so glad you're okay. Your doctor just released you to go home. Your father will get the pod and pack your things. Luca will take good care of you while I sign the paperwork."

"Thanks, Mom." She smiled, but it didn't reach her eyes.

The pair turned to leave just as suddenly as they had appeared. Aria's dad paused in the doorway to peer at his daughter. His eyes were glazed over with a sadness she had never seen in him before. He broke eye contact and walked away. Aria's lip quivered as she watched her parents disappear. Their precious, overachieving daughter had become an alleged terrorist overnight. A knock on the glass sounded before the door slid open. The rhythmic clacking of high heels on quakestone echoed through the room.

"Pres...President Gray?" Aria stammered.

Two men in dark suits stood a pace behind her on either side.

"Oh, Aria darling," she said softly, "I've been so worried about you. We care very deeply about the safety of our students. You've been through something horrific, and if you're to return to the Academy in the fall, you'll need to make a full recovery."

"So I can go back?" she asked, not daring to hope.

"That depends on you, dear. You committed serious crimes."

"Did my friends tell you what happened? President, we saved thousands of enslaved people from all over the galaxy. That's hardly something to be expelled over!"

"You're a little bit confused about some of the details," the president said softly. "It's okay. That's to be expected with your condition. Manuel Morales wasn't a perfect man, by any means, but he was a beloved pillar of the community. I don't know where you got your information, but it was wrong. All you and your friends did was kill over a dozen locals, injure countless others, and damage Drammat's relationship with Sratta."

"But—" Aria protested.

"No, dear," Gray said sharply, cutting her off. "We don't know how you got mixed up with Morales, but we don't believe you killed him. You were surely set up by someone who would see the Academy's reputation destroyed. It's my own fault, really."

"What do you mean?" Aria asked.

"I signed off on letting you attend the Academy a year early. No one had ever allowed it before because young people are prone to frivolous actions. I thought you could handle the responsibility, but I was mistaken. Especially for a person with such a complicated history of mental illness, it's no surprise you were so easily deceived. I should have seen the red flag on your record and barred you entirely. Alas, I'm a believer in advocating for the weak, so the full responsibility for your unraveling and psychosis rests on my shoulders."

"Psychosis?" Aria asked, eyes widening. "Are you kidding

me? You think all of this was a psychotic episode? How do you explain away all of my friends' accounts of what happened? Or my missing hand, for that matter?"

"Watch your tone with me, Miss Blake," Gray snapped. She smiled again and returned to her overly sweet tone. "If you want to return to school, you need to play by the rules. You have an incredible knack for leadership and persuasion. Several of our brightest students chose to follow you, even when it meant they had to take innocent lives. I hope to nourish that gift and help you use it for good instead of evil, but first, your mind needs healing. Our experts have put together a strict schedule for you this summer and your parents are fully on board. If you're still experiencing symptoms by the time school begins, you will forfeit your place at the Academy so another, more worthy student may have the chance you seem determined to waste."

Aria stared wordlessly at the sweetly smiling woman. Something in her cold eyes betrayed her true nature. She hadn't recognized it before this very moment, but it had always been there—Gray was in on it. Regardless of the impressive string of profanity that was dying to burst from her lips, Aria clamped her mouth shut. There was no convincing someone who already knew the truth.

President Gray turned and left the room with her head tilted upward. Her entourage followed her out, leaving a vacuum of silence. Aria turned to Luca and let her tears of frustration overflow. Luca tapped the air in front of him several times and nodded, indicating they could speak freely. He closed the gap between them and wrapped her in his arms again. The electric buzz of his skin on hers calmed her instantly, and she rested her head on his shoulder. For so long, she pushed her feelings down, afraid to open up to him, to depend on him. Her fear of the what-ifs hadn't disappeared, but she didn't want to let it hold her back anymore. He was the only person who knew her completely, good and bad, and somehow, he loved her anyway.

"Thank you," she whispered.

"For what?"

"For never giving up on me—on us. For being patient with me even though I couldn't explain my reasons very well. For coming right at the moment I needed you. I could go on forever."

"Always," he said, looking into her eyes, her soul. "You may not have explained it, but I think I pieced it together pretty well from your feelings. You're afraid, and there's a lot to be afraid of. Our situation makes it impossible to have a clean break. If things go bad between us, we have to stay in each other's heads for the rest of our lives, no matter how far we try to run from each other. That's intense."

"Exactly," Aria said, expelling a long breath. "But it's not just that. How am I supposed to know what my true feelings for you are if your feelings are always in my head?"

Luca shrugged. "I guess we can't really know. But that's the amazing part. How many people get to be one hundred percent sure of someone's feelings for them? We get to know each other more completely than anyone else ever could."

"I still don't understand what you see in me, other than the fact that I'm the girl you're linked to. I don't want either of us to feel like we're each other's only option. I want to choose you, and I want you to choose me."

"I do choose you. You're kind. You're loyal. When you believe in something, you're unstoppable. You're stubborn, impulsive, and unrealistically idealistic, and I even love that. Your compassion and empathy for others are unmatched... except when it comes to self-obsessed human traffickers."

Aria laughed through her tears, grateful he could joke about it. Morales was the only kill she truly didn't regret.

"You might not be ready to hear this," he said. "But you

make me better. You make me feel more alive than I ever dreamed I could be. Aria, I love you. With every particle in my body and every breath I take, I love you, and I'll spend the rest of my life trying to prove it if you let me."

The power behind Luca's words filled Aria's soul. He wasn't saying pretty words because she needed to hear them. He meant it, and his wasn't the only surge of love she felt coursing through her. For the first time in longer than she could remember, her own feelings were clear. Tears flowed freely down her face and fell to the blanket on her lap. The boy standing in front of her was the most kind, genuine, and loyal person she knew, and he gave her strength like no one else could. She reached for his face and wiped a tear from his cheek.

"You don't need to prove your love," she said. "I know you love me. I love you, too."

She pushed her fingers through his tight curls and slowly pulled him close. The electricity in the air sizzled as the space between them disappeared. The buzz of Luca's touch slid across the small of her back as he pulled her toward him. His lips parted, and finally, they collided with hers. A burst of energy flowed through them both, stronger than anything that came before. Aria deepened the kiss, not worrying who might see through her glass door as tears ran down her face. When they eventually broke apart, Luca climbed into Aria's hospital bed and wrapped his arm around her.

"I knew you loved me," he said, bumping her lightly.

"Well, good," she said, resting her head on his chest. "Because things need to change, and we can't wait around for some magic savior to fix everything. We're gonna fix it ourselves—you and me. What do you think? You ready to go rogue?"

Luca smiled down at her as he wiped away her remaining

tears. "Aria Blake, I would follow you to the end of the universe."

The story continues in Fate Born: Kingdoms of Kartzel

ACKNOWLEDGMENTS

To my God, thank you for giving me a small talent, inspiration, and the strength and perseverance to grow that talent. I have felt your guiding hand through every stage of this journey, and I pray that my words and stories will always glorify you.

To my husband, thank you for supporting this crazy dream of mine. From the day I told you I wanted to write this story, you believed in me, helped create time in our busy schedule for me to write, and always wanted to understand this new part of my world.

To my children, you are my reason for everything. Quite literally, this book wouldn't exist without you. I may never have gotten back into reading and writing if not for those many late nights feeding my hungry babies. I can't wait to read this story to you someday, but in the meantime, I'll enjoy how you fill my days with craziness, love, and laughter.

To my mom, you gave me the confidence I needed to do something I always saw as a pipe dream. Your unconditional love and support is something I hope everyone has the chance to experience. You taught me right from wrong and to always stand up for the weak, and that has influenced every part of my life.

To my dad, you gave me the skills I needed to succeed in this life, including the knowledge that I could do anything I chose, as long as I worked hard consistently and always glorified God in my successes. Thank you for inspiring my love of stories and the art of storytelling.

To Bri and Louis, my ride or dies from day one. You both know how much you mean to me. It shouldn't have been a surprise that you two were among my first readers. Not only did your feedback impact this story, but your excitement gave me the confidence I needed to move forward.

To my brothers and sisters, both by birth and by marriage. Thank you for putting up with my many polls and for always giving me useful feedback. Thank you for being endlessly supportive—the best siblings anyone could ever ask for. A special thanks to Jacob, Josh, and Mylee who made my childhood wonderful and full of make-believe.

To my entire extended family, your support means everything to me. I am blessed to have the best humans on Earth in my corner rooting for me. I love every single one of you dearly.

To Karen Hopkins, thank you for inspiring generations of Rye kids to dream big and put good out into the world. Thank you for believing in me as a writer and as a human being.

To P.J. Hoover, your skill helped me take my work to the next level. Not only is this book infinitely better because of your editing influence, but every project I work on from here on out will be impacted by the many things I learned from you.

To Cheyenne van Langevelde, thank you for being a kind friend and a thorough, patient, and honest proofreader. I learned more from working with you than I ever imagined I would through such a seemingly simple process.

To my street team and the friends who helped me get the word out, I couldn't have done this without you. Thank you for believing in me.

To the reader, thank you for taking a chance on an indie

author's debut novel. There are so many books to choose from, and the fact that you picked this one up is humbling. Thank you.

ABOUT THE AUTHOR

Michelle L Robison is a self-proclaimed story addict. She is a sucker for a binge-able show or series of novels, so it's no surprise that her debut novel is the first in a four-part series. Michelle spends her days wrangling her two young children while simultaneously building the family business—training piano teachers to use their app, Piano Marvel. She spends her evenings writing and honing her craft, except when she's watching *Survivor* or binging the latest season of *The Last of Us* or *Stranger Things* with her husband. Besides her love for writing and music, she enjoys fitness, volleyball, traveling, time with loved ones, volunteering at her church, anything outdoors, and being in the sunlight as much as possible—something she finds quite easy living in Phoenix, AZ. Despite now calling the desert home, her heart will always belong to the tiny mountain town in Colorado where she grew up.

NOTE ON HUMAN TRAFFICKING

Human trafficking is one of the issues I feel most passionately about, so I wanted to do the horror of it justice without being too graphic for young readers. This was a tough balance, and most of the commentary on what the victims of human trafficking go through and how it happens was cut in the editing process.

It is estimated that nearly fifty million people are under modern slavery, from forced labor to forced marriage. There are countless organizations that help in the fight to end human trafficking, but these are some of my favorites.

OPERATION
UNDERGROUND
RAILROAD

THE POLARIS
PROJECT

NAT. CENTER
FOR SEXUAL
EXPLOITATION

Milton Keynes UK
Ingram Content Group UK Ltd.
UKHW030957140324
439440UK00005B/221

9 798989 177110